President Henry Wallace

AND THE SLEEPING PROPHET

Doug Moore

with

Chris Moore

Beacon House – New York

Beacon House LLC.

1511 Route 22

Brewster, NY 10509

ISBN: 978-0-9861310-0-4

ISBN : 0986131008

Library of Congress Control Number: 2015904367

Beacon House LLC, Brewster, NY

Moore, Doug N.

Moore, Chris R.

President Henry Wallace and the Sleeping Prophet

Dedicated to George E. Moore

Chapter One

Spy

July 1st, 1944
Foggy Bottom, Washington D.C.

A muzzle flash lit the darkened alley.

Agents Chipton and Dunbar dropped to their knees as a second shot concussed the narrow lane followed by heavy footsteps heading away.

"On three," Agent Joe Dunbar loud-whispered in a cold Minnesotan accent. "Three!" He then lunged around the corner, gun outstretched. The red headed Agent Chipton followed, covering the left side of the brick corridor for a clean shot.

There they saw the vice president's aide, Mike Barton, twisting in a slick of his own blood, head awkwardly craned against the wall, legs outstretched – a square-headed vagrant fled the other end of the alley.

"You get Barton!" Leroy Chipton called in an Appalachian twang and sprinted passed Dunbar, leaving footprints in the blood as he went.

Dunbar, in turn, rushed to the man lying in his own gore on the grimy bricks. Kneeling before the aide he found two perfect holes in the vest and shirt.

"You're going to be all right," he said coolly, and then squawked into the walkie-talkie for an ambulance.

"I don't think so, agent." Mike Barton responded with a wavering voice.

He was right. He would die before the ambulance arrived.

Dunbar ignored the comment and asked, "What were you doing here?"

The vice president's aide sighed. He wrenched a manila envelope from his pocket and declared, "Vice President Henry Wallace is a spy."

"And you snuck out of the West Wing to Foggy Bottom to impart this knowledge on a tramp?"

"We've been watching the vice president for some time now," the aide added.

"Who's we?"

The young man ignored the question and continued, "My dead drop was compromised. I've seen that man at the Soviet Embassy."

"The bum."

The young aide looked nonplussed and coughed.

"What's in the envelope?"

"Information that will turn the heat up so the VEEP doesn't become . . ." he trailed off.

"Who do you work for?" The dark haired Dunbar asked again.

"Since Pearl Harbor plenty of groups try this work." He paused to cough and added, "You wouldn't believe me."

"Try me."

The young man then began to shake. Dunbar would have thought him dead, but his breathing continued.

The agent in turn pulled open the envelope and removed its contents. It contained three documents. One was a letter addressed to the vice president with no return address, an oddly twisted double-corncob covered one corner. The second was a memo marked "MANHATTAN DISTRICT," with one line that read: "AUTHORIZED TO PURCHASE ADDITIONAL 1,000 ACRES IN NEW MEXICO . . . NECESSARY?" With the question mark circled. The third was simply the draft of a speech Vice President Henry Wallace gave to a small group of donors in June regarding the possibility of phasing out the Marine Corps after the war.

"Do you know who he is now?" Barton suddenly said. "Do you see what we see?" He gripped the Midwesterner's hand. His fingertips were cold but Dunbar still felt warmth in the palm. "Do you understand what should be done?" the aide shouted. Agent Dunbar attempted to withdraw his hand from Barton's dying grip, but the Yale alumnus would not relent. He was stronger than he looked. "Keep the envelope," he shouted, "Bring it here!" He pressed a blood-moistened business card into their mutual handshake.

It was for a Laundromat nearby.

Then Barton wheezed. His eyes lost focus and he died pointing down the alley. Whether he pointed in the direction of the Laundromat or something else would go to the grave with him.

Sitting down and out of the way of the blood, Agent Dunbar took the envelope and card and placed them inside his own jacket pocket as Agent Chipton returned from chasing the killer.

"I couldn't find him," Chipton called with a twang. "He dropped the hobo outfit when he hit K Street."

Dunbar simply nodded.

Chapter Two

The Sleeping Prophet

July 5th, 1944
Virginia Beach, Virginia

"Mr. Vice President, you're going to be the next president of the United States," the small balding man said. He took off his wire-rimmed spectacles and rubbed one of the lenses with the handkerchief from his breast pocket. Then, looking directly at Vice President Henry Wallace, he said, "But I have something more important to tell you."

"Well, you've got to give a man more time to digest something like that before you hit him over the head with another thing." Wallace replied, observing the frail man before him on the divan with suspicion.

Wallace had been reluctant to come to Virginia Beach to meet Edgar Cayce at all. In fact, he would have stayed away completely if it wasn't for the note that Cayce sent. Mr. Cayce had tried to reach Wallace on other occasions, but Wallace ignored him, knowing that if the vice president of the United States was seen at the home of Edgar Cayce, the so-called "sleeping prophet," his career would be over before he got back to Washington. At the very least, Roosevelt would cease backing him as the vice presidential candidate in the upcoming '44 Democratic National Convention – Roosevelt himself was already a foregone conclusion on the Democratic ticket.

There was also another reason Wallace stayed away. He thought Edgar Cayce was a charlatan. Wallace was willing to entertain supernatural ideas more than most men, but since his reputation had been damaged by an affiliation with another so-called "guru," he was very careful with whom he associated now. And a man who read the fortunes of people while he slept on his couch in Virginia Beach was on the top of that list.

But then there was the note. The first note came on Edgar Cayce's personal stationary and simply asked Wallace to come to the house in Virginia Beach. "I have something important to tell you," he remembered it saying. Wallace got correspondence of this type all the time from people throughout the country who thought they knew Nazi battle plans, or where the Japanese were stationing their fleet. Wallace paid little attention to these letters, and for the most part his staff kept these notes away from him. But because Edgar Cayce was famous, someone on his staff let the note through.

Wallace threw it into the wastebasket as soon as he read it. He wasn't even sure why he gave it that much attention. He would have thrown the second letter away as well, had he not seen the illustration on the front of the envelope. As he sorted through the mail his secretary brought, he saw the design beside his name and address. On the plain white envelope lay a sketch in blue ink of two corncobs entwined like a corkscrew with a single husk pulled back at the shank.

Wallace knew this image from long ago. It came to him first as a dream. He spent so much of his time in Iowa working to create better corn strains that he had even begun dreaming of corn. But this was different. And the image, and the idea which came along with it, helped him to begin hybridizing corn, and eventually to found the Hi-Bred company. The company's success made him a very wealthy man and afforded him the luxury of entering politics and financing his own campaigns, thereby eliminating any dependence on fat cats and local machines. This freedom allowed him to be eccentric without penalty, for Wallace was, inexplicably, an Episcopalian mystic from Iowa. The country loved him for it, though he had to be careful how *eccentric* he allowed himself to be seen to be.

Despite his success with hybrid corn, Wallace knew the mysterious image from his dream meant more than what he so far understood, but he had done his best to forget the glyph and what implication it had for the future.

Yet there it was again.

Wallace noticed his hand shaking as he read Cayce's letter. Anyone who knew that image, and had sent it to him in the mail, needed his attention.

He had to see Edgar Cayce, regardless of the political consequences.

"I've known about you for a very long time," Cayce now said. "Often when I'm doing a reading for someone else I see you, and what's to come. My wife tells me later what I've said. I remember very little myself."

"And what will happen?" Wallace asked.

"The end of the world." Cayce sighed without moving a muscle.

"You really don't give a man a chance, do you?"

"It's already here." Cayce added. He gazed directly at the vice president. "I also know that you are working on the project to build a bomb bigger than any in the world." Wallace kept silent and looked straight into the man before him.

"I couldn't make that up." Cayce said. Wallace knew that only two hundred people in the world had heard about the project Cayce described. Even the current Chairman of the Senate Wartime Finance Committee, Harry S. Truman, knew nothing about the bomb. Wallace himself knew about it because he kept President Roosevelt apprised of the progress the scientists made on the bomb, often sitting with Vannevar Bush, a scientific genius with oversight on the project, for hours discussing the bomb's implications. Some of the scientists feared that splitting the atom would cause a chain reaction and consume the world, while others questioned the morality of annihilating an entire city in one crack and the precedent it would set for future wars.

All these questions weighed heavily upon Wallace's shoulders as he sat in the parlor of the sleeping prophet that afternoon.

"And how do I stop the end of the world?" Wallace asked, somewhat ironically, as if he were playing along for the sake of argument.

Cayce took a long and labored breath and said, "It might not hurt for me to give you a reading today."

"I don't think that's something I'm comfortable doing right now," Wallace said.

♦ ♦ ♦

When they finished their conversation, Wallace left through the basement door of Cayce's house carrying a folder containing the sleeping prophet's various readings into his life. Some were cryptic, and to his mind questionable, while others were as straightforward (and as accurate), as the description of the bomb. Combined with the drawing of his secret corncob, the readings made Wallace uneasy. He worried about what would happen if someone got hold of these papers, and resolved to lock them away as soon as he got the chance.

As he left the walkway and joined the sidewalk, he noticed a man in a brown suit and hat watching him by the bumper of a parked car. The man had his trunk open and was partially blocked by it. He obviously wasn't looking inside the car. He was watching Wallace.

As Wallace approached, he saw the man had a gun tucked into his alligator leather belt behind the trunk door.

"What is this?" Wallace asked. At first he thought the man looked like a gangster in his double-breasted suit, but he had the clean features of a college athlete, which Wallace didn't associate with that kind of criminal.

"We know what you're doing here, Mr. Wallace."

Wallace didn't say a word in response. If this were an assassination, he'd already be dead. The man continued, "Mr. Cayce has known communist associates."

"Who are you with, son?" Wallace asked, feeling relief that this man was not with the press, or an assassin. "You do know I'm the vice president, right?"

"We're watching you, sir." The man said.

"Son, if only you really were," Wallace retorted, and brushed by the man to get to the black Studebaker he'd taken instead of his own car in an attempt to lose anyone who might have followed him out of D.C. Now he wished he hadn't slipped his Secret Service detail in the first place. He would have felt safer.

Chapter Three

Eyes Only

July 10th, 1944
Hyde Park, New York

The president leaned back in his wheelchair and observed the man across his desk. He sighed. At no point since he contracted Polio had President Roosevelt felt so tired. And now the man in his office approached a topic he found distasteful.

The president's breathing was a bit louder now and the bags below his eyes drooped just a little lower than in months past. He had been the president of the United States for almost twelve years, but in that period he learned something important: even presidents can't have their own way all the time! Though he'd still like it if they could.

For all the talk of "imperial presidencies," Roosevelt was beginning to realize that he couldn't win on this issue. The party was going to force Vice President Wallace off his ticket, whether Roosevelt liked it or not.

If only he could go out for a ride, he thought, maybe as far as Rhinebeck, he might feel better today. He put his head back against the green leather chair and imagined the drive around the countryside outside his family home in Hyde Park, New York.

"Mr. President, sir," the man across from him interrupted, as the president had been silent, looking at his tray ceiling for nearly an entire minute.

"Well, then," the president said, suddenly breaking his train of thought, as if prompted by something internal, "we'll just see how our boy does at the convention. As Secretary of Agriculture Wallace's understanding of farming, drought, and crop rotation damn well saved the world from starvation?"

Robert Hannegan, the incoming chairman of the Democratic National Committee, smiled ever so slightly at the president's comment. Roosevelt took notice. Despite poor eyesight, the president had a keen eye for such things. He didn't comment.

Hannegan smiled. He had been around long enough to know how the president operated. Roosevelt was very rarely straightforward about his intentions, preferring to keep them to himself until the last possible moment. What Hannegan took from the comment was that Roosevelt wouldn't help Vice President Henry Wallace win the necessary votes at the convention to remain vice president. That's all it would take to elect someone else instead. And Hannegan, from Missouri, had just the man in mind.

"Thank you, sir." Hannegan said and then stood to leave, thinking that he had gotten all that he had come for.

But the president wasn't finished. "Oh, Bob," he called as Hannegan got close to the door, "Would you mind leaving those papers you brought here with me? If you don't mind?" He smiled casually as he asked, flashing his Cheshire cat smile with his teeth clinched on a black Bakelite and silver cigarette holder.

In fact, Hannegan did mind. He had been told that the documents he had on Henry Wallace and had previously shown the president were for "eyes only." This translated to: "Don't leave them with Roosevelt."

Hannegan then turned back to the ailing president and smiled, but Roosevelt recognized the man's hesitation and so added, without the warmth his Dutch patrician accent normally carried, "Of course, I could get it from the 'College of Cardinals' myself. But it can be difficult with the war on you know, and they play so many fascinating games that what gets into my hands won't exactly be what you're holding there. You did get that from our *spies* in the OSS didn't you?" Roosevelt said the word "spies" with a playfulness that suggested the men of OSS, who conducted wartime intelligence and espionage for the United States, were rambunctious Boy Scouts who had gone a little too far afield.

Despite his light tone, Roosevelt understood the serious nature of the Office of Strategic Services. In fact, he conceived the idea to centralize intelligence gathering under one roof as the seriousness of the war and America's place in it became clear. The former ad hoc system in which different military bodies gathered information, distributed propaganda, and attempted to route out spies, as existed before Pearl Harbor, appeared to Roosevelt inadequate for the realities of the current war. It was therefore he who, in June 1942, signed the military order that established the OSS. The same order designated the gathering of intelligence abroad and the power to engage in espionage across the globe as within the agency's purview. Of course, the OSS was playing "catch up" with the well-established MI6 who quietly confounded Germany while the OSS taught itself introductory tradecraft and munitions on a commandeered golf course just outside Washington.

Roosevelt was further amused by his espionage agency because the OSS's central intelligence board was known collectively as "the College of Cardinals," partly, he thought, because William "Wild Bill" Donavon, who was the on-the-ground founder of the organization, was Catholic, and partly because the group wielded the same kind of power. However, the president found the degree to which the agency appeared to take interest in domestic issues of little relevance to the war somewhat less amusing.

"Surely they're supposed to keep focused on events overseas now for the war," Roosevelt said. "But very recently they've decided that anyone who comes into contact with a Russian's just a bona fide communist. They're absolutely crazy for communists, Bob."

Hannegan acquiesced and reached out his hand and gave the papers to the president with a look that appeared almost ironic. Roosevelt smiled, "Thank you, Bob." Then Hannegan stood awkwardly as the president read over the documents again.

"So, Wallace met with Molotov while he was there in Siberia," he said, in reference to Vice President Wallace, who had spent nearly a full month in the "Wild East" of Russia back in May when the Soviets showed him around several working towns and villages. It was a good-will tour to one of America's strongest allies, who had done the bulk of the heavy lifting against the Nazis.

"He's a nice enough man," Roosevelt went on to say.

"Who is, sir?"

"Molotov. Wallace was impressed by him. And Wallace has always been so curious about corn and agriculture. He's a brilliant man you know, made a fortune when he invented a new hybrid breed of corn. His connection with Molotov is nothing more than a way to further his understanding of agriculture. If anything, Wallace might care more for plants than people." Then Roosevelt jumped to another topic as he turned the page on the intelligence report. "And no more guru papers I see," he said. "You know I was worried that old Henry would meet up with Roerich again while he was there. I had a slight suspicion that's why Wallace wanted to go. That man Wallace was connected with, Roerich, was famous in the 30s, but he's fallen out of favor now."

"I think the guru Nicholas Roerich is *persona non grata* in Russia now too," Hannegan said.

"Well, he is. So far as I've heard, Uncle Joe won't have him around," Uncle Joe was the term Roosevelt used to refer to Joseph Stalin, "but Wallace went over to Mongolia and China. Anyway, you never know where that man's going to turn up. He thinks he's gotten ahold of a stone that brings about the end of the world, or the Messiah, (the Maitreya I think he calls it) and I had this fear that somehow he would meet up with the vice president, and the controversy would begin all over again, that's all."

"Now that you mention it, Mr. President, page 27 has something about a gift the Tibetan delegation gave to the vice president in a small town at the edge of the Tibetan plateau."

"Tibetans?" Roosevelt said and quickly turned to the page Hannegan referenced. The papers he held in his hand were obviously copies of the originals. Roosevelt instantly realized that this story wouldn't just die in his office if he held onto them. He reached page 27 and saw a photo paper-clipped to the back of the page; it showed Wallace standing in front of a three-legged table. He was in a town square; dry land ran behind the town and beyond that vast mountains loomed. On the table sat a rectangular object wrapped in linen. There were two oddly dressed men, whom Roosevelt guessed were Tibetans, facing Wallace. Behind the two men and the table stood several horses and other Tibetans. Wallace's back was turned to the camera.

After considering the photograph a moment Roosevelt remarked, "They're very colorful people, the Tibetans. I always wanted to see Tibet when I was younger." Then he paused to think about what the photograph might mean, politically: "This *was* a Tibetan delegation you said?" He flipped the page and began talking again as if his question were to no one in particular and didn't require an answer. "But there was no meeting with Tibetans on Wallace's itinerary, I can tell you that," he picked up the thread again. Roosevelt had a way of jumping around in his conversations that had gotten more pronounced as he got older and sicker.

"No . . ." Hannegan answered.

"And he didn't mention to the State Department that he received any gifts either."

"The rules regarding gifts given by foreign dignitaries to members of the government can be confusing, sir," Hannegan added somewhat cynically. Roosevelt peered at him over his glasses. The rules weren't confusing at all. Then the president looked back down to the report on his vice president, a report for which he had not asked. He didn't mind that Wallace didn't report having received the gift. He knew Wallace wasn't a corrupt man; and aside from that the Tibetans had nothing of great material value to give. At least nothing he could imagine. What he did worry about was what a skilled propagandist could make of this information, and what that could do to the certainty of his reelection.

"Who else knows about this?" Roosevelt asked.

"Not many," Hannegan responded.

"So it will get out if I don't remove him from the ticket?" Roosevelt asked, which was a more straightforward question than Hannegan expected, especially considering that he thought the issue was already settled.

"No. Nothing will get out because Wallace doesn't have a chance of winning the nomination unless you throw your weight behind him, sir."

Roosevelt smiled. Then he coughed. He glanced again at the report he had thrown onto the desk. It was open to a page headlined "SOVIETS" that had a picture of Wallace meeting with Molotov, Russia's Minister of Foreign Affairs, and with one General Nikishov who was in charge of the small Siberian town where the picture was taken.

"You do know we're allied with Stalin, don't you, and Wallace went over to Siberia with my blessing?"

"Sir . . ."

"Is this a consensus, then, about Wallace?"

"As far as I can see."

"Now what is this Edgar Cayce business?"

"He's been to see him several times, and with Wallace's earlier trouble with this kind of man, and the Guru Papers . . ." Hannegan let his sentence hang as though its meaning was evident. "There's also some worry that the Soviets, or even the Germans, are interested in Cayce."

"You think they fancy a psychic reading, do you?" Roosevelt jibed. "You know even Thomas Edison went to see Cayce some years ago. It wasn't that uncommon for people to seek a reading with the Sleeping Prophet."

"Cayce's wife writes down everything he says. They worry that Stalin might be interested in what people have revealed to Cayce, or, rather, what he's revealed to them. Not to mention the Nazis' interests in the information, as we can tell, for more *occult* reasons."

The president chuckled. "So you believe Cayce knows the future and that the Russians or the Nazis may get ahold of state secrets through Wallace's reading?" He was back to appearing warm and generous, but

Hannegan was on his toes and uneasy. He wasn't sure where the president would go now.

For Roosevelt's part, he laughed because he saw how nervous Hannegan had suddenly become when pressured. *The man is just new to his job*, the president thought. Then he handed the papers back to Hannegan. "I'm sure you've been told, in so many words, to return these. They seem to have too much fun with this intelligence business now. And their club jargon . . . they sound as though they're in school. I wonder how useful this all is. You know I've seen papers like this before, don't you? There was another group over at Navy told me Eleanor was a communist. Their other accusations are best left unmentioned. Imagine that, my wife. Well, I like the OSS and Donovan better than that group, though please do let them know that they should keep their noses pointed east. If I recall correctly, their intelligence said the Japanese would 'do nothing to provoke a threat' just a few weeks before Pearl Harbor."

"I will, sir."

Roosevelt leaned back in his wheelchair as Hannegan walked out of the room. The president was uneasy. He liked Wallace personally. He thought of him as a "real American." There was no doubt that Wallace loved his country. But politics could be an ugly business, and the war was generating this type of paranoid, military mindset that unsettled Roosevelt. The president didn't know exactly what he could do about it either. So long as all these men focused on the Nazis and the Japanese their strength was not much of a threat. But the boogeymen would soon be gone. The war would be over and America would just be crawling with this "type," as the president thought of them. *Whom would they point at then?* He thought.

Chapter Four

The Dentist

July 14, 1944
Washington, D.C.

Henry Wallace walked across an open cornfield with his friend Franklin Roosevelt. Mountains loomed above them. Roosevelt watched a bird take off from a lone tree beside the old stone wall ahead of them. He pointed to the bird and Wallace watched it fly. He felt delighted. He was happier than he could ever remember being. Then he looked back to Roosevelt who smiled ear-to-ear beneath his glasses.

Franklin had a cigarette in a long, black holder clenched between his teeth. He inhaled and blew a ring of blue smoke which seemed to float across the horizon like a white cloud against the endless blue backdrop.

That's when Henry Wallace noticed that Roosevelt was walking without crutches. Henry looked more closely at his president then and saw that there were no braces holding Roosevelt's legs from giving way either. Wallace was astonished.

Roosevelt took to bed with a fever in August of 1921 after exercising. He and his wife Eleanor were vacationing at the family home on Campo Bello Island, Maine. He was only thirty-nine years old. Little did he know when he climbed into bed that afternoon that it would be the last day he would ever use his legs that way again. From then forward, he would be nearly paralyzed from the waist down. Only with great effort could he walk even the shortest of distances.

"Franklin, you're walking!" Wallace stopped beside Roosevelt and exclaimed. Roosevelt continued striding along, and over his shoulder, said, "I am, indeed, walking Henry."

That's when Henry Wallace awoke in a cold sweat. He looked around him – all was white and there was a man leaning over him also in white. It took a moment for Wallace to remember that he was at the dentist's and not in some somber mortuary somewhere. He thought he was dead and walking with . . . but what was he walking with?

"You were sleeping." The dentist said, "Must be the sound of the drill's soothing. It happens."

Wallace put his hand to his jaw where the man had just finished filling a cavity. He wasn't sure whether the dentist was joking or not about the drill being soothing. He had never thought so. But the fact remained that he was asleep.

Then the door burst open and one of his aides entered.

"Mr. Wallace, I'm sorry, Mr. Vice President . . . or . . ." The aide was obviously frightened. He had the look of a child who has just lost a parent.

"What is it?" Wallace asked.

"The president is dead! You are the president!" And then Wallace understood the look on the man's face. He knew it was true. He never allowed himself to think that he would be president, but he always knew that Roosevelt chose him because, as he said, Wallace was the spirit of the New Deal, and would maintain that spirit after the great president was gone. Wallace just never believed that time would come; even in spite of what the Sleeping Prophet had told him. Roosevelt seemed to him to be almost too great a man to die.

"The president had a stroke in the Oval Office and died less than an hour ago, sir." The aide continued.

But he was interrupted. Behind him poured a flood of Secret Service agents, most of whom Wallace had never seen before. This was not his typical detail. They seemed unsure what to say at first. Since acquiring this position and sitting one breath away from the office of president of the United States, Wallace had been dubious about the methods and protocols of the Secret Service. He knew there was a need for men like this, but he feared them as though they were the Roman Praetorian Guard, a group who had fostered assassination and power shifts in the late Empire. Wallace often wondered when the Secret Service would enter into an age of treachery like that in Rome. Probably, he thought, when the United States itself became the modern Roman Empire, complete with a Caesar president and imperial wars of conquest.

Today was not that day; these men had no designs on him. They were here to ensure his survival. One of the agents stepped forward. He had red hair, and Wallace recognized him as the agent who was present at Mike Barton's murder.

"Sir, please come with us to the White House," Agent Chipton said in a tone both forceful and dutiful.

Henry stood, pulling the bib off of his chest, and followed along blindly behind the pack of agents, all of whom, at first glance, appeared to be dressed in brown suits. Wallace couldn't help but mark the coincidence and remember the day just a few weeks prior when he sat before the man they called a prophet. When he left that day, he was terrified that what Edgar Cayce told him was true, and he had struggled to rid his mind of the thought ever since.

"Mr. Wallace, you will be the next president of the United States." Cayce had said. These words only bothered him at the time. It was what Cayce said after that, however, which had sent him to a church to pray. But none of it could be true. The transcripts of the prophecies that Cayce handed him, and that he kept in his safe now, had to be works of fiction, the writings of a madman; a man who was adept at misleading housewives and widowers, charming them out of their money.

But now the president was dead, and Wallace stood next in line behind Roosevelt. As they ushered him out of the building and into a waiting car, Chipton said to him, "Don't worry sir, we'll keep you safe." Wallace doubted that was even possible. Agent Chipton was at least sincere, he thought, and the warmth of his accent made him seem even more so. The two men then exchanged a glance, and as Wallace thanked Chipton for his kind words, he was engaged in a struggle to push from his mind the idea that his future could be so important to the future of the country, the future of the world, as Edgar Cayce seemed to think it was. *It couldn't be true. It can't be true.* He thought.

The fact that Cayce had predicted that he would become president was ludicrous. The prediction was even more burdensome because he was afraid to confide in anyone else what he had learned from the Sleeping Prophet. He knew that many people thought he was a crank after his correspondence with the guru Nicholas Roerich had been revealed. And he feared that Cayce's prophecy would only prove to be a further cause for embarrassment. Now, as president, the stakes were exponentially higher.

At every intersection, he watched the police cars stopping traffic. Their flashing lights made his convoy feel like a funeral procession. But even with all the business now at hand, all he could think about was seeing Edgar Cayce one more time.

Chapter Five

Swearing In

July 14, 1944
The White House, Washington, D.C.

Henry Wallace repeated the words, "I, Henry Wallace, do solemnly swear that I will support and defend the Constitution of the United States against all enemies, foreign and domestic."

When he finished administering the oath, Chief Justice Harlan Stone stepped back from Wallace and toward one of the eagle sconces that lit the outer edge of the Cabinet Room. The staunch Republican and native son of the Granite State made two loud clicks with the soles of his shoes as he passed from the key patterned carpet to the hardwood floor. But for those sounds, the room was silent.

A group of fifty or so cabinet members and family were assembled in the Cabinet Room for the swearing in. As Roosevelt had died only hours earlier, the short notice limited the number of people who could be present. Wallace thought it was just as well this way, he wanted as little fanfare or celebration as possible.

Eleanor Roosevelt, the former first lady, had made it a point to be present. When she first saw Wallace she rushed to him and took both his hands in her own. He felt remiss for not consoling her immediately, but she hadn't come to him for his condolences. She wanted to let him know how glad she was that he would succeed her husband in the office.

"You always were his favorite," Eleanor said, "You will be his legacy."

"I truly hope so," he then paused as he cast his eyes toward the floor. "I'm so sorry Eleanor. It's such a shock, but I know that he's in a better place."

Eleanor seemed to take his last comment as just a formality that certain people muttered in times of sudden death, but for Wallace, the dream he'd had at the dentist's was certain proof that Roosevelt had gone to another world.

"I don't mean to keep you, Henry," Eleanor then said. "You have so much to do now."

"I don't know where to begin."

"You'll manage, but you'll have to be careful of our growing military, Henry. They are no longer just the naïve and patriotic boys Franklin imagined them to be. You'll have to be vigilant. They are already antagonistic toward the New Deal. They are antagonistic toward you, Mr. President." She said looking at him pointedly. "Before he died there was tremendous pressure on Franklin to remove you from the ticket."

"There was always talk," Wallace interjected. "If the president asked me I would have stepped down in an instant."

"This was more than talk."

"I would have known it."

"Be that as it may," Mrs. Roosevelt continued, "there are forces within your own party who do not want you in this office."

When she said this she turned to look over the room full of people who had just witnessed his swearing in. He followed her eyes and surveyed the group.

The long, polished boardroom table sat to his right, and a small group of cabinet members and other government officials stood to his left. Except for his wife Ilo, the former first lady, and a few secretaries who stood behind the cabinet members against the wall, everyone in the room was male. Wallace thought this was something he'd like to change as president. Then his eyes fell upon the conference table, which, to him now as never before, seemed to look like a fine coffin.

A flashbulb went off on the camera of the photographer kneeling beside the table. The first face Wallace saw after his eyes readjusted from the flash was that of the Secretary of the Navy, James Forrestal. He was smiling, but Wallace only noticed the white buck shoes he wore. Wallace also had a good idea that Forrestal had planted Mike Barton in his office to spy on him. Agents Chipton and Dunbar trailed the young Bostonian after Chipton watched him pocket some papers from Wallace's office. They did not recover the papers, however, and the assailant escaped on foot. Part of the unofficial record claimed that a West Wing temp secretary who filled in at the press office was also Mike Barton's lover. Barton confessed to her that he frequently met with a man from the Navy Department. She, in turn, had passed the information along, so agents kept the young aide under close watch. It was unclear to Wallace how the Secret Service came to learn the information.

What he knew instead was that as Secretary of the Navy, a position which also oversaw the Marine Corps, Forrestal was suspect number one for having planted Barton. The secretary had grown increasingly antagonistic toward the Soviet Union over the years, and suspected Wallace of having Soviet sympathies. In turn, Wallace saw Forrestal as a symptom of a disease that was now gripping the American mind, and especially the minds of men in power; namely, paranoia with regard to the Soviets in particular and with communism in general.

To Wallace, Forrestal was a zealot with an inflexible mind, who looked at both the new president and the New Deal with suspicion. Forrestal had come from Wall Street, where he was one of the more successful bankers of his day. He was also a formidable political presence, with friends and allies in both houses of Congress and in business. This meant that Forrestal would be a fixture for the foreseeable future.

As it stood, the moment he uttered the last words of the oath and the chief justice stepped away from him, Wallace felt as though the entire world crashed onto his shoulders. It had been just over one month since American men landed on the beaches in Normandy, France. The Nazis were making a determined effort to defeat them there, but the Nazis were as good as extinct now; Wallace was sure of that. And with the Russians invading from the East, the problem would soon become what to do after the peace was won. Wallace didn't even want to contemplate what it would take to end the war with Japan.

He couldn't worry too much about that now. The war was like an orchestra already in progress. He couldn't just begin making changes. Aside from the war, one of the most pressing upcoming decisions, he knew, involved the Democratic National Convention, which would begin in under a week in Chicago. Wallace had already gotten word that party operatives had a VP candidate for him, Harry S. Truman of Missouri. Curiously, the "S" stood for nothing. And Wallace had every mind to go along with the pick, wanting to avoid any unpleasantness at the convention.

But more important than the Democratic National Convention was the Bomb and what he would do about it. He knew he had to discreetly bring in Vannevar Bush, who worked on the project, to talk options.

As the witnesses to his oath of office began to leave the room, Wallace wondered which of them he could trust. And as much as he wanted to call Vannevar in to speak today, he also wanted that meeting kept quiet. He didn't want to frighten the military unless he was ready to act.

That's when he saw his wife Ilo across the room and made his way toward her. She was holding a polite conversation with Secretary of State Cordell Hull.

"I can't believe the Japanese had the audacity to send their ambassadors to you on the day of Pearl Harbor," Wallace heard Ilo saying as he got near.

"It was part of their Samurai code I think. I had some very choice words for them then," Hull said. They were referring to the two Japanese ambassadors who kept their appointment with the Secretary of State just after the attack at Pearl Harbor ended. Roosevelt told Hull not to let on that he knew about what had happened until they delivered whatever message they were sent to deliver. "It was outrageous," Hull said. "They pretended to know nothing of the attack and brought a letter, which officially ended further discussions between the two nations. In all my fifty years of public service," Hull suddenly became visibly moved, "I have never seen such a document more crowded with infamous falsehood and distortion." As they left, the Secretary of State, a man born in a log cabin, called them a "bunch of pissants." He left that part out of his explanation to Ilo. After Pearl Harbor, the entire Japanese Diplomatic Core was hustled off to the luxurious and isolated Homestead resort in Hot Springs, Virginia. It was feared they would be lynched by a Washington mob.

Hull now looked up and saw the new president approaching. "Mr. President, my condolences and congratulations," he said.

"Thank you Cordell, though I don't know how happy I am that I should take Franklin's place. This situation, with the president's health, had crossed my mind in the past, but now that it's here . . . " He paused for a moment and continued. His face looked drawn, as though he was undergoing a great ordeal. "Now that it's here, the responsibility is terrible."

"I know you'll do what's right, Mr. President," Hull said.

"That's what I'm afraid of," Wallace replied without irony. Hull appreciated Wallace's sentiment and raised his chin in his high, starched shirt collar, in a kind of symbolic gesture of respect to the new president. Then Wallace said, "I wonder if I could borrow my wife for a few minutes?"

"Certainly."

Cordell walked away and Wallace held onto both of Ilo's hands. "Whenever you do that, Henry, I know you're going to ask me for a favor."

"And you'd be right this time, too. I need you to get Vannevar for me. I want to talk to him, and soon."

She paused for a moment and turned her head, "And why can't one of your aides go?"

"I'd rather keep this meeting quiet."

"You're certainly more paranoid than you need to be, Henry. These are perfectly good boys you have working for you." She could tell that he grew slightly impatient, and so she said, "Where would you like to meet him?"

"The Oval Office."

"All right." She said. "I'll go and fetch him."

Chapter Six

Jonathan Sparks

July 14, 1944
The White House, Washington, D.C.

When the cabinet room emptied Wallace stood looking out the window thinking about his former aide, Jonathan Sparks, and remembering the day they met. The first thing Wallace had noticed when he met Sparks was what could only be termed Sparks' "cowboy swagger." To Wallace, raised in Iowa, this swagger appeared rather absurd. Wallace was also hard pressed to see in the young man a New Deal Liberal, but a friend had recommended Sparks to him, and so Wallace gave him a personal interview. He liked what he heard.

"I grew up in a cabin in West Texas. We drew water from the stream a mile from the house." Wallace had only asked where Sparks was from, but Sparks wasn't going to miss an opportunity to paint his entire history for the vice president. "Times were hard on my father after the Great War, even though he had been an officer with an education, and they got harder when my mother died of Tuberculosis." At this point Sparks almost paused long enough to let Wallace offer a word, but then he continued in his slow-paced and methodical Texas drawl. "I was five then, and daddy raised us on his own, but he moved us to Midland and made a living in the oil business and things turned around. I got a good education at the University of Texas and went to study art history. But I never forgot what I learned when we were poor. I've been up and down this country, and I know what good Mr. Roosevelt is doing, and I want to help."

He was looking directly into the vice president's eyes when he said these last words. But unlike so many of the young and well-educated elites whom he interviewed, Sparks seemed to mean and to believe what he said. He was a young man who had lived the depression, like a real American. He hadn't just read about it at Harvard. In this man Wallace also heard echoes of his own family history, and in particular his grandfather, who had moved around the frontiers of America until settling in Illinois and then finally Iowa. Some of the frontier still lived in Jonathan Sparks.

From the day of their first interview forward, Wallace had a strong relationship with Sparks. He was like another of his sons. Wallace missed the young man when he went off to war in part because he had been so loyal and tenacious as his aide, but also because Wallace knew that he could trust Sparks. As Eleanor had tried to caution him, politics had gotten rather more treacherous than he remembered.

Each branch of the military was also running its own intelligence division, both at home and abroad, with or without White House, or congressional, consent, on top of what the OSS or the FBI was doing. In other words, everyone was spying on everyone. And there was so much money appropriated by congress for the war that a significant proportion of it could easily be funneled to secret, extra-military programs (like spying on the vice president of the United States), without the monies having to be accounted for, or by being accounted for in dubious and peculiar ways, as in hiding the cost in a $200.00 toilet seat for a latrine in North Africa.

What this meant to Wallace was that there were very powerful and secretive groups operating within the United States who were bold enough and organized enough to reach into the White House itself. He was face to face again with United States Secretary of the Navy James Vincent Forrestal.

This brought Henry's mind back to Sparks. As president, Wallace needed people he could trust if he was going to stand up to the kinds of pressure men like Forrestal could bring to bear against him. The problem at the moment was that Sparks was in Italy.

Sparks left in January of 1942, just after the Japanese struck Pearl Harbor. Wallace didn't want to see him go off to war. And for a week or so he had some hope that this wouldn't happen as Sparks headed up to Yale in late December to pursue a possible opening for a Masters in Art History, which he was told might also include deployment in Italy if the Allies ever got there. Wallace wasn't entirely sure how the new program was going to work, but he knew that Yale had old connections in the Navy and War Departments. So he didn't put it past them to establish a program that would allow its graduate students to earn a portion of their credit serving behind the lines in Italy taking stock of damaged art.

But the program never panned out, and Sparks signed up to fight instead. Sparks was the kind of man who was going to fight in the war one way or the other. As it happened, he had an uncle in North Dakota who was longtime friends with an Army recruiting officer there. Sparks joined the Army in that state and left for the Pacific Theater with the 164th Infantry Regiment.

He landed at Guadalcanal on October 13, 1942 and saw fierce fighting as part of the first Army unit during the war to engage in an offensive. The regiment fought alongside the Marines and was nicknamed the "164th Marines." After the battle, now veteran Private Sparks returned to Fiji. From there he would have joined *"Merrill's Marauders"* to fight in Burma had not Vice President Wallace intervened, with the backing of the Commander in chief, Roosevelt, and recommended that Sparks become a so-called "Monuments Man," in the freshly minted Monuments, Fine Arts and Archives Program. Wallace gave Sparks no chance but to accept, having Sparks' commanding officers pull him from the barracks and physically put him on the plane that would bring him to the plane that would fly him to Italy. Wallace had made the bold claim that Sparks' knowledge of Western art and architecture made him indispensable to the newly formed division, and because he was vice president at the time, he got his way; even over the protest of Douglas MacArthur. Fortunately, no one in the Army had thought to check Sparks' record to learn that he certainly wasn't the most qualified man for the job. What they did know of him, however, was that he could fight, and some men just assumed that excellence in one area naturally carried over to other fields. Despite his only having his Bachelor's degree, the change order was made, and Sparks was a Monuments Man. The deployment was ostensibly much like the program he interviewed for at Yale, so he should have been happy.

Since then, the last word Wallace had gotten was that Sparks was moving up the Italian peninsula and had been at the battle of Monte Casino in May.

Wallace now knew he was going to recall Sparks from his Monument's Man position. He needed him too much not to.

Chapter Seven

The Secret

January 1942
New Haven, Connecticut

One of Sparks' old professors from The University of Texas contacted him just after Pearl Harbor. He was a Yale man himself, and told Sparks that Yale was going to offer a Master's Program in art history that might include deployment abroad now that there would be war. Sparks took the day off from Vice President Wallace, and the following morning drove to New Haven.

He had the street name and number written down, but when he arrived the number he was given turned out to be an abandoned lot surrounded by a rusted fence. There were two cars parked inside the fence and a sign by the entrance painted with the address: 322. He pulled up to the larger of the two vehicles, a four-door Ford.

"Jonathan Sparks?" The heavily dressed greying man on the passenger side said through the open window. When Sparks nodded his assent, another man stepped out from the back of the car. He motioned to Sparks and said, "Professor Mann told us to expect you. Come with us please, we have something to show you." The man's hat nearly blew off in the winter wind, exposing his balding, grey head. He slapped his hand upward to catch it. Sparks stepped from the car onto the snow and ice left by a small winter storm a few days prior. He was apprehensive. "Is this the Masters course?" he asked.

"Yes, this is the Masters course, now please, it's cold," the old man said, holding open the passenger side rear door while waiving Sparks into the back seat. Sparks climbed into the Ford, noting how sharp the man's New England accent was. Inside he found himself next to a man his own age and dressed, much like the older man, in a Herringbone Tweed blazer with a heavy wool overcoat. As the first man climbed in behind Sparks, Sparks moved to the middle seat between the two. No one introduced himself. They were all dressed for the Connecticut winter in heavy coats and so the men were snuggly fit together in the Ford. But the car didn't move. Instead all the occupants were looking at Sparks; the driver included.

Suddenly the young man to his left said, "I'm sorry, but we have to ask you to put this on." He held up a black, silk handkerchief.

"What do you mean?" Sparks said. He was growing angry.

"Over your eyes. I know this seems strange, but there's a war on now and we have to be careful. If you trust Professor Mann then trust us."

"This is a hell of a way to greet somebody," Sparks said.

The man sitting behind the polished wood steering wheel up front became angry, "You can get out of the car and go back about your way."

Sparks defiance immediately perked and he leaned forward. The driver wore glasses. He had cold blue eyes and a protruding chin. Sparks was close to shouting. No one in the car struck him as the rough type, and he wasn't afraid to lose his temper here. These surely weren't Al Capone's men. But his curiosity eclipsed his better judgment. He'd heard certain things about Yale; about the secret societies the school housed and seemed to foster, and their practices and connections with government. The talk of such societies had made its speculative way to Texas: they ran the world, fomented wars, worshiped Beelzebub. He disliked Yale alumni generally, but mostly because he wasn't in the club. And like all American boys, he was more than curious and wanted to be part of the group.

Sparks leaned back against the leather bench seat. The young man to his left was lighting a cigarette and observing Sparks as he did so.

There was something in the man's eyes that was unsettling to Sparks; even beyond the older men surrounding him he seemed almost predatory.

Sparks then reached out and pulled a cigarette from the man's open pack without asking. He put it into his mouth and then tied the handkerchief over his own eyes.

"Let's go!" he said with the same swagger he'd displayed for Henry Wallace.

The young man beside him held up his lighter and lit the blinded man's smoke. Then he audibly tapped the seat in front of him. The heavy car lurched forward, sliding slightly in the packed slush of the parking lot as it went. Sparks heard the smaller car behind them also start its motor and begin following along.

Chapter Eight

The Oval Office

July 15th, 1945
The Oval Office

When Wallace entered, he instructed an aide to close the door behind him so that he could be alone, then he stood looking down at the desk for several minutes before he moved.

This was Roosevelt's room. No other president had ever sat here before. He had the Oval Office designed and built, along with the entire West Wing, in the early thirties. Whenever Wallace had come here in the past, he had thought of the office strictly as Roosevelt's domain, just as the presidency was Roosevelt's job. The entire country, to Wallace, had also begun to have this same kind of feel, and had become Roosevelt's country in a way that no other president had made it before.

Wallace was no stranger to death and its finality. When his own father died he was overawed by how final it really was, and yet he believed that there was a place somewhere where all souls went. But Roosevelt's death felt unreal, as if the president's heart still beat somewhere else. And standing here in the room that Roosevelt built, among his things, made this sense, like an odor, even stronger.

Wallace walked behind the desk and looked at the door where he would soon receive his guests as the president. His thrill at standing in this spot was muted by apprehension and sadness. Surprisingly, or maybe not under the circumstances, no one had thought to clean off the desk, and Wallace now turned and looked over Roosevelt's things that he found there. There were a few memos, a fountain pen with gold cap and a bronze eagle paperweight.

When he sat in Roosevelt's chair, he felt a shock and stood up. This was the chair that Roosevelt died in. That great man simply slumped over and died right there – his wheelchair off to the side. It wasn't as if Roosevelt remained in the chair for very long. Still, Wallace had the unshakable feeling that he had to wipe his clothes off after sitting down. He couldn't use that chair anymore, that was for sure; it was too close to the president. He needed his own chair.

Then as he stood, he put his hands flat on the desk. *The desk will be okay,* he thought, *I can still use this, but not the chair.* As it stood, it was as though the Oval Office was bending to the outside pressure, like the hatch of a submarine, which had sunk well below its maximum depth and was creaking from the stress of the structurally fatal pressure.

Now there was a knock at the door leading to the anteroom where the secretary, Betty, sat. It startled Wallace. He was already standing because he was uncomfortable in the Roosevelt chair and said, "Come in."

His aide, Ellery Martin, entered.

Ellery was the scion of a New York banking family whom Wallace had inherited as a favor to Roosevelt some months before. "I can't use him Henry, but I can't get rid of him either. You'd be doing a very good deed if you'd take him on," Roosevelt said. And so he had, but Ellery's allegiance to Wall Street made Wallace question the young man's fidelity to him.

"Mr. President, sir, Mr. Vannevar Bush is here to see you, sir."

"Thank you Ellery, please let him in. But would you do me a favor?"

"Yes, sir."

"Would you find me another chair for the desk? I feel uncomfortable sitting in this one. It was . . . well, it's just too close to the president. I don't want to wear his clothes either, I guess." But Wallace immediately felt that he said too much; as though he had indulged in an unpresidential outburst.

If he had, it didn't seem to register with Ellery, who said, "I understand, sir, I will have one sent up immediately."

"It can wait 'till after Mr. Bush leaves, thank you. And the desk too, please have it emptied out would you? His things are still in it."

Then Ellery withdrew from the Oval office. As Ellery did so Wallace questioned the logic of sending the first lady to get Vannevar in order to avoid tipping off his aides, when it was an aide who would eventually introduce the man into the office anyhow. Wallace just accepted that from now on it would be impossible to meet with anyone in true privacy. The White House was simply too public for the president to be private, although he racked his brain to come up with a means of meeting people in true privacy.

Vannevar Bush entered. He was a slender, well-dressed man in glasses. He was also extremely accomplished and wore this sense wherever he went like a hat or a necktie. Wallace knew Bush well because Mr. Bush reported to him and few others, members all of the so-called "Top Policy Group," on the Manhattan District which was what the atomic bomb project was named.

"How are you, Vannevar?" Wallace asked as he walked around the desk to greet him.

"Mr. President. I'm so sorry to hear about Franklin, I know you were close."

"Thank you. You're the first person to say he was sorry to hear of his death. I think other people were worried I'd think they meant they were sorry that I became president."

"I'm sure." Vannevar demurred. Then Wallace motioned for Bush to sit in one of the chairs in front of the desk. He himself walked back behind it and lowered himself down once again into Roosevelt's chair. He did so without a thought to what he was doing, but as soon as his body made contact with the leather, he remembered that he had intended to sit beside Bush in one of the two chairs on the opposite side of the desk. He immediately had the feeling of sleeping in another man's unmade bed, but pushed this sense aside and got down to business.

"I'd like to know where we stand with that bomb?" Wallace asked.

Bush's response was as concise as possible: "We will have a working bomb by this time next year. Maybe before." Bush spoke with what

Wallace considered a patrician, Boston Brahmin accent. Wallace, always the Midwesterner, generally recoiled from the accent whenever he heard it socially. It wasn't that he disliked people from Boston. He simply distrusted the way they talked, and could never get comfortable with it. However, Roosevelt himself had a patrician Eastern accent not entirely unlike the Boston one, and so Wallace did his best to forgive them this. But with Vannevar it was different. The accent seemed an outgrowth of this excellence rather than an attempt at it.

Then Wallace said, "What's the likelihood we'll have to use it?"

"It's your call. The Germans are putting up a determined effort to repel us, and the Japanese are . . ."

"How close are the Germans to getting this bomb?" Wallace interrupted.

"There's no way of knowing with any certainty. The *Alsos Mission* has been looking into that question for some time now. But as we get further into German territory it will be easier to know for sure if they're close to a bomb like this. It's accurate at this point to say that our estimates regarding the Nazi nuclear program were exaggerated. They certainly don't have it now or else they never would have lost at Stalingrad. They would have used a bomb like this without hesitation."

"It's my intention not to use it at all, Vannevar," Wallace suddenly interrupted, pulling his hand back over his graying hair in a motion that suggested an overstretched man who's uncertain what to do. "I can't stop thinking of what a terrible power this bomb is. I dream of it even." Vannevar cringed at this last confession, though he did his best not to show it. He was aware of the president's embarrassing friendship and string of letters with the Russian guru and mystic Nicholas Roerich that had nearly cost him his vice presidency before it began, so the mention of "dreaming" struck a false note with Bush. Of course, Roosevelt had continued backing his strange vice president from Iowa, despite his bizarre associations, effectively silencing criticism. But now that Wallace was the president, there was quite a bit of talk in Washington circles regarding those letters and certain other strange aspects of Wallace's personality.

For his part though, Vannevar Bush could see where President Wallace was now going with his comment. Bush himself had had some second thoughts regarding the wisdom of making of a bomb like this at all, but simply told himself that the United States was fundamentally different from other countries and could handle the responsibility.

"I just want you to know how uncomfortable I am with this whole thing." Wallace said, "Now, I believe we've got to do whatever we can to beat the fascists and imperialists, but I also don't want to open Pandora's Box in the meantime. I'm just not sure what to do."

Vannevar cringed again, because now he knew the president was not well disposed to the bomb project, one which he thought, despite his misgivings, was imperative to the survival of the free world.

The president sensed Vannevar Bush's diminishing eagerness to respond to his questions. This hesitance on the part of Bush left Wallace with a bad taste in his mouth. They talked for a few minutes further. Then he dismissed the head of the OSRD cordially, and called for Ellery.

Chapter Nine

The Secret Service

July 15, 1944
Oval Office

It was growing late, but his work wasn't done. His work would never be done as far as he could see.

He had already had some thirty meetings since Vannevar left earlier in the day. People all over town wanted to know how the change in president would affect either their jobs, or their political interests, or their futures, and so they arrived in droves. The White House switchboard was flooded with calls.

Ellery kept good watch and was turning away more people who sought the president's counsel than he gave time to. It was overwhelming. The day felt to Wallace like a train with no brakes, and so he called Ellery and told him to hold everyone for fifteen minutes. "I need time to draft this letter," he said. Ellery didn't bother to ask which letter the president meant. He merely assented to the president's wish and held the wolves at bay.

At this point, Wallace stood from his chair. Ellery had forgotten to bring him the chair he'd requested after Vannevar left. Instead, Wallace had walked to the front of the desk and pulled around one of the two green-pinstriped, upholstered chairs typically used for guests. He pushed the president's old chair to the right side of the room by the door leading to the terrace.

Now the president walked to the window and peered out at an angle between the overlapping curtains to look at the lawn and walkway leading to the rear drive. It was strange this yard could look so peaceful with all the pressure outside his door. And that's when the thought struck him. *How did the Secret Service know of Barton's confessions to his lover? By what means did they watch the West Wing?* Wallace had read the report, which had almost made it seem as though Barton was under surveillance. And no one had yet answered these questions for him.

Everything else could wait. He knew that Agent Chipton was on duty tonight and picked up the phone from the desk. Betty, the secretary who sat just outside his door in the anteroom answered.

"Send Ellery in please!" he said.

When Ellery entered, Wallace asked, "Do you know where Agent Chipton is?"

"Should I get him?"

"Please."

"What's this regarding?" Ellery asked.

For a split second Wallace was unhappy that his wish had been questioned at all. But he brushed aside the anger Ellery's question aroused and said, "Just get him, please."

When Ellery returned with the agent, President Wallace put his hand on Chipton's shoulder and walked him over to the table and chairs immediately to the right of the door in front of the fireplace, leaving Ellery sitting out with the secretary.

Wallace motioned for Agent Chipton to sit. Neither man said a word. But Wallace couldn't help but think of Roosevelt and his famous fireside chats held in this location. Then he looked from the fireplace to the agent, noting how the man's red hair gave him an aggressive look. He remembered too that Chipton was the agent who had tried to comfort him the day he learned the former president had died.

An awkward silence had developed between them and the president broke it by saying, "Where's back home for you, son?"

"Plains, Georgia."

"Can't say I've ever heard of it," the president said.

"No, sir, I wouldn't expect you would, not many people have."

"I've done a little campaigning down there for the president, well for Roosevelt, but I don't remember Plains. What do they do there? Farm?"

"Cotton, but they just started peanuts since the Boll Weevil laid waste the land," the young man said ominously.

"Corn was really my area of expertise but I've known a lot about the introduction of peanuts to the South since I was Ag Secretary, mostly because I was friends with George Washington Carver. My father was one of his professors in Iowa, and we became friendly when I was younger. He was a very kind man; a black man living in Iowa near the turn of the century, who made peanuts part of his life's work. He went after peanuts because he understood, before anybody else did, the poverty of soil that came with raising strictly cotton. It was really just a legacy from slavery that the South was so invested in cotton anyhow."

"Well, I never heard that," Chipton said. Wallace listened for any trace of the racism he often found in men from the South. But if it was there, Chipton didn't betray it. Instead, Agent Chipton said, "I knew there had to be a reason behind peanuts cropping up everywhere. I didn't know it was a Negro man that did it, but without peanuts, we were in rough shape, I know that."

Wallace was happy Agent Chipton didn't show any signs of the overt hatred that marked so many of his countryman. And that's when he got around to asking the agent why Mike Barton had been under suspicion in the first place.

"Do you remember seeing Mike Barton leave my office with papers?"

"Yes, I do."

He obviously did, but Wallace just wanted to break the ice.

"You were there when he was shot."

"I chased the man that did it. He dropped his hobo outfit and got away."

"I know that," Wallace said. "But there's something that's been bothering me ever since. Why did you suspect him in the first place? You were looking at him, weren't you? He worked in my office, what would be odd about him leaving with papers?"

Chipton sighed. He looked toward the windows and then back to the president.

"Sir, Ellery tipped us off."

The president thought for a moment and said, "If he saw him take the papers, why didn't he just confront him then, or tell me, instead of putting the Secret Service on him? I realize that he was shot, and that by following him you might have even saved his life. But why were you focused on my aide in the first place?"

"Sir, Ellery repeatedly told the officer in command to watch Mike Barton over the course of several weeks. Reynolds put the word out to all the agents on your detail. On that day, I saw Barton leave your office with a look like he just stole something. I relayed the message to the desk. They told me to follow him. My partner, Dunbar, and I did so."

The president sighed and asked, "Who was the temp he was sleeping with?"

"That I don't know, sir."

"You're sure that it was Ellery?"

"That what, sir?"

"That put you onto Barton."

"Without a doubt."

The president squinted when he thought about Ellery tipping off the Secret Service to his aide Mike Barton, and wanted to ask the obvious question. But why not ask the man himself? He stood from the chair he was in and poked his head out into the anteroom where Betty sat.

"Ellery, would you come in here for a moment?"

"Yes, sir."

Ellery followed the president into the room. Wallace went back to the chair he had been in. Agent Chipton stood, looking confused about what he should do. "Stay there for a minute, Agent Chipton. Ellery, I want to know why you thought Mike was spying on me."

Ellery looked down at his feet and looked uncomfortable. For his part, Wallace wasn't thinking about Ellery's comfort. He had trusted Mike

Barton and didn't trust Ellery, and thought it very strange that Barton was involved in such a thing at all.

But Ellery wasn't answering right away. Wallace got impatient.

"Well, you better start talking, Ellery!"

That jolted Ellery out of his stupor. "Sir, the president told me that he thought there was a mole in the vice president's office. That people were leaking information damaging to you and that you didn't know about it. He sent me to you because he wanted me to confirm what he already knew."

Wallace stood from his chair and said, "Franklin sent you to me?"

"Yes, sir. I'm sorry. He was very sure that he was right and he didn't want you to think he was spying on you." He said it very quickly, jumbling his words together. Ellery was getting emotional at this point, and Wallace could see a clammy sweat breaking out where his brown hair overlaid his forehead.

"All right. All right," Wallace said, walking toward the young man. "Now settle down."

"I was just doing what I was told."

"That's fine. But why Mike Barton?" Wallace was animated now. As much as he had liked watching his young Ivy League aide squirm, he felt much worse at the fact that Ellery seemed to be telling the truth and hadn't done anything wrong.

"I don't know how he knew about Mike Barton, sir."

"Then who's the girl he was sleeping with?"

"I just know what President Roosevelt had me do."

"The girl!" Wallace shouted. "Barton told her that he was spying for the Navy."

"Sir, if there was . . ."

Wallace interrupted, "It can't be that hard to find out which one of the girls in the West Wing he was sleeping with."

"I don't think he was. President Roosevelt had his own information. I don't think it came from a girl here at all. The girl was Roosevelt. I mean whoever said there was girl was covering for Roosevelt."

"You know that?"

"Roosevelt told me that he learned about Barton from his close ties in the Navy. He used to be secretary."

"I know he was Secretary of the Navy." Wallace looked into the fireplace. "The girl was a ruse, a rumor," he said to himself. Then he turned back to Chipton, "What do you know about Barton's background?"

"I don't have his file. You'd have to ask Reynolds for that, but I know that we looked into him when Ellery first brought it up and he had no connection to the Marines or to the Navy, or even to the Army that we could find. He has no Wall Street ties either." At this last part Ellery blushed a bit, but Chipton continued, "Or anything that would tie him with anti New Deal sympathies."

"Then who the hell was he?"

"He was a college boy. He went to Yale. From Brookline Mass. He's from an old New England family. We don't know who he was working for with any certainty, or that he was working with anyone, or who shot him, or why President Roosevelt suspected him of working for the Navy Department"

"An aide to the vice president was shot and the Secret Service doesn't know why." Wallace said.

"No, sir."

Chapter Ten

Camposanto

July 27, 1944
Pisa, Italy

He watched the lead roof bubble and melt from the fire below. The liq-uid metal dripped down the interior walls of the *Camposanto,* destroying some of the oldest frescoes in the world. Sparks had studied the building in college. It was a magnificent cemetery. He'd never imagined he'd be standing here to watch it burn.

He was positioned about one hundred feet back from the inferno with a .45 automatic on his hip, a notepad in his hand and a camera around his neck, though he had already taken all the pictures he was going to take of this site.

It made him sick to see the building burn. Just an accident really: one bomb drifted off course and ignited the rafters on the roof. If the roof had only collapsed that would have been one thing. But instead, the heavy timbers burned and melted the lead, which was in turn destroying the ancient frescoes. The rafters would cave in in a few minutes, but by then it would be too late.

He would almost have rather seen this place totally destroyed than see its own roof drip down the walls and erase its frescoes. There was something about it that sickened him.

Sparks wasn't happy that he was here to see this place burn this way. And he didn't have to be here either. He had gotten a letter from Henry Wallace, just a day after he became president, asking Sparks to return.

"I need men I can trust," the president's letter said. "And I'm damn short on them right now. I'm sending a letter to Eisenhower. However they have to do it, you're needed here."

And that was that. Once the letter filtered through Army bureaucracy, Sparks was told by his commanding officer that he was to leave Italy immediately. But unlike in Fiji, Sparks had more leeway and asked that he be allowed to accompany the Army until they broke the Nazi's so-called "Gothic Line" in Italy, on the theory that if he was going to leave the fighting early to return to civilian life, he could at least see the current fight through. The commanding officer agreed, and sent word back to Eisenhower that Sparks was "indispensable in his duties for the moment, as we are short on these 'Monuments Men' and long on broken art, but as soon as fighting ceases on the Gothic Line we can circulate him out."

Now Sparks questioned his push to remain "in country" at all. He should have done what Wallace told him to do.

It was then that he looked and saw another American looking man observing the fire from the north of the *Camposanto* compound. He was a strange looking man – not quite civilian in his dress, but not a soldier either. The man then looked up and began walking toward Sparks over some of the rubble strewn on the pockmarked lawn. It wasn't totally out of the ordinary for another soldier, or whatever he was, to walk toward Sparks under such a circumstance. After all, they were the only two peo-ple here at the moment. And since they were both witnessing this terrible event, and both were Americans, Sparks figured they might as well talk. But there was more to his approach than that. There was something in the way the man walked. It was like he was looking for Sparks.

And then the man spoke, "I work for OSS," he said.

"Well, good for you," Sparks said, put off by the guy's approach. "What can I help you with?" He had never heard of OSS before. The Army was full of abbreviated departments and the abbreviated men who thought they were important.

"You're Jonathan Sparks." The guy from OSS said, not as a question but a statement.

"They call me that." Then they both stood there observing the other. The heavy black smoke obscured the sun, and their faces glowed beside the red and yellow firelight of the burning roof. Sparks was looking down at the man. Sparks was three or four inches taller. But the shorter man didn't exactly look like a pushover. He seemed cruel in a way that made Sparks think of a predatory bird: an Osprey or Red Tail or something.

Still neither said a word. Sparks could hear the lead hiss as it struck the stone floor inside the burning building, followed by the sound of gunfire in the distance. At that point, he wondered if the guy was going to introduce himself, or even whether he was going to say another word at all.

For the moment the man in olive-drab slacks and shirt and no insignia of rank just observed Sparks. In most other circumstances, Sparks would have taken offense. But under these conditions, he decided to be a little more polite than he would have been otherwise, and started to talk as if the two knew each other.

"It looks like the end of the world in Italy."

"All over really," the man said as he broke from staring at Sparks and gazed off toward the *Camposanto*. "We're winning, but there's no telling where this will go," the man from the OSS added.

"The Nazis will surrender," Sparks said.

"But what will the Russians do? After the Nazis fall there'll be two big armies with all their guns pointing at each other. And of course, we don't really see eye to eye with the Bolsheviks. Patton wants to push straight through to Moscow."

Sparks had considered this possibility before. What else would the apocalypse look like if not the all-out destruction of people and culture?

He knew about the ovens they'd set up for extermination in Germany. He knew about the millions who died on the Eastern Front, and the millions before them who died in Stalin's purges and forced famines (the happenings in Russia since the previous war was one of his father's obsessions, although he wasn't sure how much he could believe). Now the Japanese were contributing their part to the rape and murder of the Chinese and of anyone else whom they decided were inferior or living on "their" natural resources. All you had to do was read the newspaper to see that the whole thing was coming apart. It wasn't so farfetched to imagine that the two great allies, the Soviets and the Americans, would suddenly break all their agreements and start fighting over who would become the undisputed world power. After all, the same thing had already happened between the allied nations of Soviet Russia and Nazi German when the Nazis broke the Molotov-Ribbentrop pact.

When you sat down and thought about it, it would probably happen sooner or later. That meant the fighting would continue on indefinitely. The situation reminded Sparks of a quote from the Iliad his father often repeated. His father had seen fighting in the first war-to-end-all-wars as an Army Intelligence officer, and Army Intelligence had served as one of the precursors to the current OSS. In fact, many of the men now running OSS had gotten their start in Army Intelligence. Now his son was here in the second such war. The quote his father recited read: "We are men to whom Zeus has given the fate of winding down our lives in painful wars, from youth until we perish, all of us."

Only now men weren't throwing spears at each other and forming phalanxes. Now they could kill whole fields of men with a machine gun in minutes, and level a city with incendiary bombs in no time at all. And there was talk of something even more powerful coming down the line. *What then?*

In short, if they didn't stop fighting, *who the hell would be left when it was done? What would be left?*

This was the future Sparks saw. And the Germans weren't even done fighting. They were still deeply entrenched outside the city of Pisa. And though they were defeated, and most of them knew it, they fought like they were the conquering army. Sparks had already seen several quick reversals on the field and witnessed Americans killed.

The Huns were living up to their reputation and then some. They weren't just backing out of the boot of Italy. They were destroying the place and killing as many Americans as they could along the way. Sparks thought, *maybe we've gotta fight them just to get to the next fight?* He feared that when the Americans were done mopping up the Nazis, half the continent would be a pile of rubble. Then they'd have to wreck the other half in the next war.

But as much cultural damage as the old Nazis caused, Sparks had to concede that his side wasn't coming out of this thing smelling like roses. Back in February, he was there at *Monte casino*. That place was a thousand-year-old monastery that stood atop a mountain just south of Rome.

The Germans were dug in all over the hill, picking off Americans from entrenched positions. It was only a matter of time before word came down to bomb the place. Notwithstanding General Eisenhower's directive that needless cultural destruction be avoided, the Army couldn't allow good men to get killed. If it came down to a choice between art-and-architecture and a man's life, you wrecked the art and saved the man every time.

But as a so-called "Monuments Man," Sparks had a vested interest in seeing these places saved. He was just an assistant after all, but even *he* couldn't disagree when word came to bomb the monastery. And that's exactly what the Army did. They bombed that place until it was just a terrific pile of rubble. A thousand years gone in an afternoon. As it turned out, the German's hadn't even been holed up in the monastery at all. They were all over the mountainsides below. But as soon as American bombs turned the mountaintop into a great big pile of rubble, the Nazis climbed in among the debris, raised their awful flag and commenced fighting.

When the Americans finally pushed the Nazis out, Sparks went in with a small group of other Monuments Men to see what could be salvaged. There really was very little left – lots of bullet casings. It looked more like a pile of mine tailings than a monastery. They found a few religious artifacts, but there was no telling what any of it was at that moment. The monastery was an archeological site now. And to Sparks' mind, the whole world might look like this soon for some later race to come back to and wonder what the hell happened. Maybe they'd imagine it was a comet.

"We're allies of the Soviets," Sparks finally said in reply to the man's last comment, but it sounded weak when he heard himself say it.

"Do you really think you can trust a communist?"

Well actually, no, he didn't, in fact. His father used to say, "The only good commie's a dead commie." And that stuck with Sparks.

"What's the alternative?" Sparks said, because he didn't want to admit that he agreed with this man. Then he asked, "What's your name by the way? And what's the OSS?" Just as Sparks said that, the roof of the *Camposanto* collapsed. The fire cracked and popped and threw bright sparks into the black plume.

They both turned to observe.

Chapter Eleven

Economic Advisor

July, 27th 1944
Washington, D.C.

Wallace was sitting with Lauchlin Currie in the Oval Office. As members of the so-called "Brain Trust," they had something in common, but outside of that designation they had built a personal rapport, which is why Wallace took Currie on as Economic Advisor without hesitation after Roosevelt's death.

In many ways Wallace admired Lauchlin, who had drafted the Banking Act of 1935, and soon thereafter became a personal White House advisor to President Roosevelt. Wallace further thought that Currie had saved the country from a deeper recession after the crash in '37, when he had personally changed Roosevelt's thinking on several important issues concerning the balanced budget and its negative effects on the economy at large. Wallace was happy to have Currie on board, though the Canadian born economist was less effusive in his characterization of Wallace. They nevertheless "got on" and had progressive sympathies that went deeper than the New Deal.

Their official meeting over, they stood. Laughlin was a dowdy looking man, who in a certain light almost looked as if he could have been related to President Roosevelt. Despite the slight resemblance, Wallace knew of no family connection.

This was the first time the president had been able to speak with Currie since becoming president. As he stood Wallace flashed Lauchlin his characteristic warm and toothy grin. He was about to thank him for coming when Lauchlin said, "From what I hear, Henry, the election looks as though it should be a rather easy affair, as elections go."

"Well, I hope so, but we have to get through the convention first," he said, referring to the Democratic National Convention with less confidence than Lauchlin expected to hear in the president's voice.

"You can't imagine that the Republicans can stand a chance this election."

"No, but a national election is a very tricky business."

"I wouldn't know anything about it," Lauchlin added, as Wallace walked around the desk and shook his hand.

Wallace had been eager to see his economic advisor for some time, and wanted to ask him for his opinion on topics that were strictly outside of Lauchlin's narrow role. The president knew that both he and Lauchlin had political, and to the president's mind economic, sympathies in common.

"There's something I'd like to ask you about, Lauchlin," the president said still holding his advisor's hand. Lauchlin nodded and even smiled to show that he was open to hearing any question that the president had. "There's a project the Army's working on. They call it the Manhattan District, but the term refers to an atomic bomb. From what I understand, it's easier to funnel money through a district than to a project, especially in the case of R&D for secret weapons' programs. Have you heard of it?"

Currie thought for a moment. His work under Roosevelt had spanned the entire arc of American interests in the 1930s and early '40s. Aside from being a personal advisor to President Roosevelt, he had also headed the Lend-Lease Program: a program that sent military aid and materiel to the Soviet Union and other allies including the British and Chinese. In the United States he had also created a training program for Chinese Pilots and had advised General George Marshal regarding the role the Chinese air force could play in defending that country. But he had not heard of the bomb.

"No, sir. Should I have?"

"There's not many people have heard about it. I thought it possible that you might have. I mention it because I think I'm going to end the project. We've wasted enough money trying to build this bomb, and I'm not entirely sure I even want to make it at all, if it can be made. I tell you this in confidence of course."

"Of course." Currie stood silently before the president considering what this bomb might mean for the world.

"I don't mean to burden you with too many of my fears," the president continued as he leaned back against his desk and released his advisor's hand, "but we're very close to building an atomic bomb based on some of Einstein's theories. The A-bomb would be able to wipe whole cities off the map in one explosion. I'm squeamish enough about war to begin with: men killing each other with rifles and bayonets, and tanks, and planes dropping munitions. But this is something altogether different. Imagine everything from here to Arlington Cemetery and beyond gone in one detonation. It's madness. I know we want to win, but this is a terrible weapon no one wants to use. To my mind, it will only be a matter of time before someone uses it."

Suddenly Currie perked up, "Are you sure they can even build the thing at all? A lot of these types of projects come to nothing."

"They'll do it. I'm sure of that. They're already very close."

"And do you know what this project will cost?"

"No, I don't even think the Army does."

"I assume this didn't go through congress?" Lauchlin said knowingly.

"No, this is one of those projects that exists on its own. That's why they call it the 'District'."

"Then cutting off funding is not the best route to take," Currie explained, "because, to begin with, having dealt with projects like this before, it's probably tough to pinpoint how it's funded even within the District. And you don't want to take this kind of action halfheartedly, or piecemeal." At this point Lauchlin paused. He took a somber air as he continued. "If you're serious about stopping the program, Henry, then you have to scrap the whole thing. Pull everybody off it, close the sites and liquidate the equipment. To me, and I don't want to be presumptuous, if the Army thinks this is such a high priority, then you're going to make enemies when you cancel their project, and the military has ways of fighting entirely outside the political system." Lauchlin took a breath and said, "If you're going to take this on then you can't tip your hand, or else the program will suddenly morph and change and continue on under a new name and in new buildings."

The president took a deep breath, and Currie waited for his response. "No, I know," the president said, "there's nothing I can do until at least after the convention, but realistically only after the election in November. This will have to remain quiet until then."

"Well then wait, and kill the program, but just know you're going to make a lot of these military people upset when you take away their baby."

"It can't be helped." The president now walked across the room to the fireplace. "They just want to win the war," he said sympathetically. "But what war is the question." He was looking into the empty fireplace. He seemed almost to be talking to himself. "Our military is full of people who think it's the Soviets next. That's who they're doing this for. They want to have something over Stalin, but the way they think they're going to handle him is all wrong." He stopped now as if he had been struck and asked, "What do you think of him?" He turned from the fireplace and looked squarely at Lauchlin.

"Stalin?"

"Yes, Stalin. What do you really think of him and what he is doing?"

Currie frowned. He looked uncomfortable and smirked in a kind of pained grimace one might see on the face of an abused child when asked where his bruises came from. He took a breath as if he were considering whether he should be honest. When he hesitated, Wallace looked sharply at him and said, "You're my friend, Lauchlin."

Lauchlin frowned and answered, "A lot of good people lost faith in him after he made the Molotov-Ribbentrop pact with the Nazis, plus what we've heard about liquidations in the USSR is disconcerting to say the least. It's shaken a lot of people to the core."

"And you?" Wallace asked in a deliberate way.

Currie didn't immediately answer. The two made eye contact. Lauchlin understood from the look the president gave that he had to answer honestly; that Wallace knew more than his smile and his appeal to friendship let on. "Including myself, yes," he said. "I've been shaken by his actions."

"You know Whitaker Chambers gave your name to Adolf Berle over at the State Department, don't you? He says he has proof you were giving information to the Soviets." Wallace could see the shock that Currie felt at what he had said, but he continued. "There's also talk that there are decrypted cables from the Soviet Ambassador here in Washington, Gromyko, back to Moscow, where you're mentioned in an unflattering light."

"I know, but no one believes Chambers. He's sensational," Currie added quickly.

"Whitaker Chambers is certainly a poor source. He's been thoroughly discredited," Wallace added in a manner that sounded objective and detached, "but the cables can't be disputed, and they will come out."

"Are you asking me to resign?" Lauchlin said. He sounded both hurt and aggressive.

"Lauchlin, I only just asked you to continue on with me. I didn't have a change of heart overnight. But I also know that Whitaker is not lying, nor are those cables from Ambassador Gromyko fakes." As Wallace paused, the Oval Office seemed to him to have become terribly silent. The president knew what he was doing, but this was the first time he had used the power of his office to push a man into undertaking what was not in his best interests. Wallace felt uncomfortable in the way he was treating his friend. He also felt he had no choice.

"What . . . what are you saying?" Lauchlin stuttered.

"What I am saying is that there are a substantial number of people in both the Army and the Navy, and the FBI for that matter, who know what you've been doing." He could both see and feel Lauchlin cringe as he said this. It was at times like these that Wallace wished he had more of the political cunning of a man like Roosevelt, who could make someone understand an unpleasantness without having to name what he was after. Wallace didn't have such a gift, although he was trying. He had seen Roosevelt handle sensitive issues on many occasions and had at least learned something of the technique. At this point rather than driving home the point, he changed his tactic and began a new line of thought. He hoped Lauchlin's response would help make it clear what he was really asking.

"The stories one hears regarding Stalin are terrible and can't be ignored or downplayed. Would you agree?"

"Yes!" Lauchlin answered, sounding almost relieved to be asked such an easy question, though he was unsettled as to where this might lead.

"Do you know many others who feel like this?"

"Like this?"

"Yes, as you do!"

"I can't be sure," Currie said.

"But there are others," the president asked. "They must feel alone by this point . . . as you do," Wallace added the last part to drive home the point, although having said it he felt it almost gratuitous.

"I . . . Mr. President, I don't know what you are asking me."

"I'll work with you, if you'll work with me." Sensing that this response was vague the president added, "What I mean is that I can help to shield you from your past and what will happen as your actions come to the light of day, which they will."

"But what do you need from me?" Lauchlin was nearly trembling at this point.

"You are a part of an international network."

"Sir . . ."

Wallace cut him off. "I want you to talk to the other ones. The ones you know you can trust. I want to assemble our own network, out of all the people who feel alone as you do. I understand why you leaned toward the Russians when you did, but their revolution is over. Stalin is now the Tsar. However, I think there is still some good that can be salvaged from all that's happened. And I think that you can help us."

Chapter Twelve

Intelligence

July 28, 1944
Pisa, Italy

Now that the roof of the *Camposanto* had collapsed, Sparks felt some relief. The ceiling was made of timber while the walls were thick masonry. In other words, with the roof gone the threat of melting lead was out of the way, and the interior of the old building, and its frescoes, were safer now than at any time for many months. A bomb might still wander off course and strike the building, however this threat was almost non-existent now considering it had already been hit once accidentally and the fighting was miles to the north.

All that was left to do was wait until the fire burned out on the floor of the building and go in to catalogue the damage. Sparks wondered what he would find when he finally went inside.

That's when the stranger in olive drab decided to speak up, "You're leaving the war effort?" he asked.

Sparks looked away from the *Camposanto* and to the man at his left. "How do you know that?"

"I told you, I'm with Intelligence."

"You didn't tell me that," Sparks said, "What do you do?" He hadn't liked this guy at first sight, now he really had a reason. But he was holding back his anger. Any American walking around freely just behind the front lines wasn't a man you yelled at lightly.

Now Sparks was staring right at the man.

"We gather intelligence behind the lines. I brought up Russia before because that *is* the next war. And I'm here because Eisenhower recently made a request to have you pulled from the front lines and flown back to Washington immediately, where we assume you can resume your duties to Henry Wallace.

"Is that what this is . . ." Sparks began, but the man quickly cut him off.

"I'll tell you what this is about," he said. Sparks' face reddened. The man continued on as if he didn't notice. "You'll soon be the trusted assistant of the president of the United States. He's a good man, Mr. Wallace, but ask yourself if he can be trusted when it comes to the new threat the Russians pose? He has a cabinet shot through with members of the international communist network."

"Of course Wallace can be trusted. Listen, I don't know what you think . . ."

"We don't need another answer now, but when the time is right. And, remember you already said 'yes'."

At this, Sparks gave him a perplexed look. "Oh, come on," the man from intelligence followed, "we didn't forget New Haven."

Sparks didn't say anything. The two were just staring at each other and Sparks thought that the man looked like he had once been the captain of an Ivy League football team. Sparks had, in the last few years, become more and more familiar with the "white shoe" personality. Then the man spoke suddenly, and off topic.

"They built the *Camposanto* around something called the 'holy field.' It was named that because the dirt in the cemetery came from Golgotha, and was brought here by ship during the Fourth Crusade."

Sparks tried to cut in and mention that the story of the dirt coming from Golgotha was only legend, but the man talked over him. "We're in something like a crusade now, only we don't know it. If this war has taught us anything, it's that both great oceans are smaller than the Mediterranean was in in the Middle Ages. We can't hide in our continent any longer. We either learn to fight them on their soil, or we'll continue to fight them on our own."

"And you want me to spy on the president?" Sparks asked.

"It's more about a point of view. No one cares what the president's doing so long as it doesn't help the Bolsheviks. That's all."

"Well, I'll tell you right now . . ." Sparks was talking loudly, but the man talked louder still, with a force that put Sparks onto his heels for a moment.

"You'll do what's best to protect your way of life, or you won't have one! That's all we mean to get across to you. We don't expect you to betray anyone, especially yourself. We had the impression you were already on board. You're one of us, don't forget it."

The man then walked off through the rubble and debris. He turned when he was twenty steps away and said, "We'll be in touch." He didn't wait for Sparks to respond. Instead he continued to walk and passed through a plume of grey black smoke as he went. At the other end of the building he climbed into a Jeep where a large man was waiting to pick him up. Sparks hadn't noticed the Jeep before.

Chapter Thirteen

The Roof of the World

August 27, 1944
Washington, D.C., White House Residence

It was 1:00 am and President Wallace couldn't sleep. He looked over at his wife whose rhythmic breathing told him she was not having the same trouble. Most nights were like this for him now. These last weeks all blended together into one terrible, unending day, even though to an outsider he should have been on top of the world.

He made it through the Democratic National Convention without so much as a scratch. The Democrats nominated him unanimously with the cry of, "We love Wallace!"

As far as he could tell, the chant was spontaneous. However, the convention *was* held in Chicago, the "windy city", so anything was possible.

The outpouring of support Wallace received surprised him. Even his advisors hadn't predicted the amount of affection he had garnered. The general consensus had been that he would get a bump in his approval ratings. The more cynical of his associates had called it the "sympathy bump." But no one knew how large that bump would turn out to be. And now he was riding high on a wave of both political and public support unrivaled since Roosevelt was elected the first time, over the despised and seemingly hapless Herbert Hoover.

Wallace's support was so great that he might have been able to pick his own vice presidential nominee. As it stood though, he followed advice and went with the safe bet of Harry S. Truman. He was concerned about the risk of political infighting if he failed to follow the script, and he sought to avoid such shenanigans at all costs.

It irritated him a bit that Truman was a party hack from Missouri and graduate of the infamous Pendergast machine in Kansas City. But on the two occasions they'd spoken so far it seemed Truman truly was a dedicated New Dealer, as Wallace himself was, and that's what really mattered.

Truman wanted to talk to him now about American intelligence gathering, and how the US needed to readjust the way in which it collected and digested sensitive and secret information. This sounded like a logical conversation to have, and since Truman, as a Senator, had headed the Senate Special Committee to Investigate the National Defense Program where he fought graft and corruption in the allocation of funds for the war effort, he was probably the man with whom Wallace should be talking.

Nevertheless, it was a conversation Wallace dreaded, so he had pushed off the meeting. But he couldn't put it off indefinitely. It wasn't even Truman he sought to avoid, but the unpleasantness of discussing the creation of a permanent intelligence apparatus in the United States, which is what he knew Truman had in mind. Wallace was not happy with the idea of creating a permanent intelligence gathering and espionage-engaging outfit. After all her previous wars, America had dissolved the intelligence units she'd created. Why not continue the tradition? Wallace knew the answer. And it was that answer which kept him from meeting with his vice president. Men in power in the military, politics, and business feared the Soviets; they feared Stalin. But Wallace feared the conclusions this fear would make them come to.

Wallace even thought about delaying any firm decisions on after-war intelligence policy by sending his vice president away somewhere. It wasn't unheard of. In fact, he himself had just returned from a goodwill tour of the Soviet Far East, which many had thought Roosevelt sent him on to get him out of his hair. So maybe he could send "Harry S." (Which is what he called Truman privately) on a similar tour; maybe to help with the reclaiming of cultural treasure as the Nazi war machine receded from the Italian boot?

But what the hell did Harry Truman know about Western cultural treasure anyhow? Probably about as much as a haberdasher from Missouri could, which was precisely nothing. He would know that Mona Lisa smirked, but would prefer Midwestern girls to her oddly European face – he might even have thought her a Jew and disliked her for it. And then he laughed to himself and imagined where on the planet he could send his vice president so as to avoid him best. Maybe to India?

And that's when he remembered it. He had forgotten it to this point, or had tried as best he could.

It had been given to him on his trip to the Russian "Wild East" several months ago when he'd traveled there under Roosevelt.

After leaving from Alaska for his good will tour, Wallace first spent some time in a little village on the Pacific Coast of Siberia known as Magadan. It was actually very nice. Their agricultural development was rudimentary, but enough for their purposes. No one was going hungry in Magadan; that was obvious, they all looked very healthy. And even the Russian General who'd showed him around, General Nikishov, was a very kind man.

Then from outer Siberia his convoy traveled to Mongolia where the vice president collected native cereal specimens he hoped would prove useful in places devastated by drought in the West. From there they pushed south into China in a caravan of military vehicles on dusty roads, stopping overnight at small villages where they were treated like conquering heroes.

But at the border between China and Mongolia, in a small village where the nomadic peoples stopped to trade with their more sedentary neighbors, a Tibetan trader handed Wallace a note. It read only, "We will descend from the roof of the world to meet you in Jiuquan. We have a gift."

Despite the brevity of the note, Wallace immediately realized who it was from. This fact led to many more questions than answers. And the question at the top of the list was how Nicholas Roerich knew that the vice president was coming to Jiuquan? This part of his itinerary had only been added in the last few days. But it would have taken this messenger weeks to arrive at the Chinese border, assuming Roerich was in Tibet at all. Maybe he was very near. And why did he need to meet with Wallace now, after all these years?

Roerich had disappeared into the Himalayas back in the 30's. He was pushed there because he had nowhere else safe to go. The Soviets viewed him as a decedent bourgeois, while the Americans wanted him for tax evasion. And so he quietly pulled back from the wider world into his great mountain abode, which seemed fitting for him, as the Great Himalayas were the root of much of the world's mythology, and Roerich always lived rather more like a man from myth than anything else.

The little town of Jiuquan, where Wallace's caravan was headed, sat at the edge of the Tibetan Plateau, which is what the note referred to as the "roof of the world." The moniker was apt, as much of the plateau sat fourteen thousand feet above sea level.

Wallace had always wanted to reach the plateau, but it would not happen this trip. Instead, he caught only a glimpse of its northern escarpment, just to the south of Jiuquan where the plateau rose over six thousand feet from the parched flatlands into the mountains.

He was hesitant to see Nicholas Roerich again at all. It had been some time since they had spoken on friendly terms. As Secretary of Agriculture, Wallace had sent Roerich on an agricultural trip to China on behalf of the United States to collect specimens of grains and seeds from the Asian Steppe. Roerich, however, failed to collect any specimens at all. When Wallace denounced Roerich publicly, someone in Roerich's camp leaked what came to be known as the "Guru Letters." These letters were Wallace's personal correspondence with Roerich and his wife. They acquired this name because Wallace headed the letters "Dear Guru," which was as embarrassing for Wallace as it was for Roosevelt. But the unfortunate leak hadn't been fatal for Roosevelt's presidency or his love for Wallace, whom he would later name his vice president. It had, however, permanently severed ties between Roerich and Wallace.

Why then would the guru want to speak with Wallace now?

After three days' travel through far northwestern China, the vice president and his retinue reached the small outpost of Jiuquan. It was little more than a crossroads, but had once sat on the great Northern Silk Road. It had also been used as a military outpost and had the feel of a place through which great armies once passed.

The landscape was otherworldly. There were hills and streams and deciduous trees of a type not unfamiliar to North America, yet it was also arid, as if the trees recently grew from the desert, or as if the land were slowly turning into one. Jiuquan was beautiful and full of fascination.

When Wallace arrived in an olive drab military convoy, flying the flag of the United States, the villagers assembled in the small central square to greet him, all colorfully dressed. They were nominally Chinese, but had many distinguishing characteristics of the Mongol. What set them apart, Wallace had learned, was that they spoke a dialect of Chinese rather than the very distinct Mongolian.

Upon entering the village, Wallace was given a great banquet. It was so lavish that he was surprised this bleak landscape could provide such a colorful bounty at all. The people were kind and rugged. They scratched their existence from the earth in a hard climate, but their personalities did not reflect their difficult lives. In fact, it was the opposite: they were warm and friendly.

The Americans had been in town for a day when riders on horseback descended the nearby escarpment. The resultant dust from the sandy mountains was visible miles away. There was some talk among the Americans regarding the riders' identities. Wallace's security detail grew nervous. They climbed into the back of an olive drab truck from their convoy and began readying automatic rifles. The locals themselves were arming, but still smiling as they slung surplus WWI rifles from the forgotten Ottoman Empire over their shoulders and turned to greet the riders.

By arming, they were simply taking a reasonable precaution without needless fanfare. This area had a history of raiders on horseback going back thousands of years.

As the riders approached it became obvious that they were not Chinese. They were distinguishable at a distance by the Tibetan Ponies they rode. The Chinese interpreter pointed this out immediately. The Tibetan Pony is a breed all its own: small, agile and strong; used to walking jagged mountain paths. The men who rode them all wore smiles and intricately patterned hats with long bright coats past their knees covering their solid colored trousers. And they all wore their hair long. One of the men carried a white flag that showed three solid small red circles inside a larger red outer ring. This had been Roerich's flag, known as the *banner of peace*. It once sat in the Oval Office when Roosevelt signed a treaty drafted by Roerich that was designed to protect cultural treasures, although the treaty had never been enacted.

The group of mounted Tibetans approached the armed Americans. Only one member of the Tibetan group descended from his horse. He stepped forward and knocked dust from his trousers, which in the breeze looked like a cloud of smoke. He then walked to the Americans and in Chinese asked to speak with the "great American." The Chinese official who interpreted for Wallace laughed when the man spoke. Turning to Wallace he said, "He speaks Chinese with an Indian accent. But he says he has a gift for the great American."

"Well I suppose that must be me." Wallace responded and turned to his friend, Owen Lattimore, a scholar especially knowledgeable regarding Mongolia and Central Asia, and said, "Unless he means you Owen. You've worked with Chiang Kai-sheck, maybe you're the great American?"

Lattimore laughed as he pulled a glowing wood pipe from his mouth. "I don't think a man would ride here from Tibet to give me a gift, Henry," he said, offering the vice president a dry smile as he pulled again on his pipe.

"Is that where he's from?" Wallace said. "But you said," turning to the interpreter, "that he speaks with an Indian accent."

"He is a Tibetan. A Brahmin. He must have *learn* his Chinese from an Indian teacher," the Chinese official said in his own broken English.

At that moment the Brahmin turned to the American delegation and said, "Henry Wallace," in clear and unfaltering American-English that rang like a bell in the spring air. "We want to give you an offering of World Peace."

Chapter Fourteen

Switzerland

August 27, 1944
Bern, Switzerland

"Switzerland seems out of the way to go to America?" Sparks said to the man across from him in the Douglas C-54 Skymaster. Inside the plane it was loud and difficult to hear. The ride was also bumpy, and so Sparks held on to a large latch that hung down from the fuselage above his head.

The plane was empty except for the man sitting opposite him. His name was Eldridge, and he was sent either by Eisenhower or from someone high up in the Monuments Division. Sparks wasn't sure about the specifics because Eldridge had not been forthcoming regarding them.

"It's not supposed to make any sense," Eldridge said. "It's the Army, but anyway, they have some other personnel they want to remove from Switzerland, so they're gonna' kill two birds with one stone."

"Well, where are we going?"

"Do you know Switzerland?" Eldridge shouted back.

"Somewhat."

"Then we're going to a base just outside Bern."

For the remainder of the ride neither man said a word and soon Eldridge moved up to the cockpit, leaving Sparks alone in the cargo hold. Sparks was happy enough with that arrangement. He disliked Army double-speak and bureaucratic insanity, and Eldridge seemed to have its lingo down perfectly.

The plane touched down in the middle of the night, depriving Sparks of the vision of the majestic mountains in the backdrop. He caught only glimpses of them through the small window in the moonlight.

The rotors slowly wound down. And from inside the plane he heard the staircase pushed into place beside the Skymaster. Soon the door opened, but no one entered from either the tarmac or the cockpit. Sparks wasn't sure whether he should leave, but he assumed, since he had no instructions, that whoever else was going to board would be getting on soon.

He was wrong. He waited about ten minutes before deciding to investigate for himself. The lack of direction was odd, as typically, in his experience, the Army never left you any time to decide for yourself. Just as when Eldridge picked him up earlier, every moment of their day up until the time the plane took off had already been choreographed and relayed to him.

He poked his head out the door and looked over the ladder to a large green Quonset hut. Both to his left and right the runway was empty and dark. A single yellow light glowed outside the huge steel building before him. The building looked like half a buried, massive corrugated sewer pipe with a single door in its end facing the runway. This type of building littered the landscape now that there was war. Sparks simply took in the scene and then stepped down the ladder and onto the black tarmac.

When his feet touched the ground he looked back over his shoulder and through one of the windows into the cockpit, but neither the pilots nor Eldridge were there. The only sound he heard was the crunch of gravel under his feet. He'd left his bag on the plane and now wondered if that was a bad idea. But then the door ahead of him opened and, along with a cloud of smoke, out walked the man he'd met at *Camposanto*.

"Come on in here," the man said. "You'd think you need an invitation." Then he turned to walk back into the hut, but Sparks stopped him when he asked, "What about my bag?"

"Leave it. Plane's not going anywhere 'till you do."

Sparks thought that sounded more menacing than it needed to. The man then walked through the open door, leaving Sparks hesitating momentarily on the tarmac. Recognizing that he had no choice, Sparks followed the other man into the light of the room. Someone else closed the door behind him.

Chapter Fifteen

The Stone of Destiny

August 28, 1944
Washington, D.C., White House Residence

He found his slippers where he'd left them and rose from the bed. It was dark in the White House, he thought – dark and lonely. He had never felt such a lonely place before. Even that Chinese town on the verge of the Tibetan Plateau where he'd met the group Roerich sent felt more hospitable than the drab Victorian arrangements of the White House, badly in need of remodeling.

He'd stood on the Silk Road in the Chinese borderlands and been handed the so-called Stone of Destiny. The place for him had almost ceased to be real, and had begun to take shape in his mind as a landscape of mystical importance and value. It was a land of vast historical collisions: the true corridor between East and West – the middle zone between divergent cultures – the place where the world's great religions, Christianity, Buddhism, and Islam, frayed and found their frontiers. Just to the north lived the Mongols, who from time immemorial had swept through the lands to all points of the compass. Time and again the Chinese sent armies of overwhelming size here to reclaim the land and install outposts and build great walls that would ensure the flow and safety of traffic coming east on "their" Silk Road. Just as often, the Tibetans dropped down from the highlands to conquer. More recently, the Muslims crossed the Western Himalayas to spread their religion with the sword. Even Christian missionaries skirted the desert and rode off to oblivion here.

To stand in Jiuquan was to stand in an otherworld of sorts. To the west stood the lengthy Kunlun Mountains marking the Tibetan Escarpment, which dropped onto the endless flatland where he now stood. From here the road went on seemingly forever, skirting the mountains west and crossing great rivers that dried when the snowmelts ceased or ended in vast salt marshes 3,000 miles from any ocean where the earth just swallowed them up. The road went on until it reached another world – the terminus of the Himalayas, Turkish People, Afghanistan, and then the West. He couldn't be farther from Iowa.

The vibrant Tibetans on horseback only helped develop the sense Wallace already felt. But when the man got down from his horse and said, "Henry Wallace, we want to give you an offering of World Peace," in clear and accurate American-English, Wallace was startled almost beyond words. He stepped out from the crowd and walked to the Tibetans, though he was not looking at the man standing in the dust of the square. Rather, Wallace was surveying those still astride their horses for the familiar features of Nicholas Roerich. He assumed the guru would be here as well. He was not.

Maybe that was for the better. If Wallace's detail had seen and recognized Nicholas Roerich and someone back home had heard of it, then Wallace would find himself in PR trouble again. As it stood, a Tibetan delegation coming out of their mountains across the greatest plateau in the world and then down off the Escarpment to where the wastes of Middle Asia began could conceivably be interpreted as a simple sign of respect to the United States vice president coming from a very religious, strange, and misunderstood people.

Wallace reached for the package with the thanks and pride befitting a foreign dignitary, but the man didn't hand it over immediately. It was wrapped in unadorned beige Tibetan Wool. Another man descended his horse, and walked to the packhorse behind him where he removed a three-legged brown table. They placed the package on top of the table. Wallace could tell now that it was heavy by the way the first man handled it, and by the noise it made even despite its wool wrap when it was laid on the wooden surface. The men then pulled back the wrapping, revealing the fourteen by eight inch grey stone. The other men in the American delegation began to crowd around, observing the grey colored object.

"Well, that is certainly interesting," Owen Lattimore said.

"Are you familiar with the Stone of Destiny, Mr. Wallace?" The Tibetan man then asked.

"I am a Wallace," he said, referring to his Scottish heritage. "The Stone of Destiny's the stone the English stole from the Scottish throne to coronate their own kings over. But that's still in England."

The Tibetan man replied, "That's what the Scottish say. Tradition says this is the stone that Jacob used as a pillow to sleep on before he became Israel. Just a part of a stone that fell to the earth from heaven very, very long ago, before any of the religions we know now. This stone has a destiny in the world. It was brought to Tibet by travelers who lost their home. They came from the West. They were lost in the mountains. They found themselves at a great monastery and this was the gift they gave and the story they told. They said there'd be a time to return it to its people. The time is now."

"But the United States are not its people?" Wallace said.

"Some would say you are the New Jerusalem."

"I'm very happy to receive this gift on behalf of the United States then." Wallace said awkwardly. He didn't know what else to say, and in part he was trying to distance himself from any personal association with this very odd object. Several of the men with him knew of his past, and Wallace was doing his best to prove a break with it and show his rational side. But then the man spoke up.

"No, Mr. Wallace, this stone is for you. It is not for the United States, unless you choose to give it to them."

"You do know that any personal gifts a member of the United States government receives have to be turned over to the government and purchased at a later date?"

"Our hope is that you won't do that. We believe this stone will be very important to you for what will happen next."

"And what will happen next?" Wallace asked.

The group of Americans now stood huddled in a circle around Wallace and the two Tibetans, who stood around the table. Wallace felt perspiration form on his forehead and knew all eyes remained fixed on him.

"The future doesn't work that way – not in historical certainties," the Tibetan responded, "but in alignments which are more or less probable at given historical cycles." The Tibetan then paused for a moment and looked over the men assembled behind Wallace. "You should have this stone with you. You will be very important soon, Mr. Wallace, more important than you can even imagine, for all of our futures."

"How do you mean?" Owen Lattimore said. He had been quietly observing up until that point.

"I mean that Mr. Wallace has a large part to play in what is unfolding."

Lattimore looked as though he was going to ask another question, but Wallace spoke up and said, "Then I will keep it with me as you say. I thank you very much for your generosity." He was looking at Lattimore as he spoke, almost to signal that he should ask no further questions; that he didn't want to know exactly what the man meant, at least not in front of anyone. They might be able to privately ask further questions, but the group of Americans accompanying the vice president included a few men of questionable loyalty.

Wallace then returned his attention to the Tibetan. "You've come all this way, why don't you stay with us and have something to eat?"

But the man declined the invitation. "I'm sorry Mr. Wallace, but we must go. The Germans, or I should say the Nazis, have sent their "scientists" to find the roots of their so-called Aryan Race. They are great murderers. It would be better if they didn't get ahold of this. They might destroy it simply because of its Israeli ties, or they might keep it and use it to bolster their lies. Either way, you're its rightful owner. Dispose of it in the manner you feel appropriate." They said goodbye and prepared to return home. Wallace wanted very much to ask this strange man where he learned his English, but as the moment seemed wrong, he said instead, "I don't even know your name."

"Tenzin, my name is Tenzin," he said, "and I learned my English in Tibet and then at Harvard University." Wallace was startled at this answer to a question he hadn't even asked.

Tenzin watched as the other man tied the three-legged table back onto the packhorse. Both mounted their horses simultaneously. Then they turned with their group and left, riding into the dust toward the Kunlun Mountains from which they had come.

◆ ◆ ◆

Wallace walked to the bureau now in his slippers. He felt a pebble in one. He pulled it off and heard the small stone rattle onto the hardwood floor. Then he continued crossing the room, careful not to wake Ilo.

It had been a custom for the First Family to sleep in separate bedrooms until this point. The Wallaces broke custom by sleeping together, albeit in separate beds – they weren't trying to cause a scandal. Now they used the second bedroom as another dressing room.

Wallace opened the top left drawer of the bureau and removed a small key. He then left the room and headed for that very dressing room. There he walked to the second panel on the right where there was a visible compartment. The woodwork was old. It had been well made originally, but this compartment had been an afterthought, probably of a much later administration. The lore of the White House was that Lincoln had it made for his son Willie. The workmanship was shoddy, and you could plainly see from up close where the "secret" door was. He wondered if Lincoln really had had this door made. If so, for what purpose?

He pushed the panel, which came nearly to his rib cage. An internal latch released and the door popped open. Inside was a large wall safe in a cavity flanked by wooden interior building pillars. He could see the marks in the age-darkened wood where the pillars had been hand hewn. He placed his key into the steel door of the safe and then turned the dial; you needed both the key and the combination to open it. It took him several tries to get the combination right after inserting the key, not because he'd forgotten the numerical sequence, but because he wasn't sure how many turns left and then right and then left again it took. That was always the tricky part for him.

This time it took three tries before the latch clicked and he opened the door. He wasn't even aggravated with himself, which was often the case when he opened his safe back home.

On the top shelf sat some of his personal effects, with the transcript that Cayce had given him lying near the front. On the bottom shelf sat the stone. He pulled back the wool cloth covering it and observed the indent in the rock where, according to legend, Jacob placed his head.

He touched the stone and felt an immediate shock of memory. Then he thought of Edgar Cayce.

Chapter Sixteen

Quonset Hut

August 28, 1944
Bern, Switzerland

The first face Sparks saw was the man from the plane, Eldridge, standing opposite him next to a card table with several well-dressed men. Then the door closed behind him. He hadn't seen anyone to his left as he entered, so whoever closed the door must have been standing behind it. This set off alarms in his mind and made the hair on his neck stand up.

When he turned back he saw a large Slavic man staring at him fiercely and holding the knob with his thick and gnarled peasant fingers. He was wearing a black uniform that on the shoulder said what Sparks thought was "*Nachtigal*." Sparks knew this was no American man, though he couldn't exactly place him. He was sure he was Eastern European.

"Private Sparks." A voice from the table said. Sparks turned. The man who spoke stood and walked toward him. There were five or six others at the table. Some were dressed like civilians, while others were in military uniforms bearing no insignia, but all, at least to Sparks' eye, appeared to be Americans. Sitting around another table further into the room were more men in black uniforms who were, like the man who had closed the door behind Sparks just a moment ago, of Eastern European extraction.

"That's me," Sparks flippantly said in reply.

"My name is Allen Dulles," the stranger said. "Have you heard of me?" He was an elegant man who looked to be in his mid to late fifties wearing a grey felt fedora and suit to match.

Sparks thought the name sounded vaguely familiar, but didn't know why and so he said, "No, sir," but hesitated with the "sir" part.

"There's no reason you should have. I work for OSS. You've already met Louis Simms," and he pointed to the man from *Camposanto* who was seated at the table opposite him. He didn't offer any of the names for the other men around the table. "Please, sit." Dulles said after a pause, which seemed designed to let Sparks know that he would not learn the names of the other men. He then pointed to a chair with its back to the man at the door.

Sparks didn't like this setup in the least, but there was little he could do about it.

Sparks sat, as did Dulles who said, "I know that you were less than receptive to Simms, and so I've decided to see you myself. I have certain assurances as to your loyalty . . . with your earlier "induction" and your father's service with Intel in the previous war. I knew him then, you know?" he said.

Sparks did not like that Dulles knew his father, but couldn't bother with their history at the moment. "You're asking me to spy on my president. And despite what you say about my father, I don't even know who you are."

Dulles considered Sparks for a moment, "We're certainly not asking you to spy on your president. We are, however, asking you to be a spy. The war is coming to a close, and right now, moving its way through Congress, is a bill that will continue the OSS into peacetime, albeit, most likely, by a different name."

Sparks leaned forward as if he had something to add, but Dulles gave him a look which implied he would not be interrupted again, though he was more tactful than Simms had been. "It's true that we don't intend for you to tell the president that you've been in contact with us, but we also don't want you spying on him. What's happening is that members of the communist network have infiltrated the United States government at the highest levels. We need to understand that there is and has been a world-wide revolution going on, and for many people that revolution is both just and unstoppable, and so they help it along. But we're comforted by the fact that a man like you is in the White House."

"And you think Wallace is one of those who help it along?" Sparks demanded, somewhat more angrily than he had intended.

"No. Wallace is an American who wouldn't intentionally betray his country, but he does not believe the Soviets and the revolution pose the threat they do. He's too kind to imagine that others would be working to-ward that goal. Though they are. We know there are Soviets as we speak operating in the United States and getting intelligence from Americans in government. In the trusted role you'll soon have, you'll be in a position to act if you suspect someone."

Sparks didn't bother to ask any further questions. He could tell Dulles didn't want to answer them. Sparks despised the idea of "ratting" on Wallace – a man who had been so kind to him. But he also suspected that there were Americans working for the Soviets from what he had seen when he worked for the then-vice president.

"You know my father came back from the War," Sparks began, "and hated the Soviets. He actually talked fondly of Russians, but he said that communism was a black hole that only brought death. I tend to think he was right. So you can count me in. I won't betray Wallace. Loyalty's everything, and he's been very good to me, but I will tell you about leaks when I encounter them."

"That's very good, your father and I saw their revolution first hand. And, as you said, loyalty *is* everything," Dulles stood from the table. He was obviously in charge. The men shook hands. But as Sparks moved to pull away from the older man's grip, Dulles said: "The first time you feel you have information we should hear, even if it's something that's small but just doesn't feel right to you, wear a green paisley tie. We'll get in touch. After that you'll work out a system of your own."

Eldridge then stood from the table and walked toward the door. The man in the black uniform opened it for him. Sparks also turned to leave but Dulles stopped him. "One more thing," Dulles said.

"There's always one more thing," Sparks said, and Dulles seemed to bristle. Sparks' Texas manner irritated the northeastern patrician, but he ignored his obvious distaste for Sparks' approach and held out a manila envelope. He unwound the red twine that held the flap closed and pulled out several pictures. At first Sparks couldn't make out what the pictures showed. They seemed to be of a stone sitting on a bench in front of a paneled wall and opened wall safe.

"What is this?" Sparks asked.

"We're hoping you'll be able to tell us," Dulles said.

"It's a rock."

Dulles rubbed his finger down the white stubble growing on his chin and smiled, "It's more a curiosity that anything else. This is a very strange object."

"I know that room from Roosevelt's time," Sparks suddenly broke out. "If you have someone close enough to the president to take pictures of his private effects, then what do you need me for?"

"Who said these came from one of our operatives? Pictures need to be developed. Sometimes they travel in the mail, or the intended recipient shares them with other people." Dulles paused with his eyes on Sparks. "You'll be the only one we have in the White House."

Sparks began to speak up, but Dulles cut him off, this time with less tact, "If you don't see it, which in all likelihood, you won't, then that's fine. But if you do, we'd certainly like to know what it means to the president."

Sparks could have continued asking questions but knew he was wearing on Dulles and didn't want to leave him with the impression that he wasn't going to follow through. Sparks wasn't deceiving the man either; he did intend to honor his end of the bargain because he believed that Wallace was in danger.

"If I hear about it, I'll let you know."

Dulles smiled and without saying anything further, Sparks followed Eldridge out onto the tarmac, nodding to the implacable Simms on his way past. The pilots were visible in the cockpit now as the interior light was on. Eldridge walked Sparks up the staircase and onto the plane as the massive engines fired up. "You're on your own from here," he said, and left Sparks standing in the doorway. Sparks nodded sardonically and then watched Dulles walk out onto the tarmac in conversation with the Eastern European man who had earlier held the door.

In turn, Sparks walked back to the same seat he had occupied on the ride over. When he settled in, the group of non-Americans in black uniforms who had been sitting at the other table got onto the plane with the man who'd closed the door behind Sparks and took seats by the cockpit. No one said a word. Several of the men stared at Sparks, but he looked away, focusing instead on reviewing the contents of his bags to see if anything had been touched or moved in any way. Sparks heard someone pulling the staircase away from the plane, and the plane began taxiing. It hadn't reached the end of the runway when he began to wonder what would have happened if he'd said "No" to Dulles.

Chapter Seventeen

The Wall Safe

August 28, 1944
Washington, D.C., White House Residence

Wallace remained on the carpeted floor of the dressing room for a few minutes before he willed himself to remove the heavy stone from the safe. He wasn't an old man, but he looked at the stone with apprehension. The weight wasn't the problem. He kept himself fit enough playing sports, especially tennis, to do it.

He was apprehensive about lifting the stone because of what it meant to him. It lay in this old iron wall-safe, behind the poorly carved panel, calling to him like a beacon. Wallace had a scientific mind, loved numbers and figures, and had had his hands in the earth since he was a boy. He'd made his life working the land on a hardscrabble farm alone with his wife. And then he converted his education into a small fortune by developing a way to hybridize corn that improved its vigor and significantly increased yield.

There might not have been a better mind for figures in the whole of the United States government during Roosevelt's long term. And that was saying something, as Roosevelt's advisors were known as the "brain trust." But there was the other part of Wallace's mind and of his success that had always frightened him. Wallace had come to his greatest achievement through a dream. It was as simple as that. And he had taken the symbol of the entwined corncobs to mean hybridization, which is what he pursued as long and as hard as he'd ever pursued anything in his life. He'd even gotten his wife to invest everything she had in his idea, and it had worked. He was now, in fact, a millionaire because of it.

But there was more to his vision than what he'd already accomplished. There was a great grey stone that the ploughshare struck in a furrowed field. The ploughshare ran aground on that stone like a ship at sea strikes a mighty reef and can't get off.

When the Guru Letters became generally known, Wallace thought he had struck the stone in the field as in his dream. He thought that part of the prophetic vision had played out as the political storm the Guru Letters caused had seemingly passed, but the meaning may have been greater than he thought, just as he feared the helical corn cobs were.

Now he heaved the stone out of the old bank vault and lay it on the bench where he typically readied himself for his work, which never seemed to end. He should have been sleeping, he told himself, but that was out of the question.

This was the stone the ploughshare had run aground on. He knew it as plainly as he knew his own face in the mirror. This half-buried stone lay in the dark, ripe earth waiting for the man and his plough to come and cut the surface in his straight lines. But this was the end. The plough could go no further. On the hilltop a great army assembled, and there was fire on the horizon. This was the great battle of the end of the world and the farmer had broken his plow on this stone. Of course, Wallace had interpreted the dream differently before, but he could see it in no other way now, especially since his talk with Edgar Cayce and what the transcripts revealed. Those papers, too, sat within the vault and seemed to be the key to the stone's meaning. Together, and in his interpretation, they pointed to the apocalypse, and he would be the president who presided over it. Yet there were hints within the transcripts which seemed to imply that the end could be avoided. The fact that the Tibetans had given him the stone at all was a sign that it could be. He just didn't know how.

The end of the world was so deeply imbedded in his mind that it couldn't be driven out. This teaching was as much a part of the soil of the Iowa religion he was raised in as was the risen Christ. How it would all end, no one knew, but since Wallace was a young man, he'd had some idea how it would happen. He had met George Washington Carver at the University of Iowa where Wallace's father was a professor. Carver was among the most famous and accomplished African Americans of his day, known for his scientific research that aimed to help poor farmers.

Carver took a liking to the young Henry Wallace and took him under his wing. He taught Wallace, and cultivated in him an appreciation of nature which Wallace hadn't known to that point. They took walks together in the Iowa woods and through the fields. Frequently they would talk, though just as often they walked in silence or the older man talked while Wallace listened. Carver believed that if you could unlock the secrets in the plants and the seeds then you could improve man's miserable lot in this world. This is what he went on to do with extraordinary success. But Carver also harbored a strong belief in the end of the world.

Carver was born a slave in rural Missouri in 1864. When Carver was still an infant, his family was kidnapped, and Master Carver was only able to retrieve baby George Washington from the kidnappers following a trying negotiation. After the war came and went, the Carvers, being somewhat more enlightened than many of their neighbors, raised George Washington as their own. They taught him his letters and numbers right alongside his belief in the Virgin Birth and the second coming. Carver took it all in with the spirituals he learned from the freedmen he knew and from the children in the all-black school he attended.

One day, as the two, Carver and young Wallace, walked a path that skirted a cornfield and an old stone wall that had been laid by the Scots-Irish before the Civil War, Wallace heard Carver singing a tune. Wallace wasn't sure if Carver knew all the words to the song or not, as he would only sing certain parts and repeat the same line several times. He often repeated the words, "God gave Noah the Rainbow sign / No more water, the fire next time."

The verse referred to Noah's flood and the promise God made not to destroy the world again by flood. As Genesis says, He left the rainbow as the symbol of this promise. But the second line, "No more water, the fire next time," is what concerned Wallace now. The world wouldn't end with water, but by fire. And to Wallace, this line laid down a fact for him. It was as much a fact as was a fossil in a field – the world would end in fire. He knew it. And knowing that made him suspect the Manhattan District and the bomb they developed there even more.

The stone sat on the wooden bench on top of its wool wrappings as innocuously as any old stone in the forest. But this stone was special. And it didn't even have a mark on it, not a letter, not a hieroglyph or a depiction. It was simply a stone, the size of a small pillow with an indent. Yes, it resembled a slept-on pillow to some degree, but in the sky, clouds resembled animals and some trees in the woods had the shape of men; that didn't make it so.

He held the stone up and examined its underside. There was nothing there that he observed other than that it was a rock. He didn't know what kind of rock it was, but that would be simple enough to learn. He made a note to have the stone tested, but aside from learning its geology, he couldn't see what else he was supposed to do with this thing besides lose sleep over it.

The sun was just rising on the horizon as he hoisted the stone back into the safe. He felt discouraged. The rock had not surrendered an easy interpretation. He bent down to set it onto the grey floor of the iron box. When he stood, he leaned on one of the wood columns for support. It broke and the president tumbled over behind the wall into a cavity alongside the safe. At first he laughed for having taken such a silly spill in his bedclothes into the closet wall. Then he cursed himself for falling down. He looked at the support he had broken. It was dry-rotted; the whole wall was dry-rotted for that matter.

He was inside a dusty hidden corridor, sitting behind the old horsehair plaster and lathe. He stood. The light from the dressing room was strong enough for him to see around the cavity. It was a hallway three or more feet across and eight to ten feet long that ended at the side of the brick chimney behind the fireplace in the room where his wife now slept. This long cavity was essentially the space between walls, but much larger than normal and had to have been built on purpose. It had been blocked from view by the vault and the wood column that he had knocked out of the way.

As he looked around the cavity he wondered what it had been built for. It seemed to be a silly waste of space. But worse than that, the White House's structure was disintegrating. Only the plaster and the paint looked sound. Everything else was rotted through. He was even surprised the building was left standing at all, as bad a shape as it was in back here.

He shuffled out between the safe and the wall. Then he turned and threw the door to the safe closed. But just as he did so, his wife, Ilo, said, "Henry!"

He jumped back, "Good God, Ilo, don't scare me like that! You're liable to kill me."

"What are you doing behind that wall?" she said with a good deal of mirth in her voice.

"I fell."

"Well I can see that, you're covered in dust. But why on earth are you at the safe at this time of night?" She glanced at the clock and then noticed that it was brightening outside. "This hour of the morning I should say."

"Oh, Ilo, don't be worried about me. . ." but she cut him off before he could finish his thought.

"It's the fire next time, isn't it?" she said with a look of displeasure, "and don't say it's not. Every time you get that pitiful look on your face, I can be sure that you are thinking about George Washington Carver and the dream you had with the plow in the field."

"You can't make light of it." He said.

"And now you have that silly stone to look at. Am I to believe that my husband was chosen to be the man who is the president of these United States when Armageddon comes? Don't say anything more, just come back to bed and get a little sleep before you start your day. You're making this worse on yourself by staying up till all hours of the night and working all day long."

The president turned, closed the wooden panel, and followed his wife back to bed.

Chapter Eighteen

The Campaign

August 28, 1944
Washington D.C., Oval Office

Wallace hated campaigning but realized when he went back to bed with Ilo that morning that a campaign stop in Virginia Beach wouldn't be out of the ordinary. This would bring him to Cayce. He might also get the chance to relax.

By 9:00 AM he stood in the Oval Office. One look at the president and you could tell he was a tired man. He called for coffee. "And make it black, please."

Betty entered with the cup in under a minute. This was the first glimpse she'd gotten of the president today as he was already closeted in his office when she arrived. "My God, Mr. President." She said. "Have you slept?"

"Last night I think I slept an hour."

"I'll put on more coffee." She turned to walk out the door.

"Oh . . . Betty? Will you please get Mike in here? I need to talk with him." He was referring to his campaign manager, whom he had frozen out of his daily schedule as much as was possible.

Since Wallace's early polling numbers were so strong, it didn't seem to anyone that, aside from campaign stops in key districts, he had to focus much on the campaign at all to win. The mood in the country was such that all the best minds on his staff thought that less-was-more from Wallace. People, when asked, just thought that President Wallace should have their vote. And that was that. There was no reason to give them any other idea.

The campaign moved ahead as planned, and the country remained fully behind the Iowa farmer and heir to the Roosevelt legacy. And in the middle of a major shooting war, the Republicans mostly held off going hard on Wallace's record, though not entirely from lack of want. His opponent, Thomas Dewey of New York, tried to paint Wallace as an "egghead mystic," but the backlash in the papers was strong enough that Dewey's campaign feared losing more votes than they gained by going negative. This put Dewey in the tough position of criticizing Wallace's policies, which in turn allowed the major radio and newspaper outlets to say that Dewey was really criticizing the dead and sainted "FDR," as the former president was now referred to. Under these conditions, it was clear that unless Wallace made some terrible blunder, he would be president.

Then Betty called. "Mike Turner is here to see you."

That was fast, he thought. But Mike was just down the hall, presumably *scheming* ways to make Dewey look worse than he already did. When he entered, Wallace stood and said, "How goes the battle, Mike? Has Dewey stepped in it again today?"

"As far as I can tell, Dewey steps in it every day. He can't seem to find a good line of attack. But we can't give him anything to use against us. For the moment he's . . . well, he's relatively hapless at this point, sir."

"That's what I like to hear just a few months out from the election. But we're still making the Southern campaign drive next week aren't we?" Wallace asked somewhat disingenuously, as he was the only one who could change his schedule. He was making the trip to shore up support for the final push to the election in the Sothern states where his backing was weakest and the Republicans were making inroads. The trip was set to begin with a speech somewhere in North Carolina, he wasn't sure of the town, but Wallace now had another idea, which is why he had called his campaign manager in to talk.

"I'd really like it if we could make our first speech in Virginia Beach." Wallace said. "I'd like to spend two or three days there to unwind a bit. I think it might be a good idea to make a speech there too, so people get the idea that I'm there to work."

"That sounds like a fine idea, sir," Turner said with a little too much enthusiasm. Wallace could tell that Turner didn't think it was a very good idea at all to go and make any kind of a campaign stop in Virginia Beach. There was almost no point, especially as this was a trip to try to win votes in states where Democrats were weakening, and Virginia, and particularly its coast, with the busy Norfolk shipyards and the Atlantic fleet, was not among those this election cycle. Nevertheless, Turner would go along with the request as there was nothing on the face of going to Virginia Beach that could jeopardize the campaign.

"Certainly we can schedule something to kick off the trip, Mr. President. Is there a specific day you'd like to go?"

Wallace still was unsure how much he liked being called "Mr. President," but he let it go for now and said, "I thought we'd go over the weekend and into Monday. We can tell the press boys we're kicking off the trip early and then I can get a little relaxation too. It kills two birds with one stone." Wallace said.

Chapter Nineteen

The Flight

August 28/29, 1944
Western Europe

They flew south and west. Below, the green land was pockmarked by sooted brown indents he knew to be bomb craters. This was France, 1944. The Nazis still controlled large swaths of ground, but the Western Allies were making their slow and inevitable push toward the Fatherland.

To the north and east, the Soviets destroyed the Nazis wherever they met them with murderous losses on both sides. The German Army had retreated from much of the land they'd conquered years before, and the Thousand Year Reich was soon to be over.

Sparks looked out over the ravaged countryside, and then up to the group of bad men sitting by the cockpit, and imagined the kind of indent his body would make in the fecund soil below. He'd heard of a man once whose parachute failed to deploy on an infiltration jump behind German lines. He fell twenty thousand feet and landed on his back in a freshly plowed cornfield. He was alive, and broke not a single bone in his body. But Sparks had no such illusion about his own durability. If these rough men threw him out the side door, he would certainly make a terrible blood-and-gut-filled hole in a Gallic field below.

Just as that thought crossed his mind, the foreign soldiers up front spoke to each other in their rough language. He tried to ignore the sounds they made but found it difficult to focus on anything else.

Soon the plane touched down in an airfield in Gibraltar. On the ground the plane taxied to an older and out-of-the-way section of runway. Sparks felt an ironic sense of *Deja vu*, but it was a feeling he couldn't share with his fellow passengers. He didn't know why they landed here, as it wasn't a common stop along the trans-Atlantic flight path. But nothing was common about this flight.

When the plane came to a stop, the men up front stood and anxiously waited for the stairway to arrive and the door to open. When it did, they formed a "bucket brigade" of sorts from the runway and up the stairs, conveying large wooden and steel cargo boxes piled on the tarmac into the plane's hold. That finished, Sparks watched them through the small window to his left as they approached a Jeep with two uniformed men parked some yards away. The uniformed man in the passenger seat did the talking, and when he finished, the rough men walked past the nose of the plane. Sparks lost sight of them through his window.

"I guess they probably want to see me now," he said out loud, and took his bags over his shoulder and walked up the plane toward the cockpit. At the top of the stairs he saw the Jeep pull around so that it was parked just a few feet from the bottom step. He smiled to the men inside, and then took his time walking to them as he enjoyed the Mediterranean sun. When he got to the bottom, the stark looking uniformed passenger said, "Jonathan Sparks?"

"Yes."

"That barracks is yours over there," he said, and pointed to a green metal building behind a high fence. "You'll be here 'till we come and get you."

"And how long will that be?" He hadn't finished his sentence when the Jeep sped off through the fence and toward the active part of the runway.

"I guess they're not in much of a hurry to get me back to my president," he said to the tarmac.

For the next several nights he slept alone in the small barracks cordoned off by a high fence and concertina-wire at the airfield's edge.

Whether the hold was designed to keep him in or someone else out he couldn't decide.

And then, suddenly, after well over a week of waiting, the same Jeep arrived and the same passenger, in his sharply pressed olive drab uniform, told him to pack and be ready within the hour. When he got back onto the plane he was unhappy to find that he was flying with the same group as before.

"And here I was thinking I'd never see you again," he said to one of the Eastern Europeans as he entered, the man still wearing his strange black uniform. The man simply looked up at him with an expression so hostile that Sparks took it to mean that he would rather kill him with his bare hands than speak with him. Sparks smiled. "This is my first time flying over the Atlantic. How about you?" But now the man didn't even bother to make eye contact, and the other men were silent as well. Sparks went back to his familiar seat as far away from these soldiers as he could get and looked out his window to the Atlantic Ocean below. He braced for the long flight ahead.

Chapter Twenty

Rotarians and the Barque Susan Constant

September 2nd, 1944
Virginia Beach, Virginia

And so it was that on a humid Saturday afternoon in Virginia Beach Wallace stood talking before a packed audience at an indoor event sponsored by the local Rotary Club, whose president was a donor of some middling significance – this was the best they could do on such short notice, Turner had said. And because the trip had come so soon and included a weekend, many of the usual press people were not present. Some even complained that they couldn't be expected to travel so quickly, having only been told of the plans on the previous Tuesday.

"That was partly the point, Mike," Wallace said when his campaign manager brought this complaint to the president's attention.

When they arrived in Virginia Beach in the presidential motorcade at about 11:00 AM, it was already a muggy, late summer day. Wallace was happy to have gotten out of D.C. altogether, as early September there felt almost tropical. He had once heard that early British members of the Foreign Service were given hardship pay to be stationed in the American capital. After living there several years Wallace could see why. He was grateful that as of late the appalling heat had been interspersed with several stretches of unseasonably cold autumn days, causing some trees to begin turning prematurely.

Today, however, was not one of those days. And though coastal towns caught a breeze off the Atlantic, making them cooler and less muggy than their inland counterparts, Virginia Beach was still hot, and Wallace felt sweat forming on his forehead as he took the rostrum. He looked out over the assembled mass of people dressed in suits, ties and hats under the unforgiving midday sun. There had to be at least a thousand or so in attendance, which was a lot as this event was so hastily assembled. But the crowd was a good sign. It meant that people were enthusiastic about the prospects of his continued presidency.

He began the speech as it was written, touching on the war and the progress of the "boys" overseas who were "fighting a war we didn't start, but that we certainly would finish." That line drew great applause. Apparently there were no isolationists in attendance. Then he went on to talk about the needed continuance of several New Deal policies, especially after the war, in order to ensure that the country stayed on the right track and "did not slip back into recession." He had flagged this last line for deletion on the way over, but Mike Turner insisted he keep it in because it was necessary for the American people to remember the Depression, and to remember who got them out of it. And so Wallace acquiesced and let it remain.

Then he was finished with the speech. It was short and to the point, calculated to be respectful and to get him off the stage before anything bad could happen. As Turner repeatedly said, "We can't have you falling down, or have any other mishaps that could embarrass you. Right now you're above reproach, which is wonderful, but it's a place that's easy to fall from, and if that happens, quite difficult to regain. It's also not always something in your control that will unseat you in people's eyes."

Wallace wasn't worried about the over-anxiety of his Campaign Manager at this point. He was more concerned about how he was going to get to see Cayce. He had already devised a plan for that little "problem," he now just had to execute it.

As he got down from the podium, a reporter in a gaudy paisley tie approached him ahead of the others. The group must have been the second string, or were tired from the heat, as reporters typically didn't waste any time in swarming him to shout their questions as he got off the stage. But this man was all alone, ahead of the slow moving group of writers. "Mr. President," he said, "You haven't addressed the Guru Papers since you've begun campaigning. Don't you think the American people deserve some clarification on this issue?"

"Which part of that was the question?" Wallace asked as he stepped past the man. The president's group of aides, Secret Service agents and campaign staffers smoothly stepped in and kept the reporter at bay. Agent Chipton gripped the reporter's collar as the reporter shouted over Mike Turner's shoulder, "We're doing a full page story on you next week. Don't you want to clear the record?" Wallace stopped then. Chipton released the reporter. "Thanks, ginger," the reporter said, then wound his way closer to the president. When he was within arm's reach, Wallace said, "They're a fabrication. I did have a connection with that man," he was careful not to mention Roerich's name as he had been coached not to do so, "but those letters are not mine. I should add that he was well connected in the government at that time. He even helped bring about an agreement to protect the world's cultural treasures in times of war. He was also avoiding paying his taxes, and failed on a mission he was given by the federal government to collect drought tolerant seeds in Central Asia. One can only guess why he fabricated the letters, but it seems likely it was to protect his own image from the damage he himself wrought. Thank you," Wallace said, and walked toward the building directly behind the field where he had just spoken. Inside he was supposed to meet with the city fathers, mostly Rotarians, who organized this campaign stop so they could present him with a gift. He wasn't sure what it would be, he was simply going through the motions at this point, hoping to get to see Cayce sooner rather than later.

He was just about to motion for Agent Chipton to discuss his plan for meeting with Cayce when his campaign manager said quietly and close to his ear, "That was great. You told them everything we wanted to get across and nothing more. Only next time, don't mention the Central Asian trip, it might remind people that you were there, which might open you up to criticism about the Soviets, and people may remember that you sent him on the trip after all. Just say 'his work for the government was a failure' it's less precise."

Wallace nodded, but he was concerned that while most of what he said was mostly true, it was a patent lie to claim that Roerich had fabricated the letters. As long as Wallace had been alive, he'd never told a lie, not one so boldfaced as that anyhow.

The building Wallace entered to greet his hosts appeared to be a large, recently finished high school auditorium. He could smell the sawdust and the paint.

As they walked over to where a group of Rotarians and town fathers were assembled next to a table with coffee and donuts, Wallace saw his opportunity to corner Agent Chipton.

He reached past the agent to grab a cup of coffee off the table and said, "I'm going to need to go to a private residence later today. There's someone I'd like to see."

He said the word "someone" with a tone that implied secrecy. Wallace hoped that Chipton would think that he was talking about a mistress, and that the whole trip would take on the light of a getaway with a paramour. Which was exactly how Chipton took it. It was obvious by the half smirk that showed on his usually stoic, hard American face that he thought the president was asking to have alone time with a woman not his wife.

Wallace knew that the other agents might talk about his secret liaison amongst themselves, but it would go no further. And he knew this because he was present when they protected FDR and kept the secret, or secrets, of his various mistresses from leaking to the press.

So that's what they'll think, Wallace thought. To him, even being thought an adulterer was a problem. His old Midwestern, Christian values were dyed in the wool, so to speak, and dyed hard. He wouldn't ever put himself or his wife through this kind of thing, and he certainly didn't want people to think that he was "like that." But now he had to behave as if he were a philanderer.

Wallace sipped his coffee as Chipton moved back toward the wall where Agent Dunbar stood slightly shadowed by the bleachers.

The Rotarians approached Wallace with a look of purpose on their faces. One man with a very large and very red nose stepped forward. As he drew close, Wallace could see the broken blood vessels high on his cheeks; the result, Wallace assumed, of years of heavy drinking. Before Wallace could think further of the man's alcoholism the man said, "Mr. President, sir, the City of Virginia Beach would like to present you with a gift. This plaque commemorates the landing of the barque Susan Constant, which made landfall in the New World on Cape Henry in the northern part of the city in 1606. The base is made from a plank from what we believe to be the recently discovered wreck of that ship."

Wallace smiled as he took the gift, inwardly appreciating the fact that he hadn't been given some minor key to the apocalypse. "Thank you," he said. "My family hasn't been in this land as long as that, but we've been here for some time. It's an honor to be given an object with such historical ties to the forming of our country."

He shook hands with the group of Rotarians who had just given him the gift, and left as soon as he thought it not rude to do so.

When it got dark later, at about nine thirty, he was escorted from a service entrance of the Cavalier Hotel into a waiting white milk truck. Wallace appreciated the agent's efforts to ensure no one would follow him. Chipton was very thorough, he thought.

Chapter Twenty-One

Return to Edgar Cayce

September 2nd, 1944
Virginia Beach, Virginia

The white milk truck pulled to the curb outside of Cayce's house in Virginia Beach. The large house sat on the corner of two streets and the backyard ran fifty feet or so to another road where a fence and tall shrubs shrouded the lawn and garden.

Agent Chipton peered out from behind the steering wheel of the milk truck he had just parked. He knew the seriousness of what they were doing. If the wrong person caught them, the resulting scandal might cost Wallace the upcoming election. And though he understood the possible significance of this twilight liaison, he couldn't help but see the humor in driving the president around in the back of a milk truck.

Chipton then motioned to Agent Dunbar beside him in the passenger seat to step out and move up the concrete path that led to the basement entrance of Cayce's house. On this side, the basement was a full story tall, whereas at the front of the house facing the ocean, only a few feet of stone foundation and short windows stood above ground.

Chipton watched apprehensively as Agent Dunbar opened the car door and carefully climbed down onto the sidewalk and headed to the next block. It was dark, but the streetlights were enough for Chipton to see the Minnesotan as he moved farther down the street. Then he turned and walked back toward the white milk truck and up the walkway to the basement door. The door was painted a dark forest green and set deep into the stone foundation.

The door opened and from the milk truck he saw a young woman peering out at Dunbar from the dim light of the thinly carpeted basement. She wore a black housedress with a wide belt that accentuated her hips. Dunbar turned and made a positive motion back to Chipton in the milk truck.

When Chipton saw that Dunbar had made successful contact, he climbed out of the driver seat. Before walking to the rear door, he first looked at the driver of the chase vehicle that had followed them here. The four agents inside that car would be very heavily armed. Then he knocked twice on the back door of the truck to let the president know he was ready. He opened the doors and Wallace turned on the wood crate he'd been sitting on.

"Nothing like riding in style, Leroy," He said.

"Yes, sir. I'm sorry about the accommodations, sir."

Wallace smirked, "They were fine, so long as I got here without a problem."

Chipton then motioned up the walkway to the house, "Right this way, sir."

♦ ♦ ♦

President Wallace followed Chipton without another word. As he entered the basement, he noticed that an agent in the car parked behind the milk truck stepped out and stood on the curb near the fire hydrant where the walkway met the sidewalk. *So much for being inconspicuous*, Wallace thought to himself as he shook the hand of the young lady who was now standing in the open basement door not that far from the sidewalk.

"Mrs. Cayce couldn't be here this evening," She said. "I'm Stella Delacroix."

"Hi, Miss Delacroix. I'm Henry Wallace."

She smiled and they walked up the stairs together with Chipton in the lead. The door at the top of the basement stairs led out into a large kitchen with a brick tile floor and pots and pans hanging from a pegboard over the wooden countertop.

Chipton, with Miss Delacroix's direction, led the president through a set of French Doors and into the library where Edgar Cayce was standing with a kind and open look on his face. Chipton then turned and left, presumably to survey the rest of the floor, as Miss Delacroix ushered Wallace into the library and closed the door behind him.

Edgar Cayce smiled as Wallace entered. He stood in the center of the room on an old and slightly threadbare Persian rug in a black suit and coat with his glasses in his hand. Wallace saw both the rug and Cayce simultaneously and couldn't help but imagine the Silk Road, the Himalayas, the Tibetan Plateau, and the vast openness outside Jiuquan. He pushed these thoughts aside as he adjusted his wide, geometric grid patterned tie and walked toward Cayce.

"I'm happy you came, Mr. President," Edgar Cayce said and smiled. He then nodded to Miss Delacroix who quietly backed out of the room as Cayce motioned to a small table surrounded by chairs near the bay window.

A single lamp covered the sitting area with a naturally diffuse yellow light. On the table sat a blue ceramic teapot with a small plume of steam rising from its spout.

"You knew I would be president?" Wallace asked as he sat down. He wanted to get to the point. "Did you know that you weren't the only one who told me that?"

Cayce considered this comment for a second as he poured tea for the president. "In all honesty," he said. "President Roosevelt was a sick man. There were many people who predicted he would die."

"Yes, but you *knew* he would die. You told me I would be president. Prior to that, while I was in China, a Tibetan delegation came and gave me a gift. They were also certain I'd become president. That's what the gift was for."

"What was it?" Cayce said almost in a whisper.

"I thought you might know that too," Wallace said. He was smirking from of an intense feeling of strangeness.

"It doesn't work quite like that," Cayce replied putting his glasses on.

"How does it work?" Wallace asked. "I guess I'm interested in knowing that first of all because understanding where you're getting this information might help me in what I have to do." The trace of a smile had left his face. He took the fact of a man accurately predicting his future very seriously, especially because of the other predictions he'd been given.

Then Cayce spoke up: "It's like there's a great river that exists in which flow the thoughts and possibilities of all human beings. Others have talked about it. Jung called it the collective unconscious. But I think of it as a river. Typically the person needs to be in the room or give me a question for me to see their flow, but with you it's different."

Wallace sipped his tea and considered what Cayce was saying. He didn't like it, but he couldn't deny the accuracy up to this point. "Well, is this 'river' accessible to anyone?"

"I think so," Cayce said. "But most people can't or won't learn how to tap it." Then he paused, "Would you let me give you a reading? So far I've only been picking you up inadvertently, as is often the case with large personalities. I'd like to do it intentionally now, with you present. You wouldn't give me the chance last time."

"That's why I came. But first, let me show you something." And Wallace pulled a small photograph from his interior pocket. The picture was in black and white and was of the stone he'd received from the Tibetans. He'd taken it in his dressing room, just after becoming president. "This was the gift I was given by the Tibetans," he said.

Cayce looked the picture over carefully. "It's not something I've ever seen before," he replied while still looking at the photograph.

"What about Jacob's Pillow, or the Stone of Destiny?" Wallace asked, becoming somewhat agitated.

"I've read my bible, Mr. President, but the meaning of this is not entirely clear to me. I mean, I don't know why people from Tibet would give you that stone, or its imitation, to celebrate your upcoming presidency." Cayce leaned forward and took a sip of his tea and then continued. "The history of the stone is straightforward enough. At least its biblical beginning: While sleeping on some stones, Jacob dreamt of a ladder to heaven. When he awoke in the morning, he called the group of stones he'd slept on, 'the Gate of Heaven.' From that point forward people revered the site. It was known as 'The House of God.' Do you mind if I ask you a question, Mr. President?"

"No, please do," Wallace said.

"Why would that stone be in Tibet?"

"I don't know. The man who gave it to me said that travelers who lost their home brought it and gave it to a great monastery, where it had lain ever since. He said it came to them before Jesus."

Cayce became visibly excited as he said, "In Szechwan Province, China, at the edge of the great Tibetan Plateau, Scottish ethnologist Thomas Torrance discovered a people whom he believed were one of the Ten Lost Tribes of Israel. They had lost their language in the 2,500 years since they'd been in China, but they still worshiped one God, and had practices oddly similar to Jewish ones."

"You're telling me one of the Lost Tribes of Israel traveled through Tibet and left that Stone there as they went on to China?"

"I'm only telling you what I know," Cayce said, "but it's not impossible, and it fits the story you've just told me."

"I'm sorry to be rude," Wallace added, "but what's it mean for me?"

Cayce took a deep breath and said, "I'll see if I can find the answer." And then Cayce went and lay down on the divan in the darkened corner of the room. He loosened his tie, and removed his wire-rim glasses. He paused for a second to adjust some of the hair above his ear where the glasses had pulled it out of place. When he finished patting his gray hair down, he closed his eyes. He opened his eyes again and said, "I typically have someone write down what I say, but in this case it's probably better if we don't." Then he said, almost to himself, "Actually, I'm glad I gave you your transcripts in our first encounter. I think someone broke in here, but nothing was missing. The only thing they seem to have done is rifle my papers."

"When was this?" the president asked, now remembering the man in the brown suit who had waited for him the last time he was at Cayce's house.

"Earlier this week."

"I hope it was nothing."

Cayce turned his head and faced the president when he said that. "And what do you fear it was?"

"I don't know," Wallace answered.

Cayce closed his eyes again, and Wallace remained seated at the table and watched as the sleeping prophet seemed to doze off. But just as it appeared that Cayce's eyeballs fluttered beneath the lids, his hands suddenly became tense. At that moment, he began talking in a flat monotone voice. "I see the dream. I see a great field. I see two twisted corncobs. And you are plowing, but you've struck a strange rock just beneath the surface and broken the plough. And on a blackened hill above, there is a man with a rifle; he stands where Pennsylvania meets New Hampshire. He's a remnant of the war, and over his shoulder is a giant mushroom. It's many times his size . . . The dream is over, now there's a flash on the horizon. It's the great bomb. All the nations see it explode, but they don't know what it is. And the two great nations stand against each other in its glow."

"Can I stop it?" Wallace interrupted. "Is there a way to stop it?"

"You are still the president when it goes off."

"But can I stop it?"

"No!"

"I refuse to believe that."

"But there's more, there were other men on the hill. They seem all twisted like the corn, and there are men coming out of them. And the men want to kill you. They are all the same kinds of men. Agents. The agents want to kill you. They're plotting already."

Wallace looked to the French doors where he could just make out the silhouette of Agent Chipton through the opaque Victorian curtains. *The*

Praetorian Guard, he thought. But the reading he was getting now was similar to what he'd already learned from the transcripts Cayce gave him.

Then Agent Chipton turned and walked to the staircase leading to the basement; his movement caught the president's eye through the curtain on the glass door. Wallace then heard muffled shouts. Chipton threw open the French doors. "Sir, there's a photographer outside," he said with a harsh twang he himself heard.

When Chipton spoke, the sleeping prophet jerked his body off the divan into a standing position as though he had been slapped in the face; his skin was ghastly white.

"Who are they?" Wallace said to Agent Chipton.

"It's the man from earlier today who asked you about the Guru Letters."

"He's following me?" Wallace asked.

"It looks like it, sir, though there's no way he could have known we were in that milk truck, unless. . ."

"Unless someone tipped him off," Wallace interrupted. "Well, who tipped him off?" He was looking directly at Cayce now who looked unstable on his feet. "People have come to you for years to ask for stock tips and other business questions. Who's spying on me? Why?"

"I can't give you an answer so quickly, not under these circumstance."

Wallace threw up his hands. Miss Delacroix now entered the room. She looked frightened, "Edgar, you have to sit. You're not well. Edgar please!" She ran to him.

Grabbing his arm, she helped him to sit down on one of the club chairs by the divan. Then she turned and addressed Wallace, "He can't be pushed like this, Mr. President. He's not well. He's not even supposed to be doing this, it taxes him too much."

"What do the doctors say's wrong with him?" Wallace asked as he tried to calm himself. He was upset both that a man was outside trying to take pictures, and because Cayce wasn't being any more specific than the transcripts he'd already given to him. It also infuriated Wallace that Cayce insisted that the bomb had to explode.

"It's not the doctors," she said, looking down at Cayce who had slumped into the chair and was sweating. "It's the readings. The readings tell him that he's hurting himself by tapping in on too regular a basis. But people come, and he can't turn them away."

Wallace put his head in his hands. He felt guilty for the way Cayce looked right now, but he wanted to know the answer to one more question.

"Cayce?" Wallace said, "Edgar?"

"Yes," Cayce answered and looked at the president.

"All those notes you gave me before went into detail on that corncob symbol. What does it mean?"

"The helical corncob?"

"If that's what you're calling it, yes."

"It's a symbol of the new world, Indian Corn, Thanksgiving. But when you twist them together like that I really don't know what they could mean. There was a god in the Baltic pagan religion named Jumis with a symbol that was like that. It's a god of the harvest. But I don't know what it means otherwise. What does it mean to you? That's where you should start. Why was it so important?"

"Because when I imagined two corncobs together like that it made me think of joining different strains of corn to make a better version."

"Hybridization?" Cayce asked, somewhat slumped now.

"Yes, exactly. That's my company. But what more does it mean?"

"I just don't know!"

Wallace wanted to ask more questions, but then there were footsteps on the hardwood floor above.

"Who's up there?" Dark-haired Agent Dunbar shouted icily as he entered the room.

"I didn't check," Agent Chipton answered.

Dunbar gave him a look which scolded him for his negligence.

"It's Mrs. Cayce," Miss Delacroix said. "She's been sick. She was sleeping. The commotion must have woken her."

"We have to go Mr. President," Chipton said. He had his hand inside his jacket. Wallace nodded and the two agents walked him out of the room and down the stairs, being careful to keep him between them at all times. When they reached the basement, Wallace saw that the side door was open onto the walkway. He could hear voices outside. An agent from the chase car was standing just inside the door and talking on a telephone connected to the basement wall, shaking his head in the negative.

"We just called it in," another agent outside the door said, "and you don't work for the paper, Mack!" He was talking to a man that Wallace assumed was the prying photographer.

"Yeah, what's the president of the United States doing at the home of Edgar Cayce, the Sleeping Prophet? The public wants to know!" the reporter asked. Then his voice changed and he shouted, "Hey, you can't take that. It's private property."

"It looks broken to me, Mack!" the agent said. They heard the sound of the camera smashing off the walkway. There was a scuffle, and the agent who was on the phone looking out the door waived for Chipton and Dunbar to go to the truck with the president. "Go now, go now!" he said.

Agents Chipton and Dunbar then rushed Wallace out onto the walkway. As they passed through the door, Wallace saw that whoever the photographer might be, he was now handcuffed with his head, shoulders and chest stuffed into one of the heavy shrubs by the door. Then they were at the milk truck. Wallace almost felt like a prisoner in the back of a paddy wagon. But he scolded himself for thinking in stereotyped terms.

◆ ◆ ◆

Inside the cab of the milk truck, agents Chipton and Dunbar sat looking at one another as the southerner cranked the ignition.

"His secret rendezvous was with a man," Dunbar said, "J. Edgar would love that." He was smirking.

"It's worse than that," Chipton said while pulling the milk truck off the curb. "Didn't you hear that guy with the camera? That was Edgar Cayce, the Sleeping Prophet in there. The president was having his future read."

Chapter Twenty-Two

The Reporter

September 3rd, 1944
Virginia Beach, Virginia

"Who was the man with the camera?" Wallace asked Agent Chipton. The president was looking up at the Agent from the couch in his hotel room. The morning sun shone in through open balcony doors.

"His name's Walter Grimes. He said he worked for the wire services, but we checked and that wasn't true. We couldn't detain him because he hadn't broken any law."

"No, that's fine," Wallace said, "He was just taking pictures after all, but what else can you find out about him? He's not just working for himself?"

"One of the agents picked up the man's wallet from the ground, so we're getting a better picture of who he is right now."

"I'm glad they did it, but I feel guilty," Wallace said, shaking his head. "He might have been *just* an ordinary citizen who was harassed by the Secret Service."

Chipton looked at the president and realized that he really did seem uncomfortable over what they'd done with the so-called reporter. Nothing had happened, really. They had broken his camera and taken his film. Marcus was a little rough with him when he had him handcuffed and jammed the man's face into the bushes, but that was a sound move. No one was around to see what happened, and it prevented Mr. Grimes from confirming the presence of the president. While being attacked by the

Secret Service is a fair indicator that the president's near, it's not the same thing as having visual confirmation, or having a picture. Chipton lowered his voice and said, "We did harass him, sir, that's true, but he's not just a concerned citizen."

"How can you be so sure, Leroy?" Wallace asked with his hands out in front of him in a plaintive gesture.

"Because, sir, for one he had a Leica III camera. That's a German camera, and made since the war began. It's not something you easily come by, and it's expensive. Of course, being German, it's a very good camera."

Wallace didn't want to ask the obvious question here about Grimes' connection to the Nazis because he knew there was no way to know that yet. It was also clear that the man was an American, or at least if Grimes was some kind of German spy, he had lived in the U.S. a very long time.

"When will we have the negatives developed?" Wallace asked.

"We're developing them right now."

◆　◆　◆

Agent Dunbar had just come back from returning the milk truck to its owner and was walking down the hotel hallway swinging his keys on a lanyard. At the end of the hall he turned and knocked on the door to the suite the Secret Service had taken as their command center.

Joe Dunbar prided himself on his detective skills, and had even thought of joining the Milwaukee police force before he entered the Army in the mid 30's. From there he entered the agency. This job involved more than just passively waiting for someone to attack the president, and from time to time even allowed agents to dig into the lives of criminals, or assumed criminals, and act like detectives. He loved these moments the most. One suspect turned out to be a cross dresser who, drunk on sherry and dressed in full lingerie, would write former President Roosevelt threatening letters that were addressed: Dear Cripple. His house contained a drawer full of pictures of him typing away. Dunbar found the pictures while searching his Baltimore apartment. He slammed that man off his desk so hard the typewriter popped up and smashed on the floor. But there were no weapons in the house and so he left him for the local police. They were a little upset about the broken nose, but they got over it. Dunbar was also fond of noting that the Secret Service was formed from the Pinkerton Detective Agency. The agency's genesis seemed to him to justify the vigor with which he probed into the lives of civilian suspects. At least on one occasion he'd been reprimanded for hurting the individuals he looked into.

He entered the suite. Red light emanated from a canvas "darkroom" the other agents had hastily assembled in the middle of the floor to develop Grimes' negatives. As Dunbar shut the door, two agents pushed their way through the darkroom flap and entered the room holding a set of small pictures in their hands. One of the men was Agent Marcus Johnston who had handled the photographer from the night before. He was a short, stout man with a quick wit and long fuse.

"What are we looking at?" Dunbar asked.

"We've got pictures of the president at the Rotary yesterday and entering the high school. Then there's this," Agent Johnston said, and held up a picture of a white farmhouse set back with a large barn and fields. "This comes before the photo he took outside the Virginia Beach house, so he went there in between the time the president made his speech and the time he went to the residence in Virginia Beach."

"Must be his farm," Dunbar said. "Can you get a number off that picture?"

"No, we checked. There's no house number visible."

Dunbar took the photograph out of Johnston's hand. Then he asked, "What did you get from the wallet?"

After Dunbar had learned what there was to know for the moment, he exited the room, crossed the long hall and knocked on the president's door. Chipton answered, and Dunbar handed him the photograph.

Wallace waived Dunbar over to him. "Come in, please, tell me what you know."

"We know he's Walter Grimes. He has an address in D.C. He was carrying a German camera that was never sold in the United States. He belonged to a few clubs in the city, we're checking them. He has a credit account with a local department store, and a pay stub from something called the Martex Corp. He had also taken several pictures of you. The one odd picture on the roll is of a farmhouse, which was taken between the time he took pictures of you at the Rotary and the photos he took of Edgar Cayce's house. We're checking to see if we can find where this house is located. It's not his own house, at least it's not the address listed on his driver's license."

"Thank you," Wallace said. "And you're Agent?"

"Dunbar, sir."

Wallace recognized the name. He looked twice at the man in front of him. Then he looked to Chipton and back to Dunbar, "You were there when Mike Barton was shot."

"I was, sir," Dunbar said.

"You two make an odd pair," the president replied, vaguely motioning to Chipton's head as if to implicate his red hair in the assessment. For his part, Chipton remained motionless by the door. Wallace added, "Thank you, Agent Dunbar." Wallace then looked away, and Dunbar took that as a sign for him to leave. As he walked past Chipton he knew that Chipton was staring at him. Both men filed out of the room, and Chipton quietly closed the door behind them.

Chapter Twenty-Three

Meeting with Truman

September 3nd, 1944
Virginia Beach, Virginia

"Sir, the vice president is here to see you."

President Wallace had remained in the room all Saturday morning after the agents had left after telling him what they knew of the photographer. He was occupying an entire floor at the Cavalier Hotel in Virginia Beach, which he thought was absurd. He would've been fine in a small room by himself and a few rooms for his aides and the agents who accompanied him everywhere now. But he didn't make the arrangements.

He was also eager to spend some time relaxing, which holding meetings on a Saturday would make impossible. He was dressed casually and hadn't even thought to tuck in the white button down he wore with tan slacks. If he could avoid it, he wouldn't even leave the hotel grounds today.

"Oh, let Truman in," Wallace said to Ellery over the phone. He was sitting on the patio outside his suite and reading the morning's papers.

"Yes, sir," Ellery said. And soon Truman walked through the doors.

Truman was less relaxed, wearing khaki pants with a baby-blue and white shirt, a tie, tan sport jacket and an absurdly rakish vacation hat. The vice president was also in Virginia Beach for a weekend getaway and their trips just happened to coincide, otherwise Wallace would have continued to put the meeting off as long as he could.

"Good morning, Mr. President," Truman said with a bit of Missouri in his voice and a large brown file under his arm. The vice presidency of the

United States can be the most thankless job around and Wallace knew it, which tempered the way he treated Truman in some respects.

"How are you taking it down here, Harry?" Wallace said, but almost slipped and called him "Harry S."

"Well, I'm trying my best, sir. I just have some things I think it's important we talk about," Truman said as he pulled off his round glasses.

"Let me have it," Wallace replied with a smile. He wanted his vice president to feel comfortable around him, even though he didn't want to see him if he could avoid it. He didn't dislike Harry S., in fact he thought he was a straightforward man, he just didn't know what to do with him.

As he was thinking these things and looking Truman over, his vice president began without hesitation, "The state of American Intelligence is not what it should be." Wallace almost rolled his eyes, knowing this talk would soon dissolve into Soviet bashing and fear mongering, but he kept composure and hoped for the best. He thought that he really did have a low opinion of Harry S. after all. The tie Truman wore, brown with beige circles, appeared to the president like something won in a bowling tournament. As Truman continued, Wallace was happy that he didn't betray his thoughts in his expression.

"We've never had a permanent agency to handle this," the vice president said. "Naturally, each branch of the military operates its own intelligence unit. We also now have the OSS and what's come to be known as their College of Cardinals, which is supposed to act as a clearinghouse on final decisions. But I think we have to begin making decisions now, before the war is over, to direct the shape our intelligence will take after the war. It's my opinion that the personnel and structure we have in the OSS and in the College of Cardinals should be made a peacetime organization."

Wallace thought this was the point where Truman would mention the Soviets, but he didn't. In fact, he waited for the president to respond.

"Harry, what you say both makes sense and makes me nervous. Now, I can see the point of view that the United States needs this, but we never had it before, so why now?" This was a leading question, and both men knew it.

Truman had rehearsed this answer already and so he was prepared, "When we're done with this war we're going to be left looking eye to eye with the Russians. Now we were antagonistic toward each other before the war, and while I hope it doesn't play out the same way after it's over, it's best for us to have an agency that's equipped to at least keep tabs on what they're up to."

He had thought, due to his military connections, that Harry S. would accuse the Soviets of treachery and so base his argument on that, but he hadn't. Wallace was starting to like his vice president.

"As you know," Wallace then added, "I was, along with the former president, better disposed toward our Russian allies than a lot of people in this country. Having said that, I don't think we gain anything by being poorly organized. We don't know who'll come after Stalin, or if he'll keep up his end of the bargain or if he'll seek territorial expansion. So if you've got a plan to put this together and some congressmen to put forth the bill, then by all means, don't let me stop you."

Harry S. smiled when Wallace said that. He would now immediately move to make some form of a central intelligence agency into law. He still thought of the new group colloquially as "the College of Cardinals."

Chapter Twenty-Four

The Farm

September 13, 1944
Destination Unknown

Now over the Atlantic, he couldn't relax enough to fall asleep. He had to keep stealing looks at the men to make sure they weren't making their way toward him. He kept imagining what it would be like to hit the saltwater after a twenty-thousand-foot fall. The massive white-capped waves would swallow him whole, and his body would end its time, not in some proper grave, but in the belly of a pack of sharks, or in Leviathan.

He was in a foul mood when he first noticed land below the plane. He didn't know where they were or where they were going. First he saw an estuary and then the river heading inland for some miles. The plane slowly turned and he caught glimpses of marshland and some sparsely settled woodlands. The longer the plane flew into the autumn afternoon dusk, the more he knew that every aspect of his flight into and out of Switzerland had been designed to make him keep his mouth shut; designed, in fact, to show him how powerful these people were and how powerless he was. Neither did the pilots see fit to mention where they now were, and when they would put down. As usual, the Eastern Europeans treated him as though he were dead.

It was in the last rays of sunlight, as Sparks looked from his portal window during the plane's descent, that he saw what appeared to be an abandoned 19th century village with a bleached white church steeple and crooked graveyard near a freshly-lain tarmac and other newly-planted military buildings. Oak forests with reddening leaves surrounded the military base and crumbling village.

The Federal Government had commandeered many such areas when war broke out pockmarking every countryside with the military machine. Typically, though, they didn't take over villages, at least not that he'd heard. So Sparks was interested to learn the history of this strange and now defunct old Main Street standing in the middle of heavy woods. He continued looking out the window and caught a glimpse of a farmhouse and barn. The farm was a mile or so behind the runway and base. It was a splendid old house and looked to have been built for a country gentleman in Colonial days. And the driveway was freshly paved and linked to the system of roads that led to the base and runway from the south, all separate from the village.

Then the aircraft crested a rocky knoll beside the old village; after a few hundred yards more the rubber wheels touched down and the plane headed toward a series of buildings. The rolling hills and autumnal hardwoods clashed with the Quonset huts and other quickly-fabricated, shoddily-built military structures, with the usual Jeeps, trucks, and flags alongside the runway. Sparks couldn't tell which branch of the military this base belonged to. It was American at least. But typically if this were an Army base he would have been able to tell. Certainly if this were a Marine base their flag would have flown beneath the Stars and Stripes.

The plane slowly turned to face a cluster of steel buildings on the north side of the runway, the setting sun bathing them briefly in light. When the plane finally stopped, Sparks saw men running alongside its belly, and felt and heard the metal staircase as it was married to the exterior fuselage.

Then the door ahead and to his left opened. A group of uniformed men, only wearing American flags on their olive drab shoulders, and pistols on their hips, entered. They greeted the foreign soldiers in black uniforms now standing by the cockpit. It seemed neither group spoke the other's tongue. Then a man dressed in business attire entered behind them. He immediately greeted the foreign soldiers in a language they understood as the Americans stepped out of his way.

Only one of the Americans looked in Sparks' direction, and then only out of curiosity. Sparks was wondering if he would again be left to his own devices as he had been in Switzerland. But as the group of foreigners and Americans disembarked, another man wearing a dark blue naval uniform with white piping along his deep-vee collar boarded the plane. On his shoulder he wore a golden eagle below a large round patch that had a bee holding what looked to be a Tommy Gun. He knew this to be the uniform of the Sea Bees, the Navy's construction battalion.

Sparks wondered what the hell he was doing on a naval base when he was in the Army?

"Private Sparks?" the Sea Bee said.

"Yes?"

"Welcome to Camp Peary."

"Thank you," Sparks said, now standing with his bag in his hand. But he thought it odd that this Sea Bee didn't introduce himself. Sparks had many questions to ask the man in front of him. He didn't know where to begin, and the man's expression plainly revealed that he wasn't going to tell him anything anyway. Then the Sea Bee said, "Right this way," in a gruff voice that had probably visited ports around the world long before this current war broke out.

As the man turned, Sparks suddenly decided to ask him one question. He said, "Where the hell is Camp Peary anyway?" The man turned and looked at him. One of his eyes was obviously larger than the other and his neck was thick like a bull's. His fingers looked rough and used like the hemp rope on the deck of a ship. The Sea Bee then said, "This is Virginia, but Forrestal will answer any further questions you have."

The Sea Bee then walked toward the cockpit and down the stairs as Sparks followed closely behind trying to remember why he knew the name "Forrestal."

Chapter Twenty-Five

James Forrestal

September 13th, 1944
Virginia

A short, energetic looking man with tired eyes stood at the bottom of the metal stair. Sparks stepped out from the airplane and saw the Sea Bee nod as he passed the tired-eyed man. Sparks knew in an instant who it was and why the name "Forrestal" sounded familiar. Standing on the fresh tarmac with a smile on his face and his hand outstretched was Secretary of the Navy James Forrestal.

Sparks knew his likeness from the papers, and remembered how angry his father had been when Forrestal was named first as deputy secretary and then later as secretary of the navy. "That goddamned Wall Street tycoon," he said to his son back in 1940. "You'd hope Roosevelt could find someone from outside that brood of vipers to fix the Navy Department."

But Sparks couldn't dwell on this memory and so he banished the thought from his mind and climbed down to the man awaiting him below. Forrestal greeted him before he stepped onto the tarmac. They shook hands.

"I'm James Forrestal," he said. Again Sparks saw that no one was around to see this interview. The Sea Bee had walked off into a nearby building and no one else was in sight. At least Forrestal had the good graces to come out and greet him in person instead of letting him languish out on the runway without a clue where to go.

"Jon Sparks," Sparks said.

The two men shook. Forrestal's nose was somewhat flattened, which added to his hard-driving appearance, but his eyes had a myopic look to them and a hint of madness. They were at once decisive and tired. Sparks hesitated to ask any questions or to say anything further at all. This was a very powerful man he was standing before. It wasn't his place to question him. But Sparks was beginning to wonder what his place really was.

Then Forrestal broke in, "I'm guessing you're curious why you've landed in a naval base? It's partly due to your special status." He said as he motioned to a parked military Jeep with no roof. "You know, they've never inducted anyone that way before . . . not up in New Haven anyhow. I guess maybe on account of your father. But they seem to think you're solid. I'm even a little jealous. Dartmouth doesn't have that kind of connection and even on Wall Street . . . I had to become Secretary of the Navy to get in the loop like that. But they brought you in. We're both upstarts, you know, and I like what I've heard about you. If they thought to pick you then there must be something there."

Sparks almost felt bad for the secretary. His desire to be in the loop seemed to drive him more than anything. He wore his jealousies out in the open, and even, it seemed to Sparks, chose who to trust based on what the right people thought.

Then Forrestal turned and climbed into the Jeep. Sparks followed, wondering what these men knew of his father, or what his father knew of them. As he'd aged, Thomas Sparks grew increasingly disillusioned by the evolution of world events and what he saw as the "Eastern power elite." When he talked of these things, which was almost never, it was always in this light.

It was chilly to be riding out in the open, but Sparks couldn't imagine they'd go far. He did notice, however, that as Forrestal lifted his foot to step into the Jeep, he was wearing silk socks. And with the three-piece suite he wore, he looked just like the banker Sparks' father said he was. He looked even stranger standing out on this isolated airfield just outside an old, abandoned town. He was the type of man who belonged in a country club on the North Shore of Long Island – Gatsby's Gold Coast – or in a townhouse in Manhattan. Before the Crash, and on into the Depression years, you would, in fact, have found him in just such a place. But these were war years. Business was slow and unfulfilling, and if you wanted to contribute then you joined the effort. But here he just seemed out of place.

Sparks then wondered why Roosevelt would have hired such a man at all for the job, but the thought soon passed from his mind as they drove down the tarmac and took a turn into the hardwoods.

"I saw the base from the air." Sparks said. "What is this place?"

"We train Sea Bees here. We also do some other special training and keep prisoners of war."

"Is that what those men in black uniforms were? But they weren't under restraint," Sparks said, but immediately knew that Forrestal didn't trust his feigned naiveté. Sparks wanted to talk to Forrestal, but on the other hand, he was reluctant to be too chatty with the secretary of the navy lest it lead to a discussion of some of the stranger things he'd come across during his trip.

To his relief, Forrestal didn't seem to mind the question. "Well, they've got nowhere else to go. They can't run, and we're not sure what to do with them. If we turned them loose someone would kill them, but they might be of some use to us here." He talked in a friendly tone, but Sparks could tell he wouldn't go any further with his comments about those men. "I was saying," the secretary of the navy continued, "that you're something special. The president wanted you back here. It's not often that men are released from a war early to join the president, and with your other, well . . . obligations, you can be of great service to us . . . to your country." He turned and looked at Sparks now and then said, "So we put you on the earliest flight we could get you on. There was some problem with Eisenhower's Army Air Force, and we had this flight taking these men back to the States, and so we put you in with them."

Sparks wanted to point out that the "earliest flight they could get" also included a nearly two-week layover in Gibraltar and a meeting with Allen Dulles, but he didn't think the secretary would find it as amusing as he did in hindsight.

At that point, they passed an old stone wall, which was a pile of rock nearly eight feet wide and three or so feet tall that ran for well over a hundred yards and then disappeared out of sight down a hill. The field it used to delineate had been abandoned years before, and now some fairly good-sized oaks were beginning to make a forest again, and probably with less effort than originally needed with all the rocks removed by hand and mule for cultivation.

They came to the end of the wall and Forrestal steered the Jeep to the left at an intersection. This area would have felt and looked much like it had a hundred years before if not for the fresh asphalt they drove on. The whole place had the feel of a colonial era country estate with fresh blacktop painted over the old mud road. Up ahead Sparks recognized the farmhouse and barn he'd seen from the plane on the way in. There were two men standing on the porch in navy blue overcoats as they went past. He could make them out in the last light of day with some help from the electric light pouring from the interior of the house.

Forrestal said not a single word, and so neither did Sparks as they passed by the house. They were headed in a northerly direction now. After the farmhouse was long behind them, Forrestal began to talk: "Most of this area used to be known as Porto Bello," he said, "and was the hunting preserve for Lord Dunmore, who was the last royal governor of Virginia. He fled from here when the war began and his land became the property of the United States when it came into being. Parts of it were parceled off for a few small towns, one of which isn't far. Right there," Forrestal said and pointed. As he did so, Sparks began to make out the silhouette of the village he'd seen from the air through the young trees that were now filling in the old fields. It was strange that years ago this land was wide open farmland. Now it was returning to its wild state, as it had been when the Powhatan inhabited the area before colonization.

Forrestal continued: "And right there, you can see the old village of Magruder." Seeing Sparks look of confusion, Forrestal explained: "It's named for John Magruder. He was a Confederate general, famous for conducting some kind of a delaying action against Union Troops. So the area was named after a Confederate, but interestingly enough the town itself became a town for Freedmen – freed slaves. The last of the descendants were just moved out to make way for the base."

"People still lived here?"

"Up until a few years ago."

Sparks didn't bother to mention the irony of a situation in which freedmen, who'd come here after the war, were just now moved out of their town by the United States Navy.

Forrestal took a left into the old Main Street, and Sparks inexplicably felt his anxiety level increase. There was no reason in the world they had to travel through this decrepit town to leave the base. He knew this because he could now see that the paved Main Street dead-ended at a new barbed-wire fence just ahead.

The village itself was immaculate – remarkably so. Though it was abandoned and in rough condition, it looked as though cleaning crews swept through on a regular basis to knock down all the cobwebs and sweep the streets and porches.

Again, Sparks was conscious of his lack of control. The Jeep came to a rest in front of a large, white-clapboarded church. There was enough light to make out the other buildings which comprised the village. He saw what looked like an old general store alongside a couple of small wood houses and a cemetery where the barbed-wire fence he'd seen earlier began. Across the street was a post office that was still marked as such. Beside the post office, Sparks noticed a light burning deep inside a long white rectangular building. The building was clapboarded and tall with a false second story. Above the front door was a white sign with black lettering, but Sparks couldn't make out what it said yet.

Just then Forrestal killed the motor. He leaned over to Sparks in an overly friendly way, in the process exposing his silk socks, and said, "They wanted someone else to make contact with you, but you might not have realized how important this is if you met with some nondescript agent. There's something you need to see inside."

Sparks smiled in a pained way in response, and Forrestal patted him on the back.

Both men then stepped from the Jeep where it was parked in front of the church and crossed the street to the building with the light on. The light from inside the structure was enough for Sparks to make out what the sign said. "Magruder Masonic Temple."

Chapter Twenty-Six

The Temple

Camp Peary, Virginia
September 13-14, 1944

Inside, though the room was well kept, the smell of dust and disuse hung heavy like a cloud. Sparks saw several rows of chairs facing what looked like a stage with a heavy, dark wood podium. A table stood to the right of the stage around which several men sat by a door at the back leading to a darkened room. The entire front room was paneled with stained wood from floor to ceiling.

Sparks hesitated for a moment as he started through the front door and saw into the room. As he passed over the threshold he almost stopped to look back and see if someone was standing behind it. He would have stopped, too, had Forrestal not turned and closed the door himself. Then Forrestal put his hand on the small of Sparks' back and led him forward through the rows of chairs like a father leading a son into some time-honored initiation.

Sparks cringed, but looked around the room in an attempt to gauge his surroundings. It seemed that the chairs were all new, military issue. They had that look, and bore no resemblance to the rest of the building which was of an older, more traditional vintage. Sparks wondered where the people from the town had gone after the Navy moved them out.

As they passed the raised platform at the head of the room, Sparks saw a large Masonic Square and Compass symbol on the wall with the capital letter "G" between the implements. The only light came from a lamp in the middle of the table they were walking toward. The lamp threw an odd shadow across the Square and Compass, connecting both ends of the upturned Square through the "G," making the top half dark and the bottom half light. This reminded Sparks of a symbol called "Yin and Yang," which he'd seen in one of his classes.

As they approached the table, Forrestal began making introductions. Three men sat at the table. Forrestal introduced only two. The first was wearing a grey hat with matching suit. "Jon, this is Mike Brady, he's working on this with us." Sparks reached his hand out to greet the man.

Forrestal turned to Brady with a warm look. "Mike, this is Jonathan Sparks, fresh in from the frontlines. We took him out of Italy, but he was at Guadalcanal with the 164th Infantry."

The two shook hands as Brady stood.

"Is that so," Brady said. "I hear it was some fight."

"Yeah," Sparks managed to say, but the only question which came to Sparks' mind was, "What is Mike's position?" But of course, as was becoming typical now, that kind of question would have been out of place. Sparks then turned from Brady to the second man at the table who sat with his jacket hung over the back of his chair. His hair was tousled as if he had run his hands through it. He wore a beige shirt with the sleeves rolled up with his hat before him on the table.

Sparks was staring at this second man when Forrestal hurried forward and said, "And this is Whitaker Chambers."

Neither name rang a bell, but Sparks had almost become accustomed to that. Whitaker stood from his chair in a labored way and said, "I'm happy to meet you, Jon. You're doing something that's not only good for your country, but for all the world."

Sparks was unsure how to respond to this statement; it seemed overblown. He looked over his shoulder at Forrestal, who was grinning, and then all the men sat down to the table together. The third man, who was sitting somewhat away from the table near the back door, was never introduced.

Forrestal pulled his chair around to face Whitaker and began talking. "We've been a little coy with Sparks. Whitaker, why don't you fill him in?" Forrestal flashed a proud smile, as if he was pleased to finally let the young man in on the secret. "I think it would be best coming from you."

Whitaker Chambers took a deep, dramatic breath and began to speak in a drawn, old New York accent. Chambers was much older than Sparks, but Sparks couldn't identify his age. There seemed to be a suffering in his eyes that made him look older than the rest of him appeared.

When Chambers exhaled he said: "I work for Mr. Luce at Time Magazine now, but it used to be that I was part of what we called 'the underground.' It may sound clandestine and somewhat far-fetched to imagine that there is such a thing as an underground operating in this great country, but I can assure you it is very real."

Whitaker Chambers paused then and took another breath and continued. "Like many other educated people of my generation I came to see the decline in western man as terminal. His religion was dead. His culture: dead. His way of life: dying before his eyes. And the only cure for this malady, I believed, was Communism and the permanent revolution.

"I saw this as the cure; one which could not only save the poor from the abuses of the rich, but also save our future. This could only happen if we were willing to devote ourselves to a rigid adherence to the object: the revolution. I worked for this revolution, devotedly, for years, but then, as someone else put it, 'I heard the screams' and couldn't pretend I hadn't. Communism is the great black hole of modern life, Jon. It is the logical conclusion when there is no God to vouchsafe freedom." As he said these last words looking into the lamp on the table, he suddenly turned to Sparks and said: "Are you a God fearing man, Jon?"

"I am, yes sir. I'm from Texas."

"That's good. That's very good." He took another deep breath. "I want you to know that I think we're on the losing team. And I look at Mr. Forrestal there and I think that deep down inside he feels the same way. I tell you this because in all likelihood some of us are going to get killed going forward. I'm not asking you to die, don't think that, that's what the revolutionaries do, but will you live for your country? That's what I want to know."

"Yes sir, I will, but I'm sorry, what's this all about?" Sparks said with some trepidation.

"Let me tell you a story. Have you ever heard of Juliet Poyntz or Walter Krivitzky?"

"No," Sparks said.

"I shouldn't expect you would, as you probably read American newspapers."

Sparks was beginning to think that Mr. Chambers sounded a bit melodramatic, though he certainly believed what he said. Sparks was young, yet he had been around long enough to know when a man was full of it or not. And Mr. Whitaker Chambers was not.

"Juliet Poyntz was a founder of the Communist Party of the United States. But then she traveled to Moscow. There she saw the face of death in the man of steel, Stalin. She returned and talked of defecting, only to close friends of course. But all of her friends were communists, and one was committed enough to pass that message on to her Soviet handlers. That's the thing about revolutionaries: nothing is ever closer to them than the revolution. Juliet walked out of the Women's Club in Manhattan and was never seen again. But they told me personally that they executed her for suspecting she was going to leave the party. Imagine that, of all things, in America."

Without missing a beat he continued on to the next name as though this story was part of the same sentence. "Walter Krivitsky was a Soviet Intelligence officer who defected to the United States after a friend of his was murdered by Stalin's henchmen. He came to the West and revealed the secret Molotov-Ribbentrop Pact, where Hitler and Stalin, both opposite sides of the same coin, agreed to carve up Europe together. Of course the Left here in America savagely attacked him as a liar, but there was only so much they could say after the pact became public when both countries invaded Poland in '39. Recently Krivitsky was found in a D.C. hotel room clutching a pistol with a single gunshot wound to the head and three suicide notes beside him. One of the notes was addressed to his wife and stated that the Soviet Government would be her best friend. This, of course, was not an opinion Krivitsky held. I sent his family to Florida with my own where I hoped they would be safe. Killing a man is easy, of course, Jon, but making it look as though he did it himself or that it was an accident is an art form to these people. They call it a 'good death.'

"I tell you this because there is a network of revolutionary spies working in the United States right now, and they'll not hesitate to murder to maintain their secrecy. Why this is important to you at all is because several of these people are in government and to my knowledge at least one formerly worked for Roosevelt as an economic advisor and is now very close to Henry Wallace. His name is Laughlin Currie. There are more of course, but for now that's a name you should know. If you don't mind, keep a log of who meets with the president. I'd like to know how many more have gotten in."

"Do you think Wallace knows?"

"I don't think Wallace knows. I think he's an American and a Christian who loves his country and his fellow man and wants to help them. And I think that revolutionaries know how to manipulate this kind of personality."

Suddenly Forrestal spoke up, "There's a war on, Jon, which has nothing to do with either the European or Japanese theaters. The Soviets have been in this country at least since the Russian Revolution, probably earlier, establishing contacts and fellow travelers. In a way, Stalin's Russia, or Lenin's, carried on the great Czarist Russian tradition of espionage, but Stalin is paranoid and murderous to a degree that makes Ivan the Terrible look tame." Forrestal shifted his weight in the chair he was in and continued, "And you should know, Jon, you're not leaving a war, but coming back to one. And make sure you wait a while before you make contact with us again. Get the lay of the land, so to speak. With this in mind, we'd like you to spend the next few weeks here at the base in our accelerated course."

When he said that the man who had not been introduced stood up. He was holding a black bag.

"I'm sorry," Forrestal said as though he were embarrassed, "but they've insisted on this part. And don't worry, the president doesn't expect you 'til November."

"This is beginning to become a habit," Sparks quipped, but he was the only one who laughed at his joke.

Chapter Twenty-Seven

Lauchlin Currie

November 8, 1944
The Oval Office

Lauchlin Currie entered the Oval Office. It was 7:00 PM and dark outside. Wallace sat at his desk with only the green domed reading lamp and a small fire shedding light on the room. That fire always reminded him of Roosevelt's fireside chats. He looked up when the curved door across from him opened. He knew who it was, as he'd asked Betty to let his guests in when they arrived.

As Currie entered, he turned and held the door for another man behind him. Wallace stood from his desk and waved the men in while he walked around to the front. He shook Currie's hand first as the door closed. "Nice to see you Lauchlin."

"Thank you, Henry, and congratulations on your election. The country really surprised me. It made me believe again in the wisdom of the people." Currie was referring to the landslide victory President Wallace won just the day before. He won forty-three of the forty-eight states: New Hampshire and Maine had gone to his rival, as had a handful of Southern states. Despite these small loses, such a victory was a major statement to a country arguing about what its postwar future would be like while still looking back to the Great Depression with fear.

"We're really very happy about it," Wallace said. "Especially since I got away with doing as little campaigning as possible. The people knew who I was and they voted for me." Then Wallace turned his attention to the man who had followed Currie in.

"Mr. President, I'd like to introduce Dr. Harris Cunningham."

"Dr. Cunningham," the president said as the two men shook. Cunningham was a smallish man, with a sharp nose, wire rimmed glasses and haunted eyes. He was born in Spokane, Washington to third generation grocers and looked like a man who'd spent the night outside in a blizzard expecting to freeze to death.

He was a State Department official of middling importance who worked mostly in the Middle East, which he thought to be a spectacularly stupid placement considering he spoke Chinese. But the State Department, to his mind, was a very confused agency. For the most part, he kept a low profile, made few friends, and was known to turn all his work over in record time while keeping his office so clean, tidy, and uncluttered it looked vacant.

He was also a devout communist. He had gone even further than that and become a traitor. He was actively involved with a network of American spies working for the Soviets, a group with which Laughlin Currie was also affiliated, but while Currie was little more than a fellow traveler, Cunningham was a zealot, and higher up the Underground ladder as well.

The president was fully aware of all these facts, and had been for some time. Wallace also knew, from what Lauchlin had earlier informed him, that Cunningham was appalled at what he thought the Russians had done with the revolution, and what Stalin was doing every day.

As Wallace walked the two men over to his desk, Cunningham suddenly burst out, "How do I know you aren't going to sell me to the Soviets?"

"How do I know you won't do the same or worse?" Wallace shouted back as he leaned his hand on the desk, looking down at Cunningham with disgust.

Both men were silent for a moment and Currie cleared his throat, but then Cunningham cleared his throat and spoke up, "Lauchlin knows me."

"Yes, and I know Lauchlin. That doesn't answer my question," the president shot back. His Midwestern cast usually didn't allow for shouting or quick explosions of anger, but the shape of this man rubbed him the wrong way. Cunningham looked like the kind of man that would sell out his friends for an idea. And Wallace was shocked that this unpleasant fellow had nerve enough to put the question to him like that. It forced Wallace to realize the power of his office all in one moment. Cunningham was undoubtedly a traitor and a revolutionary – he didn't ever have to see the light of day again.

"I just mean that this is not how clandestine operations work. It's highly unusual that the president or anyone like that would speak personally with an operative."

"I think that's the point." Wallace replied. "You don't come into my office and ask me if you can trust me not to give you up to the Soviets and then tell me what's proper and what's not!" he was shouting again. "There are some things you just have to do yourself, that's why you're here!"

Currie then spoke up, "Mr. President, sir, Harris came to me months ago. He's trying to get out, but he doesn't know how. Stalin kills anyone he even suspects of such things. And he kills them all over the world." He had already told Wallace this leading up to the meeting, but he was reinforcing the point now in light of the unpleasantness.

"I know he's trying to get out, but that's not my fault and it's not my concern! Do you hate Stalin? That's all that matters!" Wallace said to Cunningham.

Dr. Cunningham was sweating. "Yes, I hate Stalin. He betrayed the revolution, and no one knows it. They think it continues. He even had Trotsky killed in Mexico with an axe. It can't go on. He's a Czar." He fidgeted in his seat and was nervous. Wallace imagined Cunningham would gladly accept torture to further "the cause" but he was out of his history now, lost and confused and full of hate.

"All right then," Wallace said, "Work for me. You'll talk with Lauchlin and that's it. Your first job is to bring in other people from the cold."

Cunningham was looking directly into Wallace's eyes now. Wallace could see that he was a fanatic with a Jesuitical devotion, but it was a devotion that had turned in the president's favor. "You're right," Wallace continued, "I have no idea how to operate anything clandestine, but you do."

"What of your intelligence agencies?" Cunningham asked, this time with a deference in his tone that was unmistakable.

"We have no great tradition in that respect," Wallace began, "We're naïve. But I feel more comfortable starting this on my own anyhow. I've given this a lot of thought. I know it can all blow up. The truth of the matter is that there's already a Soviet network in this country, and it's full of people who feel Stalin betrayed them. On the other hand, all the men in our military intelligence community are eager to start a war with the Soviets. They'd just as soon side with fascists to do it. I don't think men like that could organize something like what we're contemplating now. Or would you like to see a war between the two countries?"

"No, sir, I wouldn't," Cunningham said.

"Then we'll work for peace and Stalin's removal, and we'll work together."

Chapter Twenty-Eight

Sparks in the Oval Office

November 8, 1944
The Oval Office

President Wallace frowned as Lauchlin Currie walked to the door to leave the Oval Office. When he reached it, Lauchlin turned, "You are the right man, Mr. President," he said, "I believe in you." Then he left. He had his hand on Cunningham's shoulder, ushering him out of the relative dark of the Oval Office into the light of the anteroom where Betty sat.

Cunningham didn't say anything as he left. He looked like a wet rat fleeing the flooded boiler room of a ship. Wallace had no pity for him. If they were going to work together, it would be on his terms or not at all. Again, Wallace felt his own power, the power of the office, and he didn't like it. It made him sick. The realization also made him wonder about Stalin. He understood that Stalin wasn't squeamish about using his own power. He exercised it – ruthlessly – and that was that. Wallace then shifted from thinking of Stalin to imagining what his own country would do with a bomb like the one they were now working on. *They would drop it*, he thought, *at the first opportunity!*

Wallace was sweating now, and unhooked the button of his collar beneath his baby blue tie. As the door closed, he leaned back against his desk and put his head into his hands as he thought about "the bomb" and the so-called "Manhattan District." He was afraid to take on the United States Army, but allowing them to continue making such a device even as the war wound down he thought was insane. Just having it, someone would use it.

Then the door opened and the light from the outside flooded in. Wallace thought that Currie must have forgotten something and returned for whatever it was.

"Laughlin?" Wallace said.

"No, Mr. President, it's me, Jon Sparks."

"Sparks!" Wallace jumped off the desk and came to him. "And drop that 'Mr. President business, you call me Henry as you always have." Wallace hit the light switch by the curved door and took both Sparks' hands.

"Who was that with Lauchlin?" Sparks asked, looking over his shoulder toward the anteroom.

"Oh, just a troubled soul. I wouldn't worry about him, but what about you? I didn't know you were getting in. No one tells the president anything if they can help it." Wallace was smiling like a child. "Well, come here, sit down. I think I've got a good bottle of pre-prohibition Scotch – Kennedy imported it – the stuff they make now is no good with the war on. How did you get in after all? I put in the request months ago."

"I landed earlier today." Sparks said. "They flew me in on a Navy plane, of all things. I guess Eisenhower wanted me on the next flight, no matter what it was. Then they gave me a Jeep and I drove up. Congratulations, by the way, on your election. I heard you really cleaned up."

"Thank you. We won because the mood of the country favored it, that's all."

They walked to the front of the desk and Sparks sat down while Wallace moved to the shelves on the right where there was a small wet bar and pulled out a bottle of Scotch. He poured two glasses, neat, and came to sit across from Sparks in the chair Cunningham had recently inhabited.

"It took Eisenhower months to get you on the next plane," Wallace said through his large, toothy smile.

"They wanted to break through the . . ." Sparks began, but Wallace interrupted him.

"I know, the Gothic Line. I heard that. And I'm sure you had nothing to do with hanging back there. How was it with the Monuments Men?"

Sparks sipped his Scotch and said, "Fine, if you don't mind watching half of Western art destroyed in a cataclysm to the Huns. Men fighting is one thing, that's bad enough, but to see these armies wreck thousand-year-old towns is to recognize the scale of this war."

"I almost can't take it," Wallace said looking up at the ceiling as if for help. "We saw it coming in the 30's. Roerich even talked about it." Sparks cringed at the mention of that name from Wallace. He had learned, after the fact, both how much the president respected Roerich, even looked up to him, and how embarrassed he'd been when the letters came out and all that happened afterward in the press. But Wallace didn't notice Sparks' apprehension and distaste and continued, "He was eager to have us sign the Roerich Pact, which Roosevelt did. It protected cultural treasures. I think he must've had some insight into what was coming." By now Wallace had finished his glass. Betty popped her head through the curved door to say she would be leaving for the night.

"What time is it?" Wallace asked.

"It's almost 10:00 PM, and Mrs. Wallace asked you not to spend all night out here again, Mr. President."

"I'll tell her you told me, thank you, Betty. Please hit that light on your way out, would you? It's easier for me to relax with just the lamp on."

She did so, and then closed the door.

"Roerich must've had some view to it." Wallace then broke the silence that had developed between them since Betty turned off the light. "He must have. If you only knew what I know Sparks. Ahhh," he said as he looked Sparks over, "I want to show you something. Well, actually a couple things. I'm not keeping you from anything, am I?" And then he stopped again and observed Sparks over his glass. Sparks looked older, and harder, though he didn't seem to carry the sadness that Wallace had felt in other men who've returned from combat. "You know I've always trusted you?"

"Yes, sir."

"Please stop the 'yes sir, no sir'." Wallace said.

"Henry. I mean, Henry," Sparks laughed a little at his own awkward formality. It was all that time in the military, he thought.

"Thank you, we have to talk like friends here. I need friends Jon, I'm short on them," and Wallace walked back over to the wet bar and poured himself another glass of Scotch. He hadn't felt loose like this in months. It was almost as if he wasn't president anymore, but that feeling never went away.

"Would you like another glass?"

Sparks nodded and Wallace carried the bottle over and filled him up as well. He put the bottle down and from behind the desk pulled out what appeared to Sparks to be a white flag wrapped in the traditional triangular manner.

"This flag was supposed to be known as the 'Banner of Peace,'" Wallace pointed out. He looked nostalgic. Then he said, "When we signed the pact the flag was to fly over cultural treasures in times of war." Then he unfurled the flag. It was all white with the large red outline of a circle in the center. Inside the red outline were three solid red circles, arranged so as to form a sort of triangle. Roerich had described it to Wallace as the trinity of past, present, and future, surrounded by the circle of eternity; or religion, art, and knowledge inside of culture.

"The *Campo Santo* in Italy could have used a flag like that."

"This image doesn't mean much now," Wallace said, "but what it might have symbolized . . . what it might have come to symbolize is really something we should all mourn now." Shadows fell across the flag in the partially lit Oval Office. Wallace then folded the flag once lengthwise and draped it over his shoulder like a Roman Senator. "He must have seen it coming. He must have known what we were about to do to the world. Do you believe that it's possible to see the future, Jon?"

"I guess I don't know what you mean, Henry."

"You know what I mean, you just think I'm a crank. That's the other thing I want to show you." And Wallace stood as though to walk out of the room.

"Should I come with you?" Sparks asked.

"To hell with it. I don't feel like going back to the residence at the moment. Ilo might give me hell. So I'll just tell you about it." He took another sip of his Scotch. "When I went to Siberia . . . Let me start a different way. A few months before Roosevelt died, I received letters from a man named Edgar Cayce. They call him 'the sleeping prophet.'" Wallace paused, wondering whether or not he should tell Sparks about the double corncob. He decided against it. "One of his letters was convincing enough to make me go see him in Virginia Beach. There he told me I would be president, and that we were verging on an apocalypse of fire. He gave me transcripts of my 'readings' as well, but they're a little dense. The basic gist is that I will be betrayed and assassinated unless I can eliminate doubt, but as to avoiding the impending catastrophe: I don't know, and what that means in the context of what's going on in Europe and Asia is beyond me."

"Eliminate what doubt?"

"I don't know. I should also avoid New Hampshire, I think. We can always read them if you want. I have them in a safe upstairs along with a stone I was given by Tibetans when I was in China just before the president died. The Tibetans were giving me a presidential gift when I was still vice president. And the stone they gave me is supposed to be the Stone of Destiny, or Jacob's Stone, or Jacob's Pillow. It has some relation to the end of the world and the return of the Lost Tribes. Either way, when you combine those Tibetans with what Edgar Cayce in Virginia Beach told me, all signs point to the end of the world, certainly the end of my world." Wallace paused now. Sparks looked stunned. "I guess that about sums it up," Wallace said. "Don't look so sad. I'm not crazy. These things happened, and along with the war and the bomb it's hard not to think we're on the knife's edge of an apocalypse. But the question is, 'What do I do now?'"

Suddenly there were footsteps outside the door, and a muffled conversation. The door flung open and the first lady entered with Agent Chipton just behind. She turned the lights on and both men squinted. "I knew you were in here, Henry. Why do you have the lights off?" Both men stood, and Ilo recognized Jonathan Sparks. "Jon, is that you?"

"Yes, Mrs. Wallace."

"My God, you look all grown up."

Then, turning her attention back to Henry, she said, "You didn't tell me Jon was coming home."

"I didn't know Jon was coming home."

"Have you been drinking, Henry?" Then she looked to the nearly empty glasses in both men's hands and the bottle on the table. "You old teetotaler, you know you can't handle your liquor. Let's get you to bed." She turned her attention back to Sparks. "Jon, the Lincoln bedroom's all made up. I'll just pick up the phone and let them know you're here."

Chapter Twenty-Nine

The Geologist

December 12, 1944
National Museum of Natural History

"Yes, the president wants to come to the Smithsonian, himself." President Wallace said into the telephone. "Don't worry, it's not scheduled so we won't get the normal media pressure."

Wallace hung the phone up and looked across his desk at Sparks who was sitting in one of the high-backed chairs. Per the president's orders, Sparks had carried the stone to the Natural History Museum over a month ago.

"Now that the good geologist has gotten some information out of it, I'm going over there." Wallace said. "But he's reluctant, he doesn't want the circus coming to town, I guess. Aside from that though he said he has some important findings regarding the stone. He wanted to tell me in person here, but I was already going to meet with Lauchlin outside the White House for lunch, so it'll let me kill two birds with one stone. Think of it as a field trip."

"I'm going?" Sparks asked.

"Why not, it should be fun," Wallace said and motioned to Agent Chipton, who was then standing off to the side of the Oval Office, to indicate that he was ready to leave.

In the car on the ride over, Wallace was talkative. Of late, and since Sparks' return, the president had been getting more and more comfortable with his job, but, more importantly, he was becoming better able to tolerate the pressure he was under. No longer did he look at the door to the Oval Office as a floodgate he could hardly close. He had begun to swim with the current rather than being dragged along by it. Taking a small field trip like this one to the Natural History Building to meet with the geologist Eliezer Berk made him feel in control in a way that fielding endless meetings in the West Wing could not. That's also what Sparks imagined as he looked across the car at the president.

Suddenly Wallace said, "You know what I'm going to do with that stone don't you? I'm going to have it used as a cornerstone in the new White House I'm having built."

"I thought it was just rebuilt after Hoover?" Sparks asked.

"The West Wing was rebuilt, not the White House. That thing is falling down. I mean you wouldn't even believe what bad shape it's in. You can grab onto the supports and pull out handfuls of dry rotted wood. I did it myself. It's a miracle the building's still standing at all."

Sparks didn't reply. When they passed the Ellipse on the way to Constitution Avenue, the president said, "Every day this town feels more and more like a military camp." He was referring to the Army barracks stationed in the center of the Ellipse just to the south of the White House. "It reminds me of reading of Lincoln during the war. Some days you could hear the fighting just to the south, and see the Army of the Potomac. Washington hasn't felt like this since the 1860s. I think we've got the same kind of opportunity for change too. The time is right, Jon, we've just got to do something about it."

The car pulled up to one of the service entrances of the Natural History Museum facing the National Mall. The president opened the door and exited the car before Agent Chipton, who had accompanied him, had a chance to open it for him. Sparks followed closely behind and made only brief eye contact with Chipton whom he thought was staring at him with suspicion.

"I'm beginning to feel like Al Capone or someone like that, always using back entrances and service doors," the president said.

They walked into the building together, with Agent Chipton and another agent following closely behind. The hallway they entered was full of behind-the-scenes activity and safe from the view of the general public. But in order to reach Eliezer Berk's office they had to cross part of the gallery.

"Why use the stone in the White House?" Sparks asked as they passed exhibits whose plaques stated they were from the Cretaceous Period.

"That stone's supposed to be linked to ancient Israel, and the Brahmin who gave it to me told me we were the New Jerusalem, so why not make it a permanent part of the United States? Maybe it will act like a charm to keep war away." Wallace smirked as he said that, then he paused a moment and looked over the assembled skeleton of a large dinosaur. He was standing before a Triceratops, which had recently been pulled from the ground in the Hell's Creek Formation, just outside of Jordan, Montana. On the plaque, under the species' name, was a short history of the dinosaur. The first line read: "The Triceratops was among the last of the non-avian dinosaur groups to develop before the Cretaceous–Paleogene extinction event." Beside that plaque was a timeline that showed the extinction event with a large heard of dinosaurs with colored bars behind them signifying their existence and then nothing moving forward but mice and birds.

The president didn't comment on the "extinction event." He was avoiding morbidity today. Then he said, "It was just an idea. I'm really not sure what to do with the stone to tell the truth. I suppose it depends on what it really is."

They continued walking through the gallery toward a door which led to the offices. For the first fifty yards or so, no one noticed the president weaving through the displays. Then one woman looked at Wallace and smiled, but she didn't say anything. In his experience Wallace had noted that the mood, and even the vote, of strangers who saw him was frequently reflected in their expressions. This woman had probably voted for him, he concluded, noting that her position as a museum employee made that particularly likely. But another woman with her small child, viewing a display of flying dinosaurs made eye contact with him twice before turning with her son to watch him pass. She seemed amused rather than happy. She had probably voted for the Republican.

They reached the Department of Mineral Sciences before word of the president's presence reached the larger pool of museum visitors, forestalling an impromptu political gathering.

Once inside, Wallace walked up to the desk and said to the receptionist, "President Wallace to see Dr. Berk." The poor woman was quite startled to see the president of the United States of America before her.

Wallace flashed a huge smile when she recognized him. "Just thought I would stop by," he said to her.

She smiled, "Before the New Deal, where I lived in Maryland, we didn't have anything, nothing. And I just want you to know how much it means to me to see you continuing the legacy of that great man."

"Thank you," Wallace said.

She picked up the phone. Soon the director of Mineral Sciences opened his door. His eyes were almost the same grey as his jacket. He looked like a sad man. Wallace and Sparks stood to greet him as he walked around the receptionist's desk.

"I didn't know if you would really come or not," Eliezer said in a quiet, throaty voice, as he closed the smoked glass office door on which his name had been stenciled in green. His English was very good for someone whose first language was German, but still he struggled. On the phone with Wallace earlier, he'd almost thought the president was joking, or more likely that an imposter was pulling his leg. Why would a president want to meet a geologist after all, and one who was not even an American?

When Adolf Hitler became Chancellor of Germany in 1933, Eliezer and his wife feared for their lives. Then Eliezer took the opportunity of a temporary teaching position in the States to permanently leave the country of his childhood. The move was difficult at first, especially so for his wife, who spoke only German, Polish and Yiddish. She had been born in the town of Radziejow, a part of Polish Pomerania prior to the invasion. The last she heard, through whispers and rumors sent from friends of friends, the Jews of Radziejow had been forced into a guarded, walled ghetto. She had heard nothing more since 1942.

After she lost word of her family, Mrs. Berk became a quiet but intense supporter of the Allies and the United States especially. She made a concerted effort to learn English and kept herself informed by reading the papers daily, almost obsessively, to the degree that her English allowed. When she read that the Russians had finally repelled the invaders at Stalingrad, Mrs. Berk screamed out loud in her kitchen. There was a picture in the New York Times that day of a dead German lying over rubble with a desolate city in the background. She nearly framed it. Recently, she had been saddened when she'd heard of the strength the Germans displayed by nearly pushing through the American front in Belgium in what became known as the "Battle of the Bulge." Her relief was extraordinary when she learned that the Americans ultimately repelled the German onslaught.

When she was younger, a man like General Patton would have seemed to her some kind of a scourge; now he was fighting the good fight. She wanted the Germans killed.

And because Eliezer knew this about her, he almost couldn't wait to get home to Georgetown to tell her of the president's visit; that Wallace had come to see *him* of all people. Especially since his position at the Natural History Museum in Washington was, short of a professorship, the best job his friends and associates could help him to get. Now he had the president coming personally to visit, and regarding an artifact that was very strange; one entwined in Jewish folklore, if not history.

He knew his father would be interested in both his meeting with the president and the artifact itself. However, the activities that would have fascinated his father were irrelevant for he was aware that his entire family was dead. Like his wife, he'd only heard rumors of the progress of events in Germany. But he knew it nevertheless. Stalin's Soviet Russia did not release facts easily, but Eliezer heard terrifying stories of what they had found over the summer in a place called Madjanek, where the ashes of men filled an entire field to the depth of six meters. He believed these stories, but kept them from his wife. He was thankful that the American papers had thus far reported nothing of the atrocities the Nazis had committed against civilians. Every day he dreaded coming home to find that she would learn the truth of what happened. For the time being, she lived in a bubble, rooting for the allied victory as one roots for a football team. Likewise, he was something like happy with his position at the museum and the quiet life he led with his wife, especially knowing what the Nazis were doing, and how safe he was from them in America.

"Can I get you some coffee?" the aging geologist asked.

"No, thank you," the president responded. Sparks didn't bother to answer. "But what of the stone?" Wallace then asked.

"Yes," and Berk motioned for the president to follow him as he began talking almost absentmindedly. They entered the hallway leading back to the gallery and then into a vast storage room with shelving that reached to the twenty foot ceilings and seemed to stretch for acres. Chipton and the other agent walked behind them as they moved down the corridor.

Berk talked in a low voice. "Yes, that stone is from Palestine. And you may be surprised to hear that it is of a type of limestone known as Jerusalem Stone . . . Meleke. This is what the Wailing Wall of the Temple Mount was made from. It is very common in the area, and the British Mandate for Palestine required its use in all new construction.

"This kind of stone was used in the ancient times because it was easy to take out of the ground and work; it also hardened in the atmosphere." Berk stopped to unlock the gate in a large metal fence at the end of one of the aisles. The gate led into a steel cage where the museum housed some of its most valuable artifacts. There, Eliezer waited for both the president and Sparks to enter and then closed the gate. Walking to a table where the stone lay out, he began. "Your stone is very unusual because it appears to have been worked into its current shape, yet it shows no tool marks. I can also tell you it's at least two thousand years old, I mean in its present form, because some fossil mold spores of about that age were lodged in the indentation. You said you found this in Tibet? That's very interesting."

The president placed his hand over the stone and replied, "Well, I didn't find it in Tibet, but in Jiuquan, China where a Tibetan delegation came and presented me the gift."

"And why would they do that?"

"They said that a group of people who had lost their home before Roman times traveled to the Himalayas and gave it to them."

"Why would they do that?" Berk asked again.

"What?"

"Give a stone to Himalayans?"

"I thought you might help shed light on that."

"What I know, sir, is that the stone you have your hand on has a better claim to being Jacob's Pillow than anything else, including that Stone of Scone in England; that's not even the right type of rock. There are also many people now who are very interested in reconstituting Israel. Prior to my research on this stone, I was familiar only with the European Jewish perspective of Zionism. Now I know that there are many Christians in this country who think that Jesus will return only after Israel does, and they seek to help this dream become reality."

"But it's just a story."

Berk paused a moment, looking at the president. Then he said, "In Germany the Nazis have traced their roots to a mythical tribe of Aryans."

"I see your point," the president said.

"The war has also changed the dynamic. There are now hundreds of thousands of Jews, the ones who are alive, who are fleeing Europe at the moment, or have fled it, and they are coming to America but they are also going to Israel – to Palestine – because they don't know where else to go. It's like the land that held them for 2,000 years has suddenly spit them out. Ten years ago, most of these people hardly would have dreamed such a thing."

Wallace hadn't previously made the connection between the Israelis of ancient times and the modern day Jews of Europe. As president, the notion of a Jewish migration to the holy land made him nervous, as did the idea of the land "spitting them out." He was relatively comfortable with the idea of Zionism, a concept familiar from his Iowa upbringing; however, his understanding of it had always been in the context of the end times.

They walked out of the cage with Sparks holding the stone under his arm. Outside of the reception area for the Department of Mineral Sciences they saw Lauchlin Currie sitting with another man on a bench in the hallway. When Wallace saw the two, he turned to Berk and asked, "Would you mind very much if I used your office for a few minutes?"

"No, of course, that will be fine, sir. Please do. Is there anything I can get for you gentlemen?"

"No, thank you," Wallace said. "Jon, would you mind waiting here?" Wallace also motioned to the agents to remain where they were and not to enter Berk's office.

Sparks agreed and sat on the bench. As the door closed, he saw Berk begin talking with the receptionist as the president and his two visitors entered his personal office. The third man looked back at Sparks as he sat on the bench. In that moment Sparks recognized him as the man with Lauchlin on his first night back from Europe.

Chapter Thirty

Foggy Bottom

Foggy Bottom, Washington D.C.
December 28, 1944

Sparks left his apartment at 6:00 AM to arrive at the White House at 6:30. This would be his first day back after his short Christmas break.

Of course the walk over from Foggy Bottom wouldn't take anywhere near the amount of time he'd allotted for it. It was a nine-block trek. Instead he liked to stop for coffee on I Street, just off Snows Court, and take in the remaining Christmas decorations as he went.

It was cold – late December. He noticed ice on the bricks as he stepped outside and looked toward the odd assortment of structures across the alley. Snows Court was isolated: all the buildings faced into the long narrow alley that snaked through the interior with multiple blind turns for the length of the entire block framed by 25th, 24th and I and K streets. Several of the small brick houses were freshly painted, despite being uninhabited. Also evident on the brick surface of the court itself were the outlines of several stick-framed shanties that had lined the inside of the court and had recently been demolished to make way for the future.

Sparks inhaled the cold air and looked down the dead end to his right where interior house and apartment lights spilled out from the windows and illuminated the alley dawn. There he saw a group of men leaving for work at the brewery, which had legally reopened, or at the Washington Gas Works; both major employers for the area. In the shadows, their faces looked hard and used. Several were black; the others' ethnicities he couldn't place. Where the men stood, just thirty or so feet from Sparks, the buildings were in various states of disrepair, but the federally imposed paint and renovations gave the neighborhood the slight air of revitalization. Sparks then turned and walked to his left where the alley took a right angle turn where it exited onto 25th Street, which was, in fact, the only way in or out of the enclosed court to the outside world.

He questioned why he had chosen the neighborhood as he exited the claustrophobic single exit from the court. It was cheap. That was the reason: just twenty-one dollars a month, and more thinly populated now that the Feds had moved in to clean the place up. But the people here were rough and mixed more than he was used to. He was also dressed for the White House, which made him look like the landlord come for his rent. But at this hour, and in the darkness, a landlord might never again emerge alive from the self-contained court.

Foggy Bottom and Snows Court were famous for squalor and over-crowding. For years the federal government made attempts to improve the living conditions here. Then they just handed out eviction notices and cleaned the neighborhood out. The idea of cleaning the neighborhood seemed like a good one, as it was a source of crime and disease for eighty years; the plan was even backed by Eleanor Roosevelt herself. However, the end result was that black families who lived in the most crowded conditions weren't allowed to return, by and large, after the cleanup was completed. Many of the cramped wood structures they inhabited within the alley courts were leveled and there was nowhere to return to. Their white neighbors also lobbied against their return, and won.

All this meant was that a quasi-industrial, former malarial slum was now open to new tenants. And as Sparks' father had raised him to be thrifty, he saw the opportunity of cheap rent in a rebuilt single family home close to his place of work, and he took it. The idea of the neighborhood's history never dawned on him before he moved in.

But on many morning and afternoon walks he questioned his decision. The spirit of Snows Court was still that of a 19th century slum village. Only the wrecking ball, federal eviction notices, and war dollars were keeping it from returning there.

He entered the diner on I Street. Inside he took a large coffee in a heavy paper cup off an old dented countertop. The place smelled of bacon and used coffee grinds.

"You seeing the old man today?" The grimy man with the scar on his cheek behind the counter asked Sparks.

"I *am* his aide."

This was their running joke, ever since Leonard, that is the man behind the counter, had asked about what Sparks did one morning. After he learned that Sparks worked for the president, he proceeded to ask him daily if he was going up to "see the old man." Sparks thought this was probably Leonard's way of informing the other customers that a guy who worked directly for the president came into his coffee shop on a regular basis, as if it were a point of pride. It probably was. Sparks didn't take any offense. Besides, it was nice to have people in the neighborhood who knew you. At least he hoped his being known would protect him from harassment.

Upon reflection, it occurred to him that Leonard was probably not the kind of guy you wanted to be known by. The owner of the dry cleaner across the street told Sparks that Leonard used to be a bootlegger, and that the little greasy spoon he now operated was once a speakeasy; at least the basement was; and that Leonard had run afoul of the owners of Foggy Bottom's brewery, where illicit brew and spirits were made locally. One hot afternoon in August some gentlemen from the brewery visited Leonard just after he'd cleaned up from the breakfast crowd. They put his head through his own plate glass window. Whatever his crime, after that the brewery owner apparently thought Leonard's experience with the diner window was adequate punishment for his transgression and left him alone.

That was all ancient history since Roosevelt had ended Prohibition over a decade ago. But Leonard never did lose his scar, and people in the neighborhood, those that remained, knew where it came from and would whisper the story to any stranger who would listen.

Sparks said his, "good morning," and turned to leave the diner. At the door he caught a glimpse of himself in the mirror on the wall, and stopped to fix his tie. Then he was off. He crossed onto 24th Street where Jefferson's Meridian once ran. There was a mark in the pavement to distinguish it now but it was almost invisible through the half-light of the early December morning, due to years of neglect. Jefferson's Meridian was once the Prime Meridian for the U.S.; that is, the zero degree from which the world's latitudes were reckoned. Many of the western states' borders were laid from Jefferson's Meridian, but like all things ambitious and democratic, this line fell to the treachery of imperialism, and the Greenwich Meridian became prime. The line now marked to him the hope and optimism of the bright young Republic in world history, and how beautiful it must have been.

In a few minutes he reached the White House. At the entrance to the West Wing, he showed his ID pass. This was a formality: they knew him by this point. Sparks was old enough to remember a time when he could just walk right into the West Wing without showing any kind of identification at all. But the world was changing rapidly. It was more dangerous now, and that knowledge was written on the faces of the Secret Service agents who trod the White House hallways.

In his first White House job, working for then-Vice President Wallace, Sparks had known the agents to be much looser. Now they all seemed nervous, ready to draw their guns, or, at a minimum, investigate anyone they saw.

Like Reynolds, who'd checked his pass this morning, this man acted as if protecting the president meant he had to be cold, mechanical and almost violent in his visual inspection of White House personnel.

Sparks nodded to him and smiled as he let him past.

The president was already in the office when he arrived. Agent Dunbar let him in. "Where's Chipton this morning?" Sparks asked the agent as he walked through the Oval Office door.

"He has a few days off."

Then Dunbar closed the door, and Wallace waived Sparks in from where he was standing by the cold fireplace.

◆ ◆ ◆

President Wallace had been waiting for his aide to arrive for over an hour, and he'd been standing looking onto this cold fire since well before sun up this morning. There was too much on his mind to allow him to relax, and he wanted to see Sparks not so much for what errands his aide might run for him, but because he liked talking to the young man.

"This afternoon," Wallace began when Sparks walked up and stood beside him, "I have a meeting with the College of Cardinals that Harry S. put together."

"Truman?" Sparks said.

"Yes, Truman."

"Henry, are we electing a pope?"

Wallace laughed. "The College of Cardinals," he said. "I think the name's silly too, but there's something endearing about it which reminds me of Roosevelt." Wallace knew that the former president loved this kind of word play, which the clandestine world, at least the Anglo one, always seemed to promote. But those were more innocent times, and Wallace wasn't sure how far into a truly cloak and dagger operation Roosevelt had ventured. In all likelihood, he was a novice who only prodded others on from necessity. Roosevelt was innocent enough to have a sense of espionage that fit well with his endeavor as a young man digging for Crusader' treasure in Oak Island, Nova Scotia. But these were more dangerous, and cynical times.

President Wallace didn't have as romantic a streak as the former president; nevertheless, he continued to talk of the reconstituted OSS in a way that reminded him of FDR. And as Harry S. had also continued to call the group by that name, at least in conversation, thus were they christened. But he'd told none of this to Sparks who knew of the bill and the agency it formally created out of the OSS only as the CIA.

"Roosevelt used to call the boys at OSS the 'College of Cardinals'." Wallace then said, "I've kept the name. Others have as well." The president paused as he looked his aide over with a curious eye. He stopped and said, "Is that a paisley tie you're wearing? I wouldn't think of you as one for that kind of pattern. Do they wear that in Texas?"

"No," Sparks said. "I thought I'd add some variety."

Wallace looked back to the work on his desk. He continued talking while looking down and said: "I'm going to kill the Manhattan District. That'll make a bad Christmas for some, I guess. They'll act like I put coal in their children's stockings."

"When?" Sparks asked. The president had filled him in on many of the program's details. That he was going to shut it down came as no surprise to Sparks.

"Tuesday. After the New Year."

Chapter Thirty-One

The Cardinals

The Oval Office, Washington D.C.
December 28, 1944

The president wasn't interested in meeting with the members of the so-called "College of Cardinals." To him the topic itself was poisonous.

No matter where he tried to let his mind travel, his peace was always encircled by facts of war, treachery and espionage. Only two members of the "College" were coming today: Allen Dulles and William J. Donovan. He didn't know Dulles personally. And as for Donovan, Lauchlin recently told him that they called him "Wild Bill."

What a clever name for one of my heads of intelligence, he thought.

Harry S. would also be in the room with them, he supposed, to discuss their strategy in the upcoming phases of the end of the world. But he was sure they didn't have a clue what they were doing. They were just puppies in a world of wolves; boy scouts among mercenaries. He'd even begun to wonder which one of them had been compromised by Stalin's men; was it Dulles? There was no telling if it was true: it was certainly possible.

He'd felt the hand of Stalin on occasion in his own life. As he shifted from his rock-ribbed republican heritage to a more democratic and technocratic cast of mind, Wallace had come into contact with others traveling a similar path, and often further down it. It was sometime in the late 20's that he first heard stories that hinted at the scope of the evil emerging in the former land of Czars. By the 30's there were more than hints of what was happening there. But compared with how the British maintained their colonial possessions or what the Hitlerites were doing or the Italian Fascists, such things could be easily overlooked as part of the moral geography of the 20th century – the Molotov Ribbentrop Pact was just a shrewd act of national protection. And when he became VP, he thought many of the reports of wrong doing in the workers' paradise were simply fascist propaganda.

But you could only believe your own stories for so long; something had changed since about the time of his trip to Siberia last spring. There was a drop in the air pressure of the human network that had changed the weather here for the ones who were formerly committed to their ideals.

Now those in contact with the communist network were afraid. They were disappearing as if the hand of death were reaching up from sewer grates and pulling them down into Hades. All that remained was the memory of what they were doing or were thought to be doing at the time, and the certain knowledge of what they were committed to. In a war you can hide many things, and death is commonplace, but there was no war in New York City or in The District, and yet socialists he knew were dying badly and regularly in hotel rooms and alleyways on U.S. soil.

The head of the FBI, Mr. J. Edgar Hoover, a man whom Wallace personally loathed, had told him just a few days prior, from the seat where Sparks now sat, that Stalin was killing "commies" in America and the crowd in Hollywood was scared to make a movie that offended him. His words weren't far from the truth. Certainly, if you had a good government post or a high profile job, they were less apt to kill you, but even Laughlin Currie worried. And Wallace knew he had a right to.

In this case a CIA was indispensable. The problem in that business was that knowing and doing were too entwined to separate neatly. Because, as he'd come around to see, you couldn't know what you wouldn't do; how else could you get men close enough to see, in which case you were committing international crimes? Now these CIA people had the power from Congress to do just that.

He dismissed Sparks to the anteroom when the three men arrived. They were suspicious of him, and there was no place for an aide in such a high level meeting. At the president's request, Sparks carried one of the cold fireside chairs to its place in front of Wallace's desk and placed it next to the other two. He then gladly left the office to take a seat near the secretary who was filling in for Betty who was out sick again.

Inside the office, Harry S. introduced the cardinals. Wild Bill wore a grey suite and Dulles a brown. Wallace wondered what that said about them. And then he came back to wondering which one of them Stalin compromised. With an upstate New York industrialist background and a Princeton education, Dulles was of the class who decades prior often began growing progressively horrified at their own potential and became committed to the revolution they imagined would bring them peace. He'd seen it in many of the upper class, eastern liberals around Washington now. But Dulles didn't look to have that kind of mind, he harkened back to an older current. He was a Crusader, and had no limit to the blood he would shed to defend his country.

Beside him sat the Catholic, Wild Bill. Wallace wondered at what drove him, but if he had never left the church while becoming part of the mainstream Protestant establishment, then he was no doubt the blood enemy of the revolution.

Before him sat the genuine article: they were ready to kill for their country.

Wallace offered them Scotch. They agreed.

"I can pour it, sir," Harry S. said through an overly large and somewhat feigned smile that Wallace thought made him look insane, especially coupled with another bowling tie he was wearing that seemed a staple of his wardrobe. His sudden onset of subservience was also out of character and Wallace took that to mean that his vice president was nervous. He behaved like an abused wife before knowing company, with too much emphasis on how happy and close to her husband she is. Once he'd handed out the drinks, and gave Wild Bill the ice cubes he'd requested, they got down to business.

Dulles began the meeting by laying a drab envelope on the desk, like something dirty he didn't want to touch. Wallace followed suit and pushed it back with the tip of his finger.

"Just tell me what it is, Allen."

Dulles flushed. Wild Bill fidgeted in his seat and took a sip of Scotch, and Harry S. looked down at his glasses in his lap. Dulles started slowly, "Those are pictures of Magadan; the camp you saw in Siberia."

"Camp?" the president queried, somewhat agitated.

"Yes, not a village. Well, not a real village. Magadan was a concentration camp where the Soviets sent criminals and political undesirables to work and to die, not unlike the camps in Russia where the Nazis first learned how it was done. The Soviets turned Magadan into a show village." Dulles wanted to add "for you," but that would have lacked tact. "The Russians who met you there were with the NKVD: their Secret Police." Dulles's eyes were clear, thoughtful. He didn't look as if he either liked or disliked sharing this news.

"And where did you get the pictures from?" the president asked.

"An aerial recon plane flown in from the Bering Sea," Dulles answered without hesitation in an almost academic fashion that befit his demeanor. He was capable of speaking about the deaths of men he knew in the same tone.

Wallace nearly asked what Dulles was doing sending planes over a sovereign ally, but held his tongue; clearly, Dulles was checking up on him, that's what he was doing. Wallace now recognized that the man before him was full of secrets. The man beside Dulles: he was known as Wild Bill; the name alone spoke volumes to the president. Again, Wallace was confronted with the reality that these men were his secret agents, and he worried what that would eventually come to mean.

He despised them, and yet there was a great pall of death in the Soviet East hiding behind triumphal and persuasive propaganda that he knew many in America believed. He no longer had the luxury of denying the fact. Stalin had passed from ideology to slaughter. The thought that this great people's experiment had turned to purges and political cleansings staggered Wallace, and the revelations concerning Stalin's methods and objectives were appalling; far from his earlier understanding of the man and the movement.

Wallace was not the only one. Many people didn't realize until their body hit the mud at the bottom of the ditch. There was now a report on the president's desk composed by Secretary of State Cordell Hull. The report had come to Hull from the Russian Ambassador. It was a bulleted statement of what the Soviet Army found as they pushed into Poland. One of the bullet points was the statement of a Polish escapee concerning a place named Treblinka. The man claimed that the passengers of newly arrived trains were told as they stepped onto the platform that they needed to be deloused in a common shower. However, when these people entered the "shower" structure at the end of the platform, they were gassed to death. Treblinka was a streamlined death factory that consisted of train tracks, platform, gas chamber, and an incinerator, for which the railroad was simply a conveyor. This occurred on a daily schedule.

Wallace had no way of knowing if the report was true, but he saw the optimism of many of the communists in this light now. They had one image in mind of what the future would be and Stalin had another, but he was the conductor. Even the Nazi guards on the Treblinka platform smiled at the passengers as they helped them disembark and led them to the showers. The Nazis had their racial death camps; the Soviets had their political ones.

Now that the president faced this fact of Europe, men like the two before him were tolerable; at the least he thought they were comprehensible.

"I probably wouldn't have bothered to tell you this," Dulles continued. "but for the fact that one of the generals you met with has been seen here in D.C. this month, meeting with Ambassador Gromyko. The general's name is Ivan Fedorovich Nikishov."

Then Dulles held up a picture he pulled from the file he brought with him. President Wallace nodded his assent and Dulles said, "We have no idea why an NKVD Agent and former head of a concentration camp would be here in the United States. He did, however, oversee the purges in

Azerbaijan, and there was talk of corruption in the camp you saw. There have been four murders in this city alone of suspected communists since his arrival."

"He's paying for his crimes with the lives of others," Wallace then said with a good deal of contempt in his tone. "I'm surprised Stalin didn't just have him killed. It seems to be the way he operates."

"Certainly the Soviets seem to be tightening their operations. We're seeing the same thing all over Europe. They're purging their network of anyone they think has questionable loyalty, and General Nikishov is carrying out the action here in D.C." Dulles added.

"Why do I need to know this?" Wallace asked.

Dulles thought for a moment, "Because if we're going to know what they're up to then we have to get more active outside of Germany and Japan."

"I see; you seem to be fairly active already."

"In some cases our interest in the Nazis overlaps with the Bolsheviks'. In others, it's just good to know what our ally is up to. But I would like to begin a new phase of intelligence gathering."

"Where you officially spy on our allies?" Wallace said.

"Yes, but they're already here in this country, we're late to this. I don't even think *you* can deny that." Dulles stopped when he made this last statement. It was too close to an accusation. He'd overstepped. That was not his style. Dulles was an elegant man who rarely made errors, at least of this sort. But then Wallace didn't seem to take great offence. "I understand," he said, "and I agree. They are our allies, but we should watch them. Just be careful what you allow them to learn about us while you're 'watching' them." Then the president smiled. The meeting was over.

The three men stood to leave. Harry S. buttoned and then unbuttoned his jacket. But as they turned, President Wallace said, "I almost forgot." He pushed a picture that his Secret Service had taken of the cameraman from Virginia Beach onto the desk. "Have you seen this man? He was following me, and aside from that he was using a German camera, made since the war began."

Dulles lifted the color photograph off the table and then put his glasses on. "I don't recognize him." Wild Bill looked at the photo in Dulles's hands for a moment. Then looking at Wallace, he shrugged and said, "No."

"I didn't think that you would. But on your way out have Agent Reynolds at the front desk hand you the file on the man. Maybe you'll come across him later in your travels."

Chapter Thirty-Two

The Prisoner

Soviet Embassy, Washington D.C.
December 29, 1944

Dr. Cunningham sat naked and tied to a chair in the basement of the Soviet Embassy on 16th Street in Washington. The grand Beaux Arts mansion had stood in this location since 1910, and was purchased by the Russian government in 1913. Since the revolution, the Soviets excavated the significant sub-basement in which Cunningham now sat; though he had little idea where he was. He might as well have been in a Civil War dungeon. The Soviets had timed their construction of the sub-basement to coincide with a restoration on the mansion's first floor, providing them access to stone to line the excavation without drawing American attention. But the stone aged poorly, and moisture pushed its way through every crack, forming calcium deposits like stalactites on the inside of a cave.

Dr. Cunningham was weeping. An NKVD General stood before him holding a heavy rubber strap; though Cunningham had no way of knowing who the General was other than that he was a general. The man had only asked one question since the interrogation began sometime days ago: "Who turned you?" A question he always followed by shouting: "THINK!" And then striking him over the tops of both Cunningham's bent knees. Several times the General stooped to strike across the tops of his bare feet. He did this now, and Cunningham cried in pain, though he said nothing.

"Okay, okay," the middle aged Soviet said, "We have time. We always start slowly. There is no reason to disfigure a man if we can find the truth another way."

Cunningham did not know how long he had been inside this sub-basement. But since he had been thrown into a car as he left the State Department, the only face he'd seen was the General's. When it was time to move him from the chair to the wall, or to lay the chair over so the General could strike the soles of his feet, the General called two men down who covered their faces.

Over this period of interrogation, Cunningham slept when he could, but that was difficult, as they chained him to the wall standing up when they were done with him. In that position his feet and legs throbbed. He only slept when he lost consciousness. Now, from hanging that way, the pain under his arms added to his agony. And the sound of rats in the subterranean walls made him constantly fear that those little ravenous creatures would come to dine on him at any moment.

"Your car caught on fire on your drive into Maryland a few days ago. They think you're dead. Your body was horribly charred. Do you understand what I'm saying? This is your home now. This is your life." He pointed to the light in the ceiling, "This is the sun. I am your god. Now THINK!" And he struck Cunningham three times over the tops of his knees, already reddish, black, and yellow from internal hemorrhaging. Then he struck him over the tops of his feet hard. "You are an American agent?"

His knees throbbed. But his feet felt like they were boiling away in oil. Cunningham fainted but the General revived him with a shot of morphine and a smelling salt from the rusted steel table in the corner.

When he was fully around again, and the morphine wore off, the General said, "Think, comrade, what it will be like to have to rest on your feet all night again. I can make it stop. This is only the fourth day. It will get worse, we will have new methods, but you will not die. Now THINK!" And he poked the truncheon down into his grotesquely swollen feet.

Cunningham began to scream, "I am an American agent and Wallace turned me."

"Who is Wallace?" The General said with his face up against Cunningham's.

"The new president."

Then the General said, "And why would an American president talk to you?" as he rested his truncheon on Cunningham's left foot. The pain made Cunningham jump in his chair, but the General did not remove the minor weight. He had been torturing men for years all over Europe and Asia and knew how to break anyone. During the great purges he forced many men to make confessions he was told to get. Stalin was very pleased. But in this case the trick wasn't just to get them to say what you wanted, that was easy, it was to get them to tell the truth, and the search for truth in men was a much more delicate procedure.

What Cunningham said was obviously a lie, but the strangeness of the good Dr.'s claim gave the General pause enough to stop the interrogation a moment. He repeated his question.

Then Cunningham began shouting in breathless phrases: "He wants Stalin dead. He thinks he betrayed the revolution. He knows there are many who think the same. He seeks them out. He knows the communists in America. I don't know . . . some are his friends. He had Currie speak to me. He met me in his office. He does not trust his own intelligence."

"Who's office did you meet in?"

"The president's. In the West Wing. In the West Wing."

Then the General left through the rusted iron door by the call box he used to summon the men with covered faces. Cunningham could hear him walking up the stone steps to the basement above, and then the sun went out.

He couldn't sleep in the perfect darkness, so thick it was like water. At first he cried. The pain he felt was transcendent. It began near his hips, intensifying by his knees and climaxing in his feet which throbbed like intense points of agony. And then he fainted. When he awoke the

General was injecting him with something. Now two men stood before him; one was the General, the other he had never seen before.

"Now you've seen my face," the second man said. "If you are lying you have no hope."

"If I'm lying then why did you take me in?"

Cunningham waited for one of the men to respond. Then the second man said, "You committed grave crimes against the proletariat, this is your only chance!"

Chapter Thirty-Three

"Jesus"

Foggy Bottom, Washington D.C.
December 29, 1944

When Sparks saw the face of the man in the booth at Leonard's sipping tea, his heart accelerated and his hands, ever so slightly, began to shake. It had been over three years since he saw him last. It was after Pearl Harbor, when he was still working for Vice President Henry Wallace, before he joined the Army. When he'd gone up to New Haven. When he'd been initiated:

♦ ♦ ♦

He agreed to put the blindfold on and the car drove away. It was growing dark, he could tell because the black blindfold no longer admitted any light. They had been driving for what seemed hours, but somewhere in that long car ride he got the impression they had been making a large circle, and that they were still, in fact, in New Haven.

Then the car stopped. The door to his left opened and he felt the cold of winter pour in. The man to his right said, "Reach out your hand, he'll help you out."

"Appreciate the kindness," Sparks said.

Sparks reached out his hand and the younger man, who'd sat on his left, grabbed it and helped him up. He could immediately smell the cold New England air. There were fallen leaves in the gutter, crunchy with ice where he stepped. His foot brushed against the curb and he stepped up onto what he assumed was the sidewalk. From the slight view he had at the bottom of the blindfold, he could see the grey of the granite curbstone meet the black of the asphalt.

Then the men took both his arms and walked him up a walkway made of large uneven slabs of slate.

"Step up," one of the voices said. He was being led up a stone staircase. He counted six steps. Ahead of him, he heard someone handling what he thought was an iron lock. The lock clicked and the door creaked open to a sound of emptiness beyond. They urged him forward, but the dank smell of earth and decay made him hesitate. "Please, this way Jonathan."

He followed them in. Their steps were loud on the cold stone floor; he heard the large metal door close and latch behind him. Then they led him down a set of spiral stairs, the sound of each step echoing around the chamber. At the landing, they turned right and walked a short distance, coming to another spiral staircase and descending further still. All the while they kept the blindfold over his eyes.

Here the floor was different. It was earth and loose gravel. They walked him forward ten or fifteen steps and then pulled his blindfold off. He found himself before a man wearing a black gown in a high-backed wooden chair who was seated next to a large grandfather clock. On the wall behind him were candles in sconces, which offered the room's only light. There was a black coffin on a stone table between Sparks and the man in the chair.

"Jonathan Sparks," the man before him then said. "You will now die and be reborn."

◆　◆　◆

The young man who'd sat beside him and helped him out of the car and into the temple and the coffin was now eyeing him from the booth of the diner.

"I thought I would see Whitaker." Sparks said.

"It's better that you see me. I'll be handling you from now on."

Sparks thought it was odd that this man would handle him, as he was sure that he was older than him. It made Sparks nervous, but if this was the one they thought to send, he would deal with him.

He sat down in the booth. The young man across from him had a long face and heavy glasses. Sporting a black, narrow tie and razor bumps on his neck, he affected a look much older than his twenty-seven years. Despite his apparent youth, however, there was something about the man that Sparks intuitively felt was menacing; it was his first impression of the man, and he still felt it now. The bespectacled young man looked aggressively observant, with a cast to his eyes, behind those glasses, so detached as to be almost absent; at least absent of sentiment.

Sparks was happy that he hadn't let them pick the venue for this meeting; they had been doing that to him for some time now, and he was tired of the surprises they pulled.

As he had left the Oval Office at the president's request earlier in the day, just as the Cardinals arrived, Agent Dunbar came over to him in the anteroom. "A meeting tonight when you leave," Dunbar said in a cold tone. Then he looked down at the paisley tie, which Sparks thought was a little too strong a gesture. He worried that these intelligence people might have more fun than they should with their secrets, and Sparks now considered himself to be a secret. He looked over to the temporary secretary to see if she was watching. She wasn't.

"Have them meet me at Leonard's Restaurant in Foggy Bottom. That's the only place I'm going," Sparks said.

Dunbar hadn't responded, and when Wallace let Sparks go later that evening, he wasn't sure if his contact would arrive or not. He almost hoped that he wouldn't; it would save him from the feeling of betrayal that had followed him like a shadow since he left Switzerland.

Then Leonard walked up to the table and smiled an odd, knowing smile. "We don't often get friends of Mr. Sparks in," he said.

Leonard was waiting tables as Petunia had the night off, although that wasn't her real name. That was just what Leonard called her. On her nametag was simply written the word: "Waitress."

"People are afraid of the neighborhood," Sparks said.

"Things are turning around," Leonard replied. "We don't have as many of the bad influence anymore. What'll it be for you two?"

The two men ordered, and then sat looking at each other until Leonard brought a coffee for Sparks and refreshed the other man's hot water and gave him a new tea bag.

James Jesus Angleton broke silence first. "We're players in the great game now." This was a poor start to make with Sparks, who had heard talk of this type before and thought it silly and too much in imitation of the British. But Angleton had a romantic sense and, though he was good at what he did, he hadn't yet learned to conceal it.

"I don't need you to convert me, I made contact because I thought it was time," Sparks said and paused for a moment, "I saw Dulles today."

"Where?"

"In the Oval Office."

"Of course. But let me ask you something. Why did you expect to see Whitaker?"

"Because he seemed to know so much, I just guessed . . ."

"Whitaker's just a writer. From time to time he comes out to talk when it seems necessary."

"And it seemed necessary?"

Angleton took a breath. He had opened the conversation with romance, now he would go in another direction. He had been getting the feel for these kinds of talks in Italy, where he had worked his way to head Secret Counterintelligence for a division of OSS known as X-2. They were still in the process of sorting out the alphabet soup of agencies within the new structure of the Central Intelligence Agency, and so chains of command or department powers were often left vague. But one thing was true about Angleton, he made few or no mistakes and reached his stated objectives. That much could be said of very few of the American amateurs now trying their hands in the "great game" which had taken place on the continent for centuries.

In Italy he worked against the Soviet elements infiltrating the country as war proceeded north. He always found that no matter how many Soviet assets he removed from the field, like water reaching its level, more Soviets infiltrated the Allied Italian borders behind them. When captured, many of them turned out to be organizers of one sort or another who had arrived to sway the upcoming elections. Others were altogether without political backgrounds and were found in heavily armed safe houses. Allied Italy would very soon be a battleground of another sort.

The networks Angleton ran were vast and crisscrossed the Middle East and Europe, reaching all the way to the States. Dulles had likely put him on Sparks because of his recent work with deep cover agents in Italy, and because of their mutual background.

"The only reason you were brought in was because of your relationship with Wallace," Angleton said. "Art history in Texas doesn't make you a top prospect to tap."

"I realized that when you let me go into the infantry. It was Wallace that got me into the Monuments Division," Sparks said through his teeth in anger.

"What good were you without Wallace?"

"Well, now he's the president."

"And you think he's done something we should know about?"

Sparks leaned back and thought for a moment. Even though Angleton frightened him, Sparks had a special sort of leverage in that he worked in the president's office.

"I want to know what you think Wallace is up to," Sparks said.

"We don't think Wallace is up to anything."

"Then why do you need me?"

"Need you? We need each other Jon, that's how this works. I know many agents in Italy and elsewhere, but none with your special access. Don't forget that."

"In Italy?" Sparks said and Angleton nodded. Then Sparks began to speak in Italian: "The president's planning on getting rid of the Manhattan District," the last two words were said in English, and then Sparks continued without pause in his passable Italian: "Whatever that is, but the idea weighs on him, and he thinks it will have consequences. And Lauchlin Currie's been bringing various government people in to see the president on what seems to be non-official business." Angleton stopped him for a moment to be sure he understood what he was saying; neither man's Italian was perfect. Sparks clarified: "The first meeting I know of occurred the night of November the 6th. I've seen the man he brought with him that night and on several other occasions at the White House. Then again I saw the same man at the Natural History Museum in December where the president met with him secretly in the office of a Dr. Berk. Dr. Berk is a fresh German immigrant and a Jew. They also never keep a record of the meetings."

"Why was the president at the Natural History Museum?"

And then Sparks proceeded to explain the stone in English. When he was finished, Angleton said, "There's a rumor around about that stone and a group of Zionists who plan to steal it. You should be aware, it's at least fairly credible." Then Angleton tapped his spoon against the edge of his saucer. "Why didn't you just offer up this information to begin with? I know Dulles told you about the Stone. You called me. What do you want? What's your motivation?"

"My motivation is that I'm afraid, and from what I saw in Europe and what I believe of the Bolsheviks, I think this war is coming here."

Angleton interrupted him to say, "It is here."

But Sparks continued as though he'd offered nothing. "But I'm conflicted. Wallace is my friend, and Wallace was my friend prior to all this. He hired me out of a stack of people on the spot. That's more than I can say about you people and your club. And you knew it before you recruited me."

Angleton had seen this kind of regret in men before, but he wasn't overly concerned with it in Sparks. Sparks was from Texas, his father was in the First World War in intelligence then, and Jon Sparks had shown a true fervor for his country even before Pearl Harbor. The fact that he was at Guadalcanal, with the 164th "Marines" spoke volumes. To Angleton, who judged men, Sparks would continue to betray Wallace because he believed it was his duty to do so.

"What do I wear the next time I need to make contact?" Sparks asked, attempting to draw their meeting to a close. Simply being around Angleton made him uncomfortable. The man brought to Sparks' mind a host of memories and sentiments, all of which made him uneasy.

"You don't wear anything. You know who Agent Dunbar is now. And if it's an emergency, call this number." He handed him a business card for a local dry cleaners.

"Clever," Sparks said.

"It's better if you just remember the number and get rid of the card altogether."

Chapter Thirty-Four

Double Agents

Soviet Embassy, Washington D.C.
December 29, 1944

"I want you to see something," the General said. Then he walked over to the wet stone block wall. He grabbed an iron bar from the corner and began to pry at one of the blocks, each of which was about three feet wide and one-and-a-half feet tall.

Cunningham was now lying on the floor beside his chair and shackles, watching. At first the General struggled to force the bar into the space between stones, but when the bar finally found purchase, the block moved. It was only about four inches deep and came out easily. Cunningham was surprised it didn't break when it struck the floor.

The General turned to him. "Come here."

Cunningham scratched around for a few seconds but could not stand. He looked like a man trying to get vertical while not using his feet.

The second man said, "Comrade, you can't hope to stand like that." Then he turned to the General. "What is it you would like him to see? Maybe you can describe it to him?"

"Ok, Andrei," the General said. Even through the pain, Cunningham's ears perked at the name because he knew it. And now he knew where he was. He'd assumed it all along, but now he could be sure. This was the basement of the Soviet Embassy. There was always speculation about what they were doing with the reconstruction of the building. And if it was true that he was inside the Embassy then that made the man standing over him now none other than Ambassador Andrei Andreyevich Gromyko. He had no idea who the General was, but to Cunningham it didn't matter. The General was another nameless torturer that Stalin had raised to maintain his dictatorship. Every jail in every large town had a man just like him: skilled in the means of bringing about confession. And he *had* confessed; now he was prepared to die. His hope was that they believed his story and would kill him quickly.

The General was pointing into the void behind the open block wall with a small flashlight, in the other hand he still held the bar he'd used to pry it open. His blunt face looked almost demonic as his large cheeks shadowed his eye sockets. "Do you see that?" he asked. And Cunningham lifted his head from the floor but could barely make out the opening. There was nothing but blackness inside: so dark it seemed to eat the light. "There is a hole ten feet deep that runs into the footings of the basement. No one ever will know you were here." Then he came toward Cunningham with the bar. He had a rage inside him that was all the more terrifying as it was controlled in an almost robotic affect. "THINK!" He shouted, raising the bar, but Gromyko raised his hand and said, "Nyet! Nyet! He's telling the truth."

Those were the last words Cunningham heard. He remained on the floor as the two men walked back up to the basement. They returned with the two others in masks, with a bed on wheels. The two helped to clean him off, and then lay him on the bed sheets. They gave him morphine and put a sponge to his forehead. When his face, chest, and hands were clean of perspiration and the dirt of the floor, they tucked the bed sheets in around him and gave him water through a straw. Then the helpers left.

At this point the General and Gromyko stepped toward him from the darkened sub-basement. "This is not the first I have heard of this, Dr.," Gromyko said to Cunningham. "Some in our network have already learned of this desire by your president. Only one person in the State Department thinks it's true. But no one else believes him. It is crazy. But you; you are actually recruiting for this, this counter-revolution."

"Wallace is no counter-revolutionary," Cunningham said, "and if he is, do you go wherever Stalin's revolution takes you, even into madness?" Cunningham was perspiring again, and felt nauseous. He coughed. He was shaking.

The two men looked at each other, and Gromyko looked back down to the man shivering in the bed. "What will you do when you leave here?"

"I'll never leave here," Cunningham said.

"Well, comrade, you can't walk in that condition, but we think you will." Gromyko said and pointed to the General. "This is General Nikishov. He is here because he has committed crimes against the proletariat; and bourgeois crimes too." Nikishov stepped away from the ambassador as he talked. "He embezzled funds for his concentration camp, he made a mistress of a guard. He lived a decadent capitalist life on the backs of other offenders of the people. So he has this chance to redeem himself here. Is that right?" He said pointing back in the direction of General Nikishov.

"Yes. They told me to slit my wrists in the tub, or I could make confessions of spies and double-agents in Washington."

The ambassador turned back to the bed and addressed Dr. Cunningham in a tone that one might use in church. "Yesterday, I received orders to shoot him to death as soon as possible and to put him in the wall. That hole you opened will be for you General."

General Nikishov looked stunned by the admission. The ambassador continued addressing the General now in an animated way. "No, comrade? You don't want me to shoot you? You see this is the dilemma we find ourselves in." He was looking down at Cunningham, who wasn't able to comprehend what he was hearing. Then he looked back to Nikishov, who held the bar in front of his body as if it protected him from the ambassador. "This is the dilemma we all find ourselves in today. I acquired my position from the liquidated and the purged. And who were they? They were all men who brought the revolution. The true revolutionary generation." He produced a small pistol from his pocket and Nikishov's eyes widened. "Why murder the entire generation?" Gromyko continued. "What did they know? They didn't even know as much as I do. And what is the big secret?" the Ambassador said. "General, do you know? You were never going to be leaving this basement again. You would disappear here with the Dr. Surely you must have found it? Or are you just as much a victim as the people you killed?"

The General was frightened. He was staring back at the ambassador as if he was a crazy person.

"But you don't, do you?" He paused but the General said nothing. "There is no communism! At least not with Stalin," Ambassador Gromyko said. "When I arrived at this post, there were still Imperial Gold Coins in the safe with ledgers from 1922. These were the remains of massive payments in Imperial Gold to the capitalists of this country; this was the treasure taken from the rapacious Czar and his cohorts during the revolution and sent here to buy food and other necessities. But why?" He paused then answered his own question. "Because the capitalists helped to fund the revolution and this was their reward. They fed starving Russia for gold. Nothing happens without money, especially revolution, and the Americans supplied it, and were paid back in contracts . . . exclusive contracts that paid in gold. These men still make the same deals, but no one whispers about it now. Now a murderer sits at the top of the whole heap, cleansing the past of the truth of this arrangement, but even he can't change it: his factories, his technology, his arms, his revolution, were bought and sold by merchants. The show trials, as the American press has sometimes called them, where he purged that generation, were only a *show* in that he made one in liquidating those who knew the truth – those who had made the deals that financed the revolution."

Cunningham didn't know what to think of Gromyko. At this moment he was enduring a searing pain in the hemorrhages in his knees and upper thighs.

"Do you have access to money?" Gromyko suddenly asked the Dr.

Cunningham didn't respond, he was starting to faint again. The ambassador struck the bed. "I am making a trade with you. Do you have access to money?"

"Yes," Cunningham said pulling out of his torpor.

"And how much?"

"Enough to start a revolution and more."

Ambassador Gromyko stepped from the bed and turned toward the General who had been slowly backing away from him. Gromyko was still holding the gun, but he put it away now. "You surprise me General, are you afraid?" But Nikishov said nothing in response. "It's very lucky for you that he has money, as it's your only way out. You've just bought a man's life, Dr. Did you ever think you would do such a thing? And you've just bought yourself a double agent – a shadow, and a double agent."

"But what about the order?" Nikishov asked Gromyko.

"I say it was nothing more than political infighting. If Stalin wants you dead, then the order will come again, at that time you can disappear. But no one will reissue the order, except Stalin. They'll imagine that it was he who overrode it. Do you understand?"

"Yes, comrade."

"I am somewhat frightened that you do," Gromyko said and laughed.

Chapter Thirty-Five

The District of Manhattan

The Cabinet Room, Washington D.C.
January 2, 1945

Wallace sat like a statue at the head of the long Cabinet Room table. He'd often seen Roosevelt sit in the middle of the table in meetings, as it was the more egalitarian place for him to be, but today's sit-down wasn't going to be egalitarian.

He had changed nothing about the room since Roosevelt's tenure. How else should a room like this look after all? The long table sat over the drab, key-patterned rug; there were enough windows to allow in light and a view to the gardens; and room for fifteen or so people to sit comfortably around the table. They wouldn't, however, need that many chairs today.

While the windows were nice to have, they also allowed in vehicle noise. The new construction on the White House also added to the din. Already the White House Residence had been gutted for the renovation, while the exterior walls were still intact and stood like the trunk of a great oak with a hollow core. The West Wing, however, was completely functional and not part of the remodeling job. Wallace and his family were living at Blair House, just a block north of the White House, during the reconstruction.

The president now commuted to work. That didn't bother him as much as the realization that the White House was completely unsound, and had probably been so for many years. When he brought a structural engineer in to get his opinion of the edifice, the man condemned the building, telling Wallace, "Sir, it's not even safe to be in here. Past presidents made so many cuts in the joists to allow for plumbing and new wiring that some floors have sagged eighteen inches. I've almost never seen framing in such poor shape still standing."

The Structural engineer's pronouncement was enough to convince Wallace that a full renovation of the White House was warranted. Wallace had no interest in modifications, save for those that were needed to enable the building to take advantage of modern construction methods. The floors, formerly supported by wood, would now be composed of steel and concrete – this allowed for higher ceilings because the new structural components were both significantly thinner and stronger.

Wallace was still undecided about what to do with his stone. He had considered imbedding it in the building itself. But the stone was the least of his worries this morning. He was early to his meeting and was waiting for Lauchlin Currie to arrive, hoping to see him for a few minutes without the others.

Wallace planned to give Currie the virtually unmanageable task of terminating the Manhattan District's funding and dismantling the entire bureaucratic mess that a venture of this magnitude created. He could think of no one else with both the skill and know-how to do such a job. Not a man that he could trust anyhow.

Wallace had taken the short walk from the Oval Office more than thirty minutes before the start of the meeting, as he wanted to be the first one in the room. This was not typically, at least in his experience, how the president of the United States showed up for a meeting. But he hoped to take the initiative, and arrive before everyone else.

The first man through the door was Harvey Hollister Bundy, who was the Secretary of War's Special Assistant. In this case, his job title meant he worked on the Manhattan District, and Wallace knew him in that capacity. He was also another Yale man. There were so many around that it seemed to Wallace they comprised almost the entire Ivy League. He wondered what the Harvard men thought of having to go to work for Yale men.

Bundy opened the heavy wooden door. He stopped short as he entered and saw Wallace. The president was sitting opposite him at the end of the long, polished table.

"Oh, hello, sir. I thought I was early."

"You are early, Harvey, please have a seat."

Based on the president's demeanor and posture, Bundy now knew with certainty what was going to happen in the meeting. He had wondered about the possibility ever since Wallace took office, now it was here.

Bundy looked away from the president, who said nothing further, and then clumsily searched for a seat along the length of the boardroom table. He finally settled somewhere in the middle and sat down in a way that suggested he was trying to become invisible. Then he placed his notepad onto the table so gently he might have thought that it couldn't support its weight.

As he was regretting having come here early at all, the door opened and General Leslie Groves walked in. Groves had arrived on an early morning flight. He had left his base in Los Alamos, New Mexico almost thirty-six hours ago. He was not happy that the president had summoned him to come all the way back to the capital and he wore that sentiment on his face like his mustache.

He noticed the president, but did not say a word. Instead, he walked to the chair nearest him, which sat directly across from Wallace at the other head of the table. He pulled the chair out, and sat down with a bit of noise.

"Good morning, Mr. President. I didn't expect you to be in already. I would have come earlier."

"That's not a problem General Groves." It might not have been a problem to Wallace; it was, however, a problem for Groves. He already had a low tolerance for the president, a man he often called "soft-headed." This was an opinion he had developed regarding Wallace since beginning work on the Manhattan District. He'd come to view the then-vice president as "pacifistic leaning." And though not a part of the Top Policy Group, which oversaw the project for Roosevelt himself, Groves had, in essence, run the thing from the ground up, and from the beginning. He was the channel through which all the funds ultimately had to come; he chose the building sites; he even approved designs. After he had completed the largest office building in the world, later known as the Pentagon, in record time, Groves was hardly going to let this equally massive undertaking get off track because he couldn't work with some eggheads and pink politicians. His president, however, had other ideas.

The door opened again and Lauchlin Currie entered. He said hello first to General Groves, who merely grumbled back, and then to Bundy, who smiled and waved his pen. Lauchlin walked up the room and sat two seats away from the president. He didn't want to sit directly beside him as he felt that that might make the table feel too much like a team playing field.

Then Vannevar Bush entered with his aide. Both men sat across from Bundy near the center of the table. Vice President Harry S. Truman, who knew nothing of the bomb, followed closely behind Vannevar. He picked a seat between Bush and Groves.

"We're all here," Wallace said. "Chief of Staff George Marshall couldn't be here today as he is in London."

Groves mumbled.

"I'm sorry, General Groves, did you have something you wanted to add?" Wallace asked across the expanse of table, made even larger by the fact that so few men sat around it.

"No, sir. I didn't say anything," he said with some sand in his voice. Then he proceeded to say, "But Mr. President, I'm guessing that since you've chosen to have this meeting in this room, even though there's only six of us, you're going to tell me that you want to close the program?" Groves was hoping to push off the inevitable with his initiative. This was a trait that Wallace admired in many of the military men he'd known, and so he didn't fault Groves for his presumptions. He did, however, cut him off.

"That's correct, general. I am, in fact, closing the District of Manhattan, or the Manhattan District, or Project. In other words, I am not going forward with the bomb, gentlemen. I don't believe in it. And I certainly don't believe it's good for mankind. I don't care to see a future where one country can blow holy hell out of all others with just the press of a button. It scares me. And I'm not afraid to say that. And it should scare you as well, especially because I don't think for a minute that this bomb will remain a secret of ours for very long, even if we didn't use the thing. I'm not going to give you a history lesson, but technology has a way of spreading. That's in addition to the fact that the Germans are about through and the Japanese won't make it through the year."

This was a top-secret program, but in some ways it would have been easier to kill a public one, because now it was only the most powerful men in government who knew about what was happening, and they all would blame Wallace. Had shutting down the project been a more public act he might have been able to try to counteract the negative buzz with stories that favored his point of view. As it was, the critical response was inside the minds of men who could take some form or another of action against him. He had been reluctant to hold this meeting for some time, not because he feared the meeting – he knew they would all go along with his wishes – but for what they might do afterward.

Just then Vannevar Bush picked his glance up from a piece of paper he had previously focused on and said, "Mr. President, how do you propose that we should unwind this program? It's not only very mature, but it's also top secret."

"Well, I expect that you'll destroy all extraneous files referring to the experiment. The rest, the core documents and findings and material, should be sealed as far away from the public's, or anyone else's, view for as long as we can keep them there. I don't want this thing getting out or getting into the wrong hands any more than I want it made. Aside from that, I've assigned Lauchlin here," he said, pointing to Lauchlin, who seemed to buckle under the weight of the president's request, "to take charge of unwinding the project. He'll need your help of course, and I expect you to give it to him, and he needs to see the accounting, Gentleman. With that said, assuming you don't have anything further you want to ask me, I'll leave you to it." Wallace looked at the face of each man assembled in the room to make sure that his point was made and that there were no questions. When no one spoke. Wallace said, "Then good afternoon, gentleman." He turned toward the door behind his chair and walked out of the room.

The men all stood as he left. They were looking at Lauchlin Currie.

Chapter Thirty-Six

The Shadow

Georgetown, Washington D.C.
January 11, 1944

Alger Hiss left work as head of the Office of Special Political Affairs in the State, War and Navy Building at 7:00 PM. There was a light, cold drizzle falling, and the sidewalks had begun freezing over in spots. He pulled up the collar on his trench coat to face the stiff breeze and then paused in the entranceway to look at the White House across Pennsylvania Avenue. Normally, he would have dreaded taking this walk just south to the Ellipse where his car was parked with the other government staffers, but today his mind was fraught with worry. He hardly noticed the treacherous conditions. There were two problems bothering him this evening, and they were entwined.

Weeks ago a friend had handed him a picture of the editorial board for Time Magazine, which the magazine itself had printed. One face among the group was circled in red, though that color was no longer apt. The face belonged to none other than Whitaker Chambers. Whitaker used to rent an apartment from Hiss, right above his own home in 1935. But in those days, this was almost ten years ago, the man in the picture was known by the name George Crosley.

Which of the two names was an alias Hiss didn't know. What he did know was that this man from his past now had a role that enabled him to direct, to a significant degree, the information consumed by much of middleclass-America. He wondered whether or not the magazine knew who Chambers really was. This Chambers name might have been his real identity. After all, there was talk recently of someone passing Hiss's name around the State Department and the FBI as a communist, and George Crosley had disappeared many years ago. Was it possible that George Crosley had turned? His former commitment to the revolution made it hard to credit. Of course, almost a decade had passed since Hiss had last seen him. Even after that length of time, Hiss could recall the way that even Crosley's eyes appeared to betray the hatred he had for the established order in the United States. *How could he have come to work for a middlebrow American rag like Time?* He wondered. But there was no mistaking the identity of the man in the magazine. This Whitaker Chambers and Crosley were one and the same: his former courier.

He had been walking for several minutes, trying in vain to wrap his head around the discovery, when he slipped on the walk and nearly fell. Someone had thrown sand onto the sidewalk which provided Hiss enough traction to remain upright, though it almost would have been better if he had fallen. Instead, as his foot slipped a few inches, he turned quickly in an awkward position and wrenched his neck. Shots of pain surged both into the base of his skull and down between his shoulder blades.

"Arghhh!!!" he cried, as he took an awkward and labored breath.

He was now walking with an apish gait, and cocking his neck to the side, as it hurt to stand in any other position. The pain had momentarily taken his mind off the sad face in the glossy black and white magazine, the kind found on coffee tables for housewives in Queens, but it didn't eradicate his worry altogether.

Now, almost to the Ellipse and his car, he began to ponder another problem.

Two weeks ago he'd met briefly with Dr. Cunningham over lunch. Cunningham was a friend of his, both at the State Department and outside of it. They knew each other from the network, and by some twist of fate had actually been introduced to one another by Crosley. This fact alone would now be cause for alarm, but something worse had taken place. From what Hiss understood, Cunningham was trying to recruit him, on behalf of President Henry Wallace, to turn against the network. It was ridiculous. But one had to take such things seriously these days.

"I agree that Stalin has gone too far," Hiss had said. "I'll do what I can to help you. But my position now is delicate."

"I understand. We have to be very careful these days," Cunningham said. And they parted on friendly terms, but Hiss immediately contacted a man he knew, and passed the information of Cunningham's "turning" up the chain.

He thought it was silly to believe that you could turn a network like this one against itself – it was rooted in reality and history after all. But the middleclass mind, he thought, was jam-packed with these kinds of romantic ideas, like believing they could turn back the progress of history. They hadn't yet realized they had lost the ground, and had lost the people; the real revolutionaries were only going to gain more power. Of course, until that happened, these kinds of notions would continue to flash before the minds of those who didn't know they were dead; raised on Robinson Crusoe, Fennimore Cooper, the Bible, and Horatio Alger they couldn't know any better. But to Alger Hiss, Henry Wallace was an unlikely candidate for this kind of flight of fancy.

As Hiss crossed the street to reach his own car, another, smaller Ford zoomed past him in the sleet, so close that he felt it go by. Had he been a foot or so farther into the road he would probably be dead, at the least he'd be in the hospital. His reflexive jerk away from the speeding car caused a sudden pain in his neck. Hiss slumped a bit further than he was already slumping and paused to look to see that no other traffic was headed his way. He then crossed the street, shuffling through the slush and ice in pain. Ahead under the yellowish light of the street, he saw that he had a newly dented bumper. *Great,* he thought, *when did that happen?*

Ahead in the Ellipse he heard men talking. Suddenly his worries returned.

Maybe Cunningham was lying? But Cunningham was a serious man who had taken real risks. And Hiss had worked for Wallace in the

Department of Agriculture years before; he was a man with a mind for figures, and a love for the people. Why would he become a counter-revolutionary? But Wallace had also been taken in by a shaman or a guru, and since he had fallen for that sort of bourgeois nonsense in the past, he must still have a soft spot for the mentality somewhere. It must have been in his upbringing.

Alger Hiss was nearly to his Georgetown home before he could take his mind off these complications. He had resolved to worry about it to-morrow. Traffic was light, but due to the icing he drove slowly, and al-lowed the road hum to lull him into an almost meditative state. When he arrived at Volta Place, he found, as usual, no nearby parking and was forced to park a block away across 33^d and P Street. It was a minor in-convenience that he was used to by now. This was the reality of living in Georgetown and he didn't let it bother him.

When he stepped out of his car he was startled by the sharpness of the wind. Sliding his foot along the pavement, Hiss could feel the sole of his shoe lose its grip on the light skin of ice. *Sure,* he thought, *all I need is to fall down and break my neck a block from the house.* He hated the morbid feeling he had, and passed it aside as an aftershock of the news that Crosley now worked for a Capitalist crusader by the name of Henry Luce, and Cunningham was fighting a counter-revolution for the president.

He walked up the sidewalk and crossed at the stop sign where Volta Place met 33rd. There was a car coming southbound at a slow clip. Hiss crossed in front of it, moving awkwardly as he tried to minimize the pain in his neck and walk at the same time.

But the car should have stopped by now. As Hiss reached the north-bound lane, he noticed the Ford drifting toward him through the inter-section. He started to run. There were sparks of pain in his neck and shoulders. The car was gaining speed, with no sign the driver was trying to stop. Alger's feet slipped and he continued across the street but began heading southward, hoping to jump onto the parked car at the corner.

The oncoming car was too fast; the road surface too slick. The bumper of the small Ford caught him in his upper thigh and pinned him against the hood and bumper of the parked car. He felt his pelvis sheer from the collision. He was panting and in excruciating pain, but he was still conscious as his upper torso flailed under the sleet. He noticed blood running into his left eye, and he thought that one of his hands had been severed against the jagged sheet-metal hood of the blue parked car he was crushed against.

Just then the driver of the car that struck him came around to his side. Hiss tried to plea for help, but the wind was gone from his lungs and the best he could muster was a gasp. He was drifting out of consciousness as the driver approached him. He'd had to walk around behind the car and was now standing on the passenger side. Then another car pulled up. The man driving said, "Hurry up," through the open window where white slush collected.

The last thing Alger Hiss felt were the driver's hands on his cheeks before his neck snapped.

Chapter Thirty-Seven

The White House Shell

The White House Residence, Washington D.C.
January 18, 1945

Sparks and Agent Chipton both gripped large, wood-handled screwdrivers. They were using the tools to take the screws from three horizontal boards that held up the temporary partition separating the West Wing and the White House. The president watched with a flashlight in his hand.

When Chipton removed the last screw, he and Sparks turned toward the West Wing and the drop cloth that was blocking them from view. Chipton then slowly pulled the cloth to see if anyone was looking down the hall toward them. It was late, so the chances that anyone was looking were diminished, yet it would also be more difficult to explain what they were doing breaking onto the White House construction site at night.

When he saw the hallway empty, Chipton nodded to Sparks and the two removed the partition. The construction divider was hinged on one side with metal straps so instead of lifting it away they swung the divider to one side like a door. When it moved, the partition gave off a metallic squeal, then stopped.

The president cringed. He said to Sparks, "Make sure you close the partition after we're through or someone's likely to notice the cold air and find out where it's coming from." Sparks nodded in reply. The president then added, "Wait here, Sparks. If anyone comes, just tell them I'm down there checking out the progress so far." Then Wallace and Agent Chipton walked down the open colonnade leading into the gutted White House.

When the president and Chipton were clear of the opening, Sparks pushed the partition back into place. Then he waited.

The sound of their footsteps echoed around the chamber at a volume that carried down the corridor and into the open residence. *So much for stealth,* Wallace thought. He was not a man used to, or comfortable with, behaving secretively. The last years of his life, however, seemed to require it, and often.

As the two were about to enter the residence down a ladder, Chipton put out his hand to stop the president. "Sorry, sir. Let me look first."

"We know who's going to be there," Wallace said.

"We only know who's supposed to be there," Chipton said and moved out of the president's flashlight beam and into the cavernous residence.

Chipton entered the house through the wide-open wall and down a temporary staircase to the gravel of the ground floor. He quickly located the two men they were meeting standing quietly in the moonlight by the buttressed front wall of the residence. Chipton didn't acknowledge them at first. He walked to the middle of the vast White House, devoid of all but its walls, and searched among the piles of lumber, stone, and excavation equipment.

Chipton worked outside of his job detail now, and was operating with the president without the knowledge of the other agents. If something happened here, he wouldn't just lose his job, he'd go to jail. But Wallace had taken him into his confidence. He felt a duty to protect his president – even in strange meetings in the empty husk of the White House late at night, and against his better judgment.

Chipton used a penlight to check the open space, taking a minute to walk among the pea stone piles and lumber and around the massive yellow backhoe. When he determined no one was lying in wait to ambush the president he returned to the staircase.

"Mr. President," he said, "the men are waiting for you." Wallace looked out over the White House job site. Car headlights flashed through the empty window openings in the stone White House façade.

"Thank you, Leroy. I'm sure that was unnecessary, but I appreciate your thoroughness."

They then walked down the temporary wooden stairs together. Beneath the excavated dirt floor he saw several layers of brick that at one point must have formed the foundation for an outbuilding. Beside the brick, he saw an old and rusted horseshoe.

"Probably the stable at one point, what do you think Chipton? I'll have to ask the architect." But Chipton didn't respond. He approached the two men in black overcoats with his hand on his revolver, hanging back enough for the president to greet the men first.

"Ambassador Gromyko, thank you for coming, did you have any difficulty entering the grounds?" the president asked.

"No, the gate was open, as you said it would be," Gromyko said and turned to his right. "Please let me introduce General Nikishov of the NKVD."

"General," Wallace said, taking the man's hand. "But we've met before."

"Yes," Nikishov said.

"That was some concentration camp you masqueraded as a village. What were the prisoners there for?"

Nikishov paused before answering, batting a bushy, gray eyebrow. He wasn't certain if Wallace's reference was hostile or not. But he didn't want to be rude and so he answered, "You never know why Stalin condemns a man. He might have remembered him from childhood. He thought he was a priest, or a Trotskyist. There are many reasons."

"And what reason does he have to dislike you?"

"I don't know if it's him or not. I'm still alive. But I don't think the Stalinists have been good for Russia."

"Well, whatever you might have done, you're serving your country now, and all of our countries."

Though Wallace believed what he said about their mission, Nikishov wasn't convinced. His own motives were murkier. He had gladly profited from the purges and the Soviet system, but Stalin, or someone else in power, had turned against him. That there was conflict over what should be done with him was evident in the fact that Moscow had seen fit to send him here, when they could have simply killed him. He still heard stories about what was in store for him upon his return, and since he knew how successful the assassination squadrons were against those who defected, he now made common cause with the anti-Stalinists, hoping to change the government rather than flee from it. He was happy to work for his own life, and the destruction of those who would kill him.

Suddenly Gromyko said, "It is very dangerous for you to meet with us, Mr. President."

"I know that, but I wanted you to see me for several reasons. The first is so that you know who this network is headed by. So far you've come along without any real proof."

"You often don't have proof."

"But I wanted you to have. And secondly: are you killing people in my name?"

"We are running the operation, sir?" he said with a questioning tone.

"A young State Department official with a wife and son was crushed to death by another car on his way home in Georgetown. The driver of the car disappeared. No one is pursuing the case as anything other than an accidental homicide with a suspect who fled the scene. However, the official didn't die from internal injuries, he died from a broken neck."

"Mr. President, sir, he knew about you and was seeking to get the message of what you were doing to Moscow. Fortunately . . ." then Gromyko paused for a moment, "the station chief of Military Intelligence, Alexander Terekhov, who handles Hiss, came to see me. A few weeks ago, Hiss told him a story about a network headed by the American president. Terekhov mentioned the account in a report to Moscow, but said that he thought that Hiss was wrong. Then Terekhov came and spoke with me. He's on our side. He was recalled recently, but remained here against orders for fear they'll murder him when he returns."

"If Terekhov thought the story was fake, then why kill Hiss?"

"Hiss knew the story was true and was going to continue making noise until Moscow paid attention. But even with what little intel he was able to pass to Moscow, this operation might start becoming more complicated. It is bad enough that Hiss got his story back to the Kremlin at all, even as implausible as it sounds that an American president is personally trying to use the international communist network against Stalin himself. Still, these are the kinds of stories that fuel purges, and if Hiss continued talking the chances of such a thing happening would only increase. It is better that he died."

"But you confirm their paranoia by killing Hiss!" Wallace said.

"Now they can't confirm it. And it was an accident."

"A very good death," Nikishov added in a tone that sent chills up Wallace's spine.

Wallace looked Nikishov over and assumed that he had performed the "good death" with his own hands. But Wallace didn't want these men to pick up any further on his squeamishness when it came to assassinations; he already had enough trouble from his own intelligence members who often perceived him too weak for the realities of espionage.

"Are you saying," Wallace began, "That the GRU is with us?" He was referring to Russian Military Intelligence. Gromyko had mentioned them in connection with Station Chief Terekhov. If Terekhov was reporting to Gromyko to protect the president's efforts, then that could only mean that he had turned as well.

Both the Soviet civilian run NKVD and the military GRU ran overlapping espionage operations in the United States, however neither the groups nor their missions were affiliated other than by nationality.

"I am saying that members of the GRU are with us, yes," Gromyko said.

"Then we have a good chance," Wallace responded. "Do you think we can reach back into Moscow with this network, and free the country?"

"I think we have fifty-percent chance. But this is better than not trying."

"Ok," Wallace said. "Whatever you need, you can have. But from now on, you won't see me."

"Then thank you for taking the time to meet with me. There are many people who feel the way we do. Stalin is more of a murderer than the world knows. He holds Russia in his grip, worse than a Czar. If you can change that, then you are great man. But be careful," Gromyko said, "Mr. President, your current government is a lot like this building." He now gestured to the White House façade that surrounded them.

"I'll remember that."

"And, as grateful as we are for your current generosity, we must ask for more money."

"Lauchlin will be with you shortly, he's got the purse strings now. You're still operating from Foggy Bottom?"

"Yes."

"Then he'll find you."

Wallace turned to leave the two men; as he did so he heard a scratching sound from the colonnade above. Then he saw rats run into the footing of the newly dug basement. He looked up the stone wall into the upper façade that appeared like a bizarre set from Hollywood. Then he looked down to the foundation and wondered where to put Jacob's Stone: which corner, on the exterior or interior? He wanted to put it outside, he just worried that somebody might steal the thing. He finally resolved to ask the architect in the morning, and turned to walk back up the temporary staircase leading to the colonnade and to the West Wing, but thought twice at the last moment. There was another issue he had to mention to Gromyko and his henchman.

"Cunningham?" Wallace asked.

"That unfortunate man had a heart attack under questioning," Gromyko said.

"He worked for me," Wallace said.

"We didn't know that at the time, but we didn't kill him. He died. But before he did, he told us about you, and now we are here."

Chapter Thirty-Eight

The Anteroom

The Oval Office, Washington D.C.
January 23, 1945

It was 7:00 PM. Betty was out again tonight. She'd had a stomach virus, and though doctors had recently treated her, the illness returned. President Wallace was upset by this turn of events because he'd come to rely on her. She was thorough, and to the point. He also knew her and trusted her.

Sparks sat in the Oval Office anteroom looking at the chair where the temp secretary now sat, waiting for the president's summons. Suddenly the temp turned and looked at him, "All right, I'm going," she said. "You tell Mr. Wallace that I'll be back again in forty-five minutes. I've just got to eat some dinner."

Sparks nodded his head and smiled. She was a young woman, and pleasant looking, with long legs she loved to cover in stockings. He imagined how she had worked her way up the temp pool so quickly, and so young. She was always chosen to fill in for Betty. Like most of the office workers now in Washington, she moved to D.C. as Roosevelt expanded the Federal Government during the Depression. Now, in wartime, government girls filled the huge manpower void. Since building materials were unobtainable, six to ten government girls shared a two-bedroom apartment. Many looked for any "edge" to get out of their cramped lives.

Her name was Myrtle, Sparks thought, although it could have been something like that, similar, maybe, or totally different. He'd been having trouble focusing on small details lately.

That's when Myrtle stood from her chair and slowly walked across the room. Actually, when he thought about it, there was something about her he liked. She had a fine figure to be sure, but it was almost as if she was unaware of it, and at the same time not. She seemed friendly in a way that only the innocent are.

At the doorway she turned and said, "Would you like me to pick something up for you? You look like you need it."

"No," he said. "I don't know if I'll be here when you get back, but thanks."

He would never have admitted it openly, and if the two pursued a relationship that lasted he would have invented another story, but what she did right then was all it took for him to fall in love. Her care cut through his endless worry and Texas bravado and struck where it counted: in his need for closeness.

When she walked through the open door, he spent a moment staring at where she had just stood. Then Agent Dunbar approached him from the opposite side of the room. You almost forgot these guys were around, and especially Dunbar, who could remain so still that when he finally moved it was like seeing a statue come to life.

"Don't stare too long," the Minnesotan said.

"I'll try not to."

"You got something for me? The way you've been looking at me the past few days, I figured you wanted to talk."

"You figured right, Dunbar," Sparks said his name the way a coach calls his players by their number: "Number 32 that was a good play!" Which is to say that he said it like he was his father. Dunbar didn't like it, but there was little he could do.

"Tell Jesus I want to see him."

"When?"

"Tonight if he can do it."

"We'll see."

"Then we will," Sparks said.

Dunbar walked back to the wall where he imitated a Doric column, and Sparks went back to thinking about Myrtle. It was nicer to think about her than it was to think of the problems floating around his universe. And that's when the president opened the door from the Oval Office. It was dim inside; the way Wallace liked it now.

"Come on in, Sparks. Lauchlin and I have something we'd like to discuss with you."

Chapter Thirty-Nine

Footsteps in the Fog

Foggy Bottom, Washington D.C.
February 1, 1945

Footsteps sounded on the pavement behind him. He no longer felt comfortable walking home at night, but he continued to do it anyway. This evening he had taken Pennsylvania Avenue up to I Street and was following that over the old brick and cobbled hodgepodge of a sidewalk.

Tonight there was fog. It was the first of February 1945. The Battle of the Bulge had recently left Hitler with nothing but inadequately armed children and World War I veterans to defend the fatherland with. The war in Europe was winding down and the one in Japan would be over before the year was out. But how the war at home ended, Sparks couldn't know.

The temperature had climbed to nearly forty-eight degrees today and the melting snow created a heavy mist that thickened as Sparks drew closer to the Potomac River.

The fog lay eerily on the street. It didn't help Sparks' sense of comfort that someone was following him. He had been followed, as near as he could tell, since he left Pennsylvania Avenue. When he looked back to see who it was, the fog reduced his vision to less than a block, and he found no one in sight. He continued walking. He was almost to Leonard's restaurant anyhow.

As he came within a few steps of the restaurant, the footsteps seemed to fall away. He approached the doorway and reached out to grab the handle, but the door opened on its own. Behind it stood James Jesus Angleton.

"We're waiting for you," Angleton said and led Sparks to the booth where he had obviously been sitting, as there was a steaming cup of half empty tea and a paper on the table.

Sparks might have felt comfortable here, despite Angleton's presence, but there was something wrong with the clientele tonight. Several of the men were dressed in exactly the same manner as Angleton: tailored suit and trench coat, with hats hung on iron coat hooks between booths. It seemed obvious they were agents of one type or another. It was also obvious that Leonard knew that his patrons this evening were not of the crowd that normally frequented his establishment. Leonard wore that news on his face when he looked at Sparks. Even the workmen were different. Their coveralls were too clean. Beneath their clothing they were pressed-suite-and-tie guys with degrees. They hadn't shed the habit of standing in a white collar yet.

To Sparks they all appeared to be dressed in costumes for the night. He guessed that's what came of typically limiting recruiting to the white-shoe set. He also knew that his insight came from a place other than paranoia.

"I hope all this isn't for me," Sparks said as he sat down.

"Of course not. But we like to be thorough."

Just then Leonard walked up beside Sparks. He was waiting tables as his girl was out sick again. "You all right?" Leonard asked, holding a notepad and pencil out in front of his dirty smock.

"Thanks, but I don't think you can help now."

"Neither do I. At least I thought I'd ask."

"That's why I keep coming in here, Leonard, you're a courteous man," Sparks said.

"There's not enough courtesy anymore in the world. You ask me, that's what's wrong."

"Just a coffee please, Leonard," Sparks added and Leonard walked behind the counter and grabbed the pot.

"It's been over a week since I made contact with Dunbar," Sparks said.

"There's something I want to show you. We can see it on the way to your place." Then Angleton paused for a moment, watching Leonard behind the counter. "Leonard's really a remarkable man, isn't he? We have some contacts who knew him in the old days. He had a pretty brisk trade with congress then." Then he stood up.

"It's too bad they couldn't help prevent the accident he had with his window," Sparks said.

"Couldn't be helped. Business is the same everywhere after all."

Sparks stood now: "I won't be needing that coffee, Leonard." He followed Angleton out into the street.

When the door closed behind him, Sparks looked back in the direction of the White House to see if he could find who it was that followed him, but even though the fog had thinned, he saw no one. For his part, Angleton walked so quickly in the direction of Snow's Court that Sparks had to jog a few feet to catch up.

"What's with all the men?" Sparks asked as he walked past a doorway where three bums were sitting. They were unfamiliar to him, but he noted that one grimy looking man was wearing a new pair of loafers. Sparks felt the man give him a knowing glance.

"Have you ever heard of the GRU?" Angleton asked.

"Nope."

"What do you do in the White House then if you don't know who the GRU is?"

"I don't take orders from you, that's what I don't do." Sparks said and stopped walking. Angleton stopped with him.

"Ok," Angleton pleaded, backing off his very special mole, "The GRU's the Russian version of the CIA, only they're run directly by the military."

"As opposed to Yale University," Sparks said.

"We're not all from Yale," Angleton replied. To Sparks, his gaunt face looked skeletal in the street light.

"Yeah, which ones aren't?"

Angleton took a long breath, ignoring Sparks' comments. "And because they're run by the military they have some highly skilled units that run operations. So far we call them SPETSNAZ."

"And what's SPETSNAZ mean?"

"It means 'Special Purpose' unit in Russian. I don't think they're an official group at all. Sometimes we get information across the wire in Europe that talks about a "special group," but we just started calling it that because it exists already. The soldiers come from Razvedke units who formerly operated on the front."

"What's a Razvedke?" Sparks asked.

"You don't do your homework do you? Did you listen at all on the Farm?" Angleton was being unfair. There was no way that Sparks could have known anything about Razvedke. They had only just evolved out of the necessity of war, same as SPETSNAZ, which wasn't a specific group the way the Marines or Sea Bees are, more like a category applied to men who performed "special" tasks and were now helping out with intelligence work because they were useful.

But Sparks took offense again to what Angleton said, "Your job is to know the Russians, mine's to know the president. And besides, no one ever mentioned anything like a *Razvekee*."

"Fair enough," Angleton said, as he resumed walking. Sparks was alongside him but turned his head enough to note two men in coveralls clearly following them. Sparks surmised they had been at the diner earlier. Another two men, out of place in the neighborhood in their trench coats, kept up with Angleton and Sparks on the other side of the street.

"Razvedke are something like Russian reconnaissance units. They fight with the partisans on the Eastern Front. But they are used more as weapons than solely as intelligence gathering operatives. Some of them have been incorporated into the GRU. Everything's in flux now with the war, even the kinds of soldiers that fight it. That's true on both sides of the Atlantic. Actually, it's very much like with us, only we don't liquidate our personnel based on the whims of the president and his advisors."

"No, you just spy on him."

They had come to 25th Street; the sole entrance to Snow's Court lay half a block up. Here Angleton turned, taking the same path Sparks did every night when he went home. He said with a strangely cheerful tone, "Behind us now, across I, is an apartment, number 22, if memory serves, that has a GRU team in it with several identified members of SPETSNAZ who operated in Belarus, Lithuania, and Poland."

"I'm happy you dropped in on me tonight, Angleton. I think I was better not knowing that."

"Maybe you shouldn't walk home anymore the way you do then."

"What do you want me to do, fly?" Sparks said.

They'd reached the entrance to Snow's Court. It was narrow, only fifteen feet wide, and dark, and led into the equally narrow Court that lay within the block. Sparks pointed into the Court. "Even if I don't walk to this point, I still have to walk through that Court."

"Only God knows why you moved here in the first place, Sparks." Angleton mocked. He picked at some rotting mortar between the ancient bricks in the arch that framed the outside alley wall. "I'd suggest finding another place to live. Of course, we don't know that they know who you are or where you live." Angleton fully stepped inside the blind alley leading to the Court now and was cast in shadow.

"Maybe I'm safe walking home, after all," Sparks added, "It seems even the hobos are on the payroll here."

"But they're not here to protect you."

After several minutes they wound their way through the Court and reached Sparks' small house. Sparks unlocked the lock on his red door and waved in the overly confident, young intelligence officer. He then turned the lights on and Angleton sat down on a stool by the kitchen counter.

Chapter Forty

Patsy

Snows Court, Washington D.C.
February 1, 1945

Once inside the small room that was his house, Sparks walked to the other side of the bar-like countertop. He poured himself some water from a glass jug on the counter, and then came back around to where Angleton occupied the only stool in the room. There was a small couch in the corner, but Sparks didn't feel like sitting down. He was angry. He looked at Angleton for a moment before erupting. "Why would you walk me to my house on a public street in full view of anyone with eyes! Do you want to expose me?"

Angleton hesitated longer than he should have, but he recovered and said, "Who do you think's watching you, Jonathan? Are you paranoid?" Angleton's use of his Christian name only served to enrage Sparks further. "We're the ones who watch," Angleton continued, but his voice sounded young and privileged. He was blushing.

"Really?" Sparks cut him off, "There's a room full of Soviet spies and killers up the street who beg to differ, and the last time I checked, J. Edgar runs a pretty powerful network in this hemisphere on his own, so don't bullshit me, you Ivy League grifter."

Sparks was close to Angleton now and saw his face change from confusion to anger. He was not used to being spoken to in this manner by anyone, ever. Angleton tried to stand from the stool but Sparks grabbed him by the collar and in one motion lifted him up and thrust him hard into the wall behind him. The cheap plaster gave way, sending pieces falling to the floor and inside the wall.

"Get your hands off me!" Angleton's voice betrayed his rage, as well as genuine astonishment at Sparks' daring. He tried to break free, but Sparks was the stronger of the two.

"I called you over a week ago, *Jesus*, so that I could tell you something. But then you spend all your time *making* me. You didn't need to stroll me down to see the GRU apartment, you could have told me about it! And now I want to know what you're up to or I'll tell Wallace, so help me God!" Feeling he had made his point, Sparks released Angleton, pushing back away from him as he did.

"You wouldn't make it out of the alley, Sparks."

"You won't make it out of this room," Sparks said, reaching beneath the counter to retrieve a snub-nose .38 revolver. He pressed it into Angleton's cheek with his right hand while gripping his collar with the left. "I'll put your brains on the wall behind you. You know the difference between you and me is that I've been in combat, I haven't just sent people into it or taken some course at the Farm." Angleton tried to slide to his left, but his back was dug several inches into the wall and he couldn't slide away with Sparks applying pressure against him. Then he tried to push forward, but Sparks shoved the gun muzzle into his cheekbone so hard that Angleton shouted in pain. Sparks looked at him with open disdain. "You ain't no different from a Jap, and killing people don't bother me much. They tell you it should, but I haven't seen too many men who actually did it get all hung up on it. Now you tell me I'm wrong. You tell me you didn't just blow my cover?"

"You can't kill me."

"You think your death will even get out? A Spymaster killed by the personal aide to President Wallace? This little problem would disappear so fast it would be like you never existed. Maybe you went to the right school, maybe you joined the right club and so people would never touch you, but I will kill you right here and now, as sure as you're breathing. You don't get to pass this doorway without passing me! You understand? Tonight *you* get reborn."

"Ok, you're right," Angleton conceded, relaxing his body.

"Good," Sparks said, as he shoved him into the wall. Sparks backed away and stooped to pick up the fallen stool and threw it at Angleton. "Now sit down and talk! And fix your goddamned suit would you, you're a mess."

Angleton brushed the dust off his shoulders and lower back and sat down on the stool. He was angry with himself. He'd underestimated Sparks. Though he knew where Sparks had been stationed in the Pacific, his time in Europe and at Yale had led him to perceive GIs as easy to control. His early observation had, for the most part, proven accurate. Of course you couldn't control the crazy ones, as their lack of interest in conforming to the military hierarchy rendered them laws unto themselves. Sparks, however, wasn't crazy. He was proud and intelligent and angry, and, more importantly, he was the president's aide. Angleton was going to have to accept what Sparks had done. And so he sat down and began talking.

"You're bait, plain and simple," Angleton said.

"That's real good, Angleton, now why would you use your man in the White House as bait?"

"To be honest, it wasn't my idea."

"Well, whose was it then?"

"That I won't tell you. But you were followed tonight, weren't you?"

Sparks just nodded.

"He wasn't one of our people. I watched him walk right by the window as you sat down in that diner Leonard owns."

"Who was it?"

"I don't know, but that's what we wanted to find out."

"And did you?" Sparks was still holding the revolver, but he no longer pointed it at the young spymaster.

"I expect that we did. I'm sure he didn't make it past the next doorway. In fact, I'm quite confident he's in our room in Snow's Court now."

"So why walk me down the street for everyone to see?"

"Call it overconfidence."

Sparks raised the gun over his shoulder as though to backhand Angleton across the face with it for his vague answer. But Angleton held up his hands, "Wait! There's no one else watching you. From the time you wake up in the morning we have people on you. From the guy who brings the mail, to the girl in the coffee shop, to strangers in cars passing by, they're all there to watch you. Sometimes we have as many as thirty people between here and the White House. Half of Foggy Bottom, including the Negroes, are employed just because you live here. And there's only been the one man ever following you. He's done it on two other occasions. And we decided that the next time it happened we would take him down."

Sparks lowered his arm. Angleton took a breath of relief and wiped his face with his handkerchief. He continued, "As it turns out, having this production here was beneficial, since the Russians decided to move in down the street. We know the inhabitants of that apartment are in contact with the White House, but we don't know what's going on yet."

"You still didn't have to walk me down the street, Angleton."

"If the Russians are watching you, number one, they saw us nab their man, and number two they saw me walking with you. They won't know what our relationship is; they'll just think we have eyes on our people, as they do with their people. But we don't even know who's involved." He looked at Sparks and said: "Now I want to know something from you, Sparks."

Sparks' stare was his sole response.

"Why did you want to see me?"

At that question Sparks placed the snub-nose on the table before him, then he slowly began to tell Angleton what he'd seen in the shell of the White House the week before when he snuck down the colonnade.

"And you're sure he called one of them General Nikishov?" Angleton asked. Sparks nodded. Both men were silent for over a minute. Then Angleton said, "He's NKVD, not GRU, so that doesn't explain the apartment. Let's go find out who our boys picked up tonight."

Chapter Forty-One

The German

Snows Court, Washington D.C.
February 1, 1945

The two men left the small wood-framed house in Snows Court and entered the uneven brick alleyway. Angleton had plaster dust on the back of his slacks and jacket, but Sparks didn't comment – in the darkness the white scuffs were difficult to see anyhow. He just followed the young spymaster across the Court, wondering if Angleton had any idea what he was doing at all.

Down the winding alley, they approached a metal door in the dark that Sparks passed daily on his way to the White House. He had assumed this was the entry to a locked maintenance room. Angleton simply turned the knob and entered. Once inside, Angleton looked over his shoulder as though he was pleased with himself for having access to a secret door in Sparks' backyard.

The door led to an open passage that consisted of nothing more than the space between close buildings bricked over on the Court side to look as though the buildings were one. At the other end of the passage, a single bulb hung above the green door. As they walked toward the door, Sparks realized they were approaching the back of Leonard's place on I Street from the rear.

"The Federal Government still owns most of the buildings on the Court from when they took over as part of the cleanout," Angleton said over his shoulder as he walked. "It's interesting to note that D.C. has no local government to speak of. It's like Soviet Russia. Anyhow, when you moved in, we checked the construction records and found an apartment building with access to both the Court and I Street, and installed a listening post. All the apartments in the building either house our people or are empty.

"It was just a good turn of fortune for us that the GRU showed up at all. These things happen of course. Once in Florence, we inadvertently set up in an apartment right next to Nazi Intelligence. It was only after one of our contacts refused to set foot in the building that we learned it. GRU would feel the same as we did, except the Abwher never knew of our presence in Florence."

Angleton knocked at the door; a large man in blue coveralls opened immediately. The man in coveralls said nothing, but turned and led them inside the apartment building to an old Victorian staircase with a view to the foyer door and its I Street stoop. They climbed three flights of creaking stairs and entered an apartment.

Inside, a team of six men and one woman stood in the center of a living room. The room was empty save for several mismatched and decrepit chairs surrounding a folding table that held a black and white tube monitor. The man who had led them in from the alley now closed the door as he departed.

Inside, Sparks noticed that the apartment's floors needed refinishing and the walls were cracked enough in places to make visible the horsehair plaster and lathe construction; the light fixture in the ceiling was comprised of a single hanging clear Edison bulb on a wire. Sparks guessed that Angleton and his people had acquired the building before the Federal Government had the chance to fix up the apartments.

As Sparks surveyed the room, Angleton turned and said, "What do we have?" An older man dressed in a blue suite and paisley bowtie walked forward. The others stepped back, seemingly mute. With a Boston accent so thick it took Sparks a moment to understand, the older man said: "He's a German for sure. His name's Ernst Hanfstaengl."

"A German," Angleton said. "Working for the Russians?"

"No, he works for the Nazis."

"He told you that?" Sparks asked.

"Oh, he's told us everything. Speaks very good English, went to Harvard actually."

"Naturally," Sparks said, "And where did you go?"

"Don't answer him," Angleton said.

The man then paused for a moment to look Sparks over. His gaze returned to Angleton. "Ernst is not shy about talking at all. He wants to defect – knows the Huns are through. He's told us that Hitler planned to have him killed before someone gave him this intelligence assignment. The boys are just re-questioning him now, and we're busy checking some of the claims he made, but as of this moment, what he says seems plausible. By the way, it's nice to meet you Mr. Sparks."

"So you're one of the people who watch me?" Sparks said with a tone that was less than respectful.

"I do more than that, and I get paid to do it too," the older man said with an equal measure of disrespect, and an anger and grit that slightly eclipsed that of Sparks.

"How's a man get into this kind of work?" Sparks asked.

"I suppose I could ask you the same thing?"

"Let's not do this gentleman," Angleton spoke up in an attempt to calm the two men. "Mr. Sparks isn't in a very good mood this evening, Perkins."

Perkins took that moment to note the plaster-dust and scuffs marring the back of Angleton's clothing. He then looked from Angleton to Sparks and said, "I'm sure we can handle that sort of problem right here."

Inside his pocket, Sparks was tightly gripping the handle of his revolver. He was considering breaking Perkins' nose with it. The man looked to be cast right out of the original Puritan mold with aquiline nose, rosy cheeks on pasty skin, and tight lips; Sparks could picture him in a powdered wig. To hell with what the other people in the room would do when he hit him. Sparks didn't like threats, veiled or not, and he'd already had enough of meeting the people who worked behind his own life. He wondered how many of the acquaintances he'd made over the past few months were as a result of Perkins and this operation. In fact, he recognized the woman now standing across from him with her hand in her pocket: she was the waitress without a name from Leonard's place. But he didn't have time for her now.

He was drawing the small revolver to smash Perkins face when Angleton stepped between them. "That won't be necessary, Perkins." Then he turned to Sparks. "You know Perkins was in the last war. You were a Ranger weren't you, Perkins?"

"That's good for Perkins. What about the German? Why's he following me?"

Perkins took a seat in one of the ratty chairs, saying, "All right then, let's discuss our Hun. He says some funny things about Wallace, and about the Nazis."

"What's that have to do with me?" Sparks asked.

"Patience. What it has to do with you is the Nazis are looking for a stone the president has in his possession. I think you know it. We've only seen pictures of it so far, but we know he was given it while in China."

"How'd you come by those pictures by the way?" Sparks asked.

Perkins considered the question a moment. Then he said, "Well, I don't exactly know, but we have people in the White House mail room and in the dark room Wallace used to develop his pictures, so – one or the other – maybe both."

"Does everyone in this town moonlight as an operative?"

"Probably," Perkins said in a flat tone. Returning to his point, he asked, "what about the stone? Does Wallace still have it?"

"He's planning to make it the cornerstone of the White House," Sparks said.

"Well, the Nazis want it, and according to Ernst, they think the story of putting it in a building's foundation is just a ruse to conceal its real purpose."

"And what's its real purpose?" Sparks asked.

"Something secret and magical."

"Magical," both Sparks and Angleton said together.

Perkins continued, half laughing, "It seems Hitler's decided that we "mongrel" Americans, and our weak allies, have a mystical way of divining German U-Boat locations, as well as other information critical to the war. Ernst, on the other hand, is certain that the allies have decoded their Enigma machine. But the Nazis think it's impossible for sub-Aryans to decode, so they've ruled that possibility out altogether."

"But what's the stone have to do with it?"

"Apparently the Nazis, on direct orders from Himmler, followed Wallace to China. Himmler and Hitler are both convinced that retrieving the stone was the actual objective of Wallace's mission there. Through some intercepted correspondence from a man named "Roerich" they learned that the Tibetans were delivering Wallace the mythical stone. I guess they just missed the delegation by a few days in Jiuquan. And since Wallace returned to Washington, the Nazis imagine they've suffered an increase in battle losses. They know about Wallace's mysticism, and what they call, 'Roosevelt's decadent bourgeois sensibilities,' and they think that the former president devised a plan to defeat the great German nation by using a mystical stone."

"That can't be serious," Angleton said. "Let me talk to him. Let's have Sparks talk to him."

"No," Perkins said waiving his hands, "our man knows all about the president and his travels and that stone. He even knows that Wallace moved it to the museum and that a Jew authenticated it. They had planned to steal it from the museum, but they couldn't approach Dr. Berk, who's no friend to the Nazis, and he was very careful to let no one know where he kept it."

"I'm still not clear on how one finds U-boat coordinates with a stone," Angleton said, somewhat exasperated.

"Well, you don't, in fact. The Nazis think the stone is an amplifier that needs a kind of interpreter."

"Wallace," Sparks said.

"No, a man by the name of Edgar Cayce. He is the stone's interpreter. And they've just hatched a plot to kill him."

Chapter Forty-Two

Mystical Intel

Snows Court, Washington D.C.
February 1, 1945

"We have to tell him!" Sparks demanded.

"That's sensitive information," Angleton said.

"I don't care what it is. That man might be a little strange, but he's a friend to the president, not to mention that Wallace will feel responsible for Cayce's death."

"The Germans are likely to make his death look like an accident, which will keep the president from any feelings of guilt. If we warn the president of the plan, we could jeopardize our operation," Perkins argued.

Sparks turned on the older spook: "You've got this elaborate intelligence set-up to keep tabs on the president, but you won't make a move to save someone close to him. He is still *your* president you know." Sparks was talking more emphatically than before. "You don't trust me - I get that - but you're the CIA. Can't you figure out a way to catch these Nazis in the act without jeopardizing your goddamned White House mole?" Sparks hoped what he'd said would have an impact, but neither man responded and so Sparks continued, "Then ask Ernst in there if he knows how the Nazis are planning to do it." He was looking at Perkins, but the older man didn't respond. "Forget it then, I'll just ask him myself." Sparks made a move toward the closed bedroom door, but the other men in the room blocked his path.

He turned to find Perkins standing behind him in a rage. "Mr. Sparks, you won't do anything of the sort. He doesn't get to see your face! Do you understand what a dangerous position you occupy? You may be new to this business, but I'm not. You don't just get to stop bad things from happening, not when they're outside the scope of your operation."

"I would say that catching Nazis in the act of killing an American citizen who's close to the president is probably within the scope of your operation. Or do you only go after communists?"

"That's foolish and you know it," Perkins shouted.

Sparks was getting angry now and pushed the men who surrounded him away, stepping forward so he was toe to toe with Perkins. "Stake out the house and arrest them when they show up!" he said. "Wallace already suspects someone's looking into Cayce. It's not far-fetched to think you guys might have learned of the plot and thwarted it. Come on, you know the president's not even sure about you; the least you could do is make him think you're earning your money for Christ's sake. Besides you'll make some headlines."

"That's exactly what we don't want to do," Perkins scoffed.

"It might not be too bad, Perkins," Angleton said; "They're not part of the network we're looking into at all, not even the same country. And if any one who 'needs to know' asks, then we'll tell them that we looked into Hanfstaengl because of the circumstances of his arrival here, and that we found him following the president's aide. Then we moved in and made the arrest, and the rest is history. Hanfstaengl will go along with whatever story we give him."

"Fine," Perkins said, "But if this thing goes off the rails, it's your ass."

Angleton simply smiled in return. In a tone that suggested some resignation, Perkins said, "Well, go in there and talk to him then and find out what you need to know. And you," he said pointing to Sparks, "don't even think about going into that room. You can watch from right over there." He pointed to a black and white monitor on the table.

"You guys don't miss a trick. You ever think about putting one into my room?" But Perkins wasn't listening. And Sparks didn't care to hear a response even if he was. He was also sure there wasn't a camera in his apartment, or someone would have come in when he started to rough Angleton up.

For the moment, he walked over to the folding table with the small monitor. He pulled up a threadbare mustard-colored chair and sat down.

When Angleton pushed the door open to the room Hanfstaengl occupied, Sparks saw a large man with a strangely squared jaw look up from the table he had been quietly staring at. "Ernst Hanfstaengl?" Sparks heard Angleton say through a small speaker he couldn't locate. Angleton asked the question with a tone that implied he might have stumbled into the wrong room. But Hanfstaengl smiled a dull smile and Angleton sat down.

After asking a few preliminary questions, Angleton began pressing Hanfstaengl, "What was it you said they were going to do to you in Germany?"

"On one occasion I was told to fly to Spain to help Franco's forces. Instead the pilot flew me around Germany, and told me he was supposed to have me thrown out of the plane. I think the whole thing was just to scare me. But then just as I was boarding the ship for America someone handed me a transcript of a meeting between Himmler, Goebbels and Goering. I still have a copy of it in my flat; in short they intended to use me on this mission and then strangle me with piano wire when I returned."

"And what was your mission?"

Hanfstaengl proceeded to explain how he had been sent as part of a wider mission to obtain the Stone. "I was following the president's aide, Jonathan Sparks, in the hope of gaining entry to his apartment," he began. "We have reason to believe he has more to do with the Stone and with Cayce than his title lets on."

"Explain."

"Your president had him moved from a combat unit in the Pacific theater to Italy. There he served in the Fine Arts Division – he was the youngest and least accomplished man on that mission. However, we believe that his true operation began in Palestine on his trip over from the Pacific, where he gathered information on the Stone, a task he continued while in Italy. Once he'd learned how to use the Stone, he was relieved of Army duty and returned to the United States and Wallace."

"And your government really believes this?"

"I am here aren't I?"

"And you'd like to stay?"

Hanfstaengl nodded.

"For that to happen, we'll need either Congress or the president to sign off. Without approval from either of those, it's a POW camp for you."

Hanfstaengl swore in German.

"Of course, I think I can help you. You just have to help the president."

Hanfstaengl frowned. Then Angleton continued, "We need to know when and how your people are going to assassinate Cayce. This is not a request. If you don't answer me now you'll go directly to a camp in Nova Scotia where I'll personally see to it that you have your rendezvous with piano wire after all."

"You don't have to threaten me," the Nazi said in a hurt tone. "They're going tonight after midnight. They have a Negro man with a heroin addiction whom they have set up to burglarize the home at the same time. They'll simply fill his pockets with jewelry, break his neck and throw him out the second story gable window onto the basement walkway. This is to take place after he stabs Mr. and Mrs. Cayce to death in their sleep. It will be reported as very tragic and pointless, with the only conclusion that the police will have to watch the Negroes in the area more closely," he almost smiled when he said this last part.

"How many will there be?"

"A three-man team I should expect, but I don't know for sure. I'm not on that end of operations."

"All this because you think a psychic is giving away U-Boat coordinates?"

"And that Wallace is also using the predictions to work more closely with the Soviet Intelligence network here."

"Soviet intel?"

"Yes."

"You know that for sure?"

"That he uses Cayce's predictions to help...?"

"No, that he's dealing with the Soviets?"

"That we do know. But we don't know what Wallace gets from them or what they get from him. We have some evidence that Wallace was in the Soviet network before he became president, and now Himmler thinks several of the decadent Soviet types are under the spell of Wallace and Cayce, and that the president has them working against their own government by accurately predicting the moves Stalin makes at home, but this is only speculation."

"Naturally the last part was speculation. But how much is fact?"

"We have some reliable sources that say Wallace is dealing closely with Gromyko in secret and that he has a liaison in the American Communist community."

"And what are your thoughts on the mystical component?"

"I think they're all crazy."

Angleton continued to ask Hanfstaengl questions but Sparks had been distracted by the ringing of the apartment's phone. He watched as Perkins answered and began to listen. He looked anxious. Perkins then hung up the phone and walked back and forth whispering to the various people in the room. Then he closed the swinging door, which made Sparks think that they were talking about him. He wondered if he would ever leave this place.

And just as that thought crossed his mind, Angleton placed his hand on Sparks' shoulder. Sparks flinched ever so slightly.

"Got the jitters?" Angleton said without humor. Looking up again he saw Perkins rushing forward with a flustered look on his face. "What's got Perkins?"

"You're guess is as good as mine," Sparks said.

Chapter Forty-Three

Hampton Roads

Norfolk, Virginia
February 1, 1945

They would have to adjust to the fact that he had changed his plans – after all, the schedule was made for him, he wasn't made for it. Aside from this conflict, he was happy that he finally found the courage to make the trip at all.

Despite the fact that segments of the press were, more or less, gunning for him, he'd noticed a tendency, since he became president, and especially now that the election was over, for the press to downplay his eccentricities. They no longer ran stories on how he played Frisbee down by the Potomac for exercise, or that he'd had a guru, or that he was, as some of the more scurrilous papers claimed, "a card carrying member of the Communist Party."

Many in the press had done the same for Roosevelt, glossing over his handicap, his mistresses, and other unflattering aspects. Wallace hadn't imagined they would extend him the same kind of courtesy once he ascended the throne.

He was happy that his new ability to move about in the open eliminated the need for rides in the backs of milk trucks when visiting less-than-traditional destinations. Now he would use the state limousine instead of arriving like a refugee. He had been shocked, however, to learn that the FBI confiscated the limo he rode in from Al Capone some years before. He'd even just remarked to his aide, Ellery Martin, that it was silly that the president of the United States wasn't allowed a larger budget for such things.

Ellery simply nodded his head in agreement.

Ever since Wallace learned that Martin had been handpicked by Roosevelt to spy on members of his office, he'd shied away from the young man, only using him for unimportant tasks. But since he decided to make the impromptu trip to Cayce tonight, just after Sparks left for the evening, he had to get ahold of Ellery. The aide had stayed late collating files from the old residence. The president had him call over to Sparks' Foggy Bottom house to no avail.

"He'll just have to get down here himself tomorrow then, but we have to locate him before we board the Quincy!" Wallace declared, "There's no way I'm going to Malta without him."

"Sir, I'm sure we'll find him in the morning. And since Laughlin's not scheduled to come down until late in the day, we can fetch the two in the same car," he said.

"You're sure of a lot," Wallace jibed. Ellery didn't respond.

They left the White House together without locating Sparks and with Ellery Martin in his place. Ellery now sat across from the president and beside Agent Chipton, as Al Capone's car headed for Norfolk, Virginia, aboard the ferry "Abanaki" with Agent Dunbar in the passenger seat.

There was a stiff breeze coming from the northeast which sent waves from the open Atlantic up the Potomac and directly across Hampton Roads. Several times the president felt the vessel pitch to an uncomfortable degree. The lights of the naval destroyers, cruisers and the like vanished below the rail with each rise. "God," he said. "I don't want to drown in my own limo." He looked out to the Atlantic. "What about U-Boats," he said to Chipton. His mind was diverted from his worries momentarily when Ellery put his hand over his mouth and lunged over Agent Chipton's lap toward the car door. As Ellery staggered into the wind to vomit over the side, Wallace watched Agent Chipton smirk.

"Guess he's not used to rough seas."

"No, sir," Chipton said. "It doesn't look like it, sir."

It took nearly twenty minutes before the president's limo arrived on the ferry in Norfolk. Ellery remained on deck for the remainder of the trip.

When they pulled to the car dock, Wallace was pleased to find that apparently not a single journalist had heard of his last-minute plans; no one was waiting for him. It also probably helped that it was well after midnight.

"Are you sure it's all right we're arriving so late?" he asked Ellery as the car pulled out from the lot. In Sparks' absence, Ellery had arranged the meeting with Cayce.

"Yes, he's waiting for you Mr. President. We don't have to worry about that."

"And he said he doesn't mind the late hour?"

"In fact, his wife seems eager to have you over, no matter the time. She said that Edgar has been talking about nothing but you for over a month, and she's pleased he'll finally get to tell you what's on his mind."

Wallace's anxiety over the late hour abated at Ellery's words. His other concerns remained. There were too many moving parts in his life. He felt like a great machine that constantly spins out even greater and more complex machinery in order to fix the problems of the older version.

They arrived at the familiar old house in Virginia Beach. Dunbar climbed out of the limo. He walked rearward to chat with the driver of the trail car now just behind them. This was the same security dance they performed so often that now it was routine for Wallace.

Dunbar moved ahead of the limo and up the sidewalk to ensure no one was lying in wait in the bushes near the house. Another security vehicle had investigated the surrounding area and was circling the block. The president felt safe. He could see the security car turning the corner ahead.

It was then that he watched Agent Dunbar pull out his .45 automatic and level it at a car parked a hundred feet away from the limo. Dunbar was backing away simultaneously and talking into a radio in his left hand. His Midwestern voice resounded over Agent Chipton's radio beside the president. "Man in the car is armed!"

The president looked forward through the partition to the windshield.

The Secret Service car that had just circled the block stopped beside Dunbar. Two agents charged out with rifles. They leveled their guns at the other car's windshield.

Agent Chipton lunged beside the president. Simultaneously, the driver up front put the president's car into gear.

Then there was a noise that seemed to come from the house. Ellery shouted in horror and pointed up to the third story where a black man fell, propelled backwards out the window and onto the pavement below. They heard his sick thud as he landed half on the short stonewall and half on the walk. Wallace saw several sets of hands in the window above.

"What's going on," the president demanded. "What's going on?"

"Sir, I don't know."

Then agents from the car behind them poured over the lawn and to the door where they checked the man on the ground. Then they quickly kicked in the door and three of them entered, while several other agents worked slowly around the house in opposite directions. Most of the men carried pistols, but at least one man had what looked to be a very short shotgun, and another had an M1918 BAR: a powerful machine gun.

On the seat beside him, Chipton had the radio up and was shouting as the president's limo accelerated off the curb and down the street past the other agents with guns drawn. They were pulling two men out of the parked civilian car as they past.

Agent Dunbar's voice came in over the radio again: "Negro man, mid 30s, deceased: neck's been broken. We have two men in custody. There's men in the house. Men in the house!" His words were punctuated by gunfire, which came so rapidly it sounded like a group of military Harley Davidsons firing up in succession. The sound both came over the radio and echoed up the street into the limo's cab.

"What's happening?" the president demanded.

Chapter Forty-Four

USS Quincy

The Mediterranean Sea
February 3, 1945

"You know there were two Americans found in that car outside of Cayce's house?" the president said over the papers he was reading. Sparks sat across from him. There was a finely carved wooden table between them. A Persian rug with a red border and golden blond geometric field pattern covered the floor. Several heavily lacquered chairs and desks filled the room, adding warmth to the cold blue steel walls of the ship's interior. From time to time a non-local, metallic echo, brought on by the pitch and roll of the ship, broke their silence. Since they'd reached the Mediterranean, the seas had calmed. So did the sound.

The president was reading a digest concerning the most recent events in Europe in preparation for the approaching meeting with Stalin and Churchill in Yalta, in the Crimean Peninsula on the coast of the Black Sea. Though Wallace was looking at a review of Europe, he was thinking about the murder of Edgar Cayce and his wife in their bed on the eve of his trip to the continent. The fact that one man and one woman (the report of two men that came over Chipton's radio had been erroneous), both members of his newly penned CIA, had been found in a car outside the home troubled him. This news came on top of the fact that three Nazi security officers and a black man named Lincoln Jefferson from Richmond Virginia were also found in and around the home. It bothered him similarly that his Secret Service agents inside the house had seen fit to take no prisoners when they'd encountered the Nazis, who, one must assume, they had no way of knowing were Nazis when they encountered them.

Just what in the hell was happening at that house? He thought.

"I can't help but believe that my own intelligence agency conspired with the Nazis to kill Edgar Cayce. And what do you think, Jon? You've been quiet since you got on board?"

"I think that makes about as much sense as the alternative?" Sparks said. The two had hardly spoken at all since Sparks came aboard.

"Which is what, exactly?"

"That they were there to stop the assassination," Sparks replied after a moment.

"But how did the CIA learn of it? And why weren't they inside?"

"Why would the CIA get some Nazis to do the job and then show up at the scene of the crime? They might be stupid, Henry, but they're not crazy." Sparks spoke in a deferent tone. This was no longer a friend he was talking with – the common man who made it to the house of the people – instead this was the fountainhead of power in the United States. And he exuded that spirit now like static electricity in a storm.

"Maybe so. It may be so," Wallace said. "It just brings the point even further home to me that it's difficult for a leader to know anything with certainty." He paused and took a deep breath. "When I worked for the Ag. Department, or as vice president, I made plans based on what I knew to be facts. There were such things as facts then. Now I don't know anything. I don't know why Germans would want to kill Edgar Cayce or what the CIA had to do with it. I don't know what kind of deal Churchill has tried to make outside of the U.S. with Stalin; or what Stalin will do with Poland or the Baltic States; or what will happen with the 4,000 pounds of gold and an equal worth in Rubles Lauchlin has smuggled in to cause a Russian coup."

"Sir?"

Wallace looked back down to his papers, and then up to Sparks, "And I don't know where you were the other night. You weren't home."

"No, Henry. I wasn't. I would have been with you if I was, but I had to meet a girl."

"A girl?"

"Yes."

"Ah." Wallace looked up at the ceiling and said, "And I can't say if you were really with a girl or not."

"Sir, I . . ."

But Wallace cut him off, "I can only act on my sense of things, as Stalin acts on his paranoia. I must believe and act. That's all I have."

"Henry, I don't know what you mean," but his voice waivered.

"I mean that I've acted to strike Stalin. He's not the savior of his people, he's their master, and he's a threat to the entire world."

"With the CIA? Is that why you formed it?"

"No, we're doing it. I'm doing it. I can't trust the CIA. They're the same people . . . or . . . let's say that most of the gold now on its way to Russia came here in the form of Russian Imperial gold coins. This gold came through the State Department from the Soviets for American firms in order to buy food and other necessities after the revolution and Civil War in Russia in the 1920s. Prior to that, American money aided the Red Army. And these same firms who profited off the Soviets, or the families behind them, now have a good number of men in the CIA." Wallace was staring at Sparks. The president had the look, Sparks imagined, of a man either running a hard set of mathematical calculations in his mind or remembering a painful episode, but he couldn't decide which.

"I don't understand what you're telling me," Sparks said.

"I'm telling you that despite the anti-Soviet talk of our Capitalists and the anti-Capitalist talk of our Bolsheviks, they're doing business with one another. They were happy to have each other, in fact. Just think what it's like to sign a contract to provide much needed cotton for all of the Soviet Union. It's almost as good as having the contract to sell cotton or munitions to an entire Army during war. Or what it's like to have an entire country under your command. And now Russia has a madman at its head who doesn't believe in the revolution any more than he believes in

God. But he's a madman who needs help building his oil wells and laying train tracks. He's a madman who needs Studebaker trucks to launch his Katyusha rockets. And he needs them because their wars and internal genocide and their corruption have impoverished them."

"But they've got their own factories."

"Even when that's the case, as many times as not, an American firm either built their factory or provided the expertise to do so. This business of supplying arms, equipment, and even factories to the Soviets is incredibly lucrative for many. Some firms even stayed afloat through the Great Depression with the profits from these transactions, which at the time were illegal and are still murky, though easier since we started Lend-Lease and since we're allied with the Russians. The Russian people, on the one hand, are being fleeced by American Capitalists while they're being impoverished by their dictatorship. Several of these American families represented in the CIA have a keen interest in preserving the status quo because they can sign no-compete, monolithic contracts with the Soviet government." Wallace tapped the desk with his finger. "Do you understand? We are sailing in a convoy of vessels bringing Lend-Lease goods, amid which is a container of guns, gold and paper money that will be received by a special military unit who will take it and disseminate it. They are going to kill Stalin and reform the country along more open lines. This is just the first shipment. And when they do that these industrial contracts will likely become null and void. It's not only Stalin we have to worry about here, but those who profit from the enslavement of the Russians."

A rapid knocking on the hatch startled Sparks and prevented him from asking his next question. The president tilted his head, and Sparks stood to answer. He opened the door and behind the open hatch stood Wild Bill Donovan. The man's white hair was neatly parted and he had a hound dog look to his drooping eyes.

"Donovan, you're late," Wallace barked, completely out of character, as Donovan walked past Sparks into the room. Sparks turned as though to leave. Wallace called him back. From the way he had just heard the president talk to one of the members of the College of Cardinals, he wanted nothing to do with what was going to take place. It felt as though the principal had called in one of his students to expel him, and both parties knew what was happening.

Donovan sat down, placing the folder he carried on the table. He looked at the president, and suddenly Wallace stood up. Sparks had never seen Wallace look menacing before. He had always been a mild-mannered man.

"Goddam it, Bill, he was a friend of mine! And what the hell were your people doing there?"

"Sir . . ."

Wallace interrupted, "I'm listening!"

"We only heard of the plot that night. The Germans had gotten one of their people into the country."

"Who!"

"Ernst Hanfstaengl. We tailed him as soon as he passed customs. We didn't know what he was doing. Then we caught him following Jonathan Sparks out of the White House the other night." At this Wallace looked over his shoulder to where Sparks was standing by the hatch through which Donovan had entered. Sparks wished he could crawl under the hatch. "Jonathan didn't know," Donovan continued. "As soon as we realized what Hanfstaengl was doing we bagged him and interrogated him. He told us about some cockamamie plot to steal the Stone of Destiny from you because you were using it in conjunction with the Sleeping Prophet to discern the location of U-Boats in the Atlantic." With this last part, Donovan stopped talking, half expecting the president to jump all over him, but Wallace didn't say a word and so he continued. "And not only were they going to steal the stone, they were going to assassinate Cayce that night. In response we sent two agents down to Virginia Beach and all hell broke out."

"Why was this . . .?"

"Ernst Hanfstaengl," Donovan said, helping the president who was struggling to find the correct name.

"Yes, Hanfstaengl, why was he following my aide?"

"The Nazis were under the impression that he'd helped you locate the stone in China, or Tibet, and that he'd taken possession of it for various errands in the past. He was hoping to catch Sparks with the stone to make stealing it easier. And the Nazis had been watching Cayce as far back as your last trip to see him. That's who the cameraman who tried to photograph you outside of Cayce's house must have been working for."

"Has the cameraman told you that?" The president asked.

"No, but this intel is fresh, and now that we have Hanfstaengl and the dead Nazis the pieces are falling into place."

Wallace sat down, "That's the craziest story I've ever heard in my life. What do you think, Jon?"

"I don't know what to think, sir."

"I think this is an honest story, at least mostly," Wallace declared. "The Tibetan man who came down out of the high country to give me that stone was afraid to run into Nazis, so it's at least possible they were looking for it back then." Wallace began to laugh. Then he banged the table, "Does it make you think that Cayce really was using the stone to find U-Boats? Considering I was there at Cayce's house, Donovan?"

"To be honest, sir?" Donovan said.

"Please!"

"I don't know what to think about your relationship with Edgar Cayce, but I don't think he's capable of finding U-Boats, with or without a stone."

"Well, good. Let's just say that he was a friend of mine. That's all," and he dismissed Donovan.

Donovan stood. "One more thing before you go," Wallace asked. "Who was Lincoln Jefferson?"

"The Negro?" Donovan asked from the hatch.

"If you insist."

"He was their patsy."

"Do you usually find that blacks make for good patsies, Donovan?"

"Sir," Donovan said.

"I mean, in the United States and in your experience, generally?"

Donovan thought for a moment. He knew this was a trap of some kind, but if Wallace didn't believe that Jefferson was the German patsy then the whole story would unravel in his mind. But admitting that blacks made for good patsies, at least traditionally in the United States, was something he didn't care to do. But he found that he had no choice but to be honest. And so he said, "Yes, sir. Investigators don't often look much further. It's open and shut."

"Thank you," Wallace said, and Donovan left the room.

Sparks closed the hatch behind him, and lingered for a moment. Then he walked back to the table where Wallace was seated. Wallace hadn't moved since Donovan stood to leave. He had both elbows on the table and his head in his hands. "Wild Bill, he's just another Wall Street Lawyer. And the Russians . . . the Russians!" Sparks looked at the president, afraid to speak and afraid to leave. Wallace continued, "How am I to know?" but clipped his sentence short, leading Sparks to complete what he believed Wallace's thought would be: "That the money you're sending will achieve its result, sir?"

Wallace laughed, "I took some of that money out of a program to build a bomb that could destroy cities in one blast – maybe whole states, maybe more. I killed the program and used its funding to end the reason we'll remain in a war economy for the next thirty years."

"This is more than a normal risk," Sparks said.

"Not from my perspective. I've known I would make this decision for thirty years, and so did Edgar Cayce."

Chapter Forty-Five

The Sacred Cow

The Isle of Malta
February 4, 1945

The president's plane sat on the runway waiting for permission to take off. There was something relaxing to him about the hum of the engines, and yet he couldn't put his mind at ease. He was watching the Mediterranean sunlight reflect off the silver aluminum wingtips on his Douglas CV-54C Aircraft. The plane had been made especially for President Roosevelt only the year prior. Though the former president had never gotten the chance to fly in it, the plane was still equipped with an elevator that could descend from the cabin to the tarmac. It was a mechanical oddity the former president desired greatly, but for which he only ever saw blueprints.

President Wallace had arrived in Malta two days prior aboard the Baltimore class heavy cruiser USS Quincy. He'd decided to stay on to talk with some of his generals in preparation for the Conference in Yalta on the southern shores of the Crimean Peninsula. The conference was codenamed "the Argonaut Conference." He thought the name was trite and wondered where these titles came from. He certainly didn't like imagining himself as Jason in a quest for the mythical Golden Fleece on the lonely shores of the Baltic, or to imagine Medea killing Jason's children for his infidelity.

In stopping in Malta he'd let the convoy he'd traveled with move on without him. Stopping here also allowed him to hear the views of the generals on the war and the future of Europe firsthand. Prior to arriving, he had gathered that there was a consensus among them that Stalin was too strong in the East to be pushed back now, and that large chunks of Eastern and Central Europe would now be under Soviet domination. As Wallace already knew what his diplomats thought of the Russians and their "position," it was useful to hear what military men thought.

General Bradley summed up their feelings best when he said: "You won't negotiate them out of land they've already won with arms, especially if you're doing the negotiating in their territory."

Eisenhower thought there was room for negotiation in some areas, but basically agreed. The greatest land army the world had ever seen was on the cusp of defeating the second greatest land army the world had ever seen. And now Hitler was holed up in Berlin for the Nazi's last stand. For a moment Wallace allowed himself to wonder what it would be like to have to fall back to Washington as the Nazis had to Berlin, while his own country collapsed upon itself from the pressure of an invading military.

General Patton, who'd recently died in a car accident, would have wanted war with the Russians. Wallace knew MacArthur, commanding in the Pacific, thought that the American forces should keep on pressing all the way to Moscow. He identified the Soviets as the enemy, and thought that America should take the initiative and crush them. While Wallace now shared part of this view, especially with regard to Stalin, he thought it was bad form to follow Hitler's lead and betray their Russian allies openly. The road to Moscow had always proven a graveyard for invading armies, as the Nazis just demonstrated.

As Wallace sat, mulling these subjects, he waited for his aircraft to take flight so that he could enter the plane's conference room with Lauchlin Currie. It had been some time since he'd talked with Lauchlin alone and was eager to speak with him.

From where he was sitting, he could also see part of Sparks' face turned toward one of the windows in his seat. He could tell that Sparks was nervous because he was biting his nails. As he looked on, the aircraft started suddenly. The president's plane, dubbed the Sacred Cow, was ready for takeoff. He heard the engines increase RPM as their hum turned to a fast-recurring chop. The plane moved down the runway, picking up speed until the wheels no longer touched ground. Soon the plane was airborne.

The blue waters below seemed like one great sapphire, and the isle, just a bit of debris in its formation. Wallace remembered a history lesson he'd received once on the Crusades, and of how the Muslims wiped the island clean of nearly all its inhabitants and buildings on their way to conquer Sicily.

As the plane pushed closer to its destination and further from Malta, he couldn't help but think of the mythical Hellespont, for which they were now headed, the gateway between Europe and Asia. Of course the narrow strait of water leading out of the Mediterranean to the Sea of Marmara, and finally onto the Black Sea, was currently known as the Turkish Straits. Wallace, however, preferred to think of it by its classical appellation.

It was also in those Straits where Athens met Sparta in a great and futile battle during the Peloponnesian War, a war which only served to weaken the classical Hellenes and ensure the rise of the Macedonians. Both sides (Athens, the democratic empire; and Sparta, the warrior kingdom) were so ardently looking for Victory that they could not see at what cost it could be gained.

Wallace knew some of his generals wanted war. He knew that war had pulled the Americans out of the Depression, and that war could keep American factories turning and her men at work. But war had consequences, as the Greeks learned. He feared pushing his military into Russia because the outcome could easily mean the devastation of both countries and the world.

Now that the plane was at cruising altitude, he removed his seatbelt and walked toward the conference room that Roosevelt had designed. As he opened the finely polished cherry doors, Lauchlin too rose from his seat in the cabin and followed him into the room. Ellery then entered and offered the men coffee, which they accepted. Sparks didn't move from his seat.

The two men made small talk: about the weather, about Virginia, about the accommodations on the cruiser Lauchlin had taken. Then Ellery returned and delivered the coffee. "Will there be anything else?"

"No, that will be all," Wallace said.

"I'm fine, thank you," Lauchlin said.

When the polished brass latch clicked behind Ellery, Wallace turned to Lauchlin. "About your accommodations on the ship?"

"They were adequate."

"And you didn't see fit to follow them all the way to Yalta?" Wallace asked with a hint of confusion.

"I? No. My presence there could only complicate."

Or embarrass, the president thought.

After a moment of consideration Lauchlin added, "Gromyko is already in Moscow. He was even given a state dinner upon his arrival, and Nikishov has a post in the Kremlin."

"How could Stalin let that happen?"

"They hate him, sir. Anyone near Stalin hates him. His wife killed herself after an argument with him. The people around him all want to see him die, even if they're Stalinists. It's hard for Stalin to know who simply hates him and who means to kill him."

"What of the shipment?"

"The NKVD are on the ground and will receive it."

"I hope so," Wallace said.

"I sincerely believe so, sir. I believe this will help coalesce the opposition inside the Kremlin, and then they'll just wait."

"Our people have heard nothing about this then?"

"We've had no word that they have," Lauchlin said. "And as far as I've seen, our intel community sees nothing odd in the Soviet's behavior."

"If it does come off as you expect, do you know how it will be done?"

"I know only by whom," Lauchlin said, with enough pride to make Wallace nervous, and then irritated.

"This is no game!"

"I didn't mean to imply that it was, it's just that the man they've found is very good. He's dedicated in a peculiar sort of way."

"How so?"

"He's Ukrainian."

"Is that determinative?"

"Well, his entire family starved in the Holodomor. He shot his own brother when he found him eating his dead mother during that famine. He will surely kill Stalin." He passed this grim detail so quickly that Wallace had to stop him. "Yes," Lauchlin said, "That's what I said. The Russians took the Ukrainian harvest in the winter of '32/'33 and withheld rations. Many thought it was an adjustment during collectivization, but it's begun to look organized in order to break the Ukrainian's will. Hence the name 'Holodomor,' or 'Murder Famine.' It may be in dispute whether it was a failure in the experiment or not, but our man certainly thinks it was organized. Gromyko said that it's his life's purpose to kill Stalin. But Stalin and those around him suppose that because they gave him suicide missions in Lithuania and Poland and East Prussia, and that he returned after fighting bravely for his country for years without a word of treason, that he has forgotten what happened; that his medals have taken away his memory."

Wallace remembered the winter of '32/'33: it was a hard one even in the United States.

"They call him Razvedchik," Lauchlin then said.

"Is that his name?"

"That's what we're calling him."

"He doesn't sound real. Stalin doesn't let many people he suspects live long. You'd think they'd either kill this man themselves or keep sending him away till he didn't return."

"I've gotten the impression that they did that with him already, but he kept returning. Eventually they gave up and integrated him into the GRU."

"But he won't take action during the conference?"

"No, the plan is to have Stalin die in Moscow."

Wallace reclined into his chair and thought for a moment. Then he said, "No one's contemplated such a world realignment since Woodrow Wilson. Let's hope we do better."

Chapter Forty-Six

The Gardener of Human Happiness

Yalta, The Crimean Peninsula.
February 11, 1945

The flash bulbs crackled and Wallace smiled at his own discomfort. He felt exceedingly awkward – unusually self-conscious, as though he was standing in his older brother Roosevelt's shoes and filling them poorly.

They sat in the stone courtyard of the Livadia Palace. The "Big Three" leaders sat side by side in ornately carved chairs on overlapping Persian rugs. Churchill had his hat in his hands in an oversized pea coat, while Stalin sat wearing both his knowing smile and a military long coat. Plain old American Wallace was dressed in drab business attire. He felt as though he should be wearing a shawl or something like it to detract from his un-statesman like appearance. Cracking jokes to win Stalin's approval hadn't helped him either.

So far he'd only succeeded in making Churchill look foolish, which was the tactic Roosevelt had used to bond with Stalin, but in Wallace's case, Stalin looked at him as though he was misguided, while Churchill looked nonplussed and often angry. Despite everything that Wallace knew of Stalin, he conceded to himself that the man conveyed a great sense of warmth with his brown eyes. Stalin appeared almost fatherly.

They struck different poses as the flash bulbs popped. This was all the Big Three leaders had to do now, as they had considered the points the Argonaut Conference was convened to discuss, and had, more or less, successfully divided Europe. Yet there was already talk back home that Wallace had given more than he should to the Russians, and that he was secretly in favor of a Soviet takeover of Europe, a point, his detractors said, that his weak negotiating proved. In truth, Wallace might have given more up than he would have had he not been awaiting Stalin's death. Still, there would be another conference at which they would finalize the new political geography of Europe, so what happened here at Yalta wasn't the end of negotiations. As of now, they had a rough outline of the shape of things to come after the war. This sense of accomplishment was the reason for the celebratory photographs they were now taking.

Several times, while the pictures were taken, Stalin said something in Russian to the group of men who'd accompanied him here. They smiled and looked back at Wallace. In his turn, Wallace joked with Churchill, but he knew that Churchill couldn't stand him. A reliable source recently told Wallace that Churchill often called him "a useful idiot," or worse.

Churchill was patting around his pockets looking for his cigars when Wallace turned and said to him, "the palace looks like a cross between the White House and a mosque."

Churchill looked at the president and said, "Yes, I must've left them inside the palace."

"Excuse me," Wallace said.

"I don't know how I left them behind."

Wallace wondered if the old man was senile. He certainly hadn't paid any attention to Wallace. As if the president cared where the prime minister misplaced his stogies. At the same time Wallace felt angry and alone. Should he let Churchill in on the plot? The answer, he knew, was no. The fact that Churchill was staring at him now in a way that was senile and rude sealed the decision in the president's mind. He now wondered which of the Russians who had accompanied Stalin knew and were in on the plot. Or which of them knew and were going to thwart it at the last moment.

When they stood from their photo-op, Wallace felt smaller than both men, despite the fact that he was significantly taller. In part he felt this way because the two European leaders were more accomplished on the world stage than he was, and they knew it. To his left stood Winston Churchill: the British Bulldog, the man who had singlehandedly revivified his empire and rekindled its flagging fighting spirit. On Wallace's right sat the "Brilliant Genius of Humanity," the "Coryphaeus of Science," the "Gardener of Human Happiness," Joseph Stalin, whose revolutionary name itself meant "STEEL." He was the socialist superman. Wallace was just President Wallace; or President Henry A. Wallace to make the name sound more official, which still couldn't hold a candle to the other two.

The three made polite small talk to pass the moments standing together, though Churchill still appeared distressed that he couldn't find his cigars. Then they shook hands, Wallace and Stalin last. When they did so, Wallace perceived an evil in the man's eye that nearly made him lose his breath. He had known of Stalin's hideous nature for some time now, but after he had found warmth in his eyes just moments ago, he was shocked to see such open malevolence there now. In response to the sudden epiphany, Wallace gripped Stalin's hand a little more tightly as Stalin was just releasing to walk away. His action in turn pulled Stalin's arm, already stiff from an old injury, away from his body awkwardly. Both in response to this and out of a self-conscious desire to hide his slight deformity in public, Stalin quickly drew his arm back, pulling it away from Wallace violently. He then turned toward him to discover the meaning of Wallace's sudden movement.

Neither man said a word, but Stalin's eyes spoke. Inside them lay a universe of terror. He was a bloodless butcher who thought of humans as instruments to be used or discarded as he saw fit. And they were discarded in the hope of shaping the human form for the revolutionary and progressive future, and for his own purposes. Stalin was carving the new man from native stock with widespread euthanasia; the way one brings about a new breed of dog, only saving and mating those specimens exhibiting the right traits and discarding the rest. And to the eyes of the murderer, the country was full of political refuse.

The look Wallace now got from the man of steel spoke of murder. The title of "Gardener" was particularly apt, as Stalin had clipped the buds of many to shape his nation in his image. Now Russia was a dull land full of bleak and tedious men; just a glance over the coterie of Soviet officers and diplomats attending the Argonaut Conference was enough to substantiate the hypothesis.

Stalin had even killed Americans. Wallace didn't know the number of Americans who disappeared in Russia during the terror years of the late 30s, but members of the American Embassy in Russia passed the word along. These were men and women who escaped unemployment and depression in the United States for the workers' paradise of Soviet Russia. They had gone and worked in factories built by American firms with American money, some even operating outside of state control. When the purges began, the Americans and their smiling baseball teams and jazz clubs were looked on with suspicion.

As they began to disappear, the remaining desperate men and women threw themselves upon the American Embassy's doors only to be turned away. Outside the gates of that embassy in Moscow, the NKVD picked them up off the uneven streets and took them to the Gulag, or worse, to execution chambers where masked men in leather aprons cut their lives out of them and buried them in mass graves. This was the end for those Americans, delirious but hopeful for the promise of a better life and a better future in Soviet Russia.

It was the architect of this horror from whom Wallace had just received that look. The files Wallace had been shown by his intelligence community and others were more than a fascist plot to undermine the movement, this *was* the movement: Stalin *was* its Spirit.

Wallace now had no doubt about assassination. His only fear was that a man like that couldn't be killed.

Chapter Forty-Seven

Palace Intrigue

Yalta, The Crimean Peninsula.
February 12, 1945

Then came a knock.

The sunlight was beginning to fade outside, and he was just about to turn on the lamp behind him. He had recently finished dinner on the first floor in the palace dining room with the other aides and staffers and was hoping that he'd had his last social interaction of the day. He wished to relax and prepare for the long trip back to Washington.

The knock dashed his hopes. There was something in the sharpness of the rap that made him anxious. If someone had come here on friendly terms, he would have made a rounder sound. Instead, this seemed the knock of a policeman serving a warrant. And since the Argonaut Conference was over, this building was solely for the American delegation. In other words, no local police were going to enter the grounds (at least openly). Whoever was knocking was an American.

He stood from the upholstered chair he was reading in and walked to the ornately carved mahogany door, looking back over his shoulder to the fire he had made, as if this would be the last he'd feel of its warmth. Beneath the door he saw the shadows cast by the light of the hall shining across the two shoes outside. Then he turned the knob and pulled. Standing there scowling was a lieutenant in the United States Navy. He recognized the man from the courtyard earlier while the fawning pictures of the "Big Three" were taken.

"Can I help you?" Sparks asked.

"Be in the lower garden in fifteen minutes!" the lieutenant said, and turned on his heel and walked down the splendid palace hallway as if he had never been at the door at all.

Two doors down, Ellery poked his head out of his room. First he looked in the direction the man had walked, and then he turned and saw Sparks. He acted startled. "I thought I heard someone talking," he said. The lieutenant had already turned the corner and was presumably walking to the service stair in the building's rear.

"So did I," Sparks said. "But no one was here. Since I'm out though, I think I'll have something to eat – just a snack. I didn't have enough at dinner. Do you know if the kitchen's still open?"

"No, but I'll come with you."

"That's fine. I'll go alone. If they're open, I'll just bring you back something."

"Whatever they have down there is ok with me," Ellery said. But he lingered, staring at Sparks before finally shutting his door.

Sparks didn't know what to make of Ellery. He knew his history: of how he had been forced on Wallace by Roosevelt to look for spies and had been integral in discovering the mole in the vice president's office. But since then, Wallace hadn't felt that he could trust Ellery. Adding to the suspicion was the fact that Ellery's poker face was unnervingly blank; one could never tell where he actually stood.

Sparks walked back to the white marble mantle and took his room key. He worried that the glowing logs might topple out onto the carpet as they settled, and so he put the ancient iron screen in front of the opening and left the room heading in the direction the lieutenant took. On the service stair landing, midway between the third and second floor, he encountered one of the maids cleaning a tray full of drinks she had dropped.

"Is the kitchen still open?" he asked, but she didn't reply and went on picking the pieces of broken glass off the green runner and stacking them on the silver tray. "The kitchen?" he repeated.

At this she raised her head and looked at him with her peasant eyes. "Is it still open?" She shook her head, "no," but not to signify that the kitchen was closed, rather to show that she didn't understand. Sparks smiled when he realized that she didn't know any English and gestured to his mouth like he was eating with a spoon or a fork. "Kitchen . . . Open . . . Still?" But she didn't understand. She smiled and blushed. He waved his hand at her in a way intended to tell her not to worry. "Thank you. I'll go look." And he turned to walk down the stairs.

"Kishen?" she said, and he turned.

"Yes, kitchen."

"No closed. Man, knocked me."

"What man?"

"The kishen closed."

At that he smiled, said "Thank you," and left her to continue picking up her mess.

He jogged the two flights of stairs to the ground floor. At the bottom he found himself standing in a narrow hallway that abutted the kitchen and led into the dining room, through which one could enter the study that led to the gardens. Sparks moved down the hallway until he came to the kitchen door. He saw through the rectangular glass window that the lights were out, and so continued toward the dining room.

There, he was happy to find the room empty, as well as the study. He could hear voices in the grand room just to the east. He walked through the large glass doors that led onto the veranda and to the garden. Several officers were outside smoking and he nodded to them as he passed. They didn't acknowledge him any more than a stranger would and so he strolled deeper into the garden. He came to a granite staircase that led to the lower terrace leading to the park below. He followed this damp stair down, now worried that he would miss whoever it was he was looking for. But then he caught a glimpse of a man alone, standing by the entrance to the forest trail that led half a mile downhill to the sea where there was a beach and several docks.

The man nodded to him before he arrived. He was dressed in a navy blue uniform and pointed deeper into the gloomy park below without saying a word. Sparks followed his direction and walked beneath the cold shadow of the deciduous trees. Here the sun was blocked by the steep hillside and palace above. Lights flanked the path at intervals, but they hadn't yet been turned on.

Ahead he saw another man, also in his dress blues, standing at a narrow, gated entrance to a path leading off at a right angle from the one he was standing on. The man motioned for him to enter. Sparks did so and found himself inside a hollow carved from the surrounding trees and shrubs. A path wound around the outside of the room-like hollow, and in its center, flanked by last year's flowers and shrubs, was a large fountain.

Sparks followed the path to the opposite side where a man sat on a marble bench facing out toward the path. The man didn't stand as Sparks approached but said, "I'm happy you're holding up."

"Thank you, sir." He had met with James Forrestal in the past, most recently months before, but now the man looked a decade older, at least. His eyes were sunk into his skull and darted quickly here and there. Running the war for the Navy had obviously taken its toll. He was not healthy.

"There are many patriots in the Ukraine who will never see their country again. But that's war. The president is soft on the Reds, here and elsewhere, and word says Wallace is working more closely with Lauchlin Currie than with anyone else."

"That's true," Sparks responded.

"I know that information originated with you. But you haven't been sending in the kind of quality intel we're looking for." Forrestal chided. "I don't know that you understand the importance of what you're doing. From where I sit it looks like you're just passing time. But we need to get a read on Wallace."

"I know, sir."

"No, you don't know! Our operatives just apprehended a group of scientists absconding with technical information on the biggest bomb in the world. That's a program that Lauchlin Currie liquidated, and the people he brought in were trying to steal the secrets and send them to Stalin."

"Who?"

"It doesn't matter who. This is wartime and they've committed the highest treason. No one will know what happened to them until the war is over, and then their families won't want the disgrace revealed." Forrestal motioned for Sparks to sit, then he continued, "I know it wasn't part of the deal you struck, but I need you to look deeper."

"What do you mean by that, sir?"

"I mean that when you leave here there'll be a package in your room that contains a miniature camera, some film, and some other material. You're familiar with these?" he said rhetorically.

"Yes," Sparks said, and thought of the farm in Virginia.

"I also need you to give us a three-hour window when we can get into the Oval Office. He does all his business from there, as best we can tell, and we need to know what's going on."

"I don't want to say no, but this is more . . ."

"I know it is Jonathan, but you have to understand how things look from our perspective. We're talking about nuclear secrets going to Stalin from people directly related to Wallace's closest advisor. This nuclear weapon would have been a trump card over the Reds when it was finished. And it would have been finished! And he's talking of accepting a conditional surrender from the Japs.

"And here in Yalta, he just gave all Eastern Europe away to Stalin without so much as a fight. What are our men fighting for, if we're just going to hand the continent over to the Reds in such a position that Stalin can take the rest when he wants it? No, we need this from you Jonathan. We need to know what our president is doing to our country, and who he's working with."

"I just don't believe he's a traitor, sir." Forrestal glared at him but Sparks continued, "He says he's used the money from the closed Manhattan District, that's the bomb you're talking about, to finance a coup in the Soviet Union."

"What are you talking about? Where'd you hear that?"

"I got it from Wallace himself on the ship on the way over. He's suspicious of his intelligence people, and he's turned against Stalin."

Forrestal looked like he'd just been hit with a bat. "How can that be? How?"

"As far as I know, he had the funds from the project converted into gold and shipped to the Crimea with the fleet, just a few days ago. He told me he sent 4,000 pounds in gold and an equal number of rubles."

Forrestal was silent for a moment. Then he said, "You're telling me that he just sent roughly five million dollars to the Russians without anyone knowing about it. Do you know how far that kind of money would go in that country?" Forrestal looked as if he were making the calculations in his head.

"I have no idea," Sparks said.

"And you think this sum is going toward a coup?"

"He told me so."

"I say no! I say, you let a man's actions speak for themselves, son. He just gave Europe away. If he wanted a coup, he'd use the CIA. What else did he just sign them into law for? The only reason they weren't pushing for something like this was because he's too dovish to go through with it. The whole point of those boys down there at CIA is to break the Russians. And you think he's making a coup all on his own?"

"This is what he told me."

"Well, what do you think?"

"I don't know what to think, but when you put it in that light, the president's behavior is awfully suspicious."

"We've had word going back to the 30s that he was at least a fellow traveler with the commies, but this is something altogether different.

What kind of man wrecks his own country?" He looked to the ground and then answered his own question. "The kind of man that believes in the revolution. That's who. He's a revolutionary!"

Then Forrestal stood. "We'll be in touch," he said and walked away. When he left the hollow he took the path leading to the waterfront. Sparks watched him through the heavy branches of the leafless shrubs.

Chapter Forty-Eight

The Great Dictator

The Kremlin, Moscow
March 2, 1945

General Nikishov laughed with the others.

Charlie Chaplin's film *The Great Dictator* played on the large projection screen of the Kremlin Theater. Chaplin, playing Hitler in full regalia, mock mustache and all, was preparing to give the movie's final speech. The film was in English without subtitles, so the people's commissar of cinema gave a running translation in insipid Russian. At times his fumbling and stuttered translation added to the picture's humor, at others it detracted.

The few men in attendance sometimes laughed, but for the most part they waited for the Boss's approval. They had to make certain their sense of humor didn't incite the General Secretary of the Central Committee of the Communist Party of the Soviet Union, for Stalin had been known to scream denunciations at whoever's laughter was off key. The commissar of cinema had found himself the brunt of the Boss's tirades on more than one occasion solely based upon the movie he decided to display. But tonight Stalin made the selection himself.

General Nikishov also laughed for another reason. He laughed because he thought by morning he would be denounced and brought before a special court, and the following day he would either be shot or strangled in Lubyanka Prison here in Moscow.

This was no surprise to him. He had lived with the expectation of sudden assassination for most of his adult life. He justified the liberties he took in Siberia because of that fear. It seemed the men here in Moscow behaved similarly. The members of the Politburo surrounding him at the moment all had great quantities of blood on their hands, as well as great houses and appetites.

Compared to them, Nikishov was an amateur and poor. And so he laughed. What else was there to do?

He laughed also because there was another possibility. High-ranking generals in the NKVD and of the party had denounced him in Siberia, and as the government was between formal purges, he was simply encouraged to slit his wrists. But he didn't want to die, and so he didn't do so. His real crime was not that he built himself a dacha with state money and made a mistress of the female guard, but that he had backed the wrong group of generals in a bid for power within the ranks of the NKVD itself.

In response to his failure to die, he fully expected to be tortured to death. Instead he was sent to the United States, and now he was back in Russia at the behest of Gromyko. But in his experience, the politics of the people didn't work in this way.

Sitting here with the members of the Politburo and Stalin, watching American movies, he imagined this night was his last: the Boss had a low tolerance for intrigue and seemed to know and suspect everything.

Just then Stalin looked over his shoulder with a great grin. He reached up over the back of the plush red seat and pushed General Nikishov's knee, laughing as Chaplin began to shout the movie's final dialogue. Stalin laughed all the more when Chaplin said, in a comic reversal of the real Hitler, "Soldiers! Don't fight for slavery – fight for liberty!" and went on to describe how men could free themselves from tyranny through shared humanity and democracy.

"Yes," Stalin said. "Yes. He is very funny, no?"

Nikishov nodded his head in compliance, but was as frightened of the movie's subject as he was of the circumstances under which he was here. For most of the movie, Chaplin could as easily have been mocking Stalin as he was Hitler, and he couldn't understand why the Boss would want to sit through this kind of film.

Nikishov smiled back at Stalin and laughed, slightly. Stalin turned to the silver screen and commenced chuckling, then coughed some of the smoke from his cigarette. Nikishov shifted his eyes from Stalin, who was still coughing, to the screen. He noticed that to his left Lavrentiy Beria was observing him through round pince-nez spectacles that reflected the movie screen. Nikishov smiled and Beria smirked. He was the chief of the NKVD, and after Stalin, was the most murderous man in the country. When Nikishov was asked to kill himself, he was made to believe that the order came from Beria.

Beria was also a notorious sexual predator. He drove around Moscow in his limo and had his NKVD guards pull innocent women off the streets. They were brought to his mansion, where they feasted. Then he took the girls to his room and raped them. Another NKVD general told Nikishov that Beria would stand before the girls and say, "You can scream or not, it does not affect my performance." In the morning the girls were released and given a bouquet of flowers to signify their acceptance of his rape, unless they weren't released. In such instances the NKVD planted them in Beria's wife's garden.

Soon the movie ended. They could hear the projector above clicking as it spun. Then some distortions appeared on the screen as the house lights came up. When this happened, the Boss stood in his stark white uniform. The rest of the group stood as well. Stalin said graciously, "I have dinner ready at the *near dacha* at ten." He then walked up the aisle, followed by two of his *attachments*, as they called his guards.

When the Boss was gone, Nikita Khrushchev, hero of Stalingrad, turned and said, "I trust you have room in your car?" he was looking a Beria. Beria nodded. Khrushchev sipped from the glass in his hand, then he followed the Boss out. The other Politburo members filed out accordingly, stopping at the doors to converse with the commissar of cinema in the lobby.

Nikishov was left sitting alone in the Kremlin Theater beside Beria. He was no stranger to violence, but he had never seen a crueler, more predatory glare than was on him now.

Maybe they won't even bother to denounce me, he thought?

"Did you enjoy living in America?" Beria said suddenly. He was leaning forward, observing Nikishov.

"No."

"Why?"

"The Americans are corrupt people."

"Yes. And your work?" he said, lighting a cigarette.

"I think I was . . . useful."

"Useful?" Beria repeated the word as though its meaning were in question.

"Yes."

"With Gromyko."

"Yes."

"Oh."

Nikishov wanted to turn away, but was afraid to look evasive or rude. And Beria was happy to leave the General in discomfort while he remained silent.

Beria puffed his cigarette. Then he said, "Yes, but there is a lot of money in America, no?"

"Yes."

"But in Russia we don't have any money. The only money we have comes from the Americans."

Nikishov froze.

Beria paused for a long moment and then said, "You will come with me now. I have something to show you."

"Yes."

Beria hadn't waited to hear his response. Instead he walked down the row of seats to the other aisle that ran the left side of the theater. Nikishov followed him. He slowed as he approached the doors leading to the lobby. The other entrance where the commissar of cinema stood was lighted, this was one was not. There was no need to light both entrances with so few people in attendance. Ahead were two sets of doors with an eight-foot space between that acted as a sound barrier. The first set of doors stood open, while the second was closed. In the dark space between the two Nikishov could see the outline of a man.

When he saw the man he wanted to run in the other direction. But he didn't know the layout of the building, and leaving through one of the doors by the screen would only take him deeper into the Presidium building where the theater was housed. Running would also prove his guilt. And so he braced himself as he passed between the doors. The man standing there smelled heavily of cigarettes and cognac, but he did not move as Nikishov passed him.

In a moment, they were out in the openness of the lobby and alone again. He took a breath.

"What was that, comrade?"

"Nothing," Nikishov said. He could feel his armpits sweating.

They continued out of the lobby and through the Presidium doors and onto the street, still within the Kremlin walls, just in time to see Stalin and Khrushchev's limos leaving with the others through the gate under the massive two hundred foot tall Spasskaya Tower.

At the foot of the stone stairs leading to the curb idled an American made limo with two guards standing beside it. Beria simply waved his hand and walked toward the Spasskaya Tower on his own. The guards looked at each other. Then the limo started to follow behind.

Ahead Nikishov and Beria walked together through the covered red-brick gate where the *Image Not Made by Hands* was once housed, and the tower clock above kept official Moscow time below the great red star at the apex of the hipped fifteenth-century roof.

The limo rolled quietly beside them. One of the thuggish guards strolled along with his right hand inside his jacket pocket.

The sentry standing in the tower simply waved Beria and Nikishov through the gate. The limo followed closely behind. Nikishov had no idea what Beria was up to. He might have him shot in the street and claim he was stealing state secrets. Maybe this was how it would be done. One never knew, and government murderers never lacked for flair and creativity.

On the other side of the gate they entered Red Square and came face to face with the building without antecedent: St. Basil's Cathedral. In the dim lights of the street and the glow of Moscow and the three quarter moon above, the building shone like a multi-spired fire. Its redbrick and brightly colored and contrasting onion domes shone like lacquered Faberge Eggs in the night sky.

"Come, follow me," Beria said, and picked up the pace toward the iconic cathedral. Nikishov jogged to keep up, unsure of himself in a palpable way that tasted like bile.

They crossed a street in front of the Kremlin wall and were standing at the foot of the covered stair leading into the cathedral. It was a museum now, owned by the state. Once Stalin had even tried to tear it down to make room for parades in Red Square. The chief architect, however, refused. Miraculously, he wasn't killed, but spent six years in camp with the rest of his countrymen.

They ascended the stairs together while the guards kept their distance behind them. The masonry was covered with Eastern art that reminded Nikishov of his youth, before the atheist iconoclasts sterilized the country. Oddly, when the Great Patriotic War with the Nazi National Socialists began, Stalin reinstated the church in Russia, cynically, as the "opiate of the people" to see them through their trial, and the building was now safe once again.

At the top of the stairs they exited the North Porch and entered the Church of the Entry of the Lord into Jerusalem. This was the only chapel, of the many within St. Basil's Cathedral, that Nikishov knew the name of. He remembered it from boyhood, with the story of how Ivan the Terrible had built the church and it's multiple chapels, each in commemoration of a victory over the Kazan Khanate; one of the dynasties of Genghis Khan.

But Nikishov had no opportunity to stop and appreciate the art and architecture of the wondrous building. Beria was in a hurry, and pushed on through that chapel into a round one bathed in moonlight from an upper window, and then through a dark and cold passage into another octagonal chapel with Christ Pantocrator emblazoned on the masonry vaulted ceiling. He then turned behind a rusticated column and moved up a staircase inhabiting the space between rooms.

At the top, Beria looked back at Nikishov, "Come on," he said, and slipped down a narrow and drafty corridor.

Nikishov looked up at the man above him on the top of the stairs and did as he was told. But as he neared the top he heard footsteps on the stone floor somewhere he couldn't locate and almost lost his nerve. Only muscle memory kept him moving onward. He was now convinced that he was going to die. They entered a dark chapel with yellow light coming from another room. Inside Nikishov turned to see that the light was coming from a dead-end corridor. This hall was without religious decoration, and was faced only with geometric symbols and designs in a way that looked like Islamic art merged with the Eastern Church. On the wall to his left hung a flaming lantern. Beyond the lantern and at the terminus of the hall leaned a large oil painting of Ivan the Terrible himself. The painting glistened under the torchlight, which gave his skin a lifelike, livid appearance. In front of the painting stood Andrei Gromyko.

Chapter Forty-Nine

Lamp Light

Foggy Bottom, Washington D.C.
March 2, 1945

He wasn't prepared for what he was going to do.

He left Snows Court that morning earlier than usual because he wasn't able to sleep, and he couldn't bear sitting in his apartment alone. Though there was no reason for him to hurry, he found himself walking faster than usual and arriving at Leonard's in record time.

When the bell above the door rang, signaling his entrance, the waitress avoided catching his eye. It seemed to him as if she had anticipated his arrival and didn't care to see him. He reflected on the fact that she had always been a lousy waitress – at least now he knew why. He also knew that the Secret Service had arrested her in the car outside Cayce's house on the night he was murdered, and wondered why she would still be in the field.

"You look terrible this morning," Leonard observed as Sparks approached the counter and picked up his morning coffee. "Are ya sick?"

"No, just stress" Sparks said, forgetting about the waitress altogether.

"Yeah, well, tell me about it," Leonard responded looking at her. "They're putting the screws to you too, huh?"

"Something like that."

Sparks then said goodbye and walked outside with a cup of coffee in his hand. Looking to his right toward I Street, where the Russian GRU had its apartment, he tried to imagine what they were doing there this morning. Then he thought about his own apartment and its proximity to these men. He assumed that if the GRU wanted him they could get him, whether or not they held an apartment down the street.

What bothered him more than anything was that the CIA knew where he lived – that they knew him at all. He wished he'd never taken the drive up to New Haven. He would have finished out his time for the president, maybe with some misgivings, but then he could have gone back to Texas, or applied to law school, and would have still had his friend.

At least then he wouldn't be trapped in this intelligence web. But he wanted to help his country. He kept telling himself that, echoing what Angleton said some nights before when he handed off the package. These guys loved their covert talk. But now they wanted more, and they were expecting him to pull it off.

He was worried. The president had been cool toward him ever since they returned from the Argonaut Conference. And there was more. The agency had Sparks photograph some of the president's papers which he had been entrusted by Wallace to take to the White House incinerator. They were memos from Lauchlin mostly, but there was also correspondence with Andrei Gromyko and a few unsigned documents. These seemed to imply that the president knew of the Russian military presence in the United States and approved. After seeing those, many people in the CIA, and certainly Forrestal and Angleton, more fully made up their minds that Wallace was in some way working in tandem with the Russians in America. They just didn't know what he was up to. Nor did they know what to do about it. He had felt a sense of fear from both Angleton and Forrestal when he last saw them.

These papers left open the question for Sparks of the GRU apartment and its connection with Wallace. If those men knew about Sparks' link with the CIA, and it jeopardized their operation, what would happen to him?

But he put the thought from his mind, deciding to believe that they didn't know. In the end he told himself that Wallace wouldn't suspect him at all, or wouldn't let them hurt him. *He's my friend*, he thought, but then again, *you're his friend.*

Soon he was entering the West Wing from street level. He looked up at the White House shell in the background; workman were already preparing for their day rebuilding the roof. He stopped and took a breath. Then he entered.

There was a guard on the door he wasn't familiar with. Sparks showed his credentials.

"You're early today," the Agent said looking at the log.

"A lot of work," he replied.

The man waved him on, but it made him nervous to see this strange face here today of all days. Again, he wondered if they knew.

Down the hall, he entered the small office full of cubicles where he worked. There was still a speech he needed to finish and he began working on it without delay. There was no one in his office bank yet, so he read out loud to find the right cadence to put on paper. After over an hour of reworking this late draft he felt satisfied. Sometime after 8:30 AM, Wallace called him in.

Sparks walked down the hall toward the Oval Office. He was sweating. He approached the desk just before the Oval Office door, and Myrtle, the temp, waved him in. He nodded to her, and she smiled.

"How are you today, Jon," the president called from across the room.

"I'm well, sir." The distance between them was obvious.

"I'm going to take Ellery with me over to the museum this morning," he said this as quickly as possible; as if it were just an unpleasantness they had to get beyond. And then he smiled and said: "Dr. Berk ran a few tests for me he was unable to run before." He leaned further back in his oversized leather chair. "He's as interested in the stone as I am now, which is fascinating because he has such a hard scientific mind that you'd imagine objects with a mystical background wouldn't pique his interest. But I guess, as you get older, the realities of history become more important to you. I want to have the stone catalogued with every test science can offer. I still haven't decided what to do with it."

Sparks frowned when he thought how simple that problem seemed compared to the confusion that faced him now.

Then the president looked up and said, "What's the matter, Jon?"

He hesitated and said, "I was just thinking of the speech, and comparing Southern segregation with South African apartheid."

"Yes?"

"Do you think people, your audience, will even know what that is?"

"I want to make sure we get across how wrong and anti-American segregation is down there. I think comparing it to a foreign vestige of colonialism may help show how alien it is, even if they don't exactly know what apartheid is. They'll know it's foreign and bad. That might be enough."

Sparks agreed with the president on this: the fact that apartheid was alien and bad was enough to get the point across.

Then they parted ways. Sparks returned to his cubicle. He had already finished the speech so he had nothing to do now but to wait. The fact that the president was taking Ellery with him might work to Sparks' advantage, but that depended on Agent Dunbar. It also let Sparks know that the president no longer trusted him, and this fact bothered him, even though what he was doing was certainly untrustworthy.

The phone rang. It was Dunbar calling from the front entrance. "He's entering the limo," he said. "I took the opportunity to clear the room." He hung up.

Dunbar wasn't referring to the Oval Office. He meant that the Security Room was empty. This room usually housed one or two stand-by Secret Service agents. There was only one on duty today, and Dunbar had him pulled off to check a rigged breach on the construction site. This meant that Sparks could enter the Oval Office through the security room, which connected to the dining room, then through a breezeway and study to the Oval Office, bypassing Myrtle.

He held onto the phone receiver for a few moments after Dunbar hung up, feeling as he had when he was in the South Pacific before an engagement, but he didn't have time to dwell on his mental state; it would only be so long before the agent returned from the construction site. Sparks then ducked outside the cubicle and saw Agent Chipton turning the corner to walk away. Now was the time.

He crossed the hall and entered the Security Room. In the cabinet by the door he picked up the heavy brass lamp that was a replica of the one on the president's desk. This was as far as Dunbar could safely smuggle the lamp without attracting attention to himself. Agent Dunbar claimed that if he was able to pull the Agent out of the security room then he needed someone else to switch the lamps. This is where Sparks came in.

At least that's how Angleton described the operation to him. Sparks felt he had no choice. Dunbar had worked quickly and taken advantage of the unexpected opportunity. The switch was actually planned for after the president returned from the museum. At that point, Wallace was slated to attend a conference in the narrow Press Briefing room just off the West Colonnade. But since the president had taken Ellery rather than Sparks to the museum, Dunbar took the opportunity and created the diversion. They explained this might happen; that Dunbar could use the "advantage of circumstance" to execute the mission. And this is what he had done.

Now Sparks was going through with it. He opened the door and peered into the dining room. His hands were clammy against the lamp's metal surface. He hesitated a moment longer, then passed through the dining room and into the small study and paused. He could back out now. On the other side of the door might be an ambush waiting to catch him. *They knew!*

But he pushed the curved Oval Office door open anyway, and found the room on the other side empty, as they'd said it would be. He then moved as quickly as possible to the desk where he set the replica beside the original. He pushed Wallace's chair back and jumped beneath the desk, where the gold colored lamp cord was plugged into one of a bundle of outlets on the floor. He unplugged the cord, and reached up and fed the new one through the hole in the desk and plugged it in. Then he fed the old cord out through the same hole and removed the lamp. It was such a silly and mundane task – swapping one lamp for another – yet if he were caught . . .

He briefly studied the lamp to find where the recording device was. Failing to find it he turned and left. It was over. He paused for a moment, and could hear some movement on the other side of the door where the secretary sat. *Oh God,* he thought, *don't come in here.* With lamp in hand, he ran out of the room and back through the study and dining room into the security room, where he placed the lamp in the same cabinet on which he'd found the other.

Back in his cubicle he sat sweating and doing little exercises to control his breathing. He didn't know why he felt so nervous about what just happened.

That's when there was a knock on the door.

He poked his head up over the drab green cubicle wall to see who was there, and standing in the open door from the hallway was the temp secretary, Myrtle.

"I'm grabbing some coffee," she said, "want me to pick you up something?"

"Coffee will be fine," he said. He hoped she would just go away, but she lingered. He looked down at his desk as if he was doing something important.

She continued, "My uncle owns a little restaurant not far from here. I was going there for dinner after work, I thought maybe you'd like to go?" She looked nervous. It was an endearing look on her. But tonight wouldn't work for him.

"No, not tonight. It just won't work for me. Not that I don't want to. Just not tonight." He felt like he hurt her, and he didn't want that, so he said, "Can we reschedule for next Wednesday? I promise I'll be able to then."

"Sure," she said. Then she left, and Sparks put his head into his hands. He wasn't afraid, he was conflicted. But that's what made this so difficult. His friend – his president – knowingly had connections with the other team's intelligence apparatus. No one was safe. And it brought home the point to him of just how low-down the "revolutionary type" was, but he never would have guessed that Wallace was a *commie*. Several minutes passed, as he debated the point.

"What's he really doing?" he said under his breath and then looked up at the ceiling; when he did so, his eyes passed over the doorway. Myrtle was standing there again, just back from getting coffee. She stepped forward with his drink in her hand in an outfit that accentuated her figure and her legs. "I didn't know how you take it, so I left it black and brought cream and sugar."

"Just black with a little sugar." He took the cup with both hands and tried to keep his eyes off her. "Thank you," he said. Her presence relaxed him. *The way to a man's heart is through his stomach, or maybe it's with a body like that,* he thought. And she was smiling at him in a caring way. He wanted to go away with her and felt some guilt over declining her invitation this evening. In his experience, beautiful woman don't ask men to dinner, and if one did, you'd better not reject her.

That's when she said, "Are you sure you won't come down to my uncle's restaurant tonight?" And the hair stood up on the back of his neck.

Chapter Fifty

Ivan the Terrible

The Kremlin, Moscow
March 2, 1945

"You look nervous, comrade," Beria said. He was peering at Nikishov and smiling. "What did you think was going to happen to you here, in a church?"

"I trust you weren't followed," Gromyko barked, interrupting Beria's antagonism. His words echoed within the windowless stone passage, the purpose of which was unclear or simply unfinished in the layout of the church, though this meeting was probably as good a function as any for the strangely decorated room, in places painted in designs like spiral spider webs. The presence of the wood painting at the end of the hall that captured so well the attributes of the maniacal and paranoid Czar rounded out the effect of the decorations.

"No, I wasn't followed. The Boss is already at the near dacha with some of the others," Beria said. "It's fine. You worry too much, Andrei."

Nikishov was trying to calculate what the relationship between Beria and Gromyko meant. It could mean one thing, but one never knew, and so his best course was to remain silent.

"You look shocked, general," Beria said to Nikishov.

"What is going on?" the general responded in turn.

"What do you think?"

Just then one of Beria's guards moved into the light in the other room. He was holding an M1911 .45 pistol. This was an American handgun that flooded the Russian military as part of Lend-Lease.

"I don't know if you are going to kill me or not," Nikishov said concerned.

"Oh, but Gromyko. Surely you don't think your friend Gromyko would take part in such a plot? He is just."

"That's enough," Gromyko said to Beria. Beira looked stung and angered by the rebuke, but he did not continue talking, and Gromyko stared at him until he was sure that he was finished. Then Gromyko said, "It happens tonight!"

"But I thought . . ." Nikishov said.

"No, it must be this way. Stalin is a god," Ambassador Gromyko began. "If he is openly assassinated the Russian people will not accept it. It has to be a good death. No one can know. You can enter the *near dacha* tonight . . ."

"I will take you with me," Beria interrupted. "Stalin is eager to speak with you about America. He secretly loves America, but he is greedy to keep their deals to himself, and in his madness he plots war against them."

"What do you want me to do?" Nikishov said.

"You'll poison him of course," Beria replied. He was smiling. "The members of the Politburo all want to see him die. No one will scrutinize what happens and the doctors will never go against our word. It will be more dangerous to know than not to know, and so we will decide that he died of natural causes and that will be the case. Though who becomes the Boss afterward? That is the question."

"No one again," Gromyko said.

"Yes, and you would make a fair leader Gromyko. I know that. But you are working out a plot to kill a man; that is the easy part. Power, Andrei, power is a more slippery creature. You can't control what will happen, even with American money."

Ivan the Terrible peered at them from his oil prison. He was standing on a royal staircase in a gown and high white collar. His beard was unkempt and his eyes were full of hate.

"I can try," Gromyko continued.

"Yes, well. For now, and if you want to try then we all have to go to the Boss's dacha together."

"But Stalin doesn't like surprises," Gromyko said. "Why should I go? How will you explain my presence?"

"I have brought friends before. It is of no account to him. He likes the company and most officials don't want to go anymore. He likes to set the menu with his cook, and he always has enough for extra guests now," Beria was looking at the painting of Ivan the Terrible as though he were reading it and scratching his chin. "He won't expect you've come to kill him. He has nearly three hundred men guarding his *near dacha*, no one would try to kill him there, Andrei." He suddenly had the look of a man who's had an epiphany, and he looked down at the floor away from Ivan the Terrible. "The power will be decided very quickly when he expires. Despite the money you've spent in the Kremlin, it will still be a roll of the dice afterward." He said the word "money" as though it disgusted him.

Gromyko ignored his comrade's contempt and said, "And you've brought the poison?"

"Yes, of course, it's in the limo."

"But how will you get him to ingest it?"

"As long as Nikishov is willing to do what I tell him, then it will be easy. You trust me."

And the group of conspirators made their way back out of the chapel. On the North Porch, Gromyko stopped and said, "I don't like changes in the plan, Lavrentiy. Why call me here, if you were just going to bring me to the *near dacha*? What is Stalin planning?"

"Where else would I meet you, comrade? Don't let what you are doing make you suspicious; you won't need to get your hands dirty. I promise. That's what we have the general for. If you want to decide what happens afterward, then you will you need to be there. Or else I will decide, and Khrushchev and Molotov alone. If you are afraid of Stalin, then how can you presume to assassinate him?"

Chapter Fifty-One

The Security Room

The West Wing, Washington D.C.
March 2, 1945

At that moment he wanted to ask her who she worked for, but he knew she would just play dumb and hurt, and flash her eyes at him. She'd played her hand too heavily, though. Women like her don't ask you to dinner repeatedly in a single day.

He went along with her game, saying only, "I really have a lot of work, Myrtle. I'd love to, but I can't." He realized he must have struck a false note because her expression changed. Or maybe she just felt anger at his rejection? Whatever it was she felt, she backed out of the room without another word.

When she left, he looked down at the paper cup of coffee she'd brought him. He pulled the lid back and took a whiff. It sure smelled like coffee. Then he walked to the small sink in the back of the room where several others were now working and dumped it out. *You really have gone crazy*, he thought. *But who the hell is she?*

He knew who could find the answer and left the office for the Security Room to find the Secret Service Agent stationed there, assuming the agent had returned from the wild goose chase Dunbar had sent him on.

Not bothering to knock, he entered. Agent Chipton sat at the long table inside filling out paper work.

"Chipton?" Sparks said with some surprise.

"That's me."

"I thought you were prowling around the halls today."

"They switched me in here for the afternoon, after Robinson ran out to the residence for something. Why, who did you want to see?"

"What I want is to find out about the temp secretary who's working in the Oval Office. Who is she? Where'd she come from?"

"You know you could just ask her on a date?"

"I got the impression she's not who she says she is, that's all."

"You already went on a date with her?" Chipton said with a smile.

"Just look her up, would you?"

"Yeah, sure." Chipton pushed the rolling office chair he was sitting in to the wall where a large file cabinet sat. "You said she's a temp?"

"Yeah."

"Who'd she take over for?"

"Betty."

"Oh, that's right. She's right here," Chipton said pointing to the file he'd just pulled from the second drawer. "Betty Getry, she's been in the hospital now with stomach ulcers for two months; had some problems late last year with the same thing. We've got the report from the hospital," Chipton said.

"And what about Myrtle?"

"Myrtle, Myrtle. Smith. Myrtle Smith. She worked on a farm out in the sticks before she came to D.C., then she started working for the Starlight Temp Agency," he said holding up the thin folder. "I have a list of the dates she temped on."

"Who vets the girls over at the agency?"

"FBI. We would have interviewed her after that. That's here."

"So she works for the FBI then?"

"I think you better tell me what you know," Chipton said.

"I don't know anything, but Betty's in the hospital with stomach ulcers and the temp agency sent this girl with almost no practical experience to work for the president. And she just asked me to dinner today, twice."

"What do you mean, like you told her "no," and she came back and asked again?"

"That's exactly what I mean."

"Well, that is something Sparks, because you're not a good looking man. But it would be pretty stupid for the FBI to spy on the president. The chances we'd find out are pretty high, in which case they would have just fired the opening shot in a war with the Secret Service and the president. I don't see what they stand to gain. We might try and find out though. Her lack of experience alone's enough to start asking her some questions."

"We can do that?" Sparks asked.

"No *we* – I can do that. And yeah, everyone who works here is subject to questioning."

"What do I do then?"

"You listen! We're going to take her downstairs. We have a room for this. You can sit outside and watch. There's a speaker there so you can listen to what goes on."

"No. Not good enough. There's no reason I can't sit in on this."

"Not a chance. I'll call over to Dunbar and have him pick her up – he loves interrogations – but you're not sitting in. You're lucky I even suggested you could sit outside the room. Chances are good she doesn't know anything worth writing home about. Then again, she might know things you're not supposed to know. We'll call up the FBI to see what they know, and we'll ask her questions based on what they have." He stopped and said. "We'll get what we're looking for."

Sparks nodded in agreement.

Chipton picked up his radio from the table. "Agent Dunbar?" he said.

They waited for Dunbar's response. There was some static. As Sparks looked over at the cabinet where he'd placed the lamp, the radio crackled with Dunbar's voice, "Yes?"

"We need to see you down here in the security room."

"I'm walking the hall by the Press Corps offices. I'll be there in two."

Chipton looked over to Sparks and said again, laughing, "Dunbar loves interrogations. He acts like it's his purpose in life."

"Well, that's comforting."

The door opened and Dunbar leaned in, but when he saw Sparks first he turned to Chipton with a look of confusion.

"What's this?" he asked.

"Oh, Mr. Sparks here thinks the temp for the Oval Office is a spy."

"I never said she was a spy."

"Well, her behavior caught his eye."

"I bet it did," Dunbar said as he closed the door to the security room. "This joker's had eyes for . . ."

"Be that as it may," Chipton said, as he suppressed laughter, "I looked at her file and she had no experience prior to her White House assignment. Far as I can tell this is her first job. The FBI's supposed to vet the girls at the agency so I want to see what they have."

"I still don't see why she's suspicious?"

"She was acting suspiciously, trying to get the president's aide to go to dinner with her."

"That is funny," Dunbar joked.

"You guys are a regular comedy team. You should work the circuit."

Chipton looked back to Sparks, "Hey, you brought this to me. You thought it was strange." He turned back to Dunbar who was impatiently standing by the door, "Go pull Miss Myrtle off her desk and bring her downstairs. In the meantime, I'll stroll over to Reynolds and let him know, then I'll call the FBI."

"Ok."

Chipton walked out of the Security Room in the direction of the front desk where Reynolds was sitting in the Booth. When he was gone, Dunbar shut the door and turned to Sparks and said, "Good job, by the way. We're getting audio from the lamp."

"Girl's not with you, is she?" Sparks asked.

"Not that I know of."

Chapter Fifty-Two

The Near Dacha

Kuntstevo, Moscow
March 2, 1945

The American limousine drove slowly through the forest. The car had left Moscow's outskirts minutes ago and was nearing its destination. Inside, Gromyko sat solemnly facing rearward holding a piece of the car's fine crystal into which Beria had insisted on pouring a shot of cognac, while Nikishov drank vodka (he had declined the cognac) and watched as the forest slowly passed by his window.

Nikishov knew the Germans had made it this far in the battle for Moscow a few years prior, but they had been repelled. The fact that Stalin kept a second home here was all the more reason for the Red Army to fight hard for their country and their leader's estates. And while the *near dacha*, or *Blizhnaya*, was well known among party members, its exact location was held a state secret. Nikishov had always been curious to get a glimpse of the mysterious house.

As they approached the tall black gate, Nikishov saw the iron perimeter fence wind away from the road through the forest in either direction. Within, he spotted lights spaced equidistantly and assumed these were guard posts that encircled the house.

He looked down the fence line as the driver rolled down the front window. The guard advanced and asked for the names of the passengers. Without saying a word the driver simply drew down the electric rear windows. When the guard saw Beria there, he instantly pulled his flash-light out of the interior and nodded, apologetically.

Beria scowled and poked the intercom button beside him. "Windows up!" And the windows went up.

They were now within a double fence, and from what Nikishov could see, there were posts every fifty yards or so all along the dead zone be-tween parallel fences. The car drove a hundred feet farther and stopped for the second gate.

At this gate there was another small guardhouse, in back of which sat what looked like barracks with an anti-aircraft gun on the roof. The guard at this gate held a red phone to his ear in the lighted booth and simply waved them along without making eye contact.

Nikishov sipped his vodka, and then sipped again.

"Relax, comrade. These are my soldiers," Beria said as he patted Nikishov on the chest.

"We're all Stalin's soldiers," Nikishov replied, "even you."

"Well. . ." Beria began but Ambassador Gromyko laughed across from him and cut him off, "Stalin could call these men to shoot you, and they would do it too. But if you called for them to shoot him, Beria, then they would shoot you as well."

"I called you here," Beria shouted.

"You are only part of something else in motion, don't pretend this is your doing!" Gromyko barked.

"How will you kill him then without me?"

Gromyko didn't respond, and Nikishov sat looking out the window. Ahead he saw the house approaching. The bright lights posted around the driveway showed that the house was green: the trim, the windows, the soffit, the siding and faux columns, all were a dark forest green. The house itself had an imperial bearing; two stories, lacking almost all ornamentation; but there was a sense of classical order in its design. This order described the Boss as well: he wasn't the new man the socialists had talked about creating; instead he was a creature of history, with one foot behind the seminary walls of the ornate past – a 20th century Russian Czar, who lived every bit as sumptuously while the country starved. The only difference was that now the people couldn't admit they were starving, or the reasons behind it. Still, the war helped from one perspective, for those who weren't killed, because it brought American money and materiel.

The car came to a stop at the low front steps leading up to the entrance. There were two other American made limos parked off to the side of the driveway. Nikishov was reluctant to move.

"Don't forget who brought you here; who organized this," Beria said. Neither man spoke. Then he said, "Here we go," and lifted up the armrest he had been leaning on. Beneath it, on the seat, was a small brown leather bag. He unzipped the pouch and removed a glass dropper with a red rubber stopper. "This," he said holding up the bottle, "You can pour it into his mouth or his nose or his ear when he sleeps."

"And how will I do that?" General Nikishov said.

"Or his drink!" Beria replied laughing. "A little joke." But when he saw that Nikishov wasn't laughing he added, "Patience, General. I will make you the time. Don't worry." He slapped the potion into the general's palm and opened the door. The men poured out of the car after replacing their glasses on the shelf behind the front seat. They all stood together in the cool night air and watched Stalin throw open his massive front doors and step onto the stone landing. He had changed his outfit and was wearing an all beige uniform. He reminded Nikishov of one of his statues.

The men held their breath as one when they saw him. Each knew that the Boss was a volatile man; he changed as quickly as the weather. Often beads of sweat formed on his forehead as he grew more and more enraged. Anything could displease him. He had a projectionist at the theater shot for breaking the projector. He called the man an "assassin" for spilling deadly mercury in the film booth. Life and death in Russia were decided on the whims of the old lunatic.

Now Nikishov felt as though he was shrinking as the Boss stood atop the steps with the lights flooding behind him. He looked like some kind of deity, as he did in the propaganda movies he had made of himself. Nikishov had also killed men and was as remorseless as the next NKVD officer, but this man of steel was the center of the maelstrom. He was death itself – his bad humor alone could have a man murdered and erased from the official records, as he had done to Beria's predecessor at NKVD. Nikolai Yezhov executed the Great Purge for the Boss. And when the work was finished Yezhov was killed and blamed for the severity of the purges. He was a man who had exceeded his usefulness. Only Stalin got to decide when that point was reached. He went so far as to have his censors erase Yezhov from the official photographic records as best they could.

They were now facing the man who could blot you out.

But Stalin's arms were outstretched and a smile broke across his face as though these three were his long lost brothers, back from war in a faraway land.

"Is that Gromyko," he shouted. "Andrei! Brother!" He rushed down the stairs to embrace his ambassador. "You should have called before," he said hugging him. Then he turned and saw the general, "And Nikishov. You are my Americans. You have to tell me more about the country. I only see their movies."

Beria put on almost as big a show of affection as Stalin did. Nikishov was horrified by the totality of his deception. Stalin embraced Beria saying, "Where did you find old Gromyko this evening?"

"He was leaving the Kremlin grounds as I walked from the Presidium. I thought it was proper to ask him along, comrade. Considering we had Nikishov here?"

The Boss's eye remained fixed on Beria for a moment. Then he said, "Good, good. Let's go in. We have a feast tonight. Georgian Kharcho with lamb. I know you will like it, Lavrentiy."

"My mother would make it, comrade. And the only way is with lamb. Beef or chicken, this is not true Kharcho. Not for the 'Son of the Mountain.'"

"No!" Stalin shouted with a smile, "No!" he said gripping Beria's hands tightly in his own. "Come! Let us drink and eat. Molotov and the others are already inside."

Chapter Fifty-Three

Interrogation

The West Wing Basement, Washington D.C.
March 2, 1945

She was crying now. The blue mascara running from the corner of her eyes nearly reached the bottom of her chin. She hadn't bothered to wipe it away. But she was very beautiful, and there was something about her pathetic state that made Sparks want to run to her. He assumed Chipton felt the same way because he made several side comments about the Minnesotan's love of interrogation. Both men remained seated behind the two-way mirror in the West Wing basement watching Dunbar work alone.

"None of us believes you're innocent," Dunbar said, his voice echoing through the small speaker on the wall in the viewing room where Chipton and Sparks sat. "So you can drop the act, ok. It's tiresome. No one's coming to your rescue."

Sparks felt anger bubble up inside him, but he controlled it. He was angry at Dunbar's smug tone, and he was also angry with himself for turning her in like this. Just to look at her was to know she was innocent.

She stopped crying suddenly and said, "I want my attorney!" She was angry. Her blue tears had already dried where they were, in the middle of her cheeks. There was nothing pathetic about her expression now. Sparks was almost shocked at how quickly she reigned in her emotions.

"You see, that's going to be a problem since this is wartime and you're a spy," Dunbar said in an icy Midwestern voice.

"We have a Constitution!" she shouted.

"It doesn't apply to you, today."

She considered what he said. Then she asked, "Do you have something I could wipe my face with?"

Dunbar smiled and handed her a towel from a table behind him. "I always bring towels to one of these. You never know what's going to happen."

She smirked at him when he handed her the folded, white facecloth. Sparks was mesmerized by what was taking place in front of him on the other side of the mirror. And because he saw it through glass, it was as though it were happening in a movie studio somewhere in Burbank, California.

Then the yellow light on the phone beside him lit up. There was no ringer. Sparks taped Chipton on the shoulder and Chipton stood and put the call over the speaker.

Special Agent Mark Fisker of the FBI was on the other end. Chipton had been waiting for this call. "From what we can see," Fisker began, "nobody vetted her. She slid right through."

"Is that the way you normally run the vetting process on your end?" Chipton asked.

"What about on your end?" Fisker replied angrily.

"In this case we did a verbal since we thought you G-men had it covered. But for you guys, is her case typical, a mistake, what?"

"I've never seen it go down like that before. I can't say with any confidence who she really is or may be, her file shows no background interview or any look into her past or associations. The family she claimed to come from in Union Bridge, Maryland doesn't exist, as far as we've found so far."

"Could it have been an oversight?"

"Highly unlikely. There's no real way for an employee file to get passed to the next level without going through the review process first. Somebody put her on the top of the list."

"Who?"

"We think she was sleeping with one of our department supervisors, and he took her file up ladder. Don't know for sure yet."

"Who?" Chipton asked again.

"I can't tell you that," Fisker said.

Chipton wanted to shout but held his voice as he didn't want the sound to travel through the mirror and alert the suspect. Instead he talked in a harsh whisper. "There's no way in hell you're not going to tell us who did it. We take precedence here. This is the president's personal secretary, and you yahoos sent us someone without a history."

"His name's Ed Markey. Been with the bureau almost twelve years. I guess he was lonely. But we don't know for sure yet, we only just brought him in in the last hour. He was likely the only one who could've done it."

"We want him."

"You can't have him. We may have dropped the ball on this, Chipton, but you don't get to interrogate our people."

"It's not going to work like that Fisker! There's five Secret Service personnel on their way over to you as we speak. Three of 'em are lawyers. They're going to want to talk to your boy."

"Fine, we'll continue our interrogation until then, and if anything turns up we'll call back right away. I'll try this line first."

Chipton thanked Agent Fisker and hung up the phone. Then he looked over to Sparks. "Someone on the inside passed her through the system." Sparks nodded his head, but he was still thinking about how she had changed from a scared and defenseless creature to an angry and aggressive one in the blink of an eye.

"Did you hear me?" Chipton said.

"I heard you. I heard him say it, too," Sparks said without looking. He was staring at Myrtle.

Then Chipton jotted the information he had just received from the FBI down on a piece of paper in bullet points. He stuck the paper into a green folder. "Stay here," he drawled.

"That looks official now," Sparks added.

Chipton pursed his lips and walked into the interrogation chamber.

Dunbar looked up as Chipton entered, and then his gaze moved to the mirror in the exact spot where Sparks sat. Dunbar's glance made Sparks wonder if he was at least partially visible in the darkened room. The thought made him lean away from the glass.

When Dunbar read the note in the file, he gave one nod and turned back to his suspect. Chipton, in turn, closed the door and leaned against the wall, holding the folder in front of him like a shield. His elbow partially blocked Sparks' view, and so he shifted his seat to the right to compensate.

"Myrtle, Myrtle, Myrtle," Dunbar began slowly. "You had to know that we were going to ask the FBI about you." He paused and said, "Now, why don't you tell me and Agent Chipton here exactly how you got lonely old Ed Markey to pass you through the system?"

"I really don't know what you're talking about. I'm just a temp," Myrtle said.

"No, you're a lot more than that; don't sell yourself short. You should be proud of your work. You got a little sloppy with Sparks upstairs, but honey, we were already on you."

She laughed when he said that. "You would have brought me in before if you suspected something."

"Maybe so, but we have you here now. And the thing is, now that we have Ed, this thing you were doing constitutes a conspiracy. So now there are all manner of crimes we can tag you with."

"I can't tell you anything," she said, beginning to lose composure again.

"Oh, come on, Myrtle, don't think you're going to start crying and melt my old heart. It's not going to change how I feel, and right now, I feel like putting you in jail. You were spying on the president, and you did so during a war. We might get to hang you; maybe even a firing squad. Those are always festive."

"I can't tell you anything. They'll kill me."

"We might do that too, but unlike the American justice system, whoever it is you're talking about will at least pay you the courtesy of doing it quickly."

"What makes you think they'll make it quick?"

"We can keep you safe. Make some of your crimes disappear. It all depends on what you do. The information we have on you is only going to grow. Right now, whole teams of government workers are digging into your life. Secret Service agents are tossing your apartment. Banking specialists are examining your records. The phone company's turning over any number that you've ever dialed or that's dialed you – with addresses – and a whole swarm of agents are going out to those people's houses to conduct interviews. Based on that information, and more, we're building a web of knowledge on you, and by the end of the week, if not the end of the day, we're going to know who you work for and what you're doing here." Dunbar was now walking around the room as he spoke. Agent Chipton had some trouble concealing his smile. Sparks was starting to feel bad for her again.

The tears started to flow down her face. She sniffled, and Dunbar walked around so he was behind her, leaning over her shoulder. "What I'm trying to explain to you is that if we have to do all the leg work, then we're not going to be so well disposed to helping you out when it comes to sentencing, and the list of things you'll be charged with is only going to grow. In fact, we're pretty sure that we can get you in front of a military tribunal. The benefits of that are clear from our perspective, and it's also in the best interests of the United States to deter this kind of behavior in the future. You ever see a woman shot before?"

"You can't protect me from these people!" she shouted.

"And why is that?"

"Because they are you!" she said, but covered her mouth when she spoke as if she were keeping a germ from spreading.

"How is it me?"

"I don't know."

"I'm sure you know that you're going to have to do better than that."

"I was arrested writing bad checks on a military base not far from here."

"Where?" he asked.

"Camp Peary. I was doing clerical work. And I didn't have money because I was sending it back to my family in Maryland."

"What's the name of the town?"

"Union Bridge."

"Wrong. You gotta tell the truth in this room."

"Just listen to me!" She was crying again, but this time she was scared. Her bottom lip quivered. "I know my family doesn't show up in Union because they're not my real family. Have your people look up the Bullocks if you want to find me."

"How are they not your real family?" Chipton said from the opposite side of the room.

"Just listen to me!"

"We ask the questions," Dunbar said.

"My family died, and I bounced around until the Bullocks adopted me, Ok. Look into them!"

"So you were writing bad checks at a major naval base and then?"

"And then MPs arrested me. They put me in a holding cell for a few days; they wouldn't let me talk to anyone. Then some men came and got me. No one said a word. They drove me into the woods somewhere not far from the barracks. It was like an old town with no one in it. And they offered me a job."

"Would you recognize these men if you saw them again?"

"Of course I would, but they weren't American. Only two men spoke to me, and they both had heavy accents; not German, but Russian, maybe, or something like it." She looked up at Chipton who was jotting down notes. "At Camp Peary I went by my adopted name. But they wanted me to revert to my given name: Smith. They knew everything about me, and the money was five times what I was making."

"Then how'd you get your file through the FBI. Was it Ed Markey?"

"I don't have any idea. They gave me the job. That's all I know."

Dunbar had crossed back to the other side of the table. "Who's they?" he asked.

"The Nightingale, but I don't know. Someone said that once, outside the room. I never knew names. They came to me. They'd be in my apartment at night asking questions. One time there was an American voice, a northerner, and he said: 'we can take the Nightingales off?' But the other man said 'no.' so I thought of them as the Nightingales."

"What did the American mean: 'we can take the Nightingales off?'"

"He was in my hallway. He didn't come in. I think he was pressuring them to get more from me. Like they weren't doing a good enough job."

Dunbar continued asking her questions, but Chipton left the room.

He closed the door behind him and stopped in his tracks when he saw that Sparks was holding his head in his hands. "What's the matter with you?" Chipton said.

But just then the door to the hallway leading to the basement sprang open and President Wallace stepped through it. Ellery was behind him.

The president entered. "What are you doing interrogating my staff?"

"Sir, it's protocol . . ."

"I don't give a good God damn what your protocol says." Then he rushed past Chipton and opened the door to the interrogation chamber.

"Oh, God," Myrtle said, still with blue smudges of mascara on her cheeks.

"Mr. President," Dunbar spoke up.

Chipton entered the room behind the president. Sparks remained where he was, watching through the two-way mirror, though he did look over his shoulder for a second to acknowledge Ellery in the hallway.

Chapter Fifty-Four

The Theft

The West Wing Basement, Washington D.C.
March 2, 1945

"I want to know why you think you have the authority to drag my people into interrogations?" Wallace was standing beside Myrtle, who had begun to shed tears again. Sparks was amazed at how quickly she could change her face. Then the fluorescent light above their heads flickered and buzzed back to full brightness.

Dunbar looked to the light and back to the president and said, "Sir, we routinely check people who work in the White House. It's part of our protocol."

"You make her sob, is that protocol? And Sparks, what's he doing here?"

At that Sparks stood from the table and walked into the interrogation chamber. "Sir, she had been acting strangely."

"Strangely. Oh, I assure you, she's not the only one acting strangely around here, Jon. That I can say."

Dunbar jumped into the conversation and said, "She's admitted to working for an outside agency, sir. She is not who she says she is."

Wallace was angry, but as he looked at the faces of his Secret Service detail, and at Sparks, he was beginning to calm down. Ellery was huddled in the doorway, observing.

"I thought, and Ellery," Wallace said pointing to his aide, "We thought it was strange that you pulled a working secretary off her desk to bring her into the basement of the West Wing to interrogate her. I've got business to attend up there. I just finished a press conference on winning the war without my secretary. And Sparks is down here without saying a word to anyone. A good portion of my staff is missing, just to interview a temp!" He looked back down to Myrtle as he said that. But she was looking straight ahead with a blank stare. "What have you been up to, Myrtle," he said? "Is this true?"

She shook her head in the negative, but instantly began whimpering. Then she said, "I'm sorry. I'm sorry."

"Well, who are you working for?"

"I don't know."

"Sir," Dunbar said, "We have to continue the interrogation. The best we can tell she's working for the Navy. But we don't know. It seems they recruited her out of Camp Peary in Virginia and placed her here, but there's more to it than that. She said the people who recruited her were foreign, had strange accents."

"What's that mean?" the president said.

"We don't know. The FBI's also checking and we have the Service looking into all her relations: phone records, bank, and family history. But for now we have to finish talking with her; we need to find out what else she knows."

"I've already told you everything I know," she cried. "I don't know anymore!"

"We'll decide that," Dunbar said in an almost empathetic tone, which he obviously put on for the president's benefit.

"Sir . . ." Dunbar began speaking, but Ellery interrupted from the doorway to point out that the phone on the other side of the mirror in the viewing room was blinking yellow, indicating an incoming call.

"That'll be the FBI," Chipton said, and went out of the interrogation chamber to answer the phone. "Yes," he said when he put the phone to his ear. After that he listened, and frowned. "I understand." Chipton hung up the phone. Ellery was looking at him as Chipton walked back into the open interrogation chamber.

"Well, what is it?" the president said.

"Sir, the stone you sent to the Natural History Museum has been stolen, and the . . . Dr. Berk who had it was shot."

"When?"

"Just now. Someone followed Dr. Berk to the storage cage and shot him once he'd unlocked it to get the stone. Those are the only details I have."

"Then I've got to get over there and see him," Wallace said.

"Sir, they're taking him to the hospital now."

"Then we're going to the hospital dammit."

"I wouldn't recommend, sir, going . . ."

"Agent Chipton, I'm the president of the United States, I can go see my friend who's just been shot."

"Yes, sir."

The president turned to leave and said, "Sparks, you come with me. Ellery, you stay here and get in contact with the hospital. Find out the room. Tell them we're coming. And stay in contact with the Secret Service."

"That'll be me," Dunbar said. He held up his radio. I'm on channel 8; Chipton will give you his radio." He turned to Chipton and said. "Do you mind finishing up here?"

"No," Chipton responded.

Dunbar turned to leave with the president.

Chapter Fifty-Five

Poison

Kuntstevo, Moscow
March 2, 1945

"We have to rid ourselves of this poisonous contagion that reaches even our own country," Stalin said, bringing the palm of his hand down flat on the table. He looked as though he was trying to restrain himself, and so didn't pound the table; instead he gave it a smack.

The Politburo members present all knew the signs of Stalin's insanity. There were subtle features that the untrained eye couldn't see. Like the way the furrow in his brow deepened, or that his brown eyes seemed to focus more tightly, or that a barely perceptible, clammy moistness appeared on his forehead. Nikishov didn't notice these signs, but like a dog sensing fear in the pack, he could tell the powerful men around the table like Khrushchev, Molotov, and Beria were unsettled. There was a palpable sense of fear lying in the air like humidity. Once the Boss's anger welled inside him it invariably erupted, and when it did, people often died.

"Here, look at you – blind men, kittens," he shouted, "You don't see the enemy. What will you do without me?"

No one responded because there was nothing to say.

"The Americans are plotting against us as we speak," he continued. "Who shed the most blood in the Great Patriotic War with the fascist Germans while the crippled Roosevelt sat and watched, promising to open a second front, which he wouldn't do until he'd seen both Germany and Russia reduced by millions of men? Yes, he helped us, but he helped us die as well. They are responsible for weakening us as much as anyone.

"And this President Wallace is surrounded by fascists who make him do as they want. He has no real power. He may have been empathetic toward us in the past, and he may have been weak in the Crimea, but he is the leader of a people opposed to us in its very blood. The revolution has never taken root there in any appreciable way. They were confused as to their identity for a time, but now they are coming to know that they are our implacable enemy. Their military and corporations knew it before everyone else, and they have embedded themselves into the very machinery of government; in the very fabric of their flag.

"Even a man like Wallace knows it. He is shrewd, and still has 1930s sympathies, but this is a new world, and we are on a collision course. I wouldn't even put it past his military to stage an event to make war inevitable for us. I know his military questions him, as he has made some cutbacks. They were working on the so-called Atom Bomb. One of his first orders was to end the program because he knew that it was a cover for secret fascist operations. Some of the scientists have smuggled us the work they did on that project, and it is nothing but chasing fancy. Some decadent scientists were playing with ideas and getting paid." Suddenly Stalin stood. He was at the end of the table, Nikishov was to his right, Gromyko his left, and the rest of the men sat farther down the long table. "You must understand the threat we face, comrades. They have infiltrated even our medical profession with their Jews and their art; their cinema is smuggled in even now, where it poisons us. And this John Wayne, Nikita, why is he not dead? Beria, why have you not poisoned him in California or Arizona?"

The men looked at Stalin, but all secretly hoped that someone else would answer the question in a satisfactory way. At that moment one of Stalin's attendants entered the room carrying a silver tray full of desserts. The party had already finished dinner, and was settling in for the night – they were drinking the whiskies the same attendant had brought in only a few minutes prior. After the dessert would come French Cognac for those who wanted to switch from whiskey, as the Boss would inevitably do.

Unfortunately, the attendant tripped on the curled edge of the Tajik rug. The crash was loud. Broken pie plates and centuries old Imperial silverware tumbled across the floor, coming to a rest at the Boss's feet. Stalin immediately turned like a man ready to kill. "You impudent, scheming son-of-a-bitch!" he shouted. "Can't you walk in a straight line without falling down? Must I do it for you! Have you been drinking my vodka or homebrew Somogon in the basement you Kulak?" He then sprang toward him like a cat and pounded the terrified man on the back of his head as he picked shards off the carpet.

"I'm sorry, Comrade Stalin!"

With Stalin's back turned, Nikishov saw that the moment was ripe. He looked across the table at the other men who were watching the abuse and retrieved the glass vial from his pocket. He pulled the rubber stopper in one movement. This attracted the attention of all the other men at the table who now turned from the Boss to see what he was doing. Nikita Khrushchev cocked his head to the side as if he were watching a strange natural phenomenon that perplexed him. Beria simply smiled, while Gromyko turned back to look at the Boss, and Molotov took a sip of whiskey.

Nikishov didn't waste more time, he reached up and dumped the vial into Stalin's whiskey and put it back into his pocket and took a sip of his own. Then he looked around the table, and into each man's eyes. Molotov puckered his lips, like he was holding his breath. Khrushchev coughed. Beria sneered. Gromyko, again, turned and looked back to the dictator, who by now had knocked the attendant onto his back from his knees. No one said a word. Those who didn't know of the assassination plot simply assumed that General Nikishov was acting as part of a conspiracy that was already too powerful to stop. Allowing the plot to move forward would give them preference later on. They all also wanted the Boss dead.

Suddenly the door to the massive paneled dining hall opened and several of Stalin's attachments entered to see what the noise was. They found Stalin leaning over the attendant who was now covering his face and crying out, "Sorry, Comrade Stalin! Comrade Stalin! Comrade Stalin, no!"

The two attachments approached the scene carefully, as they would a chemical spill or undetonated mine, but they were afraid to say a word. Then Khrushchev said, "Boss, let's us finish our whiskey."

"Ok," Stalin said, and scratched his chin as he stood upright, tugging down the ends of his jacket. "Let's do that." The request seemed to shake him from his violence, but he teetered on the edge of returning to his tirade. "The whole world is caving in, and this man can't keep his footing!" He then stepped back toward the man, breathing in a labored way, as heavy smokers do. But he thought better of attacking the man again and turned. His hair was out of place and he smoothed it back over his head as he came to the table and took his whiskey in the crystal glass and drank the double in one gulp.

"American Whiskey is shit!" he said when he finished. "Who brought me this?" and fixed his eyes on the fallen attendant who now put his hands up and pushed himself backward, across the floor to evade the Boss's stair. "I'm joking, comrade. I like it."

Chapter Fifty-Six

The Hospital

Interrogation Chamber, West Wing Basement
March 2, 1945

President Wallace left the interrogation chamber with Sparks, moving quickly down the hallway toward the staircase. Agent Dunbar followed behind as Agent Chipton called to arrange the car and the Secret Service detail to accompany them.

In less than thirty seconds Chipton could hear the agents' footsteps on the floor above him as they scrambled from their posts to prepare for the trip to the hospital, leaving a skeleton crew behind to man the White House. The Secret Service was designed to follow and protect the president, and though the difficulty of their jobs made advance planning preferable, they could move quickly if they had to. A car full of agents was already leaving the White House, headed for George Washington University Hospital in Foggy Bottom, where they would "scout" the building and immediate area for any potential threats. More importantly, they were there to learn the building's layout and safe ingress and egress points relative to the patient's room.

Ellery had left the interrogation chamber with the party, but had stayed on the grounds; he was upstairs somewhere, making plans for the president's arrival at the hospital and coordinating with Agent Dunbar over the two-way. Agent Chipton would have headed out with the other agents had he not had Myrtle to deal with. As it was, he stood in the doorway between the viewing room and the interrogation chamber waiting for the phone to light up.

"So what happens now? I just have to wait here?" she asked.

"That's exactly right Miss Smith, you just have to wait here. This is a turn of events that has no bearing on you. Agent Dunbar had to leave. I'll recommence the interview . . ."

"This is no interview," she said. "If it were, then I could leave."

"Call it what you want, but you can't."

"Why'd they leave you behind?"

The blinking of the phone forestalled his response and he closed the door and locked Myrtle in the interrogation chamber before picking it up. He was surprised at how soundproof the glass was. He couldn't even hear her scream with the speaker turned off, though he saw her doing so through the glass. Now he assumed that not having a ringing phone down here was overkill.

"Chipton," he said as he answered.

"Chipton, it's Fisker. I've got news you guys want to hear."

"Go."

"First, Ed Markey, the department supervisor, is definitely our man, but it's more complicated than a case of your girl sleeping her way to the top. It seems he passed several files through, including hers – all girls, all good-looking. She was the only one that got that close to the president. Markey never met them. The files were all given to him, and he did what he was told. They were using the FBI to get into the White House."

"Who was?"

"Ukrainian Communist group. They operate from a flat in Foggy Bottom. Or at least he thinks so, since he picked up the files at a coffee shop there."

"How would a Ukrainian communist group get all the way to the United States? Doesn't make sense!"

"I can't answer that, Chipton, but from what we're getting, Markey was a long-time fellow traveler, and these guys just looked him up one day. They said the right things, and they offered him the Red Star Medallion as compensation. They knew him, too, because giving him a star was the gesture that sealed it for him, that and their accents. He felt like he was really part of the international team because they hadn't offered him money. He was in it for the right reasons, he said."

"Good, we'll give him a prize then."

"The real news is that he thinks this is all leading somewhere. It's speculation on his part, but he seems happy to have gotten caught, it validates his experience. He's a real second stringer: can't keep his mouth shut. He's under the impression that they want to kill the president to start the revolution here, and he's not so sure that's a good idea."

"You're telling me the girl I have here was sent by communists, Ukrainian communists, to rub out the president. I'm looking at this girl right now. She ain't the one. She was recruited out of Camp Peary Virginia."

"Not her; she's just Intel, part of the web. It's what you do in cases like this: implant as many of your people as you can. When it all goes down, they don't even need to know the plan, just your people's presence can help massage the thing along."

"You sound like one of these intelligence types."

"Just know the ropes. As for the information, it's what Markey believes is true, not necessarily the truth, but we'll cross him after I get off the phone. And about the attempt on the president's life, I asked at the Bureau here if we'd picked up any credible threats to the president in recent weeks, and it turns out that a large military contractor just sent in a memorandum, I guess out of good will, or fear, or patriotism, or for some other reason. His firm is also doing rebuilding work in North Africa, Sicily, Southern Italy and France, anywhere the Nazis have receded; mostly reopening airports and naval terminals, and he's got ties to the CIA and the intelligence communities around the world. His memo reads." He then spoke to someone off the phone, "Where is it? Is that it? Here, here, I have it." Then he began to read:

We have been advised that some misguided anti-communist group might capitalize on the present situation of uncertainty regarding Europe's future and assassinate President Henry A. Wallace in the hope of inaugurating Harry S. Truman, which will have the result of hardening U.S. policy toward the Soviets before war's end. Sources know of no specific plot, *per se*, but have heard credible word that a special group, *The Nachtigall Battalion,* formerly operating under German intelligence, and now believed to be in U.S. under the aegis of a military contractor, are currently exploring the feasibility of such an action. The substance of the foregoing information was orally furnished to Mr. John Coxe Martens.

"And I asked around the office about the *Nachtigall Battalion,* and it turns out they're Ukrainian fascists. Now, what this means for you Agent Chipton, I don't know, and whether it's true, I can't say, but be on your toes."

"Now, how does he know all that? Who is this guy that wrote the memo?"

"Sometimes intel works like this. He's a contractor with big connections, and I can't say what his motivation is for putting that on the written record, but he did. That's all I know, and if we learn anything further then you'll be the first to know. By the way, the Secret Service never arrived here."

"I know. We pulled them off to cover the president."

Chipton hung up, and glared through the mirror at his girl Myrtle, before flinging the door open so hard it banged against the cinder block wall. Myrtle jumped from her seat and cupped her hand over her mouth to suppress a scream. He closed the door, moved a chair so that it was right beside her, and sat down.

"I want to know more about these foreigners you say handle you."

"I already told you, I DON'T KNOW WHO THEY ARE!" She spoke slowly and deliberately, as though she were communicating with an idiot.

"I'm sure you don't, but what did they want to know?"

"About what?"

He jumped up from his seat and turned her so she was facing him, her chair legs screeching against the concrete floor. "DON'T PLAY DUMB WITH ME! On a day-to-day basis, what were you here for? What's your function? They didn't just slip you into the West Wing and pay you five times what you got paid before and make your felonies go away because they liked your legs. What were you doing?" Then he pulled his own chair back to the other side of the table and sat down.

She turned her chair back to face him, frowned and said, "They wanted to know where the president *was* during the day."

"Like an itinerary?"

"Sometimes. I would bring them a detailed itinerary of what Wallace did day to day."

"And where would you bring that?"

"Foggy Bottom. A Place called Leonard's. But that was only for a few weeks. Recently, what they were really interested in knowing was where the president was at any given moment. If he went somewhere within five miles on short notice they wanted to know right then. I couldn't always make the call, but they didn't seem to think that was a problem. They had somebody else. And don't ask me who, because I don't know. I just get the impression that a lot of people in the White House aren't who they say they are."

"Impression? How?"

"When I left my desk for dinner once, I turned back to use the ladies room after I left the office. I saw Agent Dunbar walk over to Jonathan Sparks who was waiting to go into see the president. He didn't know I was there, and it seemed he'd waited till I was just out of the room to approach him. It looked like Dunbar was asking him something. I don't know what it was – maybe nothing – but I didn't trust either of them after that."

"And that's why you thought your Europeans had more people in the White House?"

"I didn't say that. And that's not what I meant. I thought they had more people observing the president's whereabouts because they asked me once why I didn't tell them that the president had left to go to the museum. I told them why I couldn't call them, and they told me that I had made a good decision and not to worry in the future the next time I faced a similar dilemma – not to make a potentially compromising call because someone else would inform them if I didn't."

"What number would you call?" Chipton asked.

"EM-3-6127. It's local," she added.

He jotted the number down and then asked her, "What do you say when you call?"

"I say: 'I need to make a delivery.' And they say: 'Where's the package.' And I say, 'It just left so and so's and will be arriving . . .' wherever he's going to be arriving."

"The president?"

"Yeah, who else?"

Chipton left the room. As he closed the locked door he heard her say, "And don't lock me in here any . . ." Then he lifted the phone from the receiver and had the switchboard call up the number she'd given him: EM-3-6127. He thought that was just west of the White House, but couldn't be sure. The phone began ringing, and ringing.

He let it ring for over a minute and then hung up and opened the door to the interrogation chamber. "They always answer?" he asked her.

"They always answer, first ring, yes," she said.

"How many times you called in the past?"

"At least twenty. That's the guy's only job. He waits around for the phone. These people are fussy. They're military or something."

"And if they didn't answer the phone, what would you think?"

"Why wouldn't they answer?" she asked.

"Because they already have what they need."

He immediately had the operator call the hospital. The line was busy. He reached to his hip and realized that he'd given his radio to Ellery.

Chapter Fifty-Seven

Where Avenues Meet

George Washington University Hospital, Foggy Bottom
March 2, 1945

"Why would Jews tell him they were Jews? Why not just steal it and leave the question open?" Sparks asked, and President Wallace just nodded. The doctors were adamantly pushing them from the room now, and Wallace had stopped arguing.

Dr. Berk was in a great deal of pain as he lay on his back in the hospital bed. He was shot through the hand. The bullet had continued traveling into his abdomen where it entered the skin, stopping once it struck and cracked his lower rib. Due to the shallow penetration of the slug, it was easily removable and not life threatening, though his hand would never be the same again.

By the time Wallace arrived at the hospital and reached Dr. Berk's room, the doctors had already taken the bullet out of his body and were delivering morphine to him intravenously. Under typical circumstances they would not have allowed any visitors to see Dr. Berk for at least 24 hours, his wife excluded, but the president insisted, and the staff acquiesced.

When Wallace entered the room, the first thing Dr. Berk said was, "I'm sorry, Mr. President."

"Please don't apologize Eliezer. I just want to make sure you're all right. You were shot because you had something of mine, and I feel terrible about it. I couldn't just send you a nice note and flowers. I had to come and tell you in person how I felt."

"No, I should be sorry, sir."

"Please don't. I never thought anyone would shoot you over the stone."

And that's when Dr. Berk said, "He was a young man, sir. And he said he was doing it for Eretz Israel; that the time of Jewish suffering had come and gone; it was time to reclaim *our* birthright. This stone would be a part of the new temple."

"And then he shot you?" Wallace said.

"No. He had already shot me. This is what he said as I was lying on the floor. He thought I was dying. I was lying in a pool of my own blood and holding my chest, but he didn't know the blood was mostly from my hand."

Now Sparks and Wallace were leaving the hospital. They were on the fifth floor, headed toward the elevator and flanked by a cadre of Secret Service personnel. There were more officers today than Sparks remembered on other occasions.

"But how many burglars tell you why they're robbing you? And how would Jewish people benefit from the stone, especially since they stole it from a U.S. president, in which case they'll never be able to say they own it?" Sparks asked.

"As he said, he thought that Berk was dying. There must have been a lot of blood on the floor of that storage room," President Wallace said.

Sparks didn't respond. The stone had never been very important to him, and he had trouble imagining that anyone, let alone several people, would be willing to kill over it. After all, it was simply a stone. But the president believed in it, and maybe that was enough.

They entered the elevator in a group, but several of the Secret Service agents couldn't fit and so were forced to take the stairs. Sparks wondered if that group of agents would run down the flights of stairs to catch the elevator or if they would hang back.

"I feel bad for him," Wallace said. "I didn't have to give it back to him. I mean, my own curiosity got him shot. Testing a rock isn't worth his life."

"You couldn't have known that some crazy person would be willing to kill over a silly stone."

"I did know that Sparks. It's more than a stone. And Cayce knew what would happen, but it's just tough to understand what he meant in the moment. Maybe I should worry about some of the other predictions he made."

"Meaning what?"

"He said a lot of things."

The elevator beeped and the number "1" illuminated as the doors leading to the lobby sprang open. Both Wallace and Sparks waited a moment for several of the Secret Service agents to exit the elevator and then they too stepped onto the linoleum floor with two agents behind them. As they crossed the room by the lobby desk, Sparks heard a door behind him bang off the wall. He turned to see the other agents exit the stairwell and smiled to himself because he now knew they had just run down five flights of stairs to catch up to the elevator.

Then they crossed the lobby. Agents were already holding open the front doors as they moved quickly to get into the street to the waiting limo. There were photographers following them now, which made Wallace, who was almost always camera shy, walk even faster.

"For a politician, you really don't like the spotlight," Sparks said, walking through the double doors to the narrow courtyard leading to the street.

"Don't I know it? I should stop and tell them how I'm visiting a friend who was shot over the Stone of Destiny and make a big thing of it like I'm a humanitarian, but I can't stomach the idea. I am a president by succession after all. It was like an accident."

"I respect you for it."

After saying that, Sparks looked up to see that the limo was actually one hundred feet or so up from the hospital entrance on New Hampshire Avenue, toward Pennsylvania Avenue, instead of directly opposite the door as it had been when they were dropped off. Now they had to follow the narrow courtyard parallel to New Hampshire Avenue rather than quickly crossing it. At that moment an ambulance was pulling in with its blare and flashing lights.

As they reached the street, President Wallace suddenly slowed his pace, as if he were going to stop walking entirely. The photographers began catching up to them at that point. He was looking north toward Pennsylvania Avenue, saying, "Where Pennsylvania and New Hampshire meet."

"What's that Henry?" Sparks said. But the president didn't respond. They were walking to catch the limo and there were people standing everywhere coming and going from the hospital, and just standing about watching the president and his cadre.

Then out of the crowd of people ahead Sparks recognized the face of a man. He knew the face as well as he knew the red front door to his house, but for the briefest moment he couldn't remember who the face belonged to, and then he realized. This was one of the men dressed in black on the flight from Switzerland. And it was this man whom Sparks assumed would be the first to grab him to throw him off the plane, the one who closed the door behind him.

Then he noticed that the Secret Service detail surrounding them had suddenly thinned. Instead of walking in a bunched formation around the president, they had been stretched into a line on the way to the faraway limo.

He heard Wallace say, "New Hampshire Avenue," but it was only noise to him. His eyes were firmly planted on the foreign man from the plane who had his hand inside his jacket.

Sparks then saw the wood handle of a model 1911 .45 shine just over the man's thumb. He didn't bother to think. He took a long stride forward reaching out to grab the gun and push it sideways. He missed and forced the gun down into his own abdomen where it fired one hot shot. The noise was jarring, and the man struggled to remove the gun from Sparks' hands as he fell forward onto the sidewalk. But Sparks wouldn't let go. The gun discharged a second time; this time into the ground.

Sparks felt a searing pain in his abdomen and the back of his shirt felt wet, indicating what he feared was an exit wound from the large caliber slug.

The two shots fired in fast succession, the first into his stomach, the second into the ground, and then men were tackling him from all sides. It was like a fumble in football where all members of both teams jump onto the ball.

There was an intense pressure on him now as he lay on the black pavement, with hands grasping at the gun. Someone was shouting, "You son of a bitch!" It sounded like Dunbar. But Sparks thought it had to be someone else shouting because then they said, "Sparks had the gun! It was him!"

Chapter Fifty-Eight

The Attachments

Kuntstevo, Moscow
March 3, 1945

"Tell the other attachments," Beria said to Krustalev, the senior attachment in the house, "that Stalin has said he is not to be disturbed. For any reason! Do you understand? Just go to bed tonight. He doesn't want you poking around his rooms."

"Yes."

"Good," Beria said and left to join the others in the dacha's center hall.

"You keep us waiting, good comrade," Stalin said. He was standing within the frame of the open front door with his hand on comrade Gromyko's back. The other men were already on the stairs headed to their limos in the driveway.

From where Beria stood at the other end of the hall, he could tell that both men were drunk. However, from the look of them, Stalin was very drunk. He thought this because Stalin looked happy.

"I'm coming, Boss. I know. I know. When it's time to go, it's time to go."

"You're paying attention," Stalin said.

"Yes."

"Goodnight," Nikishov then said from the stone landing a few feet behind the Boss. "Goodnight," Stalin replied, taking both of Nikishov's hands into his own. "And good morning."

And the Politburo members along with Nikishov and Gromyko left in their limos, the two non-members riding with Beria, as they had come, into the predawn Moscow night.

It was 4:00 AM.

◆ ◆ ◆

When Stalin hadn't moved by 10:00 AM, there was little worry among his attachments. It had been a late night. 11:00 AM came and passed, and then noon, and though Stalin usually pulled himself from bed by this time, regardless of when he'd gone to sleep the night before, there were those occasions where he remained in bed for much longer. He was a heavy drinker, after all, who kept his own hours.

By 2:00 o'clock the attachments had begun to worry, but they were afraid to enter his rooms because of the command they had gotten from Krustalev on behalf of the Boss. And they had been around long enough to have learned not to violate one of the Boss's commands, even if it contradicted their daily routine, for Stalin did not live for the routine of his attachments, they lived for him. But this was a command they had never received before.

And so it was, until 6:00 PM when they received a call from the guardhouse telling them that the light had come on in Stalin's dining room; this meant that the Boss was at least up and moving about. And yet still he did not come down.

By 10:00 PM their worry for him outweighed their fear of his order and so two of the attachments entered his rooms.

They made sure to stomp their feet as they moved down the hallway toward his dining room, and as they crossed from the hallway into that room they caught their first glimpse of the Boss. He was lying on the wood floor in a puddle of his own urine with his left arm outstretched as if he were beckoning the men to help him. His eyes were open, but not moving, and he began making noise like he was going to talk but proper words failed him. Instead he made an angry noise: "Dz-Dz-Dz-Dz." That was the only sound he seemed able to utter.

Beside him on the floor lay a copy of Pravda, and an open bottle of mineral water. He continued making the noise as his loyal attachments, who by now were nearly in tears, began asking him questions in the hope that he would suddenly rouse. Instead his eyes closed and he began to snore. With that, they lifted him from the floor and placed him on his sofa, covering him with a blanket because his skin was cold to the touch.

Then they called the Kremlin, but couldn't reach any of the Politburo members from the night before, so they left a message.

Thirty minutes later, Beria called back. They told him what they found.

"I will be there soon," Beria said.

◆ ◆ ◆

Over an hour later, Beria and Gromyko arrived at the *near dacha*. When they entered the house they asked to be alone with comrade Stalin.

"Of course," came the reply.

They walked down the long hall leading to his rooms together. But when they reached the door Beria said, "You go first."

"I can't believe this," Gromyko said. "A coward," and he flung open the wood-paneled door and entered. They found Stalin on his couch. The blanket was on the floor, and the cushion he lay on was soaking wet with urine.

Beria followed behind Gromyko. "Is he dead? Is he dead?" Beria asked.

"I don't know. He's not breathing," and Gromyko leaned over the Boss and listened for his breathing. He heard none, checked his pulse and thought he felt nothing. Then he said, "Comrade," turning to Beria in earnest, "Stalin is dead."

"He's dead!" Beria shouted with a smile and began to dance. "The scourge his gone," he said, and leaned over the Boss, "You are finally dead and your corpse will rot like your memory!"

But then Stalin coughed and opened his eyes and looked directly into Beria's. He tried to speak, but again made an indistinguishable sound. Like Rasputin, he was impossible to kill.

Beria immediately grabbed his hand and kissed it saying, "Oh, father forgive me. Oh, comrade."

But Stalin grabbed him by the collar and was trying to shout, but couldn't make the words to do so. The best he could muster was a long and furious "DZZZZZZZZZZZZZZ – ZZZZZZZZZZZZ!" Despite his incapacity his grip on Beria's collar was like iron. Beria was frightened. "Help me!" he shouted back to Gromyko. "Comrade?" But Gromyko didn't move. He stood in amazement.

Stalin pulled Beria in close so the men were face to face. Then he opened his mouth. With that, Beria violently pulled away from the Boss and took the pillow that lay beneath Stalin's head and smothered him with it in one vicious movement. For a minute or more the old man's arms stood raised on either side of the pillow clawing for the face of the man who murdered him. And then they became stiff, and suddenly went limp altogether.

He was gone –

◆　◆　◆

Later, when they were certain, they called in the doctors.

The Doctors would proclaim that Stalin died from a stroke, despite evidence to the contrary.

At that moment, behind the Kremlin walls and among the Central Committee of the Party, the Council of Ministers, and the Supreme Soviet, a plot to take over the country was underway. The effort was backed by American money and directed by Gromyko.

Lavrentiy Beria, however, had a little over a month to live before he would be shot in the head begging for his life in an NKVD execution chamber.

◆ ◆ ◆

Before they left Stalin's rooms that day, Beria turned to Gromyko and said, "We are finally free comrade."

"Yes, we are free, of Stalin."

Chapter Fifty-Nine

Coma

George Washington University Hospital, Foggy Bottom
March 23, 1945

Sparks' eyes fluttered for the first time since the president had entered the room nearly an hour before.

Then he began moving his mouth. His eyes trembled more rapidly now, and suddenly he was staring at the ceiling.

Wallace stood from the chair he had been sitting in, and slowly made his way over to his friend. "Can you hear me," he said quietly. And Sparks slowly turned away from the ceiling tiles and focused on the president.

"Mr. President," Sparks said in a whisper.

"Whatever happened to Henry?" Wallace replied and chuckled.

"Henry?" Sparks corrected, with what looked like a smile on his face. Then he looked upward as if recoiling from internal pain.

"I'll get the doctor," the president said, responding to the pain he saw in his friend's face.

"No, please," Sparks said. "Sit with me a while."

"They should know you've come around. You've been in and out now for the better part of five days, but this is the first time you've been coherent."

"Five days?" Sparks said. "I was out five days?"

"No. You've been out three weeks. Just in the last five did it start to look like you'd live. But I should really get the doctor," Wallace said and looked back over his shoulder to the closed door leading to the hallway.

"No. Tell me what happened."

"You don't remember?"

"I do. I remember the man who shot me, but I don't understand why or what happened."

The president considered Sparks' condition for a moment; he was partially turned toward the door as if he might walk into the hallway at any moment, but now he squared his shoulders with the bed Sparks was lying in and said, "To start with, the first week and a half or so that you were under, there was some evidence you were the one trying to shoot me. I had no idea what happened myself; one of the agents tackled me into the car so hard I thought I broke my ribs. And there were various proponents of the theory that you were the shooter. But they were all based on Agent Dunbar's claim that he'd tackled you when you pulled a gun, and that you were shot in the stomach while the two of you wrestled. When the FBI kindly brought us some pictures from a photographer who was at the hospital that day, they showed otherwise. The man was lucky to get the camera out of Foggy Bottom at all, as the only other journalist had his taken as evidence, which was then lost.

"Needless to say, Dunbar has been reassigned for having what we're delicately calling a "flawed perception of events," which is to say that we're letting the Secret Service off the hook since there's no evidence as of yet that they were compromised beyond Agent Dunbar."

Sparks propped himself on his elbow when Wallace said that, grimacing a bit from the pain.

"Yes, I know about you Sparks, and I know why you were working for them, and what you thought you were doing."

"Henry, I . . . Mr. President."

"Don't bother. It's all come out now, maybe not publicly. That would probably be impossible, or be the end of my presidency. But when you botch an operation this badly and get openly caught trying to assassinate a president then there are consequences. The College of Cardinals is gone. Wild Bill had a nervous breakdown. Some of the people you would know from the organization have even died: killed themselves or otherwise disappeared on assignment in Europe.

"Of course, I know you didn't think they were going to kill me. You certainly didn't think they were going to frame you up, even though no one can explain whether that was part of the plan or just something Dunbar cooked up when he saw that their man had failed. And since he says he didn't know what was happening, then we won't know why he did what he did."

"What about . . ." Sparks began, but the president answered his question before he finished his thought: "The shooter?" Wallace said. "The Ukrainian? Well, he was just a lone gunman. They brought him in for questioning right off the bat, but it was only after we got hold of the photos that we focused on him. Turns out there was a paper trail that says his mother was American, which explains how he got to the United States. And he was disgruntled because he felt I'd given his beloved homeland over to the Soviets. And so, as the story goes, he tried to shoot me for some misguided retribution," Wallace said.

"But I saw him before. He was on the plane that took me back from the war."

"I know that too. This is the way this is going to go, Jonathan. You've seen what kind of people these are and how far their power goes; in some ways they can make up history. And I might feel more like bringing out the truth if I didn't think they already lost the future, or at least that the point will be greatly contested." At this Sparks made a face that indicated he was confused as to president's meaning. And so Wallace continued, "I was working with Russians in the United States as I had told you I was, and we were successful not only in eliminating Stalin, but in putting the right men into power in that country; at least that's how it looks for now.

"No one will ever know what I did," Wallace continued. "They think Stalin died of natural causes. I'm not happy with the means I used, but the greatness of the evil we prevented on both sides of the Atlantic is immeasurable.

"Regarding the CIA, Congress has rewritten their charter and separated intel and espionage into separate federal agencies. It adds some checks and balances to their apparatus, which means they'll be greatly weakened for now."

At this point Sparks finally got a word in, "But Henry, how could the story about the Ukrainian fly? What did he say? Why did Dunbar think it would work to blame me?"

The president smiled. "For your part, you grabbed the gun so quickly from that man it almost looked like it was you, and Dunbar and the other agents hit you so fast that by the time I looked at you, I thought you were the one they were wrestling with. The Ukrainian had fallen away at that point. Dunbar claimed he turned the gun around and you shot yourself. And the Ukrainian, he didn't get to say anything; somebody shot him in the head as the METRO Police moved him from a holding cell for questioning. Anything he knew landed on the pavement on Pennsylvania Avenue. The man who shot him was a great patriot who wanted to avenge me. Then J. Edgar Hoover gave me a verbal briefing in which he called the man a crooked METRO cop, who was dying of cancer, and whose family suddenly paid off their house just after the shooting. But this is the way it works. Hoover also explained that there were at least one hundred and fifty men and women who are known in intel circles, which he was able to learn from the photographs. Nearly anybody within sight of the shooting was on somebody's payroll."

"How can nobody go to jail?" Sparks asked, and Wallace laughed.

"The METRO cop went to jail, but he'll die soon anyway. We organized the outcome. I just had to let go of the fact that some of the people who work for me really did put together a quiet *coup*. I can let that go though; there were signals that I was corrupt and working with the Soviets which pushed some of these people to think it was for the greater good to liquidate me. But from that we learned that the CIA had too much of a paramilitary power, so we trimmed it back. Some people who would have otherwise complained held their fire, both because of the botched coup and because I elevated Secretary of the Navy James Forrestal to the newly created position of Secretary of Defense."

"But Forrestal's got his hands all over this thing!"

"Indeed, but he's too powerful, and he's got the Marine Corps' propaganda arm with him. I've since learned that a lot of my troubles began when I publicly questioned the need for a Marine Corps at all. As penance, I just had to let Forrestal move up the ladder in exchange for remaking some of the government's architecture, they love him. He's also been chastened. Since he saw what happened in Russia, and since he knows I had a hand in it, I think he's developed a new admiration for his president. However, he's still a rabid anti-communist and sees what happened as merely a setback for Stalinism, and possibly a plus for worldwide Communism, as he calls it. He almost believes in the death of Capitalism as much as the Soviets do.

"I also know," Wallace continued, "with some certainty, that he was running that Ukrainian who shot you, and that Forrestal further had a group of them here in Washington. The day I was shot, he sent a team to kill the Ukrainians. They fought back. Three of them even escaped. There was a shootout in Foggy Bottom.

"The papers said it was over heroin. The fact of the matter is, nobody knows where they are. You'd think it'd be hard for a group of Ukrainians to hide in wartime America, but they were well trained: all of them spoke English, and they might have had connections in the Heroin trade after all." Suddenly, the president stood up and looked out the window.

"As for you Sparks, I think it might be the right time for you to go back to Texas."

Just then there was a knock on the door. "Come in," Wallace said, and a small young man who looked like he belonged in blue overalls on a farm somewhere entered. "Sparks," Wallace said, "I want you to meet my new aide, Elmer Wood, he's my wife's nephew."

"Nice to meet you Elmer," he said and shook the young man's hand. "But where's Ellery?"

"Ellery jumped through the closed window of his sixth floor apartment. It seems he was distraught at the state of world affairs. There was no sign of forced entry."

"He's dead."

"I didn't ask for this, Jon."

Then Elmer spoke up, "Sir, I'm sorry, but we really have to go."

"Ok then," Wallace said and turned back to Sparks. "Jonathan, feel free to stay here as long as you need."

"Thank you, sir," Sparks said.

And the president walked out the door.

Chapter Sixty

A Secret Service

July 9, 1947
Lake of the Woods, Minnesota

Joe Dunbar propped his foot against the dock rail as he dropped his fishing line into the warm summer water of Lake of the Woods, Minnesota. This was his yearly trip to his family's old camp. He looked forward to it every year. This year though, only he and his girlfriend made the trip.

She was at the store now. He was just letting time go by with a beer in one hand and his old wood fishing pole in the other when he heard footsteps on the shore-end of the wood dock behind him. "You're back early," he said without looking. "There a problem with the Willys? She breakdown?"

"No problem," a voice said.

"Chipton!" Dunbar stuttered, spilling his beer, and hopping to his feet. That's when he noticed the small revolver in Chipton's hand.

"You know you can't get away with what you did," Chipton said.

"I did it for my country," Dunbar said, angry now, and holding the fishing pole in his hand as though planning to swing it like a sword. It didn't concern Chipton, who was out of reach and had a gun leveled at his midsection.

"You don't get to decide what's right for your country. What's right is protecting the president."

"I don't know what you mean!" Dunbar responded.

"We know what you did. Other people know and that's it. There can be no question about our service."

No one heard the two shots Chipton fired. It took four days to find Dunbar's body; it had floated away from the dock and became entangled in a fallen tree on an island a few hundred yards away. A grandmother in a canoe found his bloated corpse when she rowed out one early morning to pick blueberries.

Chapter Sixty-One

"Nightingale"

May 22, 1949
National Medical Center, Bethesda Maryland

He noticed the guard was no longer outside his door and put his pen down.

It was 1:30 in the morning and hardly a soul stirred in the hospital. James Forrestal's radio buzzed dead air beside him. The station he had been listening to went off hours ago. But the background hum hadn't bothered him. He was intent upon re-working what remained of his memoirs. In fact, the static sound helped to relax him. He laughed to himself when he thought the drone might even drown out any listening devices.

Now he leaned forward in his bathrobe and turned the volume knob down on the wooden box so he could hear what was happening in the dim hallway. The radio was familiar to him, but he didn't know why. Then it struck him. As Under Secretary of the Navy during the war, the department purchased thousands of these small, art-deco clock radios. The sight of this one caused a vague sense of nostalgia to surface within him.

Then voices out in the hall broke his train of thought. He leaned from his chair so as to see better through the glass rectangle in the door. He was certain the guard no longer stood at his station now. He saw the wooden chair back through the chicken-wire window without anyone in it.

The fact that his regular guard was off tonight had already heightened a sense of apprehension in him. And now there were footsteps outside the door.

It doesn't take much to kill a man. Even the nation's first Secretary of Defense was vulnerable. But he was only a private citizen now, and one sitting on the 16th floor of a naval hospital for psychiatric observation. The man at the door 24/7 was there for suicide watch, they said. But Forrestal just hoped the "guard" could keep him alive.

And there was something else that worried him. James Forrestal was leaving tomorrow. Someone had put restrictions on whom his visitors could be and how long he had to remain "locked up" as he was. But in the morning he was going to defy the orders and leave with his brother. He was sure that President Wallace or someone else close to the White House had put those restrictions on his incarceration and that those who placed the orders were intent upon destroying him.

Thinking of the president made his blood pressure start to rise.

President Wallace let Forrestal move into the newly created position of Secretary of Defense when there was nothing he could do to stop it, but as soon as the climate was right, Wallace threw Forrestal out on his ass. And then he ended up here. He had been paranoid, he had to admit. But watching his country being given over to international communists was something he couldn't abide. Stalin was the best thing that ever happened to America because it gave them someone to hate. With his threat gone, the poison of the revolution was even more insidious and was now working its way into the very fiber of the nation. This was especially true since Wallace had won reelection. A man would never forgive an attempt on his life so easily, and as soon as Forrestal started to have "trouble" his enemies aligned against him. Even the doctors were working for his downfall.

Ever since Forrestal's brother had written to let him know that he was coming to get him, there had been a change of regular guards on his floor. They were all new faces now. That was also part of the reason Forrestal was up so late. He thought he had to ride out the night awake if he wanted to stay alive until the morning.

That's when a voice from the doorway said, "You are still working on your diary, I see." The man carefully enunciated his words.

Forrestal had earlier found that pages were missing from his lengthy diary. To the doctors, this was only further proof that he was paranoid. But to Forrestal the fact that his accusation of theft and the doctors interpretation of it leaked to the press within 48 hours was further proof that he wasn't crazy and that there were powerful forces at work against him. He had been breaking down under the pressure of his job and he knew it. But he wasn't broken in the way his enemies made it sound. They'd even said he tried to kill himself down in Hobe Sound, Florida on vacation. That couldn't have been true. Even his wife, he thought, must have been part of the conspiracy against him.

"What do you want?" Forrestal asked.

"I want you to jump out the window." When the man said that another man appeared in the hallway behind him, but with his brim down a shadow fell across his face, and Forrestal couldn't get a read on him.

"Just like that?"

"You're not a beloved man, Mr. Secretary."

"What is that accent? Russian?"

The man shook his head. He considered Forrestal for a moment with cruel satisfaction. And then he said, "Nightingale."

♦ ♦ ♦

James Forrestal was found dead on the roof of the National Medical Center's cafeteria. He'd fallen thirteen stories. His body was found at 1:50 AM. In his room investigators found a partially transcribed poem, which Forrestal had been working on. Due to the subject matter, investigators took it to be an implied suicide note. The poem was from Sophocles' tragedy, *Ajax*. The handwritten section read:

> Fair Salamis, the billows' roar,
> Wander around thee yet,
> And sailors gaze upon thy shore
> Firm in the Ocean set.

Thy son is in a foreign clime
Where Ida feeds her countless flocks,
Far from thy dear, remembered rocks,
Worn by the waste of time–
Comfortless, nameless, hopeless save
In the dark prospect of the yawning grave....
Woe to the mother in her close of day,
Woe to her desolate heart and temples gray,
When she shall hear
Her loved one's story whispered in her ear!
"Woe, woe!' will be the cry–
No quiet murmur like the tremulous wail
Of the lone bird, the querulous nightingale–

Epilogue

Ex-President Henry A. Wallace was mentally lucid but physically debili-
tated by ALS, commonly known as Lou Gehrig's disease. On the table
next to him was his deathbed diary: "Reflections of an ALSer." His robust
routine of tennis, vigorous walks and tending his beloved garden, where
he would never see the fruits of his most recent strawberry hybridization,
was over. He only had enough energy to scrawl a few final remarks in his
bedside diary.

He thought about his legacy. He really had two legacies, one of which
only he and very few others would ever know about. This first legacy was
his conspiracy with President Gromyko to engineer a bloodless "coup
d'état" which ended Bolshevik Communism and prevented both the im-
minent Cold War and nuclear holocaust. This, with the help of dear Edgar
Cayce, was his grand achievement. Henry Wallace was no egomaniac,
and even if he had tried to reveal what really happened, his critics, who
already thought he was crazy, would double down in condemnation.

His second legacy was very public and very well accepted, even by
his harshest critics. "Pax Wallacia" was the new normal and would remain
so for decades. Essentially, Henry Wallace and his confederate President
Gromyko had put an end to formal Nation State wars. Religious conflict persisted in Ireland, Palestine and along the Pakistan-India fault line.
Warlords and tribal chieftains struggled for power in the third world, but
Nation States no longer declared war on other Nation States.

There were two reasons for this. One was economic: rebuilding the
devastated Eurasian Continent with the help of the expanded Marshall
Plan provided worldwide full employment. The United States of Russia

(USR), led by President Gromyko, used their expanding GNPs to fund infrastructure and quality of life improvements in a complete reversal of the Communist policy of building arms and missiles at the expense of quality of life.

The second reason was that the United Nations, which replaced the impotent League of Nations, had real power. In perhaps his greatest known public accomplishment, Henry Wallace drafted the United Nations Charter. The UN Security Council, which would condone and legitimatize worldwide police actions against rogue nations, was composed of the USA, the USR, England, France and Communist China. Henry Wallace made sure that two vetoes were needed to block an action. Since the USA and the USR were allies after the Wallace/Gromyko accords were signed, China was alone and powerless.

This became obvious in the early 50s when a communist dictator in North Korea, Kim Il Sung, gained power and attempted to occupy the southern portion of the Korean Peninsula. The UN Security Council immediately voted 4 to 1, China dissenting, to initiate a police action. The remnants of the United States Army led by Douglas MacArthur invaded the Southern Peninsula, while the US Pacific fleet deployed in the Sea of Japan. At the same time, China mobilized hostile communist forces west of the Yalu River in support of the Northern dictator. But the most important move came when President Gromyko ordered Marshal Zhukov to assemble one million battle-hardened ex-Red Army soldiers along the Great Wall of China. Although the wall was a hindrance to Genghis Khan, it was not going to stop the brand new MIG jets and heavy armor.

The casting of Marshall Zhukov was obvious for this job. He had methodically and viciously pushed the German army from the outskirts of Leningrad, Moscow, and Stalingrad all the way to the garden of the Reichstag building in Berlin. A similar march to Peking would have been a cakewalk. Once he realized what he was up against, Mao Tse-tung recalled the troops from the Yalu and changed his vote at the UN. Kim Il Sung then took sanctuary in Peking, where his descendants started a basketball team and raised dogs.

The Democratic Republic of Korea occupied the whole peninsula, and within a decade along with Japan, Taiwan, Singapore, and eventually China, became an economic powerhouse, joining the so-called Tigers of the Orient. These countries had no interest in militarism or warfare. Life was good without war. Pax Wallacia.

So the UN had "bite," they demonstrated that in Korea.

But after the Korean incident, President Gromyko felt that President Wallace's successor, President Eisenhower, had done little or nothing to discourage dictatorships in his own hemisphere, and pointed to the Dictator of Cuba, Batista, as a case in point. The Eisenhower administration, beholden to the United States sugar and fruit interests, had propped up many Latin American dictators who would allow the USA to monopolize, sugar, coffee, bananas and tobacco. Given what Gromyko had accomplished in terms of snuffing dictators in Eastern Europe and Korea, Eisenhower had to yield.

The UN Security Council voted 5 to 0 to impose worldwide sanctions on the Cuban Sugar crop. The American sugar lobby was livid, but within one month, Batista had no choice and held a Democratic election, which was won by a bearded intellectual who loved baseball – of all things. President Castro was repeatedly re-elected through reputedly fair elections.

With Eisenhower's help, an exhibition baseball game between the world champion New York Yankees and President Castro's pride and joy, the Havana Cubans, was arranged. The Cubans won 12 to 3. After that, Spanish speaking players, who were formerly treated as outcasts, flooded into America and became gods and idols in the Spanish speaking world. Roberto Clemente was the first to leave the National League for Cuba, where he was treated with the dignity he deserved. After him, Orlando Cepeda, Juan Marachal, Vada Pinson, Tony Oliva and others jumped ship. The Havana Cubans eventually joined the American League and dominated the second place New York Yankees for years to come.

The UN was effective at thwarting and overturning nation state tyranny, but the world still had problems; religious intolerance, organized crime, opium warlords and tribal genocide. The Wallace/Gromyko accords had little or no effect on anything other than Nation States. Nonetheless, Gromyko, not Wallace, received the Nobel Peace Prize.

Henry Wallace was raised an Episcopalian, but also had a verifiable experience with supernatural forces that was undeniable. On his death-bed, he wondered about the afterlife he would soon enter. Was God going to be the muscular, bearded, white God of Michelangelo, or the collective unconscious that might combine Buddha, Jesus, and Mohamed into an understandable supernatural unity? He would soon know the answer.

He was groggy from medication and drifted into a restless sleep. He entered a dream state. He was still reclined in a hospital bed, but now he was in an operation theater. A surgeon and a scrub nurse hovered over him. There was an elevated gallery looking down on him. He knew that the observers were important, and he now recognized the surgeon. It was Edgar Cayce, and the scrub nurse was his long suffering but dutiful wife, Ilo. Instead of asking for a scalpel, Edgar demanded a pencil.

One was crisply slapped into his hand. Next he asked for a slate. He then drew a sketch on the slate. Henry knew Edgar was communicating in symbols, as before, but the picture was curious. It looked like two par-allel rectangles standing on end. Edgar penciled in wavy lines at the top part of the rectangles. Were they supposed to symbolize halos, clouds, smoke, or even fire? Henry was confused, but he knew the image was important, very important.

Then Edgar Cayce uttered three words.

Henry gradually awoke from his trance state, his first real dip in the "river" Cayce had once described to him. He struggled to find the energy to transcribe the image and the three words into his "Refection's of an ALSer". The manuscript was open to a blank page. It was difficult and very painful, but Henry Wallace drew the two upright parallel rectangles with smoke and flames at the top of each. He initialed and dated the pic-ture at the bottom to give his drawing provenance:

HAW 1965.

He had to rest before writing the three words. As a man of peace he knew he had to write the words before he collapsed and entered the afterlife. He slowly but methodically wrote the words before collapsing on the bed: PRESIDENT ALBERT GORE.

As was his custom, Henry dated the document, but before he completed the entire date he fell back into the bed from exhaustion. He only got the month and date onto the paper............. 9/11.

Made in the USA
Middletown, DE
01 October 2017